The Old Man's Boy Grows Older

THE OLD MAN'S BOY GROWS OLDER

ROBERT RUARK

illustrated with line drawings by
WALTER DOWER

A Holt Paperback
HENRY HOLT AND COMPANY   NEW YORK

Holt Paperbacks
Henry Holt and Company, LLC
Publishers since 1866
175 Fifth Avenue
New York, New York 10010
www.henryholt.com

A Holt Paperback® and ⬤® are registered trademarks
of Henry Holt and Company, LLC.

Library of Congress Cataloging-in-Publication Data
Ruark, Robert Chester
The old man's boy grows older / Robert Ruark ; illustrated with
line drawings by Walter Dower.—1st Holt paperbacks ed.
p. cm.
ISBN-13: 978-0-8050-2974-1

1. Title.
PS3535.U15043 1993   93-9037
813'.54—dc20   CIP

Henry Holt books are available for special promotions and
premiums. For details contact: Director, Special Markets.

Originally published in hardcover in 1957
by Holt, Rinehart and Winston

First Holt Paperbacks Edition 1993

40 39 38 37 36 35 34 33

*This book is
for two grown-up small boys,
who once shared an idea in a rowboat.
I do not recall that we caught any fish,
but the idea was a beaut.*

Contents

FOREWORD

A Word from the Boy

It's a popular pastime among adults, when the hair begins to gray and the aches of middle age grow more steadily persistent, to look back on the prodigious deeds of their youth and proclaim that we've all gone soft and that they don't make boys like that any more. The Old Man had a theory about this. He said that as a man grew older the miles that he used to walk to the Little Red Schoolhouse grew longer.

"I am convinced," he said, "that what schoolin' I had took place no farther than half a mile from the homestead, but the older I get the longer the trip seems to get. If you asked me right fast how far I walked through the snow I reckon I'd say ten mile without battin' an eye."

I wasn't paying too much attention to what the old gentleman was saying, except I caught the word "snow." It was steamy August, and I was torturing the crank handle of an ice-cream freezer. Or, rather, the crank was torturing me. Sweat was streaming down my face, and only the promise of being allowed to lick the dasher kept me grunting at the task, as the cream in the cylinder, surrounded by a mixture of cracked ice and rock salt, got stiff and stiffer.

When it became almost immovably stiff the ice cream was done, and I would be onto that smoothly creamy wooden paddle like a duck on a June bug, and there would be wonderful chunks of frozen peaches making lovely hillocks under the satin surface of the ice cream. This was known as solider's pay or extra incentive, and I was allowed an even start on the bulk of the ice cream with the family. I usually came out ahead despite impost.

It seems to me that this was the best ice cream ever tooled by the hand of man, when you consider the miracles one used to work with Jersey cream, sugar, eggs, and vanilla extract, with a few peach nuggets or cherries stirred into the mixture. They don't make ice cream like that today. They don't make life that way today either.

This sobering thought occurred sharply as I was smitten by a violent crick in the back the other day, when I was trying to recapture my misty youth by producing some home-churned ice cream instead of sending somebody to the store for a carton or merely reaching down into the freezer for a rock-hard package that generally tastes of the same old sawdust, no matter how brilliant the stripes.

I reckon that in recent years I've ruined an awful lot of good meat cooking out of doors in pursuit of youth. I will go fishing or camping just for the fun of being frozen or sunstruck, fly bit or mosquito chewn—anything at all as long as it's uncomfortable. I am a sucker for picnics, and savor anything at all to eat if it's either raw or burnt and has sand in it.

In recent years I have consumed elephant heart, raw antelope liver, and half-cooked sand grouse or gazelle chops—meat that had been flying through the air or gamboling on the plains a few short minutes before. Let me catch a fish and I'm not happy until I've given it a clay pack and shoved it into the coals. If it comes out half raw it doesn't hurt the taste, even on a tongue that may have been jaded by thirty years of nicotine and honed smooth by prohibition gin.

But it is true that things were different when I was a boy, and the Old Man represented the irretrievable mystery of yesteryear. I do not suppose that I would get very far in interesting today's crop of nippers in what to me was high sport and great fun some thirty to thirty-five years a-past. It was altogether too simple then for this age of television and ballet in the circus. Progress, like nearly everything else, is relative, and I often wonder if its benefits are entirely undiluted.

Most of the fine things we did in the long-buried days happened out of doors. The seasons were sharply etched on the calendar as to potential. Winter was the infrequent snow, with icicles to suck and snow ice cream to be made, and traps for rabbits and the little snowbirds and waxwings that miraculously appeared with the first powdering. The traps were simple. A box was tilted and propped with a stick that had a cord attached. A trail of bread crumbs led to the box, and when the prey entered the trap you gave the cord a twitch from your hiding place and the box fell, imprisoning your quarry. Then the only problem was getting the birds out, and they usually flew free.

A thin skin of ice on the sweet-water ponds made duck hunting easier, because the ducks rafted in clumps and bunches in open water and were loath to fly in the flurrying snow. Somehow all animals and birds seemed tamer and easier to hunt in the snow, and it was tremendous fun to track a deer instead of running him with hounds.

Springtime was strawberry time and green peaches time and bellyache time and—blessed of all the blesseds—getting-out-of-school time. As May nudged lazily into June and the bobolinks swayed atop the long grasses and the black cherries sweated sweetness as their trees oozed jewels of gum the medicine cabinet took quite a thrashing and the castor oil lowered its level in the penance bottle. And it was time to swim again, strictly against parental orders, so you swam anyhow, and the goose-pimpling waters were rendered doubly pneumonically delicious by their very illegality.

Summer, with the horrors of the schoolhouse all but forgotten, was a steady diet of fishing and swimming. There were some summer camps, even in my time—up in the mountains mostly. These were basically created for parents who wanted their children out of their hair for six weeks or so, and so remanded them to a kind of benevolent concentration camp with supervised archery, boating, swimming, hiking, campfire-making, basket-weaving, and suchlike.

The nicest thing about August was that it was a sort of preparatory school for September, when the real adult action started: when you started to train the puppies seriously, when the dove season opened, when the big nor'easters swelled the tides and fetched the marsh hens into sight, when the big blue-fish and the channel bass supplanted the inside fish as a point of interest.

October gave you squirrels and chinquapins glossy brown on the bushes, alum-tart persimmons wrinkling, and the quail calling sweetly in the dusk, still innocently secure from the fusillade that would greet them in November. That was when it really got frosty and the undergrowth withered. The necks of the buck deer swelled, and you could hear the big fellows scraping the last of the velvet off their antlers and snorting in the thickets.

I tried to put some of all this on paper, and once it got going it came with a rush. It was exactly as if the stuff had been locked away, waiting for someone to shove a key in the door and let it all come tumbling out. The first of this outpouring made a companion book called *The Old Man and the Boy*.

Often the material almost wrote itself. I suspect that in reporting the fevered present I had somehow forgotten the old things: the smell of Christmas in a country house; the bugling of hounds hot after a coon; the sight of the wizened old Chinaman's face of a possum curled in a tight ball in a persimmon tree; a colored boy singing to keep off the hants as he drove the cow home through the lowering evening woods; the spumy smash of norther-driven waves on a lonely beach; the rich swelling of song at a colored camp meeting; the convivial gaiety at an oyster roast, when the fruit jar passed freely in the shadows and the square dancers struck up a slightly unsteady reel.

The Old Man and the Boy made me think, made me fine-tooth-comb my memory. The smell of Christmas is a case in point. The old-fashioned Christmas smell was predominantly that of crushed evergreens against the constant resiny scent of a snapping fire. One was a cool smell, the other hot, but both joined forces in delightful companionship. This aromatic backdrop was overlaid by the heady odors that drifted from the kitchen, the sage which went into the turkey stuffing predominating.

The whole was tinctured with spices and by alcohol, because brandies and wines were lavishly used in the preparation of sauces and in building the fruit cakes. There was, as well, an infusion of tropical scent, as the infrequent Christmas citrus fruits—the opulent golden oranges—added an oily sharpness to the mixture. This was counterbalanced by the clean, cidery bite of the hard, white-fleshed, scarlet apples. Bright Christmas candies—the clover-shaped and heart-shaped sugary ones you never saw at any other time of the year and the striped hard ones with the soft centers—helped the greasy Brazil nuts along, as did the winy aroma of the great clusters of raisins, sugary-sticky to the touch. The spices that went into the eggnog or the hot Tom and Jerrys stood off the warm friendship of the rum that gave character to the cream.

Now I had to turn back the clock a far piece to sort out all those various effluvia in my mental nostrils, and in the process I ran onto other stimuli. I could suddenly remember what it was like going to bed between icy sheets in an un-steam-heated house, and the torture of leaving a warm bed to crawl into your clothes in the black predawn of a duck-hunting day—of the tiny furnace that a hunter's big breakfast built in your stomach when your ears were dropping off from cold and your legs were numb from the knees down.

It was easy, then, to reconstruct the bright droplet that always hung at the cherry end of a boy's frozen nose, as he shivered in a duck blind and prayed for the mallards to come in. And such things as the dewdrops of spray standing distinctly on the Old Man's mustache, and the smell of an old man—"old men and old dogs both smell bad"—which seemed compounded of tobacco juice, corn whisky, open fire, and just plain old man.

I was moved to think again, for the first time in many a year, of just how hell-conscious a small boy can be, and of that frightening span of two or three years when I was sure I was going to hell for telling a lie or for cutting Sunday school or for saying damn, and of how I was sore stricken with the enormity of eternity. These severe strokes of conscience generally took hold during a late afternoon in a swamp, when the doves mourned and the early evening snaps and pops and hoots began. Even today, as an adult, during a late fishing afternoon in a darkly mysterious swamp, surrounded by cypress knees and Spanish moss, I feel something of the old fear of the wrath of God, and a chilly finger runs up and down my spine.

Practically nothing of what we did in the old days was artificial or contrived. I shot a bow and arrow, but I had made the bow and the arrows according to a recipe in a book by Ernest Thompson Seton. I didn't need a counselor to teach me archery. We could sling a hatchet, tomahawk fashion, and throw a spear, and make a deadfall, and hurl a knife, and row or sail a boat.

The barn walls in winter were generally tacked full of rabbit skins and the hide of an occasional coon or possum, and I daydreamed violently of meeting a bear to add to the trophies. I never did, but I saw one's tracks once, and that was almost as good as seeing him and shooting him.

There was also a secret life that adults never shared—a life of interlocking caves, of out-of-the-way islands where pirates surely once had buried their loot, of tree houses and even log cabins, their beams out of plumb, to be sure, but a power of cozy comfort to the weary pioneer.

The train from Southport to Wilmington, North Carolina (called the W.B.&S., which meant "Wilmington, Brunswick and Southport," but was corrupted to "Willing But Slow"), consumed the best part of half a day to travel thirty miles, but the trip was fraught with high adventure and a sense of vast travel. The trip on the river boat, of which my Uncle Rob was engineer, took longer, but you felt pretty near like Columbus once you passed the stinking fish meal factory. It took longer to make that thirty miles than it does to fly from New York to London today.

The Old Man and the Boy dealt with a small local segment of the American scene, so it is rather strange and rather amusing that its components should have been produced in practically every corner of the world. The first two chapters were written on a steamer bound for Genoa; subsequent ones were recorded on an African safari. In the years that followed, *The Old Man and the Boy* was written in such disparate places as the Hotel Savoy in London, the Hadden Rig sheep station in New South Wales, and in a camp in Goroka, high in the mountains of New Guinea, as well as in Rome, Paris, Madrid, the Philippines, Tokyo, Hong Kong, and a number of other places I won't take the time to list. Altogether it has been one of the best-traveled pieces of work in history, and it is odd that the only place in which it has not been written is the locale where the incidents happened—Southport and Wilmington. Most of the contents of this book were written in Spain, Africa, and India, airplanes being what they are today.

It is probably perverse and cranky of me, but I can't understand what the modern youngster sees of interest in rockets to the moon and satellites and such when there are still so many things to discover in the tangible sea. Nor how the extravagances of television can claim precedence over camping trips, or even over the limitless, understandable adventure to be found in books that do not deal with space cadets and moon dwellers.

But as a boy grown old I do not seem to be lonely in this appraisal of things not being like they used to be. The weather's changed, and everybody talks about whether or not it's the atom bomb's fault. The safari business is booming, and is patronized largely by old boys with prominent veins and pot-bellies, men trying to torture themselves into a misty remembrance of things past. You never see any bluebirds any more, and the red-headed woodpeckers have joined the dodo. Things are definitely not the same as when I was a lad, and if you asked me right smart how many miles I walked to school through the snow I would probably top the Old Man and say, "Twenty." That would be a lie, because all the time I had a bicycle and the schoolhouse was just around the corner. It wasn't red either. That was the color of the seventh-grade teacher's hair at just about the time the birds and the bees took on a slightly different significance.

Come to think of it, they ain't making red-headed school-teachers the way they used to either. Not the last time I looked.

1

All He Left Me Was the World

The streets filled as far as you could see; past the oak grove one way, down toward the river another way. Most of the faces were black, the black bulk accented here and there by a white face. There were dogs in the crowd, too, and children as well as adults.

They had come to see the Old Man off, to "say good-bye" to the Cap'm. The only face among his kinry that was missing was mine. I had said good-bye to him; he had said good-bye to me. I didn't want it all confused with a lot of mourners. I went and got the oars from under the house and rowed over to Battery Island. There didn't figure to be anything on it but birds.

There is no way, absolutely no way, to describe the desolation I felt. The Old Man was gone, and I was fifteen years old and alone without a prop in a world that was too big for me without the Old Man. I rowed the boat hard, trying not to think of him dead, but not succeeding. Then I thought of what had sent me onto the water—his old axiom that a boat and open water would come pretty close to solving any problems you had at the time, if only because water cleared your head, fishing calmed your nerves, "and you can always eat the fish." I suppose that some people would think it odd that I skipped the Old Man's funeral services and went fishing. The Old Man would not have thought it odd.

I noticed that from force of habit I had brought the cast net, and there were hand lines in the locker. I drove the boat over into the shallows, jammed her into the bank with an oar, and looked about the marsh for some schools of shrimp. In a bit I had bait, and I pushed her free of the beach and went out to a fishing hole I knew, where there were plenty of croakers and often sea trout. I anchored, baited the line, and proceeded to fish. What I caught I cannot say. I assume I caught something. I usually caught something on these expeditions.

"March is an awful month," the Old Man used to say. "Best you use it for remembering." So I sat in the boat and methodically fished, and remembered.

"I ain't going to leave you much," he had said, when it got bad toward the end. "This sickness cost an awful lot of money. The house is mortgaged, and there's a note in the bank, and the depression is still on. There won't be much left but some shotguns and a cast net and a boat. And, maybe, a memory."

All of a sudden the sun came out in my head. What did he mean, he wasn't going to leave me much? Who was kidding whom? I was the richest boy in the world. Croesus was a beggar alongside me. I had had fifteen years of the Old Man, and nearly everything he knew he'd taught me. I started to take a check on my assets.

First he had raised me as a man among men, without condescension, without patronizing. He had allowed me companionship on an equal basis with himself and with his men friends.

He had given me pride and equality. He had taught me compassion and manners and tolerance, especially toward the less fortunate, white or black. That sea of black faces which appeared in the street had not heard desegregation or any other "ation" except starvation. They came because they loved the Old Man, their friend. All but the younger ones had been born of slaves.

The preachers, white and black, had been in the crowd. And so had the bums. These were the hairier types who had taken a part in my education, the drinkers and the fighters and the loafers. They were there, together with the city fathers, and the Coast Guard boys, and the Pilots' Association, plus the relatives and the hound dogs. I reckoned that the Old Man must have had something that rubbed off on people, including me.

What else was there?

Well, he had given me the vast gift of reading. He had made reading a form of sport, like hunting was a sport and fishing was a sport. He had unleashed all the treasures of the knowledge of the world, so that I always had my nose buried in a book. It didn't matter what kind of book so long as it had words in it. I was reading Macaulay and Addison and Swift and Shakespeare for kicks. I never read the Bible for religious reasons. Reading the Bible as a straight book, and not as a tract, I had found it to have more action than Zane Grey's woolliest westerns. I read history as avidly as fiction, and the ancient Egyptians got away with very little I wasn't hep to. Everybody else called her Venus, but I knew the lady that rose from the sea was called the Aphrodite of Melos a long time before Dr. Harland got hold of me in college.

So the Old Man had also given me the gift of avoidance of boredom. If there is any piece of paper anywhere, whether it's a patent-medicine bottle or a soap wrapper, and if it has words on it I will read the words and not be bored. I am well past forty now, and do not remember a moment of boredom, because, among other things, the Old Man also gave me eyes to see—to actually *see.*

"Most people," he had said, "go through life looking and

never see a thing. Anything you see is interesting, from a chinch bug to a barnacle, if you just look at it and wonder about it a little." Then he would send me to the swamps or out in the boat or off along the beach with a firm command to *look* and tell him later what I saw. I saw plenty and in detail, whether it was ants working or a mink swimming or a tumblebug endlessly pushing its ball.

I saw male squirrels castrate rivals in the rutting season; I saw a sea turtle laying eggs and weeping great tears. I saw the life of the swamps and the marshes, heard the sounds and watched the lives outdoors change as the climate varied. I learned to listen to the night sounds: the dogs barking in concert when the moon was right for it, the mournful hoot of owl and plaint of whippoorwill, the querulous yap of fox and the belling of a lonesome hound on a trail of his own devising. I learned to love the mournful coo of doves as the evening approached, the desperately forlorn call of quail as they tried to reassemble a scattered covey.

I became acutely conscious of smells: crushed fern, dogfennel, the bright slashes of split pine with the oozing gum, bruised Jimson weed—the little smells apart from the major ones, like jessamine or magnolia or myrtle. The smell of summer differed from the smell of autumn. Summer was languid and milky, like the soft breath of a cow. Autumn was tart and stimulating, with leaves burning, frost on the grass, and the gum trees turning. Spring was a young girl smell, and winter was an old man's smell, compounded of grate fires and tobacco juice.

Cooking? The Old Man had taught me that food can be something more than fodder to distend a growling gut. We had had as much fun out of preparing food as in the procuring of it with gun or rod. He had taught me to make an adventure out of cooking a catfish on a sandspit, of making an oyster roast or eating raw clams busted on the gunwale of a boat. I was proud of me as a cook—and grateful for the knowledge that hawg-and-hominy, if you're hungry, or a bait of turtle eggs or a fried squirrel or rabbit is better than the fine-haired saucy stuff you eat when you get wealthy enough to traffic with restaurants.

What else had he left me, apart from these things?

Well, good manners, painfully impressed, and once or twice with a lath. I said "Sir" and "Ma'am" and "Please" and "Thank you," and was more or less silent in the presence of my elders and at table. I didn't try to hog my shooting partner's bird shots, and I never infringed on another man's right to command his dogs. I was quiet in the woods, and I left my campsites clean, with all the refuse buried and the fire raked neat.

I could throw a cast net, shoot a gun, row a boat, call a turkey, build a duck blind, tong an oyster, train a puppy, stand a deer, bait a turkey blind (illegal), call the turkey to the blind, cast in the surf, pitch a tent, make a bed out of pine needles, follow a coonhound, stand a watch on a fishing boat, skin anything that had to be skun, scale a fish, dig a clam, build a cave, draw a picture, isolate edible mushrooms from the poisonous toad-stools, pole a boat, identify all the trees and most of the flowers and berries, get along with the colored folks, and also practice a rude kind of game conservation.

That seemed to sum it up, as far as legacy was concerned; two shotguns, a cast net, a boat, and a house with a new mockingbird in the magnolia—a house that wouldn't be ours much longer. College just around the corner, if I could figure out a way to work my way through it.

I heaved up the hook, picked up the oars, and rowed home. By the time I got there the funeral crowd had dissipated, and there wasn't anybody there but a few relatives and close friends. Nobody appeared to have missed me.

I was hungry, and in the South funerals are always accompanied by food. The idea is slightly macabre, but everybody pitches in a cake or a turkey or a ham, and if you can conquer the funereal smell of the flowers the dining-room table is groaning. I made myself a ham sandwich and was pouring a glass of milk when one final thought hit me, wham!

On the rainy days or driving the Liz or rowing a boat or in

the off seasons where there wasn't anything to hunt or fish the Old Man had made a habit of what he called indoctrinating me into the world of human beings. This consisted of the sum of his travels and his reading. He was a shark on the old West, for instance, and he knew a great deal about Coronado's treasure and the people who had wasted their lives looking for it. He was a bug on the great trek westward, when the prairie schooners set out on a prayer and a venture. He knew all about what happened to the buffalo and about the passing of the carrier pigeon. He was an old-timer who was modern enough to know he was the last of the old-timers. He knew about all the world as well, whether it was ancient Egypt or Stanley looking for Livingstone in Africa, and he had fed me these stories like cakes ever since I was a toddler.

It suddenly occurred to me that I was educated before I saw a college. I made up my mind right then that someday I would learn to be a writer and write some of the stuff the Old Man had taught me. There was only one thing I had to do first, and that was to get educated and make enough money to buy back the old yellow-painted square house with its mockingbird in the magnolia and its pecan trees in the back yard.

This took a lot of time, and included a war, outraged peace, and a lot of written words. It included Washington and New York, London and Paris, Spain and Australia, Africa and India, lions and tigers, hope and despair. But the Old Man's house is back in the family now, and the mockingbird—lineal descendant of the one I once murdered—sings cheerfully on the moonlit nights in the magnolia, the pecans are bearing again and so is the fig tree. The oak grove hasn't changed.

There is gray in the boy's hair, but the Old Man persists, and you will be hearing more about the things he told me. And perhaps the gray will momentarily depart, and I shall not be the Old Man, but the boy again, because it is all coming powerfully clear.

2

Nobility Is Wrecking the Country

Some five years from the day I told the Old Man good-bye Mrs. Eleanor Roosevelt was saying—for about two hours—to several hundred bright-faced young people in the football stadium, ". . . and the future of the world rests solidly on your sturdy young shoulders," as the University of North Carolina prepared to thrust the graduates of 1935 out into the jungles of commerce.

Three of these sturdy-shouldered young men were not, I am afraid, treating the graduation exercises with proper respect. Among the three R's grouped together on the hard stadium seats was a scientist. Working secretly, just at dusk, he had managed to hide a large crock under the middle R. By way of individual rubber hoses, run from the crock underneath our scholarly robes, we could siphon sufficient home-brewed happiness to relieve the ceremony of some of its tedium. I am afraid that at least three young plumed knights wore their mortarboards at a rather rakish tilt when they marched bravely up to receive the sheepskin that declared them to be World Saviors (j.g.).

During the lengthy orations—or exhortations—I kept thinking how much more fun a colored camp meeting was, which conjured up the kind of graduation speech the Old Man might have made. Once he had said, "You're going to be a man soon. There never was anybody fit to tell another man how to be a man. Free advice generally accomplishes two things. If you take the advice and it turns sour you hate the man that gave it to you. If it works out sound you still don't like him for telling you how to run your life. And if you refuse the advice and make out all right he'll never forgive you for making him look bad." He paused to fire up his prop—the pipe.

"I plead guilty to having tried to teach you a few things I know, like not blowing your foot off or shooting me for a deer or killing all the quail instead of just a few. You were raised honest and decent to the best of my notion, and if none of it took, why, it's too late to do anything about it now. What you make of your early raising is strictly up to you.

"But I would ask your permission to throw a couple more thoughts at you, which might keep you out of jail or the loony bin. Don't be noble—it's wrecking the country. And try to remember that having a little fun as you go along ain't no sin. It's just as necessary as sleeping. Don't take yourself seriously, because you're competing with about a hundred billion people, including Chinamen and Ubangis, who think that they're just as important as the next Chinaman or Ubangi, and they never heard of you at all.

"Speaking metaphorically," he concluded with a flourish, "I will look down on you from wherever I'm at and smile if you manage to struggle through the next fifty years or so without setting fire to the bush, leaving a messy campsite, or hogging the shots from your fellow man. Selah."

The old gentleman had already read me a lecture on turning personal tragedy into high adventure (and sometimes low comedy) if you could only manage to regard yourself as somebody else, which I have found a handy aid over the last triple decade. At least if you can laugh instead of cry the troubles will either kill you or go away, and it is a bit better to die laughing than to die crying.

From the first days I was old enough to toddle into the woods the Old Man was able to make the tiniest occurrence—things that many people pass by—seem adventurous. He could find a symbol of life's struggle merely by watching a tumble-bug struggle with his ball.

"There," he would say, "is Everyman, trying to shove that ball uphill as a life's work and never quite making it. But you can't say the little devil ain't giving it his best effort, and he don't seem to be whining for any help."

He broke me into life as you'd teach a child to walk or a puppy to respect an older dog's point. He suggested rather than ordered, and he was diabolically oblique in his methods. Havilah Babcock once wrote a piece in which he cured an obstreperous puppy of breaking a back-stand by eventually beating the old dog that was suffering the indignity. The puppy's papa finally turned on the puppy instead of humoring him, and trounced the daylights out of the sinner. The sinner immediately conformed to the society of decent bird dogs. (The Old Man would have loved that piece as did I, because I could read me very easily into the puppy's part.)

The only thing the Old Man was intolerant of was intolerance. He construed intolerance as several things. Basically he was highly tolerant of other people's rights, whether it had to do with race, creed, or property. He respected Posted signs, but sometimes, when he figured the end justified the means, he was not averse to calling another man's turkey across the

road to where there weren't any POSTED signs—if nobody was
shooting the turkeys anyhow. He was intolerant of impolite-
ness, whether it was in the house or in the field, whether it involved hogging a shot or leaving a filthy campsite or setting
fire to a forest. He taught me humility in a darkening swamp,
when the doves moaned and the shadows fell and all the spooky,
late-afternoon swamp noises set in.

About this time of year, when I had been bucking and rearing
like an overfed colt all spring, he calmed me down by letting
me help him build a boat, and then sent me off for a summer on
the waters all by myself. He was the original do-it-yourself
inventor, especially if doing-it-yourself—such as scaling the fish
or chopping the firewood or shooting quail in the rain—involved me.

"Boys," he would say, "belong to do a lot of men's work,
out of respect to their elders' rheumatiz, and also as a kind of
apprenticeship toward manhood. It's the price you pay for being a boy."

Curiosity, he reckoned, was one of the cardinal virtues of
life. "They say curiosity killed the cat," he would opine, "but
more likely it was an overdose of mice." He looked under logs
and peered around the corners. He wasn't satisfied until he
knew all there was to know about anything that crossed his
path, and that included everything from Greek mythology to
the nesting habits of a tomtit.

He had a strange sense of beauty and a stranger sense of
humor. One time I deliberately stepped on a caterpillar.

"Don't let me see you do that again," he said sharply. "You've
just squashed the daylights out of a diurnal rhopalocerous lepi-
dopterous creature—a thing of beauty."

"A which?" I asked.

He grinned. "A butterfly that ain't born yet." He was full of
that sort of foolishness, because while he used "ain't" and
double negatives for emphasis he read encyclopedias for fun,
and very early he had my nose stuck into Bulfinch's *Mythol-*

ogy, which I found fascinating. He had me reading Shakespeare for fun, instead of yellowbacks of blood and thunder.

"Shakespeare's got more blood and thunder in him than Nick Carter and Ned Buntline put together. And stay away from the Horatio Alger books. All them heroes are namby-pamby bores, and anyhow it didn't happen that way. Bosses are a little choosy about who marries their daughters. You can't build a life hoping to find a pocketbook on the streets so you can return it to the boss and get to be president of the bank."

Fun had several definitions. "No man belongs to play until the work's done," he would say sternly. And then slyly, "But there ain't nothing wrong in turning work into fun if you can get away with it. I see nothing wrong about pretending you're a high-rigger in an Oregon fir forest, two hundred feet above the ground, when all you're really doing is chopping kindling."

He dearly loved his toddy, but he was very stern about mixing up drinking with hunting or any other kind of sport or work that needed a keen eye and full concentration.

"You either come to hunt or you come to drink," he said. "It's all right with me if the drunks want to stay in camp, but I don't aim to have my head blown off by no damn fool in a duck blind. Drinkin's for when the work's done, too. Nothing I admire more than a cup of corn at the end of the day—or even," with a wink, "in the case of old men, when the morning's bitter and the stars are still up and it's colder'n a mile into an iceberg. But not while you're hunting. Or fishing. I know many a man to get himself drownded when he was drunk. Or fall off a hill and bust his neck."

He would continue on his favorite topic—fun. "Fun is a little present you give yourself as a reward for what you've earned. You can turn work into play, but you can also turn play into work if you don't balance it off with a little honest toil. You run out of things to play at, and you run out of play toys. Them rich playboys are as useless as tits on a boar. A bum is a bum, whether he's rich or poor."

On the topic of what constituted a gentleman: "A gentleman don't necessarily have to own a necktie or shave every day. There's some ruffians around this town that don't wash too much and might get drunk on Saturday night that I would call gentlemen. On the other hand there are some stiff-collared, nondrinking, church-going, clean-necked folks I wouldn't trust as far as you can sling an ox. A gentleman is what the word means, a *gentle man*."

The Old Man never held forth much on formal religion. He said he reckoned a man knew best what his own God was and how to work with Him, and he was never much of a reformer. He said he reckoned Somebody, no matter what name you called Him, was responsible for sun, moon, mountains, sea, stars, heat, cold, seasons, animals, birds, fish, and food—"even small boys, although that may have been a basic mistake"—and whether you called him God, Allah, Jehovah, or Mug-Mug didn't make much difference as long as you believed in Him.

On the sexes: "Man is a simple creature—a very small boy who wants to be patted on the head and told he's a good boy and a nice boy and a smart boy. You can lead him anywhere. But as for women, I don't know. They got a sort of contrary, different chemistry of brain and action from men, which makes them unruly and subject to strange fits. My only advice on women is to stay out of the house when they're cleaning and don't say yes too often."

The young people who are exploding forth from the citadels of knowledge in any lovely month of June will have a tremendous heap of exhortation flung at them, and they will be told, in varying terms, that the world's future rests on their stanch shoulders. They will feel, possibly, that this has not occurred before. But I can think they might do worse than heed some of the Old Man's advice.

I had no bad conscience that night more than a quarter-century ago, when the three R's inhaled a little home-brew while we sweated through the platform rhetoric. After all, the work of education had been finished and we were entitled to a little fun before we plunged into the future. I went to work that same week and have been steadily at it since. But it has not been work unleavened with fun. And I have heeded the old gentleman's advice as well as I have been able. At least, I haven't been noble, and so far I haven't managed to wreck the country.

3

Uncle Rob Had Humphrey Bogart Beat a Mile

The world of a boy who lives beside a river is limitless in scope, if the boy is blessed with imagination and there is some older, romantic head around to encourage the boy in what some grown ups dismiss as tomfool daydreaming.

We lived by a river, and the river rolled snaking out to sea. It was a broad, broad vista, seen by a boy's eyes, and the Old Man's tales about what might lie on the other side drove me into a frenzy of youthful torment. My people were born of the river and of the sea, and they spoke a language which fed more from seafaring English than Southern drawl. We drank strong black tea and ate raisin duff; the surnames of St. George and Newton, Adkins and Guthrie, Davis and Morse were only a jump removed from another Southport in England. My relatives ran the river, and some of them had strode the seas. My imagination surpassed them, until Samarkand and Far Cathay were at my beck.

All of this was fetched sharply home a few years ago when somebody steered me onto a moving picture called *The African Queen*, which had to do with Katharine Hepburn and Humphrey Bogart running a wild African river on a dilapidated old scow called "The African Queen."

All through the picture something kept bothering me, and it wasn't the fact that the director, John Huston, opened the action with Bogart's belly rumbling as some missionaries were leading the wretched heathen to the light. Nor, exactly, was it the anguished look on Bogart's face when Miss Hepburn threw all the gin over the side and Bogart watched each square-faced bottle as it disappeared to eternity in the "Queen's" bubbling wake.

What struck the basic reminiscent note was Bogart using his foot to kick the ramshackledy old engine into life and his primitive means of preventing the boilers from exploding. Whiskers and all, Mr. Bogart, now gathered to a land where the woodbine twineth around free gin bottles, drew me back to my Uncle Rob and some voyages I made with him when he was chief—and only—engineer of an old passenger tub called, I think, "The Steamer Wilmington." I could be wrong about the name as it was something more than thirty-five years ago.

Uncle Rob was my favorite relative, apart from the Old Man, but Rob was kind of a raffish relative, somewhat given to profanity and occasionally to strong waters. Not until later years was he addicted to steady work. Not that he was triflin'— far from it. Rob was a man of far horizons, but limited opportunity to reach them.

Uncle Rob, from young manhood until the day he died, looked like a whisker-shorn Scotch terrier, with a terrier's temper. He was a man of motion. When Rob was a boy his father would hitch up the buggy, and cart Rob off to some boarding school (his father was what was known in those days as well-to-do), and Rob would generally take a punch at the headmaster and beat the old man home, sometimes a distance of a couple of hundred miles. Rob did not lean kindly toward education, and education did not consider Rob a likely candidate for distinction.

But there was very little Rob could not do with his hands. They were strong, callused hands, with square-tipped fingers and nails that always wore a clean rim of grease, because Rob's hands were always plunged deep in the guts of an engine. He would tinker, and tinker, and if the cussed thing wouldn't go he would haul off and fetch her a kick. The motor would catch and settle down to a steady hum. They said Rob had "a knowing foot," and so he did.

Rob was blunt with a Scotsman's bluntness, which sometimes lost him friends. He had a habit of saying what he thought, regardless of consequence. On one occasion, when Aunt May had trapped him into going to church, he glanced down the prayerful aisles to a female relative who was somewhat lacking in beauty.

"Damn, that's an ugly woman," Rob muttered.

"Shhh, Rob," Aunt May said. "The poor thing can't help it if she's ugly."

"No, she can't help it if she's ugly," Rob muttered back, "but God dammit, *she could stay home.*"

Rob eventually turned highly respectable, and worked many years as chief engineer of government dredge boats on the Mississippi and elsewhere, and seldom jeopardized his professional standing on the strong waters without by his old fondness for the strong waters within—*within* Rob, that is. He kind of settled down after one bout with John Barleycorn caused him to lurch into a Christmas tree, scattering the burning candles and nearly setting the house afire.

"God*damn* Santa Claus," Uncle Rob muttered, and tottered off with something other than sugarplums dancing through his head. What pounded through his skull next day was a withering hangover and the combined censure of the steadier element of yuletide celebrants.

But somewhere in his earlier days of sketchy employment Uncle Rob enjoyed a brief span as engineer of this hand-knit passenger liner, the "Wilmington," and as his favorite nephew I was allowed to go voyaging occasionally with Uncle Rob. Thereby opened the vistas of far places, which have caused me trouble ever since.

I had some seagoing experience—as unpaid supercargo on the Coast Guard rumchasers and on the fertilizer-fish boat, the old "Vanessa," that the Old Man skippered from time to time in the pogy season. But I reckon my trip from Southport to Wilmington on the Cape Fear River was my first experience with a vessel on which people actually paid passage, and certainly it was my first run on the river.

I can clearly remember the thrill of being in the cabin (the cabin!) of the "Wilmington," and hearing the pulsing of the engines, and knowing that my Uncle Rob, greasy to the ears, was one-half of the human forces which kept us afloat. I was not concerned with the captain and the deck hand. The Cape Fear was wide enough to accommodate ocean-going freighters and needed little skill in the steering. What intrigued me most was that teakettle below decks, which kept me from the gaping maws of the imaginary hippos and crocodiles which undoubtedly thronged the river.

That first voyage was notable for the fact that I was deep in the vitals of *Tarzan of the Apes*, possibly the most fascinating book ever written for young or old. (I read it again with vast satisfaction the other day, and it loses nothing with time.)

In this instance the "Wilmington" had been renamed the barque "Fuwalda," by me, and I was John Clayton, Lord Greystoke, about to swim through the croc-ridden waters to the forbidding African shores. As a matter of fact there probably *were* a few sharks in the Cape Fear, and, as the water changed from salt to brackish to fresh, the odd alligator lurking in the rice marshes.

Uncle Rob cursed steadily and feverishly in the stinking heat of the engine room, and kicked the engine into sputtering life when its dying gasp was imminent, so I did not have to swim through the crocodiles and hippos into the waiting arms of shrieking savages and fierce beasts. And thus, with one of my first impressions of man against the sea, was born an abiding respect for anybody who could do anything with his hands which would make a piece of dumb machinery respond sufficiently to conquer the elements.

A trip down the river was quite a sight in those days. She is a strong brown river, the Cape Fear, roily with filth, and subject to whimsical current. The entry from the ocean, between the islands of Baldhead and Caswell, was jagged and marked by sand bars, to a point where the big foreign ships had to hang off the light and wait for the pilot boat to chug out, board a pilot, and then answer the pilot's con in the wheelhouse or on the flying bridge, as she ran the river to the discharge-and-loading port of Wilmington.

You would see the big ships, sea-weary and rust-scabbed, their stacks salt-grimed and their paint scaly, butting down the river. Their high poop decks bore their names in rusty gold, magical port names, "Hamburg" and "Liverpool," "Bremen" and "Antwerp," "Marseilles" and "Rotterdam." Wilmington was on the North Atlantic run, which touched Jacksonsville, Savannah, and Charleston, all names that were nearly as foreign to me then as the Rotterdams and the Bremens.

It was a powerful thrill, then, treading the quarter-deck of the stanch ship "Wilmington" to know that blood kin was driving the engine which throbbed and rattled beneath your feet, and that the guiding hand at the helm of the big, ocean-battered freighters that passed you belonged to another blood relative, Uncle Walker or Uncle Tommy or the Old Man himself, with a whole dynasty of younger blood relatives—someday, perhaps even me—coming up to guide the big ships and perhaps to sail away to the far places as master or man.

The entirely ersatz Africa of Mr. Edgar Rice Burroughs' Tarzan then seemed no more distant than the duck-tremulous rice fields of the fabulous Orton Plantation, with its moss-dripping live oaks and stately white-columned main house. A river is just as broad as a sea to a boy, and limitless depths of the ocean no more peril-fraught than a greasy, rolling brown river, which can wreck a big ship and has yielded its toll of bloated drowned men, just as dead as if they were swept ashore off Hatteras, the ships just as wrecked as if they were tolled to doom by the decoying lanterns of the wreckers at Nags Head.

My Uncle Rob—my Uncles Tommy and Walker, the Old Man, and me—were all part of what was a most exciting state, if only a boy realized it at the time. Blackbeard the Pirate was no stranger to our off-coast sea islands. British troops knew the old town of Wilmington, and old Fort Fisher had seen a power of Rhett Butlers running blockades. We had our own lost Indian tribe of Roanoke; we still had the Croatans upriver; and a solid reservation of half-naked blanket, bownarrer Cherokees upstate in the mountains.

Rumrunners used our coastal coves to dump their cargo, and our Coast Guard had a cutter, the "Modoc," which called Wilmington a home port. Baldhead and Caswell had its Coast Guard stations, from which beach patrol, surfboat patrol, and rumchasers operated. It was not unusual to see apprehended rum being smashed in the street in front of the Customs House, and I can remember the sight of one drunk dabbing the wasting rivulets of good whisky with a handkerchief and wringing out the booze-soaked cloth in his mouth.

Deeper, farther in the swamps, a few counties away, we had a strange race of people called Brass Ankles, a mixture of Indian, white, and Negro, who were as handy with knives as some of their relatives amongst the Croatans of the Lumberton area.

Not too far away, close to a township called Waccamaw, we

had the Green Swamp, big enough and impenetrable enough to be called abysmal. On some islands in this vast sea of tangled growth were clumps and clusters of humanity who had escaped first from the French Revolution to Haiti, thence from Haiti to Wilmington, thence from Wilmington inland to sanctuary in the swamps. Some were inbred and idiotic from isolation. Nearly all had French names and spoke a French patois not unlike the Haitian creole. In that swamp, the Green Swamp, there were panthers and bears and alligators, wild hogs and wild cats.

All of these riches, these excitements stretched before a small boy whose uncle drove the craft on which he strode the waters, whose other relatives piloted ships from far-distant places, ships whose crews gabbled in strange tongues and whose captains often gave the pilots a gold-foiled bottle of strange liquor or a sandalwood chest to take home as a souvenir of the trip down the river.

Yet for some reason, some obscure reason, only a handful of men from this area had been abroad, in the sense of having seen the Mississippi or the phosphate-loading port of Fernandina in Florida. They shrimped and they fertilizer-fished and they piloted other people's ships on the river, but they stayed home. One man named Lockwood built a boat on a big creek with some inchoate urge to take it down to the sea, but he built the boat too big for the bridge, her draft too deep for the channel. The locality is still called Lockwood's Folly, as an admonition to stay home and not go off mingling with the furriners.

My own people had been away and had mingled with furriners, but they had come home. Home was a salt-rimed fishing village, whose oak grove was called simply "The Grove," and any voyage to the post office or the store was called "going up the street." Even Wilmington, thirty miles away, was a foreign country, whose people spoke a different language, lived different lives, and were regarded with scorn as city people, freshwater catfish.

Some of this must have rubbed off on me as I made my first run as a river-boat man with my Uncle Rob. Some of it must have bitten deeply as I breasted the bar with the "Penton," the pilot boat, went fish-chasing on the "Vanessa," or fingered the cold-greasy guns on the cutter "Modoc." Some of it must have itched and burned as we danced on the treacherous edges of Frying Pan shoals, sailing perilously close after bluefish and mackerel, within easy view of the lightship, a floating light-house, with its mournful bellow to keep the big ships away from Frying Pan.

All this, I suppose, came surging home when Humphrey Bogart kicked the engine alive in the moving picture *The African Queen*, reposing partially in the memory of Uncle Rob, who finally conquered a bigger river than Humphrey Bogart vanquished—a river leading to a considerably larger body of water.

But I will say another thing for Uncle Rob over Humphrey Bogart. Uncle Rob would not have stood idly by to watch Katharine Hepburn dump a case of gin over the side for the crocodiles to puzzle over. If Uncle Rob had been engineer of "The African Queen" Miss Hepburn would have joined the gin.

4

The Old Man Paid My Passage

The waves crashed against the bow of the ship, spreading sheets of water over the foc'sle head. The old Hog Islander was running bow on into the gale. As she plunged she suffered and creaked amidships, and when she buried her prow in a sea her screws came clear of the following waves and thrashed painfully half out of the water.

The night was blacker than the water and as cold as the Arctic that supplied the sea on this northern passage to Liverpool. The night watchman was braced against the anchor chains as they stretched taut from the chain locker to crimp round the winch. The night watchman was really two people—the Number Two Ordinary Seaman and the cadet. They each worked an eight-hour shift, from eight bells to eight bells, or from

8 P.M. to 8 A.M.—two hours on lookout, two hours stand-by, two hours lookout, two hours stand-by, seven bitter-cold nights a week, each week.

The night watchman wore smelly long drawers, two pairs of pants, two wool shirts, two sweaters, a sheepskin coat, oilskins, a knitted cap pulled down over his ears under the sou'wester, two pairs of socks, and hip boots. The sheets of water hit him full in the face, streamed back over the iced foc'sle head, and went cascading over the deck cargo of lashed-down logs, chained tautly to the hatch and bulkhead and tightened by turn-buckles.

The Ordinary Seaman, who was paid ten dollars a week, no overtime, who stood eight-hour watches at sea, who shortly would begin to rot his hands in a mixture of lye and water called *suji-muji* with which he cleaned the whitework, who helped shift the ship at night from dock to dock on his own time, who painted over the side in port, who swept the remains of sheep manure and phosphate rock and sulphur from the holds, who cleaned the stinking bilges in the deep tanks, who helped batten down open hatches in company-timesaving de-fiance of maritime law when the ship was already at sea, who was part of the poop-deck gang when the ship tied up or cast off, who had been shot at by strikers in Antwerp (strikers who had rifles and who climbed grain elevators for better aiming vantage), who ate biscuits from which cockroaches were knocked, who worked under a Danish bosun named Svendsen who hated him and was doubly hated in return, who lived with seven other men in one room under the poop next the grinding of the steering engine, who shared one toilet with the same seven men and washed out of a bucket into which a steampipe had been turned to heat the water, and who had been forced to fight half the men on the ship to defend his right to be a former college boy at sea during the great depression—this ordinary seaman walked into the crew mess and bled a cup of overboiled coffee out of the huge zinc urn in the corner, sat down on a bench by the mess table, observed that the "night lunch" had already been eaten, and lit a cigarette. Hungry, he cursed again —cursing ships and men and the sea and the spirit of high adventure that had gotten him into this mess.

The Ordinary Seaman Number Two was a little over twenty years old. He had been a college graduate on the bum for nine months. The year was early 1936. The Ordinary Seaman Number Two was me.

After I had my coffee I warmed my hands over the fiddley heat again, and then I got the *suji* bucket and the rags and went into the passageway to freeze my hands and open up the cuts the lye had already made in my fingers. I closed my mind to the freezing cold and the burning lye and began to think. I had found on the foc'sle head, where you weren't allowed to smoke, that I could control my thinking, and by channeling it along pleasant lines I could make the time pass more swiftly. Mostly I thought about the Old Man—not the captain of the ship, but *my* Old Man, dead now for six years.

"The Old Man got me into this," I used to say aloud. (You got used to talking aloud when they switched the watches to four on, four wheel watch and stand-by.) "He got me into it, and I might as well make him pay part of my passage."

He had, too, in a way. He had a master's license in sail and steam, and once he was on a trip around the Cape of Good Hope that took three years. He bottle-fed me on seafaring stuff. He told me all the hardships, all about the lousy food and some of the lousier people, and I refused to believe it wasn't romantic. I had one thing in mind: when I finished school I was going to sea. I was going to see the world.

"You ain't going to like it," the Old Man had said. "But you might as well try it and get it over with. You won't be happy until you do."

Oh brother, thought I, taking half a foot of paint off a plank with the *suji* rag and the same amount of skin off my hands, *he didn't tell me the half of it. He didn't tell me that the second*

*mate was going to wake me up once with a kick in the belly
or that I would ever entertain a serious idea about killing a
squarehead bosun named Svendsen in an alley with my bare
hands.*

I guess the Old Man saved me from being hanged for murder
at that, for when the mutinous madness came on I could drive it
off with the thinking. I thought of all the nice things we had
ever done together: the first shotgun, what Christmas cooking
smelt like. I thought about the first double on quail and the first
deer and how to make a good camp and how a bird dog looked
winding a covey in the broom grass. I thought about the quiet
of a Carolina swamp with the bass biting, and an autumn afternoon on a lonely beach with the blues ravenous and the wind
howling pleasantly outside a snug cabin whose walls shook
with the gale and trembled from a roaring fire, with ham spitting in the skillet. But I never thought about it all at once. I
rationed it. I would say: "All right, Ordinary, what do we
think about tonight?" and then I'd pick one thing and think
about every little bit of it. I suppose people in prison do the
same thing.

This particular cold night I was back in Louisiana, where the
Old Man took me on a duck-hunting trip. I was down a bayou.
We were living on a big boat with some of his friends, mostly
Cajuns, and I never saw duck hunting like this before. You
hunted in a singlet, and your face got sunburned, and all you
worried about was mosquitoes. We went to a lot of fuss over
blinds in the Carolinas, but here in the Louisiana marshes you
went to no trouble at all. You just climbed into a pirogue, with
the Cajun who poled it standing, from the stern, and the decoys
jumbled together in front of you. The Cajun could push that
flat-bottomed pirogue over solid mud, if it had a bead of moisture on it.

There were four pirogues in all, two men to a boat. We—or
rather, they—poled slowly down the bayou, letting the tide take
the boat, until we came to a kind of track that led into what

appeared, in the gray of the early morning light, to be a broad sweet-water pond set in the middle of the marsh.

My Cajun, named Pierre, shoved us into a patch of roseaux or reeds. He got out, in his boots, and then pulled the pirogue up onto a grassy tussock, where he braced her with the pole athwartships, each end of the skiff jammed into the reeds. Then he pulled the roseaux in bunches round us until we were beautifully hidden. He waded out into the finger-shallow water and flung the weighted decoys here and there. Across the pond I could hear the *skush* of the other pirogues as they slid across the ooze, and occasionally a muffled Cajun "By gar" drifted across the quiet water as the poler got his pole fouled in a water lily root. Then the splash of the decoys, and silence until the sky began to pink at the edges.

The most exciting sound in the world cut the stillness, and you forgot the persistent mosquitoes as the high wings whispered through the sky and dim shapes made faint marks against the low gray clouds as they passed out of range overhead. The torture was heightened by the thin whistle of teal coming by, low and turning, and the faint splashes as they set down among the decoys and the tiny gurgle as they swam. Then the watery flap of wings as one drake stood on his tail to challenge the world made the semidarkness well-nigh unbearable.

But the pink spread to red and crowded higher in the sky, and suddenly an enormous gray blur darted past the blind. I shot the blur more or less in the pants as it passed, and it fell with a soggy bump onto the water-covered ooze.

"Must of been a goose," I whispered to Pierre.

"*Non, man,* dat no goose," he whispered back. "Dat beeg bull peentail. Beeg lak a goose, though. Look, you, here come some more."

A flight of pintails came in and swirled, and I raised the gun, but Pierre touched me on the arm. "*Non,* don't shoot yet," he said. "Dey mak one more turn, den come seet down weeth decoy."

Pierre was right. They went away, turned, came in low and perfectly, and locked their wings. I shot at the feet of one big drake as he dropped his legs, dumped him, and pulled away to a fast-climbing bird—another drake. I aimed at his sky-seeking bill and dropped this fellow, too. I was out of breath—three big pins on the deck in half a minute—the most beautiful of all the ducks, with russet head and herringbone gray suit, showing white-breasted as they lay belly up, feebly kicking in shallow water. Pierre seemed impressed, although he said nothing, just nodded. He had a gun but hadn't fired.

Now the boom of guns was coming from the other blinds, and ducks were dropping out of the sky. You could hear the splash as they hit, and the rattle of shot on wing as some carried lead. It was full light now, the sun a red ball, a light breeze freshening and rippling the water, making the water lily pads bow their edges in a tiny little minuet. High against the cloud-gray were black strings of ducks, wedges of ducks—big mallards, more pintails. And higher still were enormous, endless V's of blue geese, honking mournfully as they passed.

The teal were working low, and Pierre touched my arm again. "When de teal dock come een, een a beeg ball," he said, "shoot de meedle. Teal docks don' count like beeg docks, but dey eat good for breakfast and mak' fine col' lunch. Shoot plenty teal docks for de cook."

A literal swarm of greenwings buzzed in and I fired across their bows with both barrels, and felled what seemed to be a bushel.

Pierre grinned a big gold-toothed grin. "*Bon, bon,*" he said. "Now we forget teal docks, shoot only beeg docks. De cook, he be plenty happy, you bet."

"Who's the cook?" I asked.

"De cook?" He punched himself in the chest. "I'm de cook, me."

A flight of mallards stuck their heads down as Pierre called plaintively. They turned, circled to reconnoiter, and Pierre called again. They swept behind us in a great curve and came around, intent now on decoying. Keeping my head down I moved the gun up higher and slipped the safety catch. . . .

A shrill whistle from the bridge hauled me swiftly out of Louisiana and back to a *suji* bucket on the hungry ship "Sundance" bound for northern European ports from Savannah. I ran up to the bridge. The mate was bending over the ladder, looking down at me.

"We've changed course," he said. "Trim the ventilators."

"Aye, aye, sir," I said, and went off to trim the ventilators that led to the cargo holds so that no nasty ocean damp would damage our lovely cargo of sheep manure, sulphur, phosphate rock, nails, and scrap iron for the Germans to make war with. The waves crashed over the decks as the ship changed course, and all the ventilators appeared to have rusted fast since they had been trimmed an hour ago. I thought, as I wrestled in the wet cold with the jammed ventilators, that Louisiana duck hunting was too good for this kind of work, and I would save the rest of it for the last two hours before dawn on that (unlimited stream of profanity) water-drenched, windswept, sea-tortured foc'sle head.

The foc'sle head was even colder, windier, and wetter after the change of course, and I had to wedge myself between the anchor chains to keep from being washed ten feet straight down into the well deck and onto the deck cargo of logs. It was still a couple of hours until dawn, the coldest, most miserable time of the waning night, when cold gray sky would merge with cold gray sea and there was nobody alive on the Atlantic but you. What they needed a lookout for I couldn't say, because you couldn't have seen the "Queen Mary" fifty yards ahead of you.

It was time to go back, mentally, to where it was warm, to the roseaux-reed blind off the Bayou Philibert in Louisiana, squatting in a flat-bottomed pirogue with a Cajun named Pierre. The sun was coming up, the mosquitoes were departing, and across the little lily-studded, sweet-water pond the Old Man's gun was booming. The sky was full of big ducks, and higher up a million geese were working. I wiped a gallon of cold Atlantic Ocean off my face with the back of a glove and longed then and there for Louisiana.

Somehow you don't associate fine duck hunting with warm weather and pleasant surroundings, but this Louisiana hunt the Old Man took me on was about the best I had ever seen up to then. We were living on a big clean launch moored at a Cajun oyster dock that stuck out of the levee, and poling out in the pirogues to hunt. There were eight of us—the Old Man and me, two of his friends, and four Cajuns who served as guides, cooks, and assistant gunners.

I thought Cajuns were just fine. They were originally the French people that the British deported from Acadia in the middle 1700's (Acadia now being Nova Scotia, the Old Man told me), and they still spoke a French-English patois that was pretty funny to the outsider. They were magnificent hunters, trappers, fishermen, and marshmen. A Cajun in hip boots could walk a marsh as though it were a sidewalk, when you would bog to your neck in the ooze.

My friend Pierre, my mate in the pirogue, was little, dark-sallow, bushy black-headed, and fox-faced. He wasn't shooting much, only when a big bunch of ducks came in to the decoys and then I could feel the rattling blast of his rusty old pump gun. Those were the days before you plugged them down to three, and Pierre could spout five out of that old sliphorn faster than most people play an automatic.

After the pintails quit flying the mallards took over. The Cajuns call a mallard a "French duck," possibly because the yellow bill and vulgar yellow shoes and green head and purple-blue wing feathers appeal to a certain Gallic appreciation of gaudiness. There was a sight of ducks flying, and we weren't having anything to do with little ducks or trash ducks. We let the shovelers and the goldeneyes and the broadbills alone, even though, there wasn't much attention paid to limits in the marshes in those days. A marsh was a far piece away from a warden. Wardens didn't have much truck with Cajuns anyhow, Cajuns being notably pepper-tempered and the malarial swamps and marshes where they lived a bit tricky for law enforcement. A fellow can get lost easy in those Louisiana swamps.

The French ducks were decoying well that morning. Allowing for the misses you make foolishly in an abundance of riches, by ten o'clock the marsh line, which surrounded the pond, was studded with dead ducks that the wind had wedged gently into a lee shore. Some of the ducks we would lose, as always—the runners that made the marsh only to meet a mink or a coon. Once that morning we saw a mink tiptoe daintily out onto the mud, seize a mallard by the neck, and disappear into the marsh.

It was almost pickup time when Pierre pointed to a lonely dot in the sky. The dot was making mournful noises and seemed to be mixed up in its directions. "Young goose. Lost hees mama," Pierre whispered. "You watch. I play the mama, call heem right eento blind. Hees eat very good, young goose. Not so tough lak hees papa, heem."

The seduction of a lost young goose is one of the simplest Cajun tricks, and one I was to see a great many times, but the first time is always the most impressive. Pierre talked that yearling goose out of the sky and down to the blind, which it circled three times. You might have killed it with a stick, but I settled for the shotgun. It fell with a crash, but I swear it wasn't any bigger than the first pintail I had taken in the early light.

"*Bon, bon*," Pierre said again. "Dat cook, he be plenty happy, you bet you. I guess we pick up now and go back to boat." Pierre said as we watched the other pirogues snouting out of the impromptu blinds. "We got plenty dock today. Dees afternoon we go shoot plenty goose on de flat. I show you some treek, eh?"

It was tough poling—or it would have been for me, who couldn't even stand up in the skinny almond shell that is a pirogue—but Pierre leaned on his pole, standing erect in the stern, and shoved his boat full of boy, decoys, guns, and dead ducks along the bayou, against the surging tide, without working up a sweat. We pulled up alongside the launch and I looked at my dollar watch. It was just 10:30.

The Old Man was in high humor. "What do you think of *this* for duck hunting?" he asked himself, more than me. "Beats that freezing to death, don't it? You hungry?"

"I could eat a muskrat, me," I said. I was already about half-Cajun myself by this time. "What have we got for lunch?"

The Old Man winked at Pierre. "Well, the ducks won't be ready to eat before tonight. All we got is some sandwich truck and coffee and eggs and such as that. It seems to me it's up to you to provide the lunch, unless you'd rather stay aboard and gut about fifty ducks. Not that there's much trick to it, the way these fellows do it. Show him, Dedée"—this to another Cajun, the one who'd poled the Old Man's pirogue.

Dedée picked up a mallard and extended the anal vent with the point of his knife. He crooked a finger, stuck it inside the duck, and hauled the whole innards clear with one jerk. He shrugged, threw the guts over the side, and wiped the finger on the mallard's back feathers.

"Simple when you know how, ain't it?" the Old Man said. "But then, most things are. Tell you what. I'll go provide half the lunch if you and Pierre will furnish the main course. No, I forgot. Pierre's the cook and he'll have to stay aboard. You go with Anatole. But first— Dedée, where's that yellow stuff?"

Dedée grinned and went below. He came back with a half-gallon jar of light yellow liquid.

"That's Cajun orange wine," the Old Man said. "Have a sip, but don't let it get to be a habit. These boys make it, and it'll bust your skull if you take too much."

Dedée poured me out a dram in a coffee cup and I sipped it. It tasted innocent enough, and I drained the cup. Whatever it was it burnt a firebreak right down my gullet. My eyes must have popped and I broke into a light sweat.

"I told you," the Old Man said. "That's powerful stuff. Now get over the side and into that pirogue with Anatole. Whether you know it or not you're going fishing. Me, I got other chores. Come on, Dedée, let loose of that jar and we'll get to work."

Anatole and I drifted down the bayou a few hundred yards, and he worked the pirogue over to what looked like an enormous straight chair built into the water at the mouth of a smaller, excited stream, which came from a man-chopped cut about twelve feet wide that wound out of sight through the marshes. The rushing, eddying water made a roll where the stream met the bayou. Anatole jabbed at the bottom, and his pole went nearly its full length before he hit mud.

"You go 'long top," he said. "Here, tak' pole an' stringer." He handed me up a light rod with a small reel and a hook with a buckshot sinker. "You wait a meenit," he said. "I be back with bait." He let the pirogue drift and unfurled a cast net. Then he disappeared around a bend in the bayou, but I could hear the cast net splash, once, twice, three times. In a moment he came poling back. The pirogue's bottom was full of kicking, bucking little shrimp. He took a bailing bucket and filled it three-quarters full of the shrimp, and passed the bucket up to me.

"What are we fishing for?" I asked, perched on a crosspiece on the platform that obviously was intended to serve as a seat.

"Redfeesh," he said. "Red drum. Best feesh we got in bayou. You just steek shreemp on the hook, let her float in current and haul in feesh. Maybe you get a trout, maybe not. I be back in mebbe-so one hour, me. 'Voir." And he was off, around the bend again in his pirogue.

I baited a hook, paid out the line, settled back on the comfortable plank seat, braced my feet on the rough rails that surrounded three-quarters of the platform, smiled at the sun and fumbled in my pocket for a pack of cigarettes. I had been smoking about a year—legally, that is—but somehow I never smoked in duck blinds. I had just managed to get a cigarette lit when a bolt of lightning struck my shrimp and headed, I guess, for the Mississippi River. I fiddled with him a bit, but not wanting to foul up dinner I fetched him back as fast as I could. He was a big redfish, three or four pounds, well-hooked and swimming around at the foot of the platform.

I didn't have a net or a gaff, so I climbed down the crosspieces that made steps up to the fishing chair, holding the rod with the line taut in my left hand, the left arm crooked under a crosspiece to hang on. I managed to swim the fish in to where I could gaff him with my hooked fingers in the gills and jerked him kicking out of the water. I climbed backward upstairs to the platform and strung him on the stringer, then let him back into the water, where he seemed to be happy.

The sun was pounding down now and I took my undershirt off. I could almost feel the freckles pop again on my shoulders, where old-time blisters had been replaced by big blotchy brown spots. My nose and forehead were already beginning to pink. I threaded another shrimp on the hook and repeated the performance. When Anatole came poling back about an hour later I had six or eight big reds swimming on the stringer, and I'd lost as many as I caught.

"That's plenty for lonch," Anatole said. "Come on, we go back to boat. We got plenty odder t'ings for eat, us. Today we got jambalaya. At least we got de making, eef dat Pierre he don' wreck de rice."

I clambered down and we dragged my string of fish into the boat, where the big reds flopped and kicked on top of whatever it was Anatole had provided. What Anatole had provided was a bushel of big crayfish, another bushel of big shrimp, and about two bushels of clams.

When we got back to the boat, sitting clean and riding high and pretty, the Old Man was already aboard. He was perched on top of the cabin, shucking a mound of fresh oysters that reached nearly to his chin.

"Man, this is the land of plenty," he grinned around his pipe. "All you got ot do is stick down a tong and drag up a peck of oysters."

"*Oui*," Dedée said from the stern sheets, where he was plucking ducks. "Plenty *huîtres*. Odder people's *huîtres*. You don't teenk deese tengs just grow *sauvage*, you? Steal de oyster very bad. Put you in jail plenty."

"Worth a stretch," the Old Man said happily. "Here, boy, have a dozen of these illegal critters to hold down your appetite until dinnertime, which is a good hour off yet. We got to get the raw materials ready for the cook. All he's done so far is fumble around with some rice and drink a quart of that jaundice-colored poison they make out of oranges."

The oysters, new-tonged from the mud and washed clean, tasted wonderful without salt, pepper, or sauce. There must have been a zillion-billion oysters in that bayou, because all the roads alongside were made of crushed shell, and right where the launch was moored were mountains of the bleached shells, just sitting like big white hills.

"Try some dees clam, you," Anatole said, dumping a dozen of the yellow-fleshed, purple-cornered, plump little clams onto my tin plate. "More better dan de *huîtres*, I teenk, me. Got more salt, heem."

Indeed, the clams tasted even better than the oysters. We all sat and worked now, me finishing up the fish and graduating to plucking ducks. Anatole tossed most of his clams onto the Old Man's dwindling pile of unshucked oysters and started preparing the shellfish. As the cleaned raw material mounted, somebody would take a batch to the cook. Certain smells began to drift out of the galley, wonderful smells. . . .

It was full light now and the ship was near awash, the deckload of logs loosened, the deep-cut well decks running with water. Eight bells hit on the bridge. I tapped the bells back. There was no need to yell, "Lights 'r bright, sir," because the running lights and the masthead lights had been doused. I could see the cadet stumble down the ladder from the wheelhouse. As soon as I'd hit the bells I secured my watch and picked my way over the loosely moored logs, climbed the ladder to the wheelhouse deck, and crossed the open midships deck to get back to the warmth of the engine room fiddley.

I peeled off my wet stuff and went aft to the crew's mess and what passed for breakfast. Breakfast would be half-baked, doughy biscuits and fried fatback and ancient eggs, badly scrambled, but at least the coffee would be fresh. But whatever it was we were going to have, if it had been plovers' eggs and caviar, I wasn't going to like it—not after what I had been expecting for lunch on the sunlit Bayou Philibert in Louisiana.

It wasn't really my fault that I got into trouble over the captain's night lunch. It was some my fault, because I was the actual thief, but mostly it was the Old Man's fault. He shouldn't have taken me to Louisiana, duck shooting that time, and the eight bells that sent me off watch to a filthy breakfast shouldn't have interrupted my train of thought. Smitty, the second cook of the "Sundance," was an enormous plum-black Negro, and a good cook when he had anything to cook. But like the old gittar song says, "the beans was tough and the meat was fat and oh, my Lord, I couldn't eat that"—which also applied to the eggs, which may have been extracted at gun point from the last of the dodos.

I guess it was one of those days. I couldn't seem to sleep in my blue-jean sheets back under the fantail, because the steering engine was making an ungodly racket as some poor freezing sailor tried to keep the raunchy "Sundance" on course. So I got up for lunch and we had curried-something, possibly ship's rat, and supper was worse. All through the three meals I had to look at Svendsen, the bosun, with his cigarette dripping out of his pursed mouth, the smoke floating upward past his squinted eye, as he held forth on the futility of hiring college boys as sailors when master mariners and chief mates were starving on the beach.

Then that night I came off the foc's'le-head lookout at midnight, frozen stiff and wet through. When I thawed out a bit I was hungry again. The night lunch wasn't much—coarse-grained cold bread, clammy salami, mummified bologna, and cheese a rat would refuse. What made it worse there wasn't anything left but crumbs, because the able seamen had eaten it all. My belly was singing a long lament, and I kept thinking about that meal I had in Louisiana, and this process led inevitably to the officers' night lunch.

I figured the skipper was in his sack, and I crept forward to the pantry. I opened the icebox and there it was, all the delicatessen my soul as well as stomach craved, and I ate hearty—stuffing it in with both hands. The stolen feast called for coffee . . . boiled-only-once coffee in a silver percolator, when I heard familiar steps. The skipper had been roused, by either intuition or hunger, and was heading for the pantry. I beat him out the door by a whisker, and for some stupid reason I was carrying the coffeepot with me. Thereupon began a chase that was never bettered by the Keystone Cops or the Ritz Brothers.

Still grasping that percolator I took off. The captain, wearing carpet slippers, took one look at his ravaged icebox, the door gaping open, and the gimbaled holder on which his purloined coffeepot once had rested. He let out a scream like a wounded banshee and took off behind me. Around, over, and practically under the ship we went, aft to fore and fore to aft, the skipper cursing, stumbling, and blowing his whistle for aid. It sounded like the Apaches had captured the fort and were scalping everybody.

I was pretty young and sure-footed and I knew that ship and its cargo as I knew my fingers, and what to me was a beaten track was an obstacle course to the captain, who ordinarily stayed close to the chartroom. He fell over deck cargo and barked his shins, slipped on the watery deck, collided with bulkheads, lost his footing on ladders, but he continued to blow his whistle and scream for assistance.

He got assistance, all right. He roused the off-watch mates and the steward's department and the deck gang and the black gang, and he also roused me. I had long since flung his coffeepot over the side, not wishing to be caught with the evidence, and I joined the protective coloration of the herd of drowsy men. I made myself busy at all sorts of things, like trimming the vents and slapping *suji* on distant bulkheads, and when the skipper herded everybody into the crew mess to sort out the culprit you might have seen the canary's feathers fluffing out of my lips.

There were over thirty men on that ship, and it's hard to pick a night-lunch thief out of thirty men, unless you stomach pump 'em all. Fortunately the "Sundance" did not carry a stomach pump, although I had a fleeting suspicion that the skipper might order the ship's carpenter to jury-rig a food detector out of the bilge pump. The skipper ranted and roared, and swore that he would keelhaul the guilty party when he caught him, and in the meantime there would be no pay when we docked and no shore leave at all. I suppose if it had been wartime he would have shot the entire crew. The captain ultimately lost his voice, swore a final husky oath of vengeance, and departed, croaking. Everybody went to bed, and I went back on the foc'sle head to announce colliding dolphins and reflect aloud that the lights, running and masthead, were bright, sir.

After the hare-and-hounds episode I had little difficulty concentrating on that midday meal on the Bayou Philibert, because I was stuffed with the skipper's night lunch and had scored my first and only victory over the anointed personnel of the wallowing bucket "Sundance" from Savannah.

I spoke aloud into the wind, addressing the Old Man, off somewhere in infinity. "I hope you're satisfied," I said. "You could have got me hanged from the yardarm. This'll teach you to expose me to Louisiana food. . . ."

That day on the bayou, after we'd finished preparing the ducks and the oysters and the fish and the shrimp and the crayfish, we saw the entire fruits of the morning collection pass down into the launch's galley, where Pierre was chef. I had stoked myself pretty well with raw oysters and clams, but there was still plenty of space in the boilers for whatever Pierre was making. What he was making was one big dish, and he made it in an iron cauldron big enough to boil a hog in.

It was jambalaya—call it *pilaf, payloo, pilau, paella,* or anything you want—but its main ingredients are rice and red peppers. Into this rice had been mixed shrimps, oysters, clams, crayfish, pork sausage, great white slabs of fish, a chicken for the stock, and the whole business cooked together until it was one great big wonderful adventure. Pierre had cooked the rice with saffron, so that it came out yellow, and the juices from the seafood and the chicken had got married in a tremendous soupy ceremony so that the rice, while dry by grain, was damp by volume, and the hunks of fish and the shellfish hadn't lost any of their flavor but were nuggeted through the rice.

He served all this with great big chunks of crusty French bread for mopping up and a gallon of homemade red wine, and we finished up with Louisiana chicory coffee that was so strong you had to cut it to drink it. Even with an elder gentleman's estimation of a young man's anaconda capacity I hesitate to recall how much I ate, sitting with a basin of this stuff in my lap, soaking in the sun, listening to the birds in the marsh, watching the fish jumping in the sparkling, breeze-ruffled bayou, and smelling the good smells of decaying oyster shell and marshgrass mud.

Pierre observed the destruction of his masterpiece with proper Gallic pride, although he played it coy. "Dat only meedleday snack, heem," he announced. "You tak' leetle sleep now and then go shoot goose. I theenk I don' go. I theenk I stay here on boat and mak' really good beeg supper, me. You got plenty of people for shoot goose."

The Old Man said he thought he'd grab forty winks below, and the other people said, "By gar, dat one hell of good idea," but I stayed up topside and just sort of snoozed on the cabin top. About three o'clock the Old Man stuck his head out of the cabin and announced that I better take some No. 2's along with the 4's if I intended to go shoot a goose that day.

"I already *shot* a goose," I said, "With a duck load."

"You shot a pinfeathered adolescent goose," the Old Man replied. "I'm talking about real grown-up geese, including maybe a honker from Canada. You don't want to mess around with 6's on these fellows. Buckshot ain't too big for a real hoary old gander. They can pack off a power of lead."

The Cajuns started piling stuff, including a bundle of reeds, into a broad-beamed, shallow-draft bateau, about the size of a surfboat but wider. It had a small engine in it. The bateau had been floating tandem to the launch.

"You don' need pirogue for goose," Anatole said. "You need beeg boat. We jus' go along bayou een dees bateau, then we park heem 'long levee, walk through muck, mak' blin', shoot plenty goose. We shoot off prairie."

We putted along the bayou for half a dozen miles. The flights of geese were enormous, and they settled in huge flocks on the water-soft savannas the Cajuns called prairie, semibogs covered with bright-green grasses. In the distance you could see the feeding geese, blue some, many white, as if they had changed their plumage with age. Once in a while a V-ended double thread of bigger, grayer geese entered the party—Canucks. I looked and saw no decoys in the boat, and finally screwed up courage enough to ask why.

Dedée laughed. "Dees ver' intelligent goose," he said. "Read all de tam'. We use *Picayune* newspaper, stick him on prairie, goose fly down to read all de news, shoot goose, bim, bam!"

I looked at the Old Man.

"You remember that time we were making decoys and you said they didn't look like ducks to you?" he said. "And I said they may not look like ducks to you, but they look like ducks to a duck? Same thing. You fold these papers, prop 'em up with sticks in front of the blind, and to a flying goose they look like a hull herd of geese feeding. You call the goose right, and the old stud gander will fetch his flock in."

We chuffed along some more, and on both sides of the bayou the geese rose with wild, annoyed honking in clouds of thousands, until the sky was filled with a hundred thousand. The noise they made was unbelievable.

Dedée, who was steering the bateau, finally nosed her into a cut, pushed a pole into the soggy turf, and announced it was firm enough to walk on. He drove his pole deeply into the turf, bent the bow painter around the pole, and let the bateau swing with the tide until she nestled against the bank.

"*Allons-nous*," Dedée said. "We go shoot de goose."

We went off to shoot de goose, each man carrying his gun, each man with a couple of boxes of shells. I looked at the Old Man and saw he was loading his long barrels with a 4, right, a 2, left; and I did the same. I'd get mixed up later maybe, but at least I'd start right.

Away over yonder the ground was snowdrifted with geese. Flocks whirled and circled lazily and then dropped the undercarriage and slanted down to feed. Two of the Cajuns, Anatole and François, started splicing the reeds together to make small repairs to a blind that had been shot over before. There was a plank, a long one, mounted on saw-horse legs inside the blind.

"Better dan get the *derrière* wet seeting een dees prairie," Anatole said. "He's look dry, but he got plenty water under grass, heem." For the first time I really noticed that I was muddy past my shins. The water seeped up from the muck and came all the way through the grasses, when you put your foot down hard.

While Anatole and François were repairing the blind Dedée was out with the newspapers, which he had been folding into a very creditable representation of a goose—the wings cocked, so, the paper extended into a searching neck, scanning the sky, or a feeding neck, crooked over and inspecting the muck for nutriment. Even at a short distance they looked remarkably like feeding geese. From the air, I imagined, they would look exactly like feeding geese. Even to a goose.

"Ees not bad," Anatole said, "but ees not de best. When we shoot a few goose, we run out queek, us, and plant de dead goose in forked stick, so we have nex' best teeng to live goose. Den de goose he come plenty, heem."

Dedée finished his paper work, gave a look around, seemed satisfied, and scurried into the blind. We sat along the sixteen-foot length of plank, each man with his shell box opened in front of him.

"Who de goose?" Dedée asked. "I teenk you, François. You call de goose, you."

François scorned a mechanical caller. He cupped his hands around his mouth and yelped. He pleaded and cajoled and attracted the interest of a big flock of white geese. They circled three times, were not alarmed at the blind or the *Picayune* decoys, and sailed in for dinner. I performed in my usual fashion. I picked the biggest, oldest, toughest, grizzliest gander I could get under my sights and gave him two. He more or less cocked an eye at me and went swiftly elsewhere. I reloaded while I listened to the soggy thump of other people's geese hitting the prairie. One was a runner that got up and shook his head, and I settled his troubles for him, figuring I'd better contribute something to the party.

We let the dead geese lie. The Old Man had a smug look about his mustaches that indicated he had scored a double. All told, there were six geese down by seven shooters. Since I got none, and giving the Old Man two, the other five boys shared four. Somebody else missed too, I thought, and felt better.

François started to gabble goosy again, and before long in came another flock. This time I committed my second mistake. I let go both barrels at the entire flock, where it was biggest, and something dropped this time. A handful of feathers. Around me was the solid *thud-thud* of geese falling like sacks. I counted and now there were fourteen. Everybody was improving but me.

Dedée held up a hand. "Now we got de real decoy," he said. "Anatole, you help me feex, you."

They scuttled out of the blind, keeping low, and replaced fourteen folded newspapers with fourteen dead geese, their necks jammed in forked sticks, their wings braced in a flap or left to fold. Some had necks crooked, some extended. They looked like feeding geese. Even more so to a goose.

Back in the blind Dedée squinted at the horizon. A small V

of birds, bigger and blacker in the distance, was headed our way. "*Les Canadiens*," Dedée said. "My goose French she's more better dan you," he said to François. "I call dees cousins from Canada."

He changed the timbre slightly and began to talk. The Canucks halted slightly as the call touched them, and the lead gander inclined his head to look at the ground. He seemed satisfied and came on. The Canadas—big, gray, black-headed, with their white collars—came on, swept round in great circles, losing altitude all the time, and then came straight in like a great covey of aircraft. While they were coming I slipped the No. 4 out of one barrel and shoved in another 2.

This time, by gar, I wasn't going to miss, me. I still went for the gander, which flew almost into the gun barrel and then flinched, shuddered, and fell when the load struck him. I watched him drop from under the gun, and switched to a male friend that was struggling for altitude and led him too much for a big goose, but managed to put the full load into his head and neck. Down he came, like a rock, and while I did not blow through the smoking barrels I felt like it. I had *my* geese for the day. The other folks could mess around with blue geese and white geese, but I had a full bag of bull elephant. Blue geese me no blue geese. The pros shoot only the Canucks.

The Old Man looked at me and grinned. "There'll be no living with him," he said to nobody at all and shrugged. Then I looked at the goose-littered terrain and there were two more Canadas, both females, lying close aboard my ganders.

"Just call me a pothunter, not a hero," the Old Man said. "We got enough geese, boys. Let us *allons-nous* the hell out of here."

I'll say we had enough geese. We had enough for everybody to make two trips from the blind to the bateau. "Eet look like we shoot a snowstorm," Pierre ventured, "except for mebbe one, two leetle spots dirty snow."

My big gander weighed fourteen pounds. That is a very large gander. . . .

It was now about ten minutes, again, from finish-lookout and the same dreadful breakfast. As I sat down to the table my foc'sle-head mind raced back again to the dinner Pierre had smoking in the galley when we arrived triumphant with a bateau full of geese.

We had oysters on the half shell. We had a tawny-red soup called crayfish bisque, with the big crays, heads and all, in the sherry-rich soup. We had tiny teal broiled with bacon, like baby chickens, which fell apart in the fingers. Each man had a big pintail, cooked to pieces, with carrots and onions and potatoes and apples and sage shoved into its inside. We had that French bread and a chicory salad, and a side dish of redfish with a sauce of tiny shrimps and sherry and cream, which Pierre got the Lord knows where, unless he hijacked a cow. We had coffee.

"Tomorrow," Pierre said, "we have roas' goose. Weeth fresh goose leever for de hors de'œuvre."

The city of Hamburg, Germany, has a fine roast goose, and it is possible to buy a good goose-liver sausage, and if you are in funds a fine goose-liver pâté that comes from Strasbourg. When we docked there the skipper forgot the night-lunch-stealing episode and paid us off. Still haunted by Louisiana memories I went ashore and blew a week's pay on just one dinner.

It was then I decided that the Germans, when war inevitably came, would lose it. They couldn't have touched Pierre's goose with the business end of a pirogue pole.

5

How to Make a Hoorah's Nest a Home

Well, I been laying off to tell you about the spring when the Old Man and I decided to rebuild our fishing shack, which had been mauled by a couple of hurricanes. It never had been much of a shack, even for fishing every now and again—some four-by-fours and two-by-fours with a tar-paper roof and some warped, uncurried boards for walls. Everybody had used it and abused it, and even in good weather the inside looked like a tornado had struck it.

The Old Man used to grumble, "That's the trouble with being nice to every Tom, Dick, and Harry that comes down the pike. They'd ride a free horse to death." Usually the place looked and smelled like a hoorah's nest—old tin cans, coffee grounds, papers, and rusty tackle scattered every which way;

the mattresses torn and dirty, and the lamp chimneys dyed black from smoke.

The last couple of big blows had really fixed her. Outside the shack looked like a bird's nest in a high wind—tar-paper blown to tatters, planks ripped off the sides, sand drifted up against the door.

"We'll salvage what we can and then burn her," the Old Man said. "It stinks like a cooter's den. Judging from the bottles the last few parties that used this shack didn't do much fishin'. Then we'll move over to another site and build us a proper lodge. We'll clap a lock on her, stick up a PRIVATE sign, and get the Coast Guard boys to keep an eye on her when they ride beach patrol. I hate to do it, but these days the only way a man can keep a decent permanent camp is to be selfish about it. Twenty, even ten years ago you could leave any door open and your provisions in the locker. People would come in, use what they needed, and leave the place clean. Later you'd find they'd put back what they used.

"It don't seem the same today, which is why, when you're my age, there practically won't be no such thing as common shootin' and fishin'. Everything will be posted and locked up, just for the protection of the farmer that's tired of having his pigs shot, and his hayfields burnt down with careless matches, and his property mucked up with old tin cans and filth. Dodlimb it," the Old Man said, "I'm just surprised this last bunch didn't set the place afire and be done with it."

The Old Man was striding up and down, mumbling and cussing under his breath. If there was anything he hated, it was a filthy camp. He was a real old maid about burning rubbish and burying leftovers and generally leaving a place cleaner and better than when he found it. I suppose a lot of it rubbed off on me, because even today a nest of beer cans and tumbleweeds of greasy paper can make me mad, just looking at the mess.

As far as we could see, up and down the beach, the shore was strewn with wreckage from the hurricanes. When she blows in that neck of the woods she rears back and blows, all the way from the Caribbean, past Hatteras, and right on up north. Anything that isn't secured pretty fast carries away. Most of it fetches up on the beach as flotsam, and a lot of it is usable. Where we used to call "down home," around Hatteras and Nags Head, the wreckers once made a considerable living gathering up the stuff that floated in off the ships that were wrecked, some by accident, some on purpose. The Old Man said Nags Head got its name from a cute little habit the natives had of hanging a lantern on a horse's neck and walking him up and down the beach during a storm. The distressed ships mistook the bobbing light for a signal light, plowed ahead, and broke up on the reefs. The flotsam came ashore, and when the weather calmed down the wreckers would go out in boats and pick the hulk clean, like buzzards. It was a long time ago, but that's how the story went anyhow.

The sand here was hard-packed, and we were able to get the Liz, the old high-axled Liz, down onto the beach. The Old Man had a coil of one-inch hemp in the stern sheets, and we went trundling down the beach looking for likely building materials. There was plenty to find: scantlings, a few tarry pilings where some fisherman's little dock had blown loose, a whole section of roofing—planks and joists and beams and the Lord knows what all in the way of innards—part of a staircase, ruined chairs, busted tables, even an old toilet seat.

A lot of it was no earthly good, but it was enough for a start. We made the line fast around what we wanted, piece by piece, bit by bit, and snaked it to the new building site, while the Liz panted and snorted and bucked and boiled over. I never saw such a car as those old T Models. They rattled and shook and made noises like coffee grinders, but they'd go places you couldn't get a team of horses in.

It took us the whole weekend to assemble the stuff and stack it in building order around the new site—one well back from the first line of dunes, one which grew enough sea oats to be anchored fairly permanent.

"We'll build her here," the Old Man said, "in that kind of

gully between the dunes. That way we'll get some wind protection. We won't have to worry about storm tides. What's more we'll set her up on pilings."

"How come pilings?" I asked. "Seems to me you're just shoving her up there in the air for the wind to blow over. Wouldn't it be better to snug her close to the ground?"

"I am no engineer," the Old Man said, "but I know a thing or three about building on a windy coast. A big wind don't fancy anything better than something that's nailed firm to a foundation, so's it can really bend a shoulder onto it and shove. I don't generally criticize the Good Book, but that business about the man who built his house upon a rock and the man who built his house on sand ain't strictly accurate for the Carolina coast. The principle is simple: You know how a big tree'll blow over and some wavy sapling will still stand in a gale? The limber log rocks with the gusts, the big stiff log or the pile of bricks tries to stand firm and shove back. One stays standing and the other blows down.

"There's another thing in favor of putting your house on stilts. It leaves plenty of space for the wind to blow underneath, and a lot of force gets diverted that way and passes on. The house'll rock a little and bend before the gale, but the gale goes round it and over it and under it. We'll shingle the roof. A blow might steal a few of your shingles, but you ain't apt to come here after a storm and find the hull roof carried away."

"It sounds reasonable," I said.

"There's still another thing you ain't spotted, from our standpoint, in terms of saving work. You know what I'm driving at?"

He had me stumped. "No sir," I said.

"Well, half or more of the work in a fishing or hunting camp can be better done under the house than in it. You can haul a boat up out of the weather for painting or repairs. It's cool underneath, out of the sun in the daytime. You can sort your tackle or mend a net or clean a mess of fish without cluttering

up your house. You can stack your rods or your oars and leave
your boots. You can dry your washing. You can tie your dogs
under the house. All over the East and in the Pacific the salt-
water people spend more time under the house than they do in
it."

"You can't keep leaving gear and boats just loose when you
go away," I said. "How you going to keep the stuff from getting swiped?"

"Simple," the Old Man grinned, "easy as pie. We build a
lattice, about six-inch squares, all around the pilings. We put a
heavy lattice door on it with a lock. I have noticed that while a
man will use what's laid out handy and not nailed down he'll
think twice before he'll batter open something that's got a door
and a lock on it. We haven't got too many bad people around
—just careless. Leave something loose and they may abuse it.
Shove a lock on your gear, and tearing down the surroundings
to get at it constitutes breaking and entering and maybe even
burglary. We run powerful few burglars to a hill in these
parts."

"All right," I said. "that's fine. You got me sold. But what
about this business of the wind blowing *underneath* the house
and passing on?"

"It blows through the *holes* in the lattice. The lattice'll be
limber, too. So what does it matter if the wind rips off a strip
or two? They're easy put back. So what you really got is not
one house, but *two* houses. One is cool and shady to work in
when it's hot, and the other is snug and warm to cook and
sleep in when it's cold or rainy or blowy—all in the same
space."

I don't know where the Old Man got all these ideas, except
he had been nigh everywhere when he was younger, and he always had his nose stuck in some book that was too heavy to lift.
But I must say most of his home-grown prescriptions for
nearly everything had a practical side and generally seemed to
work.

School let out in another week, and we went into the house-building business on a full-time basis. We took a little fly tent over to the island and some cooking gear and a cast net and a rod or so. We lived off the country. The big sea turtles were laying, and when you walked the beach in the moonlight it wasn't much trouble to get yourself a mess of fresh eggs for breakfast, if you just followed the big old herringbone marks the female made when she lurched across the wet sands to deposit her eggs. There were mullet and shrimp and pan fish in the creek, and an occasional puppy drum or little blue or Virginia mullet in the sloughs, working on the sand fleas. The big stuff was still up north or away off at sea using around the big shoals, but we made out. We had a hard-cured ham and some canned salmon and sardines and truck like that, and we ate pretty good.

Brother, we worked. The Old Man had sweet-talked somebody into sending over a truckload of stuff we hadn't been able to scavenge off the beach: cedar shakes for shingles, heavy-duty strips for the lattice work, creosote for the pilings, fittings for the innards. You'd have thought, the Old Man remarked, that we were building the Taj Mahal, which turned out to be some place in India. "But I must say," he said, "we'll take less time than they spent on the pyramids."

We sank the pilings about halfway to China, seeing as how I had to dig the holes, poured in a little cement to anchor the bottoms in the sand, and then built a platform across the top, which was the floor. There were good pine planks, and the Old Man shinnied up an improvised ladder and planed them smooth. He said his feet hurt bad enough without collecting splinters in his sock feet.

We reared the walls to six foot six, left room for a big window fronting the sea, and put what you might call square port-holes on two sides. We installed a plank ceiling, and then built a shingled, pitched roof about a foot above the ceiling. The Old Man had got hold of some ratty old mattresses and he ripped the stuffing out of them and shoved it between the false roof and the regular roof. He said that was insulation and would keep the shack cool.

We cut the living quarters into two parts. One was the kitchen-living room, and the other was what the Old Man called the bull pen or sleeping quarters. The Old Man said he didn't like the idea of confusing slumber with grub.

He built—this called for fancywork—a hinged drop-leaf table that fell vertically against the wall and was out of the way when you weren't using it. He built cabinets all along one wall to hold the permanent stuff—canned goods, coffee, sugar, salt, pepper, mustard, catsup—that kind of camp truck. He built a perishable-food safe, with wire sides port and starboard, that fitted into one of the windows and could be hung outside in the breeze. We installed a two-burner cookstove that would feed off oil, and when it got hot it jumped up and down on its legs and filled the room with heat. Later on he arrived with two wicker rocking chairs—stolen from Miss Lottie, no doubt—and a couple of straight kitchen chairs. He built in lockers all around the room, for cups and saucers and frying pans and glasses, and he built one bookshelf the length of the room. We hung hurricane lamps from the ceiling. That was the living room-kitchen.

The bull pen was simple. It contained four beds—two double-decker bunks built right onto the walls on opposite sides of the room. Under each bottom bunk was a double set of lockers for clothes, and at one end of the room was a crosspiece for hangers. There was no running water in the shack, but in the kitchen he stuck a sink with a drain for inside dish washing and face washing.

It took near about all summer, building a rude staircase up from the ground, fitting the doors and storm windows, and building the lattice for the underpart. We sank a well about two hundred yards back toward the brush, and while the water was brackish it was usable. We put an old-fashioned stiff-handled pump on the well with a pumpshelf. Then he built a small rain water catcher—a reservoir—and put drains around the roof leading into it. He reckoned we could catch enough rain water to drink. About the last thing we constructed, back in the brush, was a two-hole privy with a deep trap. When we hung the Sears Roebuck catalogue on a nail we reckoned we had finished the job.

"She may not be much to look at," the Old Man said, as he dumped the mattresses into the bunks and hung the cups on the hooks and stuck the dishes in the racks, "but she's sound and weatherproof and she's ours. Anything you make yourself has a little bit more significance than if you got somebody to do it for you."

I rubbed a sunburnt nose with a palm that had long since seen its blisters change to horn. It seemed to me about the handsomest fishing lodge I ever saw—everything what they used to call shipshape and Bristol fashion. We had a power of fun in that little shack for as long as the Old Man lasted.

It's been about thirty years since we built it, and there have been a lot of hurricanes along since—Alice, Ethel, Helen, I don't know how many. But I am willing to bet that unless somebody tore the house down on purpose, the best part of it is still there. Certainly they haven't built a hurricane yet that would make it do anything more strenuous than take a bow.

6

If You Don't Care Where You Are You Ain't Lost

The Old Man and I were sitting in front of a driftwood fire we'd built down on the beach close to the water, and although it was late August the fire felt mighty good and looked prettier. You know how those old salt-sodden driftwood logs burn, light blue fairy flames that seem to dance over the wood, as alcohol burns. Sometimes you can't see the flickering flames at all the blue is so fragile against the night sky.

A sizeable mess of medium bluefish made silver stacks alongside the fire, and there were a couple of respectable puppy drum. An unseasonable nor'-easter, not due until September, had raised a ruckus and brought the first fish into the fresh-cut sloughs, where they were having a roaring fine time with the small bait and the sand fleas. We'd also had a roaring fine time with the feeding fish, until they knocked off biting when the tide came full flood. A little moon was shoving its way up over the horizon and any minute the water would start to ebb, and we figured we'd fish the ebb for another hour before we packed a mile up the beach to the shack.

"I wish we'd brought a wheelbarrow," the Old Man said, rummaging in the tackle box for his anti-sea serpent lotion. He found it, uncorked it, and blew drops of moisture through his mustache. "You're going to be powerful tired, sweating all those fish all the way back to the shack. I'd help you, but I'm too old and feeble and full of dignity to go around toting fish like a common peddler. Shouldn't be surprised if you didn't have to make two trips."

He snorted at his idea of a joke. I didn't laugh. I knew he'd help me lug the fish back to camp, but I had a strong suspicion about the identity of the fellow who would scale and gut 'em, and that fellow did not own a mustache or drink anti-sea serpent lotion out of a tackle box.

We sat quiet for a spell waiting for the tide to change, and the Old Man fired up his pipe and took another small precaution against moonstroke from his anti-moonstroke lotion. Then he hit me with one of his sudden questions. "What do you want to be when you grow up, now that you're past the policeman, fireman, cowboy stage? What do you want most?"

"I dunno," I said. "Money, I suppose. I want to have a lot of money."

"At least you're honest," he said, rubbing his chin with the pipestem. "Not that I admire it—your wanting to be rich, I mean. How do you figure to get rich?"

"Somehow. I dunno. But some way'll work itself out. I won't steal it, if that's what's worrying you."

"I wasn't worrying about you stealing it. You ain't got the makings of a good thief. You like to tell everybody your business too much. A thief keeps to himself. He don't gab. But he don't have any fun, either, because when he starts to spend what he stole and brag about it somebody ketches him at it. The lawyers get all the money, and he winds up breaking rocks in the jailhouse. What do you want to be rich *for?*" He threw that one at me hard.

"I don't rightly know. But there's a lot of things I want that take a lot of money."

"Such as?"

"Well travel, for one thing. I want to see all the things I've read about and you've told me about. I want to go hunting in Africa and India. I want to buy cars and guns and good clothes and houses. I want to send my young'uns, if I have any, to college, and I want to grow old without having to worry about it. That all takes money."

"That it does, that it does," the Old Man said. "But there's other ways of being rich without worrying so much about money. If you ever do get rich, and I ain't saying you will or you won't, but if you ever do you might find yourself worrying so hard about keeping the money that you wouldn't have time to do all these things. You know any real rich people?"

"Not firsthand, but I seen some. Them fellers that come in with the yachts from time to time."

"Willies-off-the-pickle-boat," the Old Man spat scornfully. "Drunk from noon on and working on their third marriage. Worried the whole time about Wall Street, even when they're out in their *yatch-its* all gussied up in brass buttons and captain's caps. They couldn't navigate a garbage scow from the pilot's dock to the quarantine station." That was about one mile over clear water.

"Well, how about those cotton people that own the big plantation? They're rich."

"Yep, they're rich, all right. I was raised with one of 'em. Used to hunt and fish with him when we were young'uns and he was still poor. He was crazier over fish poles and shotguns than you are. I bet he hasn't baited a hook or fired a shotgun in forty year—ever since he started getting rich. He don't even live on his plantation. Hasn't got the time. Seen him the other day in town and stopped for a talk. I asked when we were going to shoot some of those big turkeys on his place. His face lit up for a minute, and then dropped all the way to the sidewalk. 'I'd sure like to go again, Ned,' he said, 'but I never seem to get the time. You remember once, when we . . .' And then he looked at his watch. 'Oh hell, I got a directors' meeting,' says he, and rushes off like there was hounds after him. I never will know what he was about to remember. You know any more rich people?"

"No," I said. I was beginning to feel depressed.

"That's where you're dead wrong," he said quietly. "You know two rich people. You and me. We're both rich, right now. Richer than them Willies-off-the-pickle-boat. Richer than any of them cotton people. Stinkin', filthy rich you are, and so am I."

"What's rich, then?"

"Rich," the Old Man said dreamily, "is not baying after what you can't have. Rich is having the time to do what you want to do. Rich is a little whisky to drink and some food to eat and a roof over your head and a fish pole and a boat and a gun and a dollar for a box of shells. Rich is not owing any money to anybody, and not spending what you haven't got."

"It still takes money," I said doggedly. "It takes *some* money."

"Well, hell's bells," the Old Man said cheerfully, "anybody with the right number of arms and legs can make a *little* money. You take Tom and Pete. They fish some when the pogies are running, and manufacture a little moonshine in the winter. They trap a bit, and hunt a lot. They drink up most of the moonshine they make, but they take in a mite of money from fish and hides and guiding the sports from time to time. They live off a shotgun. They always got a smokehouse full of venison—most of it illegal, it's true—and other people's hogs that got lost. But their women tend the pea patch and the collards pretty good, and hominy don't cost much. They got a yard full of hounds and plenty of time to run 'em. I'd say they were pretty rich, wouldn't you?"

"I suppose so, if you look at it that way. But they won't never get to Africa or have a big car."

"For that matter, they won't ever get out of Brunswick County," replied the Old Man. "But the point is, they don't *want* to go to Africa, because they ain't got the right guns to shoot lions. They don't want a big car, because you couldn't take it into a deep swamp to tend the still. They got everything in the world they crave, including a set of cast-iron innards and the ability to sleep standing up. Many a rich city man would trade his millions for a house-broke belly that would let him eat a mess of fat pork and collards, chase it off with corn likker, and then lay down with the hounds and sleep ten hours in the yard. You know what I would of like to been, if I had been born in a different time?"

"No sir. What?"

"A kind of early-day Tom or Pete. One of them mountain men, they were called, about the time of Lewis and Clark and later Kit Carson and Jim Bridger and all those hairy old goats. The men that opened up the country west of the Mississippi. There's a lot of literature on the subject. Man, they were a rough lot of cobs. They thought they were lucky if they got back out of the Crow country with their hair on. They trapped virgin beaver streams and crossed mountains no white man ever crossed and charted rivers no white man ever seen. They were the advance people for traders like Frémont and Sublette and all those fellers, and they carved a trail through the Blackfoot country that left many a bone to bleach, but they wound up in Oregon and California.

"They were all rich men—not in their beaver plews, because they largely lost their profits gambling or pitching a big drunk when they come back to the outskirts of civilization—but rich because they were self-sufficient. They looked down on the traders and the soft city settlers that come later with the covered wagons, because the mountain men were a breed of he-coons apart. You interested in all this?"

I just nodded. The Old Man went on, dreamylike, and I could pretty near see it, the way he talked.

"Mountain men," the Old Man continued, in front of the blue-dancing fire, "were probably the most self-sufficient, uncurried boar hogs that ever lived. Most of them took to the small-bore, long-barreled rifle, with a cap lock instead of flint, after Dan Boone made the Kentucky long rifle a legend.

"Them fellers took everything the Injuns had to offer and improved the score considerable. They could throw a hatchet or a knife as well as any Injun or better. They rode bareback, Injun-fashion, with just a braided-hair loop around the pony's lower jaw to steer him by. They wore buckskins and long hair, and by the time they'd spent a winter in a buffalo-hide lodge, tanning skins and smoking themselves over a slow fire, you couldn't of told one from an Injun, either by sight or by smell.

"Some of them took squaws, if they were on good terms with the local tribes—Crows or Blackfeet proper or Shoshones or whatever—and the little, fat brown gal cooked their meat and sewed moccasins and chawed the buckskin to soften it for new clothes and scraped the beaver and the buffalo hides and slept 'em warm in the cold nights, even if the ladies were a little bit louse-infected. There was no disgrace attached to being a squaw man—that come later with the civilized back-easters, who wore linsey-woolsey and hickory shirts instead of buckskin. But some of the wilder mountain boys thought a feller who'd tie himself to a squaw and a half-breed family was going a little soft and sissy.

"These lone men were out in the West and Northwest for the spoken purpose of trapping beaver, but the beaver and the buffalo were just an excuse for roving free and unhampered by all the things they didn't like about law and order and rules and regulations. These fellers liked to get up on a bright morning in a place no other white man had ever seen, and look out to watch a million buffalo black on the plain as far as the eye could see, and to spin down a stream in a bullboat and take a prime beaver plew out of every trap.

"They lived off a steady diet of meat, when the shooting was good, and they never ate much fresh meat except buffalo hump, tongue, ribs, and what they called boudin—intestine stuffed full of chopped meat. The rest went to the wolves or got jerked into thin, dry strips, if there was a squaw handy. She'd pound a few dried berries into the pemmican and they lived off that all winter, that and a few carcasses shot during the cold and hung up in a tree to freeze. When they were off on the prowl they didn't need much provisioning. Buffalo chips made a fire to warm up the jerky, and if the jerky run out they could make it somehow on roots or prairie dogs or bear or mountain goat or whatever come under the gun sights, including horses and Injun dogs. If there weren't any roots or berries or prairie dogs they could make it for a spell on buckskin. Many a man ate up his last pair of spare moccasins.

"Where a man stood or rode or built a fire was home. He paid no taxes, saw no white people, obeyed no laws, spent no money. If his gun bust, he whittled a bow from wood or horn and strung it with a thong clipped off his hunting shirt; he chipped some flint and tipped his arrows. He only had two real enemies—Injuns and weather. Injuns could lift his hair, and weather could starve him first and freeze him second. But he never got lost, because a man that don't care much where he is ain't lost. He's exploring.

"They were a hairy, dirty, lice-ridden, mean, cantankerous, antisocial, and in some cases murderous lot of hopeless cases for civilization. When they come to the trading posts they spent their beaver money on watered-down trade whisky and foofaraw for their squaws, if any.

"They gambled and they fought with knives and cheerfully killed each other when the pannikins passed from hand to hand, and a man kicked his heels, let out a war whoop, and allowed he was a stud bear and could lick any other two- or four-footed animule that ever walked, crawled, or flew through the air. But when they got back on the plains and in the hills they owned all the space and sky and wood and water, and they were the freest, least dependent critters that God made recently. In that respect they were all rich."

The Old Man paused and looked at the sea. The ebb had started and the moon was riding high. In its light you could see the wet brown stain on the sand where the water had receded.

"I kind of got carried away," the Old Man said, a little sheepishly. "I would have probably made a terrible mountain man, and the first fat Kiowa that come along would have had my hair for a trophy. But it's nice to think about what it must have been like, especially if you never will see it again. That's where books come in handy. A man can be rich retroactively, if he can stand off the Armada with Drake and fight the Injuns with Jim Bridger. The water's going out. Let's try the fish again."

We walked down to the water's edge into the chill sea up to our thighs and cast. Each of us had simultaneous strikes. From the way the rods bent, we both had tied into good ones. We walked backward, reeling in, as the angry blues fought on the other end. The Old Man turned his head and asked, acidly, "You still want to be rich when you grow up?"

"That I do," I said stubbornly. "At least if I'm rich I can hire somebody to tote the fish and clean 'em afterward."

We toiled backward up the beach, and as usual the Old Man's fish was bigger than mine. I guess he might have made a pretty fair mountain man at that.

7

Stories Grow Taller in the Fresh Air

"A liar," the Old Man declared one day when I had stretched the truth a touch on some matter involving nonattendance at school, "is a person I cannot abide. He is like a suck-egg dog. You can't trust him out of your sight."

"Yes sir," I said, having been caught out handily.

"However," the Old Man said, gnawing at his mustaches, "there are certain exceptions to the rule."

"Yes sir," I said, looking hopeful.

"Now I wouldn't give a nickel for a truthful hunter or fisherman," the Old Man continued. "A hunter who ain't a liar, a fisherman who won't toy with the truth is generally the kind of man who will do you one in the eye on a cattle trade, foreclose a mortgage on a widder, and sneak stamps out of the petty-cash box. He will steal a horse and possibly kick his dogs. He will also have a small, tight, mean mouth and carry his money in a snap purse."

He fired up the pipe and shot one at me fast. "How much did that big puppy drum you caught the other day weigh?"

"Thirty-five pounds," I said.

The Old Man positively glowed with triumph. He cackled. "I weighed it behind your back," he said. "It weighed thirty-two pounds. You see, you're an automatic sporting liar, which I think is commendable. If it had been me, I'd of said forty pounds. But you're young yet and don't know the difference between a cheese-paring fib and a good, strong, hairy-chested falsehood. If you got to tell one tell a good one. I ever tell you about Elwood and Corbett and the doe deer?"

Elwood and Corbett were two brothers who lived near the Green Swamp and like many another, including my friends Tom and Pete, were known to make and sell a little white lightning, and thought that game laws were an invasion of civil liberties in Onslow County. They had a smokehouse that was full of meat the year round, and very little of it had ever seen an abattoir. There was a limit of two deer a year, and once I asked Elwood how many deer he'd shot so far (this being before Christmas). He scratched his head, and replied, "Well, I bought a box of shells in October. That's twenty-five, and I got two left. That means I must of shot twenty-three deer. No, dammit, I forgot. I had to shoot one deer twicet."

The Old Man went on. "I was hunting with the boys one day close to Waccamaw, and I was waiting on a deer-stand when I heard a gun go off. There wasn't any mistaking it, it was Elwood's; he was the only man around that had a single-shot .32 rifle. When I heard the crack I moseyed over, about half a mile, to help him skin and gut the deer. As I came close I heard voices, and there is this game warden talking to Elwood.

" 'You shot this here doe deer, Elwood,' the warden said.

" 'What doe deer?' Elwood replies.

" 'This here doe deer here. The one you just drug into the bushes and was fixin' to cover up with bresh when I come by.'

" 'I never shot no doe deer.'

" 'You must of shot her,' the warden says. 'Her neck's broke with a bullet and they's a .32 shell a-lyin' over there by that stand. The deer's here and the cartridge is here and you're here and you're the only feller around with a .32 rifle that always breaks deer's necks arunnin'. I say you shot this here doe deer, Elwood.'

"Elwood put another bullet in the rifle and hauled back the hammer. It made a nasty click. 'Warden,' he said, 'anybody that'd say I shot a doe deer is a suck-egg dog, and I'd *shoot* ary suck-egg dog I ever seen in the woods.'

"The warden looked at Elwood and then he looked at the gun and then he looked at the dead doe. He shuffled his feet and cleared his throat. 'I reckon you didn't shoot that there doe after all,' he said. 'But hit's a nice day, ain't it?'

"You know those cold gray eyes of Elwood's. He looked the warden straight in the face a long time before he answered. Finally he spoke. 'Hit *mought* be,' he said. 'Good day, Warden.'

" 'Good day, Elwood,' the warden said, and disappeared into the trees.

"Elwood got out his knife and started to gut the deer.

"Now that," the Old Man said to me, " is what I would call a very special lie, and one I don't approve of, because Elwood was wrong in the first place and he was backing up his lie with force. That's what starts all these wars you read about. A feller'll tell a lie and get caught at it, and then he's got to shoot his way out of it unless the other feller falls for the bluff. There's a little moral in that, too. There ain't any use bluffin' unless you're prepared to shoot your way out of it, and I am convinced that Elwood would of shot that warden. Those are hot-tempered boys down that way."

The Old Man got out a plug of tobacco and whittled a little clump of shavings into his hand. He stuffed them carefully into his pipe, after knocking out the dottle, and fired up the infernal machine.

"There's a lot to be said for some kinds of truth-stretching," he remarked vaguely. "A lot of mischief-making goes on from telling the pure-T truth that could be avoided either by keeping your mouth shut, giving an evasive answer, or telling a teensy little white one. This here kind of lying is called diplomacy, and is practiced the world round by diplomats and statesmen. At home it's a little simpler. I mean, if your ma asks me if you cut school the other day—which you did—I would merely say, 'I don't know. I haven't seen too much of him lately.' This would save you some trouble at home. But if I go running to your ma blabbering that you been cutting school, without her even asking me, then I am a meddlesome old man, but still I am technically telling the truth and should be had up for being noble beyond the call of duty. You see the difference?"

"As far as I'm concerned I see it," I said. "It's the difference between a week's lost allowance and a swat on the tail."

"It wouldn't be a lick amiss," the Old Man said.

"I know where you got that phrase," I said, sort of cocky. "You got it out of Tom Sawyer, when Aunt Polly whipped Tom when he really wasn't guilty."

The Old Man looked at me in amazement. He shook his head. "I cannot really believe that education is beginning to sink in, but there are signs—there are signs. Where was I?"

"Different kinds of storytelling," I said.

"Well now," the Old Man said, "we come to the sporting liar. He ain't really a liar. He is kind of an artist, like a painter. The difference between a photographer and a painter is that the photogtapher uses a machine that captures a subject exactly as it is. If the subject has got a wart on his nose the camera records the wart. But a painter only makes an impression—his impression—of what the subject seems like to him. If a man is painting a woman he loves or if he is painting for money and the woman has a wart on her nose or too many chins there is no law which forces the painter to leave the wart or dutifully record the chins. He can exercise a little artistic license because paint's cheap, as cheap as talk."

The Old Man yawned and scratched himself. "There are a great many fine things about hunting and fishing," he went on. "You can look at a deer-foot knife handle and remember what time the sun rose, how late the dew lasted, what the camp was like, how the food tasted, how the dogs sounded, when the sun set, when the moon rose, how the owls hooted, all the sounds and sights and tastes and feels. There is that moment of triumph when you boat the trout or haul in the bass or shoot the deer or score a snappy double on the birds. But it is really anticlimax to the other stuff. The adventure is ended with the bird in the coat, the fish in the creel, the deer gutted and hung in the tree. It is sad, a little bit, because all the anticipation is gone, the fact accomplished, the sport over. And that's where lying comes in.

"It is a sin to call it lying. It isn't, really. It's taking a piece of nice, honest cloth and embroidering a pretty design on it. You can't do the embroidery without you got the cloth first. You sit around and you remember and you talk in front of the fire, and gradually you swindle yourself into believing that the deer had eighteen points instead of twelve. You shot thirty ducks instead of fifteen. You only used half as many cartridges as you actually used, and all the fish were world records.

"This is a highly healthy thing. When you are a man grown you are too old for fairy stories, for folk tales, but any man is only a little boy with creaky joints and a bald spot, a mortgage and dyspepsia. He still needs to be amused, and this excessive use of imagination which we call fish stories is just an old little boy telling himself fanciful adventures to keep the hobgoblins away. Without these little embroideries life is mostly a matter of getting up in the morning, staggering through the day, going to bed at night, and thinking about the bills you haven't got the money to pay. When you get older," he said gently, "I think you'll understand what I mean."

"Where does it start and where does it stop?" I asked him. "Where does this embroidery leave off?"

"A man can overdo it," the Old Man replied. "I know a lot of bums who have managed to talk themselves into the idea that nothing's their fault, that they ain't lazy, and the world owes them a living. I know drunks that blame what's wrong with them on the state of the cosmos or the boss is down on them or their wives don't like 'em, when all the time they're drunks because they drink too much liquor. That is when you are really off with the birds.

"But a little self-delusion is good for the digestion, aids sleep, and improves conversation. It don't hurt a man to tell himself that things would've been different if the dog had a cold nose that day or the wind was right instead of wrong or that if he'd led it another foot he would have had it in the bag. And bimeby you believe it and are happy with it and it isn't a lie or a self-delusion any more. It's a fact, because you made it so by constant practice."

Of course, I see now that the Old Man was right, as he was mostly right. I have been to a war and I have written a great many words. I have hunted and fished and traveled the world. And I find that without any intent at real falsehood I have managed to embroider. So few true stories are letter-perfect. All need a little lacework, a little padding here, a little decoration there.

Recently in Africa I shot a leopard and that was quite a feat, if I do say it myself, as it had eluded the best six white hunters I know for a matter of more than two years. It steadfastly refused to appear in daylight. More by luck than design I got it to come to the tree in shooting light, nailed it precisely through the shoulders, and celebrated for a week.

In my mind that leopard is already becoming a legend. I did things to attract it that I really didn't do, but almost did—if I'd thought of the things at the time. The leopard has already grown about a foot in length and is easily another thirty pounds heavier. We stalked it a hundred yards at most but the distance has moved up to half a mile, and the other difficulties, from the pig as bait to bees in the tree, have grown apace.

A friend of mine shot another leopard, a big female, under most unusual circumstances on a recent safari. He shot it charging and growling and moving as only a hurried leopard can travel. Since that day I have heard the story about fifty times. (The exaggeration is mine—actually only about twenty-two times.) But the tale has changed as many times as he has told it. He is now referring to "she" as "he," and the beast has doubled in size, ferocity, and noise. We went together to the taxidermist one day in Nairobi and inspected a male leopard whose hide was as big as that of a medium-size tiger.

"I'd say mine was a little bigger, wouldn't you?" the friend said, believing it.

"I think yours was a lot bigger," I said, compounding the felony and believing it.

Back to the Old Man. I once declared my intention to hunt in Africa when I was a big boy, if the gods would so allow.

"I hope to live to see it," the Old Man said. "But most likely I won't. But I will make you a bet right now: By the time you get through talking about it and thinking about it, all the lions will be as big as elephants, all the elephants as big as houses, and when you go to sleep at night you will count the ammunition and find you never missed a shot."

The strange thing is that the Old Man was right. There was one day when I shot at a buffalo with a .318 and killed him and another standing behind him. Or was that a .300 Magnum and did it happen to Harry Selby?

8

Same Knife; Different Boy

Every time I pick up a paper and read about the teen-agers doing this and the teen-agers doing that and some young maniac shooting people or beating them up for fun I have a hard time reconciling it with the fellows I knew when I was a teen-ager. In days not so dead teen-agers meant somebody between twelve and twenty, but today it's gotten to be a term that certainly connotes problem and may connote criminal.

When I hear "teen-ager" today I almost immediately think in terms of switchblade knives, zip guns, gangs, rebellion, violence, and psychologic difficulty. The emphasis we put on certain examples of adolescence certainly far outweighs the indisputable fact that there are millions of good kids in jeans, who have a lot of fun with and without their folks, who know wind from water and how to build a campfire, run a motorboat, or catch a fish.

The Old Man had a saying about young'uns. He said they were fit to bust with energy, and unless you let the energy loose they *would* bust. The trick, he said, was to channel that energy down some road that wouldn't lead to window-breaking and car-stealing. He was a master at diverting energy and fetching the adolescent home so tired from the diversion that he didn't feel like getting into trouble.

I think today, even more than thirty years ago, that an interest in and knowledge of all dangerous weapons, including knives and pistols—brought out into the open and carefully supervised—is a healthy deterrent to misuse of those weapons. Possibly this does not apply to some social structures in the greater cities, but it never did really.

As the Boy I owned a knife from the time I was six. "The knife," the Old Man said, "is a tool, and a dangerous one. You ain't supposed to carry it open, and when you cut, always cut away from you. Keep it sharp, because if it's dull it ain't any use for what it's made for. But whittle *away* from you."

Thirty-five years later I still bear two magnificent scars on my left thumb. After acquiring those wounds I heeded the admonition and collected no more scars.

We all carried knives—starting with the twenty-five-cent barlow and working up to things with really wicked ripping blades —for skinning animals and cleaning fish. There was also a special saw-toothed, fish-scaling-and-bait-cutting knife in the tackle box, and as we grew a little older a sheath knife that we wore proudly as a sign of our frontiersmanship. But I would rather have gone without my pants than my pocketknife.

There wasn't a day when that dangerous weapon didn't come into use a dozen times—just plain whittling, cutting some cane to make arrows for the bownarrer, fixing a leader on a fishline, opening a can, cleaning fingernails (not very likely) or once, in my case, performing a bit of impromptu surgery on my own foot. I expect if you asked a really expert outdoorsman to name the last weapon he would abandon in the wilds he'd say, "Knife."

With a blade of sufficient temper there is nothing you can't do with a knife except shoot. And you can even make an acceptable substitute for that. The old Boers of South Africa used to kill zebra and wildebeest for their hides, meat, and tallow by riding in among the herds and stabbing them in the withers, a rather risky business if the horse stepped into a pig hole.

You can make a bow and arrows with a knife. You can literally make a canoe with a knife, and you can make a shelter with a knife, merely by cutting down small trees and using anything from a strip cut off your shirt to some tough twisted bark to tie the saplings and the sheltering foliage—whether it's palm frond or pine branches—together.

I reckon the stone knife was man's first important tool. It really became a weapon when he cut down a short sapling, whittled it smooth, and tied the knife onto the end of it, so he could throw it straighter. In a way, it was kind of a Stone Age zip gun.

When I was last in New Guinea a benevolent gentleman of the modern Stone Age, a former cannibal, gave me a magnificent ax. The blade is of greenstone and sharp enough to fell a tree, split the skull of an enemy, kill a pig, or build a house. The handle is shaped like a big T with a curved top, and is made from a single root or branch of hardwood. The greenstone blade was whetted by a warrior sitting in a river and using sand and rushing water to bring it to an edge. It fits into one arm of the T and is balanced by the branch that forms the other arm. The whole thing is bound together by a decorative cross-hatched sennit of the tough-barked *pitpit* palm, and is as tightly woven as cloth. The modern New Guinea Stone-Ager, discovered only in the mid-1930's, depends on this ax as the foundation of his entire economy.

Point is, it was put together with a knife.

The greatest archers of modern time I know are the Kuku-

kuku tribes of the New Guinea highlands. Their bow is a five-foot number made of black palm. It is strung with a fiber about half an inch wide. The arrows are unfletched, unnotched, un-tipped—merely fire-hardened. But they are deadly if only because of filth, and when fired in salvos they are something to see. I have watched one little black gentleman shove four into the air before the first one hit ground.

I have a spear from New Guinea and a shield made from a root. That shield will turn a bullet, unless it is centered dead on, and you can throw that spear entirely through a man's soft section. The spear is not tipped—just plain fire-hardened wood. And I have seen knives of tempered cane that cut beautifully.

Here again the knife, whether of wood or stone, made the other implements and weapons.

This is how I first came to regard a knife as something you used to keep the wolf from the knife-made door, not as something to stick into a stranger for fun. As far as I can remember us kids fought as kids will, but nobody ever drew a knife on anybody.

The same respect applied to guns. We started out at about six with a Daisy air gun, and by the time we hit seven or eight we graduated to a single-shot .22, and at eight or nine we got a 20-gauge shotgun. The care and feeding of these weapons, as I may have mentioned before, was forcefully impressed by a stout, whippy stick on the seat of your pants. In a very short time we learned to respect the tremendous power for harm, as well as the tremendous power for fun and positive enjoyment. I think the worst hiding I ever got was when the Old Man caught me and some cousins playing cowboys and Injuns by shooting each other in the pants with air rifles. My stern tingled for a time, and not from a BB pellet either.

Respect for what could kill you was hammered into our hides. Every summer, when the upcountry people came to the beaches, there was always somebody being hauled out of the water, drowned or half-drowned, because of being swept off-shore by the vicious currents that were formed by tide and two inlets to the major island. There is no such thing as undertow, but there are these currents, dictated by wind and tide and inlet, from sea to sound, and the wise guys always managed to die in defense of not appearing chicken, as they call it today.

My tribe comes from a long line of seafaring folk, and the first thing the Old Man impressed on me when I was a nose-holding, feet-first-jumping moppet was that the big stretch of blue stuff out there could kill unless you kept an eye on it every minute.

"Be frightened of it," he said. "It's a hell of a sight bigger than you are, and twice as ornery, twice as tricky."

Perhaps I am not very clear here, but what I am getting at is that my teen-age group possessed, legally, all the death-dealing, injury-wielding weapons that are now owned clandestinely by the "bad" kids. There was a certain pride in being trusted. My cousins and friends and I used to go off on a Saturday picnic into the local wilds with enough armament to conquer the county—rifles, shotguns, knives, scout axes—and were not regarded as a serious menace to the community. Or to each other.

It is perfectly true that we were free of the modern boons of child psychiatry, television, and progressive schooling. We denied ourselves much parental supervision, since we were out from dawn until dark. We cut Sunday school whenever possible, and the people we knew were rough—watermen, bushrangers, and city toughs. Mostly we came from medium-poor to poor families.

Why aren't we all in jail? I confess I have raided other people's watermelon patches and learned to chew tobacco at a very early age. I once jacklighted a deer and got into terrible trouble. But that seems a minor list of sins when you remember that I—and my chums—were all posssessed of formidable killing machinery. And if it came to racial tensions, God knows there were enough people of another color around to work out on.

We never traveled in packs. Cliques—yes. Three or four boys of an age group generally hunted and fished, and, when we were older and the sap began to rise, dated together. But

the cliques never fought one another. Moonshiners and boot-
leggers I knew by the score, yet they never taught me any
nastiness. And then we came out of the teens in the teeth of the
depression, which, Lord knows, showed a glistening set of
fangs.

A moral is not intended here. I know a flock of modern kids
with a cut of jib similar to ours, and they have been handi-
capped by all the helpful aids to growing up that prevail in
this decade. They still remain good kids, and do not run around
killing each other for kicks.

. . . all of which leads me to the fact that during the summer
they bagged John Dillinger in front of that Chicago theater
everybody was making a lot of noise about this brave Robin
Hood of the underworld and The Lady in Red and a lot of
similar nonsense. You would have thought this thug was a combination of Davy Crockett and Mike Fink, and that his contem-
poraries—Pretty Boy Floyd and Ma Barker and her brood—
combined the nobler portions of Dan'l Boone and Hannah
Somebody, who stood off the Injuns in the blockhouse raid.

I didn't take much stock in all the hullabaloo. The Old Man's
memory was a bit too fresh—that and a dressing down he gave
me one time when I did something bad. I disremember exactly
what sin against the commonwealth I had committed, but the
Old Man narrowed his eyes and sort of sneered.

"Who do you think you are?" he asked. "Judge Roy Bean?
The law west of the Pecos? You make your own rules?"

"Who? What? No sir," I said.

"Your ignorance of your country's folklore is lamentable,"
the Old Man said, coming even closer to a sneer. "I don't suppose you ever heard of Joaquín Murieta or Billy the Kid or
even Jesse James"

"I heard about Jesse James," I said. "He was an outlaw. He
robbed the rich to give to the poor, and he was shot down in a
dastardly fashion."

"Oh my God," the Old Man said, and clapped his brow. "In a dastardly fashion.' A *dastardly* fashion. You know what dastardly means?"

"No sir," I said. "I read it somewhere."

"You get a dictionary for Christmas," the Old Man said grimly. "But right now you get a little lecture."

I settled down for the long winter.

"I called you Roy Bean because there was a hanging Judge by that name one time, when the West was rough and they were building railroads with a lot of ignorant riffraff. There was so much murder and mayhem about that there was a saying: 'No law west of the Pecos.' So a scallywag named Roy Bean—a gunfighter, drunk, cowpoke, blockade runner, and saloonkeeper—set up shop in a place called Langtry, Texas. He opened a saloon called 'The Jersey Lily' after Lillie Langtry, and got appointed justice of the peace. He held court in the saloon, and announced that *he* was the 'law west of the Pecos.' In a way he was, because he would try you, fine you, and hang you all in the same motion. He set himself up as law, and justice didn't enter into it."

The Old Man snorted through his mustache.

"This bum was a hero when I was a boy," he said "We are a peculiar people, us Americans. All a fellow has to do is take the law in his own hands and we make a hero of him. Like this Billy the Kid. A nasty little bucktoothed rat, who'd shoot his mother in the back, who wasn't even a very good murderer, and who got killed by Sheriff Pat Garrett when he was twenty-one. Now they got songs about him.

"And this California bandit, Murieta. He is still famous, since 1853, but they ain't even certain it was him they killed and cut the head off of to exhibit around at the fairs. There was about five Joaquíns—all bums, all rustlers and back-shooters—working at the time, and they seized onto the first Mexican they could bushwhack who looked like his name might of been Joaquín.

"One thing you will find running through all these tall stories about bandit heroes. They were all supposed to be kind, generous, handsome, happy, chivalrous, kind to women and children. They were all supposed to be forced into a life of crime because of some outrage society dealt 'em off the bottom of the deck. I don't know what it takes to make a legend, but honesty, decency, and a reasonable obedience to law and order don't seem to qualify."

"How about Robin Hood, from the olden days?" I ventured. "I read a lot about him, how he robbed the rich to give to the poor."

"Fiddlesticks," the Old Man said. "There never was a highwayman would give a plugged nickel to a blind beggar. As for Mr. Robin Hood, he got in trouble first because he was a poacher—a rustler, if you will—and stayed in trouble because he couldn't keep his paws off other people's pokes. His pleasing personality was an invention of time and people with vivid imaginations."

"How do you know all this, for sure?"

"I *don't*," the Old Man said, "but it figures. When a man sets himself up bigger than the society he lives in anything he had nice for a start wears off him as he goes along, and he winds up a rat in a hole until somebody removes him from serious consideration."

"There must of been somebody from the last hundred years you admired," I said, figuring that the Old Man was so mad at Roy Bean and Billy the Kid and Robin Hood that I was off the hook for my own misdemeanor.

The Old Man smiled. "I kind of fancied a couple folks," he said. "I reckon I would go along with Jim Bowie. He was wild but he wasn't no outlaw, and he died with the knife he invented in his hand in the battle of the Alamo. Like everybody else in the fort. You must of read about that in the history books, General Santa Anna and the siege and all?"

"Yes sir, we had a chapter on it."

"Well, that chapter didn't tell all about Bowie, not by a durn sight. This was a cold-eyed, soft-voiced gentleman, from all accounts, and a real ring-tailed wildcat. He was born gentle and raised rough. He rode alligators for fun in Louisiana, and he had slave dealings with Jean Lafitte, the pirate, on Galveston Island. He was a colonel under Andy Jackson. He ran wild cattle and speared them, and he was a great dark-room duelist with that wicked knife he thought up. He was maybe the greatest Injun fighter of them all. One time a hull flock of Comanches aimed to ambush him, and he and ten men accounted for fifty dead and thirty-odd wounded, against one white man dead and three hurt. The books say there was a hundred and sixty-some Injuns against the eleven whites. He was a sick man at the siege of the Alamo, but they say there was Mexicans stacked up like cordwood alongside his bunk before they finally got him.

"No man I ever heard about lived as big as Jim Bowie. He married the prettiest girl in San Antonio, a Spanish gal, daughter of the vice-governor when the Mexicans still had Texas. He went out and got himself adopted by the Lipan Apaches. These Lipans did a heavy traffic in silver at the trading posts, and Bowie had himself a keen eye for old Spanish treasure.

"He worked hard at being a good Injun. He was a fine shot and he killed a lot of buffalo and fought a lot of the Lipans' enemies. He stood so high with the chief and the tribe that they finally showed him their treasure. The historians don't quite agree as to whether they showed him a galore of smelted Coronado ore or an ocean of natural veins. But they showed him something that drove him mad, and he spent the rest of his life trying to locate the lost San Saba mine.

"Some think he found it, but didn't have time to exploit it, or else he was biding his time until he could work it without cutting the country in half. But the Texas War of Independence came along and Jim Bowie died with all the other men in the Alamo. Even today the Texas people around Santone think he died knowing the whereabouts of the San Saba treasure, whether it was smelted ore or natural vein. And they're still looking for the lost mine."

"Your Mr. Jim Bowie sounds about as raunchy as the others you're so down on," I said. "I mean he was a killer and a slaver and a real roughneck."

"There's a difference," the Old Man said. "Bowie was a gentleman and most of his legend is founded on fact, not on what a bunch of latter-day sentimentalists and maudlin outlaw-worshippers wove around some drunk cowpoke, who managed to shoot six Mexicans and make himself a reputation as a bad hombre. Most of the Kids and Jameses were just murderers and stick-up artists, before they hung halos on 'em. There's been more lies told about the olden days and the tough guys that inhabited those days than I like to think about. Seems like all a fellow's got to do is die with his boots on and he gets to be an archangel, when all the time he was just some ignorant bushwhacker with a mean streak."

"How do you account for all the hero worship then, in modern times, if they're all so no-account?"

"Son," the Old Man said, "a fellow named Thoreau once remarked that the mass of men lead lives of quiet desperation. The average fellow is stuck so firm under the thumb of his wife and his family and his job that even a hyena sounds romantic, if it happened to holler yesterday. These hairy ruffians would have seemed pretty commonplace, disgusting, and possibly full of lice if you'd lived in the same neighborhood with 'em. When they got drunk you ducked out of their way, and wished they'd move off someplace else."

"All the same," I said stubbornly, "I would like to have lived in those days."

"I do not doubt it in the least," the Old Man said. "You would have been one of the first victims of the James boys or of Billy the Kid, due to being a basically law-abiding type and a little slow at fanning a gun."

About that time a female voice sounded strong on the evening breeze.

"That's your grandma requesting that we wash up for supper, Judge Roy Bean," the Old Man said. "I'll say one thing. If she'd of been around in those days, there would have been law west of the Pecos, and they wouldn't have made a legend out of your namesake. She'd have made a great peace marshal without firing a shot."

9

You Got to Hurt to Be Happy

It was one of those freezing Southern days, with the wind slapping harshly against the clapboards and riffling the green shingles on the roof. The house seemed to shake a little as the gale buffeted the tiny town, and there was a flurry of snow amongst the magnolias. The Old Man hunched his rocker a little closer to the fire, and we both listened to the wind screaming down the chimney and raising tiny cyclones of loosely shifting ash. The Old Man mock-shivered and hunched his shoulders. He was wearing a ratty old gray sweater hauled up under his chin.

"If you pinned me right down to it," the Old Man said, "I don't like nothing very much but a hot fire and a warm bed and a quiet woman to fetch me my food. I can generally manage the first two, but I been looking constantly for the basic ingredient of the third. Quiet, I mean.

"What I really like is more or less bearish. I mean a cave, a snug, warm cave. Let the winds howl and the snow fall and leave me safe inside my cave. The bear is a mighty intelligent animal. He's got sense enough to come in out of the winter weather and wait for the pretty flowers in the spring." The Old Man spat a sizzling jetstream into a fire that was fairly shaking the chimney.

"Listen to that wind," he said. "It'll have the planks off the house by tomorrow. Nobody but a damned fool or a hungry Eskimo would go out in weather like that. You better go to bed early tonight, boy, or us damned fools will be late for the ducks." He grinned and spat again. "Try to remember you're a hungry Eskimo when the alarm clock rousts you out tomorrow. It makes more sense than being an idiot."

That was the Old Man for you—full of contradictions. He would be praising the comforts of the fireside one minute and then deviling you to buck weather that would have put old Peary off his program.

The Old Man had a lot of favorite topics, and one was that a hunting-fishing fellow hated comfort, that he welcomed pain, that he was never so happy as when he was miserable. He was like the gent in the old joke who kept hitting himself over the head with a hammer, because it felt so good when he quit. The Old Man ranked duck hunters with mountain climbers for damfoolishness; said he never climbed a mountain and didn't want to. He hadn't lost nothing up there in those clouds.

The Old Man had stomped in with his pipe frozen solid, rime on his mustache, and his nose a brilliant cherry red. He seemed as bright as a boxful of birds at a time when the dogs were indistinguishable from the logs on the fire, they were that close to the blaze.

"It's a lovely day today, ain't it?" said he, shaking the snow from his overcoat and warming his chapped hands before the fire. "And by all indications it'll be lovelier tomorrow."

Grandma regarded her mate with disapproval. "Quit dripping all over my rugs," Miss Lottie said. "A lovely day for what? Pneumonia? Hang that wet coat on the back porch."

The Old Man smiled. "It's a lovely day for ducks," he said. "I never saw a nicer day for ducks. The wind will break up the rafts, and the snow and ice will freeze up the big ponds. The ducks'll fly low and come into any little pothole that isn't frozen tight. They'll decoy to anything that looks free of wind. If I was a meat hunter I'd make me a fortune in the morning, just creeping up on a few unfrozen patches and letting fly with a 10-gauge or some other murderous weapon. Slay 'em by the hundreds."

The Old Man scowled at the idea. "Fortunately," he said, "I ain't a pothunter, and I don't own no 10-gauge shotgun. But all the same I intend to take advantage of the weather and shoot rather selectively with that old pump gun that's standing in the corner. Tomorrow I shoot nothing but canvasbacks, bar the occasional pintail and a Canada goose or so. Have I got any takers or are you just going to sit here and shiver and feel sorry because it ain't April?"

The Old Man used to reckon that one man's weather is another man's poison. "The only way to handle weather," he said now, "is to know what you want to do with it and use it accordingly. Quit complaining about it and put up with it for what it's worth. And be prepared for it. The trouble with city people is that they freeze when it's cold and boil when it's hot, because they dress the same way for all seasons. An Eskimo knows it's going to be cold, so he stokes himself up on boiled walrus or blubber, builds a house to match his mood, and only interrupts the long dark winter to thaw out another chunk of seal. The African savage knows it's going to be hot the year round, so he wears a strip of banana leaf to hide his nakedness and seeks his coolness under a palm.

"You get a big unseasonable snow like this, and the man who owns a pair of long-handled, red-flannel drawers hollers hooray and goes for a sleigh ride. The fellow that's still stuck into summer BVD's whimpers and wails that the weatherman's betrayed him personally. There ain't no such thing as bad weather, if you come right down to it. Some's just better than others, as there ain't no such thing as a real ugly woman. Some are just prettier than others."

I had seen that pointed pipestem before. He strictly wasn't aiming it at Grandma.

"What time do we get up?" I asked. "Before dawn, as usual?"

"Let's don't overdo it," the old buzzard grinned. "It'll be black night until seven o'clock, and they'll fly all day in this wind anyhow. I should remark that if you had breakfast ready by six-thirty we'd have ample time to cope with all the necessities. But dress warm, boy, dress warm, and don't bother to get me up till the coffee's boiling. I aim to sleep in my long drawers, too. That way you start off warm."

One thing the Old Man taught me: You dress warm from the inside out, not the outside in. You start with a hot breakfast—ham and eggs and toast and a lot of coffee—and then you surround the breakfast with long drawers and a soft sweater and a couple of flannel shirts and two pairs of socks. A pair of woolly britches over that, and hip boots to keep the wind and water off you, and an oilskin jacket and a cap with earmuffs, and you don't need a bearskin coat. Once that inside furnace starts working you find you can sweat in a blizzard.

"I know it sounds kind of sissy," the Old Man said, as we mopped up the remains of the eggs with the toast, "but certain creature comforts can make a power of difference in how good you shoot. You go get that little kerosene stove we used on the beach this fall, while I tend to the coffee thermos."

He tended to another kind of thermos, too, but I suspect it contained no coffee. It didn't *sound* like coffee. It sounded thinner to the naked ear, and possibly contained a vitamin tonic whose sale, at the time, was highly illegal. In any case it was too special for boys.

We had two or three blinds to be used according to wind and weather, and this freezing morning we chose a nearby one, with me poling the boat and freezing my fingers through the mittens, my nose running droplets onto the scarf around my neck, the marshes cold and gray and windswept, as only salt marshes can be on a day like this. As I shoved the skiff up the little avenues of what was water day before yesterday the boat's keel made a crackling noise, forcing its way through the thin crusting of last night's ice. The narrow lanes were frozen bank to bank, but when we hove onto a semisweet-water pond it was only iced around the edges. A mighty flock of mallards took off with irritable quacks when we approached the blind, and the darting *squish-wish* of frustrated teal swept low as we shoved the skiff into the little tunnel behind it. The Old Man more or less slung a dozen decoys into the water helter-skelter, with nothing of his usual attention to meticulous placement.

"Today," he said blandly, "they'll decoy to a couple of old tin cans and some milk bottles. Fire up that stove, sonny, and hand me the jug—the *other* thermos."

I swear we could have gotten a limit of anything with a couple of old brooms and a slingshot that day. It was almost— but not quite—as if the ducks were trying to come into the blind to get warm. You know Canada geese as wary birds. We collected our limit of the old honkers in two flights, and didn't even bother to change to goose loads; they came in that close.

The roaring wind had filled the skies with disturbed birds, all looking for a place to set. None of the usual artifices which the Old Man employed, and which I knew by now, were necessary. It was a mere matter of choice of breed. We got so persnickety at one time that we made a bargain: I would shoot only canvasbacks and the Old Man would specialize in pintails. We sneered at mallards—as it was late in the season, and we suspected a tendency to fish eating—and simply stood up and shooed away the teal and the goldeneyes and broadbills and trash ducks that fought their way to the little space.

Time has passed, but I would swear we were out of that blind with the boat loaded to the gunwales and the special jug only a quarter diminished before an hour was up. I have only

seen it that way once since, when an old friend named Joe
Turner, a Washington rasslin'-boxing promoter, and I dared
a snowstorm on the Eastern Shore of Maryland. You had to
look between the snowflakes to see the ducks, but Lord save us
there were more ducks than snowflakes.

Well, the Old Man and I snuffed out the little kerosene stove,
broke the skiff free of the ice that bound her, and shoved happily off for home and fire. The snow had started again but the
wind had dropped, and the sky was still filled with enough low-
flying ducks to have provided a hundred years' imprisonment
for a man who wished to overshoot his quota. When we dragged
the boat up on the shingle and shouldered the strings of fowl
and the guns the Old Man smiled sort of sardonically at the
putty-gray skies.

"Your grandma ain't going to believe it," he said, "but I think
this was one of the prettiest days I ever saw in my life. Any argument?"

"No sir," I said. "I ain't arguing. You can have them bluebird
days."

I don't ski, as I would rather contract pneumonia without
breaking my back in the process, but I can see now where a
snowfall that wrecks a city's transportation can be a thing of
beauty to a man who straps staves on his feet and goes hurtling
down a hill to sudden dissolution.

The older I get and the more places I have hunted, the more I
figure the old man was dead right, as usual, about suffering.
Ernie Pyle, the late war correspondent, once wrote that he had
been sicker in more hotel rooms than any living man, and I
swear I have been scareder, hotter, colder, dizzier, more exten-
sively bug-bitten, sunstricken, breathless, witless, and generally
unhappier than any of the old Penitentes, who used to climb
mountains wearing hair shirts and beating themselves rhyth-
mically over the shoulders with whips for fun. And all in the
name of happy outdoor sport.

I get vertigo just crossing a plank bridge over a six-inch-deep creek, but now it seems everything I hunt is placed on top of a peak that would make a molehill out of Everest. I took up grouse hunting once because I thought a moor was a kind of lowland bog—at least a marsh—and found out that a Scottish grouse moor is always placed on the highest peak of the highest range, and that no matter how the cards fell for the draw of butt position I drew the one nearest the top.

I took up elephants as an art form once because I thought you could find them on level ground. You *can* find them on level ground, all right, but you've got to climb Mount Kenya first and then walk a rough hundred miles before you discover that the owner of the big fat track you've been following has only one lousy tusk.

In the hunting business there seems to be no pleasure without excruciating pain. You got to hurt to be happy.

I was mixed up in an Alaska brown bear hunt not too long ago, and it seems to me all I did was crawl through thick bush on my belly, trying to make the summits of mountains I never cared for even pictorially, in order to sit glumly in the rain and let the mosquitoes bite me. I had heard of Alaskan mosquitoes, but never believed they actually carry four motors. They do.

I shot a bear eventually, and nearly got hit on the head by it. I shot it in the heart, and it had enough adrenalin left to run straight away from me up the face of a mountain for about sixty yards before it decided to die and come roaring down again like a Sherman tank out of control. One thousand pounds of bear bounced between me and the guide, and later I reflected that this would have been a silly way to die. Sample conversation around the cracker barrel:

"What happened to Ruark?"

"Oh he was hit in the head with a bear. Always said he'd come to a bad end."

Whoever might have made this snide remark would not have included the fact that in order to get hit in the head with a bear you have to push a skiff about half a league in shallow water, breathing the delightful aroma of rotting salmon, and then stumble another half a league onward over moss-slick stones, feeling the gruesome, fleshy squish of the same rotting salmon under booted foot, before you get to the base of the mountain you must climb in order to see the bears in a nine-foot jungle of lush grass.

A bear is not a bear; it is a far-distant black grubworm on a piece of ragged yellow carpet, and shortly it will go away never to be seen again. That's if it is worth shooting. You fairly have to fight your way through the she-bears with half-grown cubs, each of which could throw a horse over its shoulder and gallop it a country mile. But the big boys are all mobbed up in the hills, eating blueberries and playing poker.

The thing most nonhunters don't realize about the artistic pain that goes into filling four ounces of flesh-and-feathers or seven tons of elephant with the correct prescription is that when you walk out thataway you got to walk back thisaway. Non-fishermen don't realize that the current is likely to run steadily in one direction, and if you float downstream, eventually you have to fight your way upstream. From rabbit to tiger, from bobwhite to buffalo, from sand perch to marlin, there's no such thing as a free lunch.

And the animals have us always stopped on a simple axiom: Nothing moves very much except in early morning or late afternoon, which means you leave camp in blackest freezing dawn and return—cursing, stumbling, bone-sore—in the chill of even blacker night. Except that now you are thorn-wounded, stone-bruised, ankle-wobbly, nose-running, lip-parched, bug-bit —and nearly always without the thing you went after in the first place.

I do not know how many dusty miles I have driven in Kenya and Tanganyika, in North Carolina and Texas, how many bogged-down vehicles I have rescued, how much mud I have slogged through, how many busted axles, how many tsetse-fly bites, how many wait-a-bit thorns, how much blazing sun or how much grinding monotony, aggravated by cracked lips and blistered feet. I do not remember the pain when I see a noble head on the wall, whether it's a whitetail or a really good buff. I just remember the triumphal coming into camp with the horn beeping and the promise of a cold Martini before a hot fire.

But I do remember the aching agony of my legs on a little twenty-mile jaunt after elephant, when we had struggled through the highest, closest-clenched grass and past the ugliest, nearest rhino I ever hope *not* to see any more to finally achieve the blessed level calm of a railroad bed. I sighed and thought, *Now we're home*, but a sadist named John Sutton smiled brightly and said, "Well, we're *almost* there. It's only another seven miles." I made it, God knows how, but the elephants have been safe from me since.

The most self-punishing hunters I know today are millionaires who have been and been and *been*, who've shot it all and don't really want to shoot any more. They just want to see and to suffer. One is just back, after searching a couple of months for what is, in these times, the almost mythical grail of an elephant that will go a hundred and fifty pounds or better per tusk. I doubt he shot anything larger than a sand grouse during the trip, because he is not interested in killing just to hear the gun go off. But he must have been spending a minimum thousand a week just to walk in foot-sucking sand, following seductive tracks through razored dwarf palm, only to end up in daily disappointment and the long trek back.

What makes them do it? Why go to all that bother? It isn't entirely curiosity, because the guy I have in mind has made at least eight safaris.

It must get back to the Old Man's theory that you ain't happy unless you're hurtin', and that somewhere in the hurt you cleanse yourself of a lot of civilized nonsense that spreads a thick veneer on the hides of people, like a scabby overpaint when what you really need first is a scrape job or a blowtorch. You scrape it off, you sweat it off, you walk it off. Your head gets clearer, your senses sharper, and when you do come back—blistered, thirsty, too tired to be hungry, too weary to wash—some of the nonsense of today has been burnt away.

Some beauty has been observed, some hardships overcome, some sympathies established, and there is a wondrous satisfaction about honest fatigue.

I remember once I took a hard-core city slicker—a man who did not like dogs, who knew nothing of guns or game—on a pheasant hunt in Connecticut, which was blanketed with a light early-autumn snow. The fellowship in the snug cabin was excellent, the food fine, and the next day the dogs worked beautifully. The birds were plentiful. We had what is generally described as a magnificent day in the blazing autumn woods, and the bourbon was beneficent when we came in, beat, with a lovely bag of birds and memories to the beckoning fingers of the fire.

Our man had missed manfully; his Stork Club training had done little for his wind as we trudged the snowy hills. Finally, if only to vindicate himself to the dogs, he more or less accidentally killed a magnificent cock pheasant and insisted on carrying it personally all the weary way back to the lodge. He leaped immediately to the phone and called all his acquaintances —and they are widespread, including Europe and Mexico—to declaim his prowess over the rumpled bird that he still stroked mentally as he talked.

He finally sat down, emotionally overcome. "How long has this been going on?" he asked. "And where have *I* been all my life?"

I don't know. Possibly somewhere beyond the point reached when the first cave man did in the first hairy mammoth for food and clothing, and then was constrained to scratch its picture on the wall. Something between gratification of the hunger pangs and some essential element of esthetic conflict between man and animal, man and bird, man and death took over to build hunting into an art form of appreciation and self-sacrifice, of a willingness to punish the hunter's body to make a point of personal egotism; with, finally, a possible tangible reward at the end—a plume to deck the cave lady's head, a fine tusk to turn into a rude plowshare.

And always the fire, the snugness inside to hold the elements aloof once the dreadful travail of the day was done. And then the old boy can sit down with the braggies to tell all the cave kids how good Papa done that day with his spear.

It is, I suppose the Old Man would say, a form of crawling back into the cave, but all I want ahead of it is a long, hard day's work in the woods, so that I'll feel I've earned it when the cave lady brings me some dinosaur broth or even a Brontosaurus hamburger. Quietly. On time.

10

Hang Your Stocking in August

"Christmas," the Old Man once said, "is a damned dull day, and generally raining. But preparing for it is more fun than a barrel of monkeys." And as a Texas friend of mine once opined, "It ain't gettin' ready that's the most fun. It's the gettin' ready to get ready."

It is maybe August elsewhere—just plain August—but in England it is something else. You can throw away all those trite flights of prose about the trees being lushly heavy with August, the lazy buzzing hum of August. In England during August a lot of people are whetted to a fine edge and are busier than they were in the blitz.

There is a day in August that is called simply The Twelfth. Nothing more, but nobody ever asks, "The twelfth of what?"

Because the Twelfth is when the grouse season opens in Scotland. Ever since the season closed last fall all the wine-purpled gentlemen with ersatz healthy complexions have been preparing for this day. Sherlock Holmes deerstalkers have been carefully rescued from the moths, tweed knickers and canvas gaiters have been hauled out of the attic, shooting sticks have been furbished to a high-silver shine, and the matched Purdeys and Greeners and Churchills have been exhumed from their plush-lined cases and searched suspiciously for a minute speck of dust. The square leather cartridge cases come out of the attic, and the state of the world is neglected. What the gentry wants to know is the condition of the heather, the amount of the hatch, the abundance of the vital quartz; and Nasser can go and be damned, together with all the Russians. I rather like the idea.

All this came up because I more or less tore off an arm one time just before the quail season opened. A recent split finger, in the middle of a working project, fetched it back strong. Just before I was supposed to leave for a safari I helped Mama in the kitchen, and wound up with a hand that was grease-crisped to the bone. I had been preparing for that safari for eighteen solid months. During the first two days I had to shoot an elephant and a rhino under rather tense conditions, and the second finger of the convalescing right hand was split open like a frankfurter that had tarried overlong on the grill.

In the strange thinking process of a small boy August was the big month, because August prepared you for September. September whipped you into shape for October, and October was the trial run for the best of them all: November. After that December and January were a cinch, and all you had to do was sweat out February and March, and then the fish bit again and school's recess was just around the corner.

In August I was sick to death of summer. I was weary of summer as a man tires of too many gooey desserts, and craves the peasant companionship of hard ham and hominy, the smell of wood smoke, the invigorating thrashing of a salt breeze, or the nip of frost that wrinkles the persimmons, browns the grasses, and pulls the leaves off trees so you can see the squirrels. Along about August summer took on the aspect of a pretty woman who had let herself go and was beginning to bulge over her girdle as a result of too much fudge.

Enough of those flowers, boy; let's hear a little hound music bugling in the piny woods.

The Old Man had said that if you just confined life to preparation you'd never really be disappointed when the actuality arrived. This was soundly cynical, but it was true—if you can accept a poet's negation of the harsh bitterness of reality. Stars in eyes have never been practical, but sometimes are more comfortable than a speck of actual grit.

It would not be very long before the bluefish were running close to the coast. One big norther in September would bring them along for you. So a man had better get up to the attic or into the closets, and see what shape the fishing tackle was in. It is amazing what manner of demons infest the secret places in which a man hides his fishing gear. They perform strange feats of tangling lines, misleading leaders, warping rods, and jamming reels. So if August had no other value it was a fine month for straightening out the mischief the leprechauns had wreaked on his salt water tackle over the winter.

The season for squirrel, marsh hen, and dove would suddenly be upon you, and the dogs had gotten awful lax. The bird dogs and the duck dogs had a little more time to be lazy in, but it certainly was time to ginger up the hounds and beat a little nonsense out of the utility crossbreeds, the squirrel-chasers and the rabbit-coursers that had done nothing but sleep under the house all summer and eat themselves out of shape.

Come to think of it, I know of nothing as shiftless as a working dog when there's no work. The finest pointer in the world, the best-bred setter, the most dedicated hound, the infallible Chesapeake, all get to be bums over the slack months. Maybe they are like writers who make sudden money and don't have to write for a while, for they sure do get out of the habit of earning their keep. When you finally kick them loose from lethargy they look at you as if you were asking them to stick up a bank or volunteer for a trip to the moon.

"You know," the Old Man used to say, "I never knew anybody who really liked his work. I knew a lot of people who *said* they liked their work, but I disbelieved it. Take one of these dogs. The setters were created to find quail. The retrievers were made to fetch ducks. The fice dogs were accidentally provided to tree squirrels and jump rabbits. But damme, none of them are satisfied. The bird dogs want to run rabbits, and the junk dogs want to be pointers. The duck dogs want to sit in the blind and shiver and look at you with them appealing brown eyes, like Eliza being sent out into the snow and ice. Any man or any dog really needs a boot in the behind to set him about his appointed task."

Part of August's preparation was to take the dogs into the woods and cure them of laziness, rebellion, and the idea that the world owed them a living. It is possible that a whippy stick laid smartly on the behind is mildly brutal, but you could more swiftly reimbue a lazy dog with fresh interest in his work by use of a switch than by all the preacherly persuasions in the world.

At that time you really had to reindoctrinate the quail in the idea that they were not nightingales paid by the state to thrill the world with song, but five-ounce packages of dynamite that shortly were going to be working on their own time, and that men, dogs, and guns were portion to their soldier's pay. I will entertain arguments, but I swear you could train a covey of quail to kind of behave at the same time you were schooling the newest puppy and informing the elder canine statesmen that they really were not Winston Churchill after a long stretch on the Riviera. You could accustom the bobwhite to use in a certain place at a certain time, and there were always some coveys that almost left you a note in a cleft stick if they decided to go someplace else to spend the afternoon.

Man, but that August was busy, and a lot of it was waiting for the drowsy heat to depart and the first bracing chill to come.

It seemed like September would never arrive, and in the meantime you had to put up with all the people who cluttered the beaches and jammed the streetcars under some sort of mistaken idea that they were having a vacation. August was a time of strangers—sunburned, pink-blotched people, people you didn't know and didn't want to know. Strangers far from home, cluttering up the local facilities.

On a hot day, with the asphalt oozing under bare feet and the air dripping humidity, the thoughts of autumn crispness became well-nigh unbearable. The dogs' tongues lolled and they panted in the heat. The sea was a solid shimmer of sun, unlike your angry gray friend that crashed onto the beaches and communicated its leashed fierceness to you, promising lean, mean, undershot-jawed bluefish and solid silver slabs of sea bass, while the gulls screamed.

The flies all came into the house in August, as I recall, and the mosquitoes, sensing winter death ahead, tried to eat everybody before they died. While scratching bites you kept telling yourself that Labor Day would bring that norther and the mosquitoes would die and the people would go away and a man might breathe again.

August was really the night before Christmas. I was not seeing the steaming, traffic-cluttered city streets or drowsing to the hum of cicadas or hearing the plaint of the whippoorwills at night. The mockingbird in the magnolia bored me with his silvery night song, and I wished he would shut up. He sounded too much like summer, and I would have preferred to hear a turkey gobble.

What I was really hearing was an angry squawk as a marsh hen flapped ungainly from the tips of the marsh grass, almost covered by the swollen tides the full moon and the northeaster brought. I was hearing the harsh whistle of duck wings as they arrived from Canada. I was seeing the dark frieze of geese before a full moon, the night trembling with honking. I was hearing a coon dog belling in the woods, and my mouth was watering, because when you could hear the hounds hog-killing time was close, the frost was on the punkin, and oysters were fit to eat again.

Then I was thinking that the summer calling of quail changed, abruptly, and that the classic *bob-white, bob-bob-white* changed to a lonely *who-he, who-he,* as the scattered coveys remustered in the dusk. I was already cupping an ear for the snort of a buck whitetail powerfully overcome by nipping frost and his own importance, his neck swollen with lust and his eye walled for all the pretty girls in a twenty-mile area.

And all the time it kept on being August, August, *August!* Where was September, the golden month, the threshold of the fine times, the wondrous days when the leaves turned gold and red and the pine woods assumed dark, spicy importance again? Where *are* you, September? Possibly you don't recall the frustration, the oil-smelling frustration, of cleaning a gun you know damn well you can't use for another month. Or you may not remember just how long it can be until the quail season opens in November. Time drags. The days, for a boy, never end, although the days end very swiftly in the three months you are allowed to shoot quail. Then it is barely morning before it's dark. Weeks tumble into one another, telescoped like an accordion. This is not all boy feeling; some several hundred years later as a man I went on my first African safari, and I swear it was over before I got there. Or almost.

But in one way August may be the best of all the months. It holds the promise of autumn, the breathless excitement of what is just around the corner, and if autumn falls down on you you have at least experienced delicious anticipation. Even if it rains on a future autumn Saturday, even if it's too calm for the ducks, even if the dogs' noses go hot it has not happened to you *yet.* What you experience in August is a future millennium, where the ducks always decoy well, the geese always come in to feed before the legal shooting hour expires, and where no dog ever runs up a covey of quail because of a dry smeller.

Whether you are shooting grouse with a thousand-dollar Purdey in November or just whistling up a yellow fice dog to

go look for a squirrel with your mail-order .22 it is always nice
to remember one thing: No matter what happens that day, good
or bad, you really paid for the day in August, the bridesmaid
of all the months, the bridesmaid who will never be a bride.

11

Good-bye, Cruel World

My boy Mark Robert, godson to me and son to a friend, has a tent pitched in the yard outside his pappy's house in Limuru in Kenya. Mark is six years old. He has his air gun and his cooking equipment and most of his lares and penates in the tent. But up to now he is afraid to pass the night in the tent, although Mummy is within easy hail and he has his lion dog, Sam (part dachshund, part cocker), to keep the carnivores at bay.

"But don't you want to spend the night in the bush in that tent all by yourself?" I asked young Twain, who is called Twain because his first name is Mark, if that makes any sense.

"No," said young Mark Twain.

"Why?" said I.

"I'm too scared," said young Mark, a tad of appalling frankness.

I admire honesty in the young, and this particular spate of a rare commodity reminded me of some days when I had a tent pitched under the magnolia tree in Southport, North Carolina, to which I retreated when the adults became too heavy to bear. It was a tent quite like young Twain's tent, and no more distant from the house.

We had a difference of opinion, as I recall, my people and I, and I determined to run away and embark on a life of piracy, rapine, and highway robbery. I was a red-hot six years old, and the Irish was showing. The whole world was wrong, and you could have called me Parnell.

"Good-bye, cruel world," I said, more or less, and departed for a life of shame.

I must say that the Old Man took it in stride when I announced my intention to trek. "You sure you going to give us all up and run off to live with the Injuns?" he said gently. "I mean, we don't get no chance to mend our ways and maybe keep you with us until you get out of the sixth grade?" The Old Man had a dirty twinkle, but this was dirtier than usual, and made me even madder.

"You'll be sorry when I'm gone," I said. "There won't be nobody around the place to fetch the firewood and run the errands and clean the fish. You'll be sorry, all right."

The Old Man heaved a sigh. "That's what I was afeard of," he said. "Without I got you, *they*"—he gestured in the general direction of Miss Lottie and the other grownups—"they'll be making *me* do *your* work. Maybe I could run away with you?"

"No sir." I was very firm. I figured even at my tender age that running away was something a boy had to do all by himself or it didn't count.

"No sir," I said. At the time I had not encountered Mr. Dickens and his Sydney Carton, and the bad gag about "it is a far, far better thing that I do" had not crept into my working vocabulary, but I was thinking it all right.

"I'm going now," I said, full of dignity and trepidation.

"Well, good-bye," the Old Man said. His tone was solicitous.

"You got everything you'll need? Matches? Hatchet for fire-wood? Air rifle to shoot birds with? You better take some eggs and bacon to tide you over until you start living off the country. And be careful of snakes. If you do get struck try to cut a cross over the bite, tie on a tourniquet, pour in some gunpowder, set it afire, and if you can find somebody to suck the poison out of the wound do so. Gettin' snake-bit is a messy business when you're off on your own, because you generally can't reach the place you're bit to suck out your own poison."

The Old Man fired up his pipe and looked at me under low-ered lids.

"You ain't going to find it very comfortable," he said. "I mind well I run away once when I was a kid. Of course, we ain't got any Injuns now, except some tame ones in Robeson County, but in them days the place was populous with redskins. A man come home with his hair on was an exception. I knowed one feller, he got scalped before he was dead. The Injun run off with his hair, and when the man come to he was prematurely bald. Had to buy a wig to cover his shame."

"There ain't any Injuns around now except some Brass An-kles," I said. "And they ain't really Injuns."

"True," the Old Man said. "But you want to watch out for such things as wild hogs and wild cats and the stray panther now and then. That air rifle is all right for robins and such—like that mockingbird you killed that made your Grandma so mad—but a BB gun don't stack up very high against a wild boar. And when you're reduced to eatin' what you can find in the way of herbs I suggest you watch out for the poisonous toadstools and the berries I don't even know about myself. What might seem like a sparkleberry to you might be something en-tirely different when they do the autopsy."

"You're just tryin' to scare me," I said. "I'm leavin'. Good-bye."

"Would you mind shakin' hands?" the Old Man said, and shoved out his paw. "We may never meet again in this life."

Feeling very noble, I took his hand, shook it, and went off

to the wilds of my tent. I figured I would mount the expedition from the tent, straighten out my gear, pack my rucksack, and depart before dawn.

"Good-bye sir," I called and choked back a sob. Frankly, I was on the hook and there wasn't any way to get out of running away except to run away.

You know how lonely it can be in a tent, even in the side yard, when the night falls and there's no place to go except the tent, with the world opening up ahead of you and no point of fixed destination?

Yes. Just about that lonely. The house was maybe thirty yards away. It could have been a million miles, because my pride had removed it from my ken. There were lights and laughter, but I, the outcast, was now not allowed to share either lights or laughter. I was stuck in a tent, ringed round by loneliness.

Night noises came on. Late-blooming mockingbirds tuned in. Bugs zoomed and swooshed and plunked against the canvas. Frogs croaked. The whippoorwills made a symphony of sadness. Things popped and cracked and boomed and snapped and crackled—and stalked by on careful feet. Over there an owl hooted. Over yonder a dog howled, which meant somebody was dead. A lonely, frightened colored boy started a sad song to stave off the demons of the dark until he got home to Foxtown.

And me? I had acute claustrophobia complicated by active fright and a vague guilt consciousness. I was trapped in a tent, and over thataway lay the far shores. And I didn't know precisely how I was going to achieve those far shores. Certainly not in the middle of the night, with all the sounds and the things—all the birds, bugs, and beasts—against me.

But I couldn't leave the tent, although the rustle I had just heard was certainly a moccasin, an adder, or a rattler. A man has his pride. Once you start to run away you got to run away. I peeked out of the tent flap and the house had never seemed brighter, gayer. Life was in the house, and there I was dead stone cold in the dark in a tent.

"Make a fire," I said aloud. But then I considered that I would have to go and rob the house of firewood, which was a poor way to start a life of crime. Also, there wasn't any flue in the tent.

Anyhow, it was too hot for a fire, although a fire might have been a heavy help against the mosquitoes, which were now beginning a concerted dive on my carcass.

Now I was hungry. Figuring that I would live off the country I had spurned the Old Man's suggestion about bacon and eggs. There was no country I could live off of at this moment It was the wrong season for figs and grapes and pecans, which were all we grew in this plot.

The mosquitoes buzzed and my belly growled. Lone and lorn in a tent, with civilization thirty yards away and me too proud to compromise. The owl hooted louder, the whippoorwill keened. The dead-man dog howled.

Footsteps padded softly across the lawn. "You all right in there?" The Old Man's voice was soft. "Anything I can do?"

"I'm fine," I said. "Don't worry about me," and I must have snuffled back half a sob.

"Well," the Old Man said, "I'm kind of a committee. I'm speaking on behalf of your ma and pa and grandma. They reckon that maybe there was wrong on both sides, and if you could see your way clear to make a parley we might be able to straighten things out.

"Mind you," the Old Man said, "we ain't askin' you to give in on anything that offends your sense of what's right and wrong. It's just that we're havin' deep-dish apple pie for dinner, and it seems a shame to waste the spare slice. You reckon you could come in under a flag of truce and we could work the whole thing out tomorrow morning after the ham and hominy?"

Even at six years old I wasn't no fool. I knew a concession when I saw one. I stuck my head out of the tent. My relieved soul wanted to cry, but I made the voice cool and bored.

"I'm willing to talk business if you are," I said, when what I wanted to do was jump up and wrap myself around his neck and weep out of sheer relief, not knowing then that the old gent had really pulled me off the hook and left my self-respect intact.

That's why, I suspect, I'm glad my boy Mark Robert was honestly scared to spend the night in that tent in Limuru. He didn't have to go through that horrible evening I spent before we called the conference next day. There is nothing as lonesome as a tent when the home fires are burning within spittin' distance, and I do not recommend running away unless there is a circus handy to join.

And there are so few circuses handy these days that running away seems scarcely worth the effort, especially if they are having deep-dish apple pie on the night of departure.

Thinking back on my first journey into fear, when I holed up in the tent, I was suddenly reminded of the second time I absconded. I don't recall now exactly what I was sore at, but I was mad as a wet hen at something, very possibly school, my parents, or the weather. Also, I had been reading *Huckleberry Finn*, who had run off down the river with the slave Jim. This is heady fare for a young man resentful of the adult currycomb. My heart was sore and my disposition desperate.

"What's graveling you?" the Old Man asked. "You look like you're about to cloud up and rain."

"I am," I said. "I think I'll run off. Don't nobody around here understand me."

The Old Man sucked on his pipe and crooked an eyebrow. "That's a prime pity," he said. "I know how you feel. If I wasn't so old and rheumaticky I'd run off with you. Miss Lottie . . ." He shrugged. "But I guess I'm too old and sot in my ways. However, you don't want to take this runnin' away too light. An absconder burns his bridges behind him, because once you've lit out there ain't no returnin'."

I muttered something about I didn't care if I never saw nobody I knew again, except maybe the Old Man, and I guess I just put that in to be polite.

"Runnin' away from your responsibility takes a power of

preparation, not to mention precautions. The old Injuns used to tie a tree branch to their horses' tails and sweep away the hoof marks as they moved camp. And any hobo'll tell you that you got to travel light, but you still got to carry most of the things you need when you're alone in the woods in the night. Seems to me we better practice a little before you run off permanent. You gonna take your gun?"

"I better. I'll have to live off the country. I better take some line and some fishhooks, too."

The Old Man looked at me. "You ain't very big yet," he said. "A gun, even that little 20-gauge, can get powerful heavy. Or was you planning to steal a raft like Huck Finn and live on that for a spell? A boat ain't goin' to take you no farther than Wilmington, unless you care to ride these reefs here on the ebb tide and hit the open sea for Charleston."

"I'll hoof it," I said, mean and stubborn. "Don't you worry about me."

"I'm not," the Old Man said, a little too cheerfully. "I just don't want you to be ashamed in front of the other hobos, for running off without the full kit. Of course, you'll need two blankets, a hand ax, a knife, a canteen, a skillet, a coffeepot, some iron rations, and some pepper and salt. With that gear you ought to be able to live off the country. Any idea where you're headed?"

"No"—even more stubborn than before. "West, maybe. Maybe to Canada. I dunno, and I don't care."

"Well, if it's Canada you got in mind you better take more than two blankets. I'd say about six. It's cold in Canada. Was you planning to live with the Eskimos, or the Indians and be a trapper, or will you fetch up as a cowboy? That's if you decide on the West."

The Old Man never cracked a smile, but I could see he was up to his old tricks of going along with my tantrums, and this made me even madder. "I'm going somewhere, all right," I said. "Maybe one day I'll write and tell you where I wind up. If I ain't too busy."

"They're a little short on communications in the Arctic," the old buzzard said. "But I would appreciate a birchbark postcard once in a while, if you can rassle down a caribou and ride it to the nearest trading post. But in the meantime we better get you outfitted, because there's no tellin' how long you'll be gone. In fact, you may be gone for good.

"Now we'll do a kind of checkoff list, and I'll see can I get you geared up for the road. I'll even do more than that. When you're all ready to roam I'll drive you a half-dozen miles out of town in the Liz. This is kind of covering your trail. People won't reckon you're running away. They'll just think you and me are going huntin' or fishin' like we used to before you got restless." The Old Man stared at the sky. "I'll miss you, you know. You got your faults, but you were a pretty good huntin' and fishin' partner. I guess I'll have to stir around some and dig me up another boy."

I ignored that one. It hurt, but I let it fly by.

"Well," the Old Man said, "there's no time like now for running away. It's pretty late in the afternoon, but it might be raining or even snowing tomorrow. It's a chance you have to take. Now you go collect all your gear, and mind you make them blankets into a tight bundle so you can strap them on your back. And you're goin' to need a belt strong enough to carry your ax, your knife, your canteen, your coffeepot, and your skillet. These things don't pack so good. Too much bulk. And then, of course, you're goin' to have to tote your shotgun and a knapsack full of things like fresh socks and underwear and a little salt pork and flour and sugar and salt and coffee. You can't hit the road without the basic essentials. You can't go off half-cocked. Get movin' now."

Well, sir, I was a sight for sore eyes. I must have weighed about ninety pounds stripped. The gun weighed six, and by the time the Old Man had strapped a blanket roll and a knapsack on my back, and draped a cartridge box around me like a bandoleer, and hung things onto one of those World War I web pistol belts with the hooks on I must have weighed two hundred pounds. It was a pretty hot day for winter, but the Old Man made me wear my Mackinaw too, because he said you never could tell when it would turn real chilly, and catching pneumonia when you were all by yourself in the woods with nobody to nurse you was even too much for a Blackfoot brave.

"We lost more Injuns from the *p*-neumonia than we ever did from the cavalry," the Old Man said, as he helped me, clinking and clanking and sweating, into the Tin Liz. "Seems like most Injuns suffered from a weakness in the chest. That and diphtheria, not to mention starvation when the big snows come and the buffalo crop run short. If I was you—after you decide roughly what you want out of life—I'd head for some place like Mexico, where you can always eat lizards and sleep out of nights if the Aztecs don't sacrifice you to one of their gods."

Not once did he twinkle. He was as stony stern as the preacher when he talked about hellfire and damnation. Mostly I could surprise him in a twinkle, but not this time. No twinkle. Nothing.

He had to help me into the car; cars had high running boards in those days and boys had short fat legs, and this boy resembled a walking hardware store more than he resembled a boy. I sat down with a clank and a rattle, and all you could see out of this mess of equipment was my face and my feet. Somehow I didn't feel like Leatherstocking or Dan'l Boone.

The Old Man cranked up the Liz and off we went, me rattling inside and the Liz rattling outside. The Old Man was garrulous as we rode. He pointed to a cornfield off to the right, with a stand of second-growth pine trees on its rim, and sighed.

"We had us some mighty good times with the dogs there, didn't we?" He was talking to himself. "I'm sure goin' to miss opening day of the quail season, with you not here. I may not even hunt. Huntin' ain't much fun by yourself, and I suspect I'm too old to break in another boy, no matter what I said earlier. Maybe I'll just give up huntin' altogether. I'm a little old to be alone in the woods, with nobody to run for help if I fall into a stump hole and bust a leg or something like that. The woods can be mighty lonesome by yourself, and if you get into trouble, well . . ." His voice trailed off.

We drove about five miles and he stopped the Liz by a creek. "You know where you are now. You've got plenty of water, and the campsite where you and me and Mr. Howard shot your first deer ain't more'n a mile off yonder. I guess I taught you enough about camping to where I ain't got to give you any advice about not setting fire to the broom sedge and leavin' a clean campsite for people who ain't so fortunate as to be running away."

He got out of the car, opened the door, and helped me out. Weighed down as I was, I couldn't have made it on my own. He clapped me on the back.

"So long, son," he said. "And good luck. If you find the time drop me a line once in a while. I'll be here if I ain't dead. And don't worry too much about me and your folks. We'll all make out."

He banged me on the back again, got back into the car, turned her around in a little sandy cut off the main road, and headed back to the village. Dusk had dropped swiftly, and I could see him switch on his headlights. The taillight winked like a malicious red eye.

I stood in the middle of the road in the night, and watched the taillight disappear over a rise. I have been lonely since, but never quite that lonely. And I often wondered if the Old Man forgot to include a flashlight on purpose, because suddenly the night fell like a great black blanket and there was no moon to lead me to the campsite. Walking through the bush was impossible, encumbered as I was by all the tinware the Old Man had tied to me.

This was, I believe, the first time I ever realized how big the world, how absent the moon, and how lonely the loner, not to mention how long was eternity, a problem that had been bothering me a lot.

There was nothing to do but make the best of the mess I'd landed myself in. I clanked a couple of hundred yards off the main road, found myself a little bare patch of ground, and un-slung about a hundred pounds of accouterment. Cursing myself and the Old Man for not remembering the flashlight I lit some kitchen matches, and managed to scrabble up some pine cones, which made the beginnings of a fire. In the faintly flaring light I was able to pick up a few dead branches, and I found a fat pine stump that granted me a few slivers of lightwood. Then, with the fire blazing, I was able to accumulate a few dead logs. Well, I thought, I had man's first friend—fire.

I took the hatchet and went round the perimeter to the little longleaf pine saplings, and cut myself sufficient butts to make a springy basis for a bed. I spread one blanket over the pine branches, weighting its corners with stones, and pulled the other blanket up over the bottom covering. At least I had a fire and a place to sleep.

But a sudden pang in the pit of my stomach told me that I didn't have anything to eat. There was about half a pound of side meat in the knapsack, and that would have to do. I put the fat pork in the skillet and browned it, mentally deploring the waste of grease, and chewed on enough of the fat meat to quiet my belly.

The stars were out now, and I lay down on my bed. The pine boughs were not nearly so springy as I remembered, and some of the butts gouged me in the back. Owls hooted, and there were the usual myriad night noises that are so terrifying unless you have company.

Dew fell, and the blankets were stiff with it and my face was wet-cold with it. The fire was flickering low, casting eerie shadows into my imagination. I was a big boy. I was big enough to shoot a gun. I was big enough to run away to the West or to Canada. But I was not too big to cry. I cried myself into a semblance of sleep. It was just dawning when the rattle of a car stopping roused me from a nightmare-ridden slumber.

In a few minutes I heard footsteps out in the brush, and an occasional curse. It was the Old Man, standing over me, looking down at a very lonely lad.

"I wouldn't of come back," he said, "but when I was helping you out of the car I lost my best pipe. You see anything of it?"

"No sir," I said, scrambling out of my uneasy bed, "but if you like I'll help you look for it."

"All right," the Old Man said. "It's a little dark yet. Where's your flashlight?"

"We—I forgot to bring one," I said.

"Well," the Old Man said, "*I* didn't. Suppose you use mine. And the next time you run away be damned sure you're fully equipped for it."

Of course he never lost a pipe, and he did not insist that I strap myself back into my running-away kit.

"I told your grandma you'd gone camping with some of the other boys," the Old Man said. "If I was you I'd keep my mouth shut about this."

"Yes sir," I said.

This is the first time I've opened it, but since everybody's gone but me it don't make no difference now.

12

It Always Rains on Saturday

The rain sheeted against the panes. Recurrent blasts of wind shook the house, rattled the doors, struck wildly at the windows. A draft crept down the chimney to loosen the ashes, to drive smoke snaking into the room, and to spread a chill around the ankles.

"It's Saturday," I said to the Old Man. "Why does it always have to rain on Saturday?"

My voice was bitter. The good Lord above had betrayed me. Here it was Saturday, and the bird season freshly opened in midweek, and I had been to the wholesale grocery where my Pa worked, and had bought some shotgun shells, and now my mind was out in the country. The soybeans were velvety gray capsules on their stalks, and the black-eyed peas had succumbed to frost, and the field peas—the peanuts—were clustered lusciously on their stalks atop the moist red earth, lying helpless where the plow had torn them from the earth. A feast lying fallow for the birds.

If it had not been for the rain—the dratted rain, the pounding, slashing, miserable rain—I would be out there on the back forty. I would be picking a handful of chinquapins and cupping a mouthful of sparkleberries, and it would just be a matter of where I sent the dogs. The quail season had opened, the dove season was still on, fall plowing was finished, and the birds would be pinpointed. All you had to do was wave at Frank, whistle in Sandy, or just nod at Tom, and you could predict to square yards where the birds would collect. Except for this rain — this I-wish-I-was-bigger-so-I-could-come-right-out-and-say-it rain.

"I go to school all week," I said to the Old Man. "Monday through Friday, I go to school. I study Latin, which nobody speaks, and algebra, which I will never understand, and read that Chaucer foolishness—you ever know anybody who went around saying, 'Whan that Aprille with his shoures soote'?—and Miss Emma Martin says I'm goin' to flunk English, and Miss Rachel Clifford says that I ain't got the right interest in Charlie-Main and the Saracens. The sun shines bright all week and then it sets red and clear on Friday, and I got a pocketful of shells and three bird dogs, and look at it! Rain! "Aprille with his shoures soote," my foot! It's plain old rain—rain on the only day I got off!"

"Here, here, calm down," the Old Man said. "Take it easy. You ain't Noah, and this ain't an ark. It's rained before and it'll rain again. What do you want me to do, ask God to stop it so that one little microbe on the face of the earth can go bird huntin'? I thought you were bigger than that by now."

"Well, it just don't seem fair. I don't care if it rains from Monday through Friday and on Sunday, too. I don't care if it snows or sleets. But Saturday is the only day I get off, and it just ain't supposed to rain on Saturday!"

The Old Man looked at me with his eyes sort of sleepy. He rubbed his nose with one finger. "Son," he said, "when you're as old as me you'll realize that it always rains on Saturday. That's the tragedy of bein' alive. Saturday is for rainin', like work is for doin', like cryin' makes up for laughin'. Believe me. From now until the day you die it'll nearly always rain on Saturday. As far as I know, Noah couldn't lick it, and he had the Lord and all the animals goin' strong for him. When he cut loose that dove . . ."

I was still mad. I had got to where I could handle the Old Man's philosophy in small swallows, but just hearing the word "dove" made me sore as a boil. I thought about all that corn still standing, all those soybeans, all those peanuts and black-eyed peas, and all those doves I wasn't shooting, and I didn't want any lectures about olive branches. The rain kept pounding down, and I thought about how long it was going to be until next Saturday.

The Old Man always enjoyed seeing me heated up, and he liked to keep it going. He had a lot of sayings that were just calculated to rile me. And he could make his voice kind of mincing, sissylike, like an old-maid schoolteacher's.

"Remember," he was singsonging now, "April showers make May flowers. It isn't rainin' rain to me, it's rainin' violets. That ain't really rain out there. That's violets, daffodils, and maybe pee-tunias."

Then he snickered. I guess the word "pee-tunias" got him. "All right," he said. "I'll let you up. I don't like rain no more than you do, because I got joints with aches you don't know about; but if you're ever goin' to be big enough to call yourself a man you got to remember one thing: There ain't any use developin' ulcers over what you can't help. Few things in this life ever work out the way you had them figgered. And there are certain things like wind and rain and high tides that you just can't control, even if you beat your brains out. Might help you someday, when you're older, to remember it. If you can't beat it, join it—or least don't try to fight it."

I'm not going to sit here and tell you that I felt any less mad at Providence for keeping me nailed to the hearthside on a day when I had my mouth fixed for bird hunting. I paced like a nervous puppy, and when the Old Man suggested I try a book I tried it, but I couldn't concentrate, even though it was a book by a man named Selous, a hunter who seemed to know an awful lot about what he was writing.

And I didn't feel any more kindly disposed toward Sunday, when the dawn broke clear and I took all the dogs out—without guns, of course, because I wasn't allowed to shoot on Sunday—and we found every covey I knew we should have found yesterday, and put up enough droves of doves to have reassured all the Arks that ever was or ever will be. I guarantee that the sun shone all through the next school week, although somebody made a bargain with me and carried it over through Saturday. It rained real hard on Sunday, and I didn't have to leave the country to go to town to Sunday school.

"You can call that a bonus," the Old Man said. "You see how everything works out for the best?"

I was prepared to agree. I had indulged my blood lust to a limit on everything but people the day before. Coming back to the house I had even shot a coon, and was figuring to make myself a cap out of the hide, like D. Boone, who "cilled a bar" on that tree. That was the kind of day when I envied a man who had not been subjected to sufficient schooling to know how to spell "killed" and "bear," and so could hunt seven days a week. At least, I thought, he could spell better than Old Man Chaucer, him and his "droghte of March hath perced to the roote." I'll take Dan Boone and that bar he cilled on that tree every time. "And bathed every veyne in swich licour," Chaucer said. I bet Dan Boone just had him a drink of hard corn likker and went out looking for a fresh bear.

Somehow I survived the educational processes, although some people would say you'd never know it, and went on to other things. I didn't really start to think about rainy Saturdays and Noah's arks and *The Canterbury Tales* until one day in

Tanganyika, a great many years later, when a Mr. Frank Bowman and I got mixed up with nature the hard way. And believe me, getting mixed up with ordinary nature in Brunswick County, North Carolina, is one nest of eggs, and taking on nature in Darkest A. is quite another.

Frank Bowman is a professional hunter, a slightly testy gentleman, and he has fought sufficient elements in Australia, where he came from, and in Africa, where he works, to know that you can't do much better than you can do. But he'll still quarrel with the process. In Swahili it's *"shauri a Mungu"* or God's will, and Frank's willing to argue the point.

Frank and I had been away up in Tanganyika in a place called Singida, shooting—or trying to shoot—greater kudu, a creature that is considerably larger than a quail or a dove. We had a variety of ornery vehicles: one jeep that eventually got put out of its misery and a big fat English truck that had a wistful habit of catching fire every time you spat.

Through some arrangement with the hunters' gods who control kudu I had shot me a nice heavy-horned fellow along about the same time a large black cloud suggested that if we did not plan to spend the rainy season in and around Singida we had better up-anchor and get the hell out of there right now. That Africa, as somebody once said, is a large chunk of real estate, and we were a fur piece away from where we were headed.

There were certain obstacles before our arrival at the promised land. One was a greasy clay hill straight up the side of a mountain, that is so bad you are not allowed into the area if it seems dubious that you can make the climb. But once allowed in and up it, you still have to go down again, whereupon you are confronted with a desert. This desert is largely surfaced with cotton soil and lava dust, in which your happy little axles can sink. It's only about sixty-five miles wide, the Serengeti, but I have heard tell of another time when one of the best hunters in east Africa spent an unhappy three weeks just simply bogged down and cussing.

In an operation of this sort rain is your active enemy. And

what makes it especially your enemy is that you can see it, see it in the black clouds speeding up on you, so that if you blow a tire, if your engine catches fire the rain is right on top of you and you can see the track turn to muck, turn to sticky goo; and all of a sudden, a profane sudden, you are just as immobilized, just as lost, just as planted as if somebody had stolen your wheels.

Also, there's precious little firewood. You are marooned, and what makes it doubly ironic you are not supposed to shoot, either to feed or to protect yourself, since it is a government park. The fact that it is a native poachers' paradise does not concern you. You are not supposed to shoot, even to avoid starvation. The sixty lions over thataway, eating their heads off on the game that blacks the plains, are a thumbed nose at your integrity. The alkali lakes are also an insult to thirst.

Certainly that last hill behind you, that one you just came slipping down, sliding slantwise from the greasy red clay to the greasier, more-suckingly clinging cotton soil, is a frightener, and then that menacing black cloud that hovers, that follows, that threatens ahead—rain? Man, nobody who ever got thwarted on a Brunswick County Saturday ever even heard about rain.

In the case of Brother Bowman and me, we were lucky, just plain-out country lucky. We slid down the mountain backward, the truck slewing in circles, and beat that rain all the way across the Serengeti. I will permit Bowman a small knock against me about our spending one extra day shooting the guinea fowl, and all would have been well if we had left a little earlier on the way from Singida; but then Bowman must yield on the fact that we constantly had to send people back for extra motor parts because the lorry kept catching fire. Bowman kept cursing the Kipsigi driver for unwarranted use of overextended intelligence, such as throwing sand on the wrong side of the truck's engine at about twelve thousand feet, with a rainstorm hotly pursuing us.

Running a forced foot race with rain in Africa is one of the most unrewarding sports I ever got tangled up with. As we crossed the desert it would look for a minute as if we'd make it, and then something would happen and it would look as if we wouldn't. If we didn't . . .

We did. We got to a river called the Grummetti just as the rains clashed, one behind, one ahead of us. We barely crossed the river with all the vehicles just before it went into flood—in flood behind us, in flood ahead of us in its other branches. Brother Noah, perched high atop Ararat, was never more precisely marooned than Frank and I. Fortunately, just as the cloudburst started, the boys managed to wrestle the tents up and hoe drainage ditches around them. Fortunately, too, *shauri a Mungu* touched my trigger finger and I accidentally managed to shoot an impala for camp meat. When I pulled the trigger the rain was coming down so hard that I couldn't have seen through a scope with windshield wipers.

We collected the poor critter and barely squished through the mud back to our dreary camp. There was no such thing as a real fire; the wood was sopping and the rain was coming down so hard that it was falling sideways. Somerset Maugham once wrote something called *Rain*. After a week in that downpour I am here to tell you I could write a series of clinical novels called *Rain*.

Brother Bowman and I had a real good time, though. For some reason we never snapped at each other once. The cook made sufficient pathetic fire to feed us fresh meat until we ran out of impala, and then he started hacking at the tins with his panga, and corned willy is not really unpalatable. I got out the Swahili dictionary and increased my vocabulary by another six or seven words, and wrote some stuff on the rusty typewriter—stuff that I would have to write someday anyhow, even when the sun was shining. The radio didn't work, but nobody cared much.

Bowman had recently come back from crocodile shooting in northern Australia, and I was not so long out of duck hunting in Spain and tiger shooting in India. We managed to sit and tell lies to each other very profitably for a week.

The rain hit that canvas like a giant slapping it with the flat of his hand, and you could hear the small roar as it went by the tent in runnels to spill into the almost raging stream below. (I will tell you a little more about African rain. In the *lugga* country of the Northern Frontier I have seen huge trees cast as high as thirty or forty feet above the banks of the river bed, and the whole Northern Frontier District is off limits, from Isiolo all the way to Ethiopia, during the wet season.)

Finally the rains stopped and the sun came out and the river shrank and we could move the vehicles again, and I was almost sorry. Frank and I had both learned a lesson in temper control. We had both learned some sort of lesson about *not fighting city hall.*

I know I tend toward the Pollyanna approach sometimes, after the temper's done, but hunting and fishing are at least two things that you can't do much about if the boss weather-maker decides adversely. And to sit in a soppy tent, with everything clammy damp—clothes, equipment, everything—is a thing to try a good man's patience, soul, and cussing vocabulary. The only answer, which I believe the Old Man seeded in me at an early age, has been aptly phrased by sage counsel to a man just joining the Foreign Legion. The old Legion hand told the recruit, "When things are bad, *bleu,* try not to make them worse, because it is very likely that they are bad enough already."

If there is a moral in this tale it is that the sun came out in many more ways than one. For the next six weeks I never had more fun or better luck, and at the end of the safari there was no bitter recrimination to spoil the good-bye part. I suspect the Old Man would say it's merely a matter of growing older, or just growing used to being wet on Saturday.

13

The Trouble with Dogs Is People

"The trouble with dogs," the Old Man once said, "is people." We had been through the dog business thoroughly—how a dog was like a boy, you had to wallop it with a stick once in a while to make it behave; how a dog could accumulate bad habits unless corrected; how a dog needed gentleness in its early months and stern discipline thereafter. Foxhounds, quail dogs, retrievers—I thought I had a graduate degree in dogs. Then he hit me with the people bit.

One thing I learned as a kid: You must play your cards right with adults when they come up with a sweeping statement that exacts attention. No adult goes around muttering wise words on his own time. He demands a question, so he can make the answer run awful long.

"Yes sir," I said. "I been thinking the same thing for a long time. What I always say is—all right, you got me. Why is the trouble with dogs people?" I gave up without firing a shot.

"The horse," the Old Man said, "ennobled man, and when you debase a horse you debase mankind. The same thing applies to dogs. In a way the trouble with people is dogs."

And in a way he was right.

Every time I see a bug-eyed, narrow-headed cocker spaniel today, all ears and hysteria, every time I see an Irish setter, nothing but red coat and stupidity, every time I see a collie, bred out of working into a mere mattress for ticks and other debris, I recall the dogs of my tenderest youth. And I think how the people have degenerated too.

Every time somebody's "tame" German shepherd snaps a chunk out of me from sheer nervous reflex, every time a dachshund disputes my right to sit down on the sofa, every time I meet a dumb French poodle I think about dogs in the days when I was not so old and you could kind of count on a dog by his brand name.

I know I must sound like the Old Man in one of those things-ain't-like-they-useter-be moods, but I swear to John I'm right. Cocker spaniels today, for instance, ain't much better than bugs for any practical purpose. They yip and they yap and step on their own ears and they got these big stupid eyes and pinheads, and if a rabbit snarled at them they'd have a fit of high hysterics.

The cocker has been ruined by mankind in exactly the same sense that the Irish setter has been turned into a kind of Liberace-type dog—all adornment. I am so old I can even remember when an Irish setter was used to find birds, and we didn't care too much whether his tail was plumy or his fetlocks feathered. He would work for you, if you conquered his Irish arrogance with an occasional whack on the behind when he ran up a covey or failed to honor a point. Now he isn't anything but the memory of Errol Flynn in a red jacket.

We had a cocker named Mickey, who was the best all-round

working dog I ever saw in my life. She was sort of sand-colored and wasn't overlong in the ear department, but she had a head as square as a cigar box and brains inside it. Her muzzle was as heavy as a boxer's. She would run a rabbit or course a deer. She was death on ducks, and she had a radar nose for quail. She would sit quiet if you were shooting doves, and she treed a real fine squirrel, possum, or coon. If there ever was an all-purpose bitch, old Mick was it.

Mickey died an honorable death under the careless feet of a speeding motorcar at about the same time cockers got to be popular, and when fanciers started breeding them to type. Twenty years later they had wrecked a sturdy working dog and turned it into a kind of beetle that couldn't find its way off it's mistress's lap, like a pug or a Peke. Except that the Peke did keep its lousy disposition; all that was left of the cocker was whine. And yip. And yap.

We had Irish setters before they got to be stylish, and though they needed a touch of reeducation after a long hot summer they were fancy in the field. They were prone to moodiness, perhaps, and not so day-in-day-out steady as a Llewellin or an English cousin, but they also had occasional flashes of genius that allowed them to find all the birds on a particular afternoon. Like most redheads they figured to be a touch temperamental.

I would invite correspondence, all adverse, on this statement: I don't believe there's a good, dependable Irish setter or an all-purpose field cocker at work these days. The springers seem to have resisted the new look and can be depended on to fetch you a duck or a grouse. But cockers—I didn't even see one working last year around the grouse moors of Scotland or the partridge shoots in Spain. And I haven't seen a dashing mick on anything but a leash in twenty years.

The French poodle was a spaniel by original intent, and was one of the finer hunting dogs. They came into France by way of Germany, and their fancy hedge-clipping dates back to hunt masters who cut their coats in various designs for identification purposes, much as you'd brand a cow-brute. The lion-mane trim evolved as a thumbed nose by France to the British lion, when the kids were having hard words across the Channel.

Offhand I would hazard that the French poodle of twenty-some years ago was the smartest of all dogs, in the field and out of it. But association with people—too many trips to the beauty parlor, too much time waiting for Mama to finish girl lunches, and too much inbreeding to cut down their size—is really making a stupid dog of the poodle. The little ones are nasty yipping beasts, nervous as the well-known lady fox in a forest fire, and the larger ones seem to have forgotten that they got their working papers in a peat bog rustling up blackcock.

At least I can say one thing without stirring up an argument: For ten years I have owned a beautifully bred standard French poodle bitch, who is unqualifiedly the dumbest dog I ever saw in my life. And before you start in to write I offer this for free: It is undoubtedly from long association with her master.

Hewing to the Old Man's thoughts about dogs being spoiled by people, I know one kind-of collie whose life has been wrecked by being named Lassie. The fact that this Lassie is male and does not want to be called Lassie has inverted him to a point where he is a mass of jangled nerves. Don't tell me dogs aren't subject to psychic pressure. I once had a male pointer named Tom, whose voice never changed, and the girls hated him, and, so help me, he committed suicide.

The only dogs I know who have successfully resisted people are the halfbreeds, the nondescripts. The best deerhound I ever saw was half bulldog. The best quail dog, for finding, stanch pointing, and gentle but ardent retrieving was a dropper—half pointer and maybe half setter, with possibly a slight infusion of cur.

The only people I ever knew who successfully resisted the blandishment of dogs were people I did not choose to know much better. There is, to me, something distastefully peculiar about people who are afraid of dogs, who dislike dogs. And the dogs know it right back.

The dogs I miss most today—and seldom seem to see around —are the true Huckleberry Finns; the part Airedale, part fox cerrier, part plain fice, with shoebrush coats and back-curled tails. The old-fashioned cur seems to have vanished from the land. For sheer street-gamin intelligence, good disposition, and proficiency in any kind of field work the mixed-salad pariah was the most. I got more hunting mileage out of a yellow semijackal named Jackie than all the purebreds I ever associated with.

The Old Man was right. The trouble with people is dogs, and the trouble with dogs is people. But somehow, one breed can't seem to get along without the other and still call it a life.

Which brings us to Sam, an animal whose very uselessness has made him an all-purpose paragon of necessity around the house. Sam is the property of a godson of mine, and he has been named Samuanensis Horribilis by the father of the godson, and I resent it. He is not horrible at all. Sam is one part cocker and one part dachshund, and he inherits the decadent qualities of each. He has long hair like a cocker's, is colored black and russet, and has a cocker's ears, a dachshund's snout, a cocker's plumy tail, and a dachshund's undercarriage.

Sam is the best all-purpose, useless dog I've ever met. He is small enough not to knock the glasses off a coffee table with a swishing tail, but not so small so that you are always stepping on him. He is an inveterate hunter of lizards in the flower beds, but is not large enough to wreck the posies.

Sam loves cats—he has three large playfellows named Simba (lion), Chui (leopard), and Somali, which is coal black. They are all as big as Sam or bigger. Sam hates strangers and loves friends. From time to time he will absorb a snifter of gin (which makes him sneeze), but steadfastly refuses whisky or beer.

As mentioned, I don't care much for either dachshunds or cockers today, but in the case of Sam the twain have met and produced something delightfully impractical, as in the case of H. Allen Smith's dream of an all-purpose animal called a bouncing pussy-pup.

Under the influence of a late night on beer (the United Press was not paying much in salaries in those days, certainly not enough to afford whisky for its serfs), Author Smith dreamed of a charming creature that was half cat and half dog. You bounced the cat once on the floor, and it became a puppy. You bounced the puppy, and it turned back into a kitten.

Smith was inordinately proud of his dream. He made the mistake of confiding its basic ingredients to a colleague, Henry McLemore, also a slave of the U.P. salt mines, and Henry promptly claimed the dream as his own, and went around promulgating the idea of a bouncing pussy-pup as the solution to all pet problems. This caused an estrangement between Messrs. Smith and McLemore, since there is no way to copyright a dream. Result was that the two didn't speak for a year or so, since both stanchly protested that the bouncing pussy-pup was his own personal dream property.

I feel more or less that way about Sam, as if I'd invented him myself. I didn't, but I would answer for trouble if someone attempted to take him away from me—in a purely vicarious sense, that is.

Having been owned by many dogs, I have a memory that's always pleasurable and nearly always on the semidisreputable side. We had the usual number of pureblooded setters and pointers when I was a kid, but whenever possible I hung out in the back alleys with the waifs and the strays and the odd amalgams.

For downright street-urchin intelligence, such as is seen among Arab children and young Parisiens, there was never a peer of Jackie, a cross between a fox terrier, a jackal, a raccoon, and a skunk, judging from the smell of him. He was colored a dingy yellow. His tail curled so far over his back it almost touched his neck. His specialty was squirrels, but he would bravely bay a bear if called on and would run a deer if there wasn't a hound handy. He would retrieve a duck, hating the coldness of the water all the time, and find, if not point, a covey of quail.

He was entirely a professional dog. You could not get him inside the house, and apart from coldly and balefully accepting his tin plate of scraps he had no time for the human race. Jackie was completely without racial prejudice: He hated people, black or white, and bit them indiscriminately. He only associated with people in the field, and his allegiance was to the gun.

Jackie was one. A boyhood friend of mine named E. G. Goodman had another mongrel, which defied description. It seemed to be part hound and part bull, with heaven knows what else cranked into his chromosomes. I can't remember the name of this beast, but I can remember that one day, in Goodman's precinct, we shot quail, dove, rabbit, coon, one possum, and buck deer over the noble efforts of this large assortment of nothing that owned a hound's bugle, a bulldog's tenacity, a retriever's sense of where it dropped, and an over-all sense of what-the-hell-boys-hunting-is-fun. This character is long gone to his fathers, but he was a power of dog.

Perhaps the greatest mongrel of them all was a dog that became named, late in life, Bonzo. This dog was basically bull terrier, with one red eye and one black eye. He had lived all his life on his own, until one day he pitched up on the veranda of the Norfolk Hotel in Nairobi, in Kenya, where a sign plainly declared that all dogs were forbidden.

He was scarred and flea-bitten and hungry. His ribs washboarded, and he had more than a touch of mange. The manager of the hotel wasn't feeling so well himself that day, and just as a big porter was about to kick the dog back into the streets the manager said a loud no, and carried the animal off to his cottage.

Some days later Bonzo emerged looking considerably better. His mange was gone (burnt crankcase oil and sulphur), and he had filled out the wrinkles in his belly. And he took over the hotel. The service, which had been drooping, improved, because Bonzo bit the waiters if they were tardy in feeding him. Bonzo improved public relations, because he had an unerring instinct for sorting out the poor types, to a point where he sometimes stood on the register and refused to let a suspicious character sign in. He treed a couple of Mau Mau in the back compound.

As Bonzo increased in power so did the manager. The manager found a better tailor and ran a better hotel, and soon became general manager of the entire chain.

Bonzo had only one failing. He was dame-happy. He would take off occasionally and come home full of battle scars, as a result of love's labors lost. His interest in the other sex finally got him gored to a point where, in his boss's absence, the assistant manager had him destroyed. It is interesting to note that the assistant manager shortly thereafter took off with all the available funds, a weakness that Bonzo must have suspected.

But Bonzo's picture hangs today in the head receptionist's office a few feet away from a sign that says "All Dogs Strictly Forbidden," because there will never be another Bonzo in anybody's time or heart.

The theme of the boy and his dog has been badly overworked and I do not propose to thrash it to bits, but I have observed my young godson with Sam, and am prepared to propound the idea that a youngster is better off with a mongrel in his early formative years than with a haughty something with Ch. in front of his lofty handle.

There is a curious communion between a runny-nosed tad and an animal out of the back drawer, a sort of Tom Sawyer-Huck Finn relationship, where the urchins share a small world of their own. My young man is learning to clean and maintain a weapon, to shoot a BB gun, and to absorb something about the fields and streams. Somehow Sam fits the apprentice pattern better as an intrepid lizard-courser and toad-nagger than if he were the best of show in any category at the Westminster Kennel Club show.

Small boys are little beasts at best, and need careful nurturing to introduce them to adult responsibility. The mongrel—the "Please, can I keep him, Mommy?" pup—fills in a gap between babyhood and boyhood, because a puppy is a puppy, whether it's human or canine.

The Old Man used to have a saying about that. "There ain't

much difference," the Old Man said. "They both need worming at regular intervals. They both need to be housebroke, with a smack on the behind to teach 'em manners. A combination of castor oil and birch tea will work wonders with any boy and any dog, because there comes a time when everybody has to learn the difference between running loose and walking to heel."

I observe my boy Mark and his dog Sam with great pleasure. Through keen parental perception and discipline both are learning the difference between running loose and walking to heel. And I think in the process, as a result of association with Sam, young Mark will grow up one day soon to deserve the companionship of a purebred.

14

Cooties in the Knight Clothes

I was reading a divorce story the other day in which the aggrieved husband called his wife's boy friend a "sugar daddy," while the wife's counsel hailed the other man as a "knight-errant who rushed to Ellen's protection after her husband deserted her."

I laughed right out loud. The last time I got mixed up with knights-errant was via the Old Man. He had a salty way of disposing of popular error, and since that particular day I have never felt quite the same about chivalry.

It was the kind of day you've got to expect sometime in May—cold, rainy. The Old Man was resigned to sitting it out, but I wasn't.

"I want to *do* something," I complained. "It's too late to

hunt and it's too cold and rainy to fish and it's too late for football and too wet for baseball."

"You could try studyin'," the Old Man said. "The last look I had at one of your report cards tells me you could do with a small bait of application. You want to grow up ignorant?"

"I don't care if I do," I said, stubborn as a billy goat. "There ain't anything for a boy to do today. You can't run off and join the Indians or take up with a circus or be a cowboy or a knight in armor or anything that's fun—and gets you out of the house."

"I think maybe you need a good sound worming," the Old Man said. "You got the nervous twitches, like a hound dog with a tape. But it's odd you mention bein' a knight in armor. All along that's just what I thought you was practicing up to be."

"How could I be a knight in armor?" I said, kind of cautious. "There ain't much call for that kind of work these days."

"Oh I don't know," the Old Man said. "You just kind of strike me as a natural-born knight. Or a highwayman. They were about one and the same thing. Maybe bum would be as good a name as any. What would be your idea of a knight-errant, for example?"

I was trapped, and well I knew it. There was going to be a moral hid out in this one, like a rattlesnake, and I knew who would get bit, and it wasn't going to be the Old Man. I'd been there before, but it seems I was never going to learn to keep my mouth shut.

"Well, a knight-errant was a kind of hero that practiced chivalry. He wore armor and rode horses and lived in castles with portcullises and a donjon keep and drawbridges and things. He had a sword and a lance and he rode around the country righting wrongs and saving maidens and killing the savage infidel and slaying dragons and giants and all like that."

"Somewhere between a Boy Scout and William S. Hart, I wouldn't wonder," the Old Man murmured. "Chunk another faggot on that fire, varlet, and I will see can I straighten you out a little bit on knighthood. The ignorance of young people these days is something fierce.

"First place, chivalry and chevalier don't mean exactly what you said. They came out of the French word for horse—*cheval*. You could apply chivalry to a hostler in a livery stable just as easy as to a knight. Chivalry just got mixed up to where it meant anything that wasn't walkin'.

"Knight started out to mean boy or manservant, and got graduated to mean a mounted man who had a shootin' license, so to speak. He could tote arms when most of the other people couldn't, and it give him a superiority complex, even though it might take half a dozen stout yeomen to raise him and his armor onto a horse's back. Once he fell off chances are he'd just lay there and kick and cuss until somebody set him on his feet again. That cast-iron suit he wore weighed more than the man."

The average knight, the Old Man went on, was nothing much more than a paid fighter when a local war sprang up, and in between wars he hung around the castles, tickling the ladies fair, getting plastered twice a day on some sort of moonshine they called mead, and lying his head off about all the brave deeds he performed last time out against the Saracens or mayhap the next-door neighbor.

A knight-errant wasn't anything better than a knight out of work. After his liege lord got sick of listening to all the gassing about how many dragons the knight had fetched with his lance and how many heathen he'd done in with his sword, after he got tired of the knight eating him out of castle and home and swilling down all the best liquor and kissing the prettiest maidens, the lord would spot weld the knight into his cast-iron overalls and gently indicate the drawbridge, with the suggestion that travel was broadening and that maybe King Theobald the Unwashed, down the road apiece, hadn't heard all of Sir Bohort's latest best stories.

"A knight-errant," the Old Man said, warming up at the mention of mead, which appeared to be some sort of nerve balm constructed mainly of fermented honey and malt and fit to blow the vizor off a headpiece, "a knight-errant was nothin' better than a bum. Him and his squire—if he had one—rambled around the countryside beggin' a handout here, stealin' a shoat there, kissin' the pretty milkmaids, and now and again moochin' a meal and a night on a pallet in front of the fire in a castle or an abbey. Often as not they slept out by the crossroads or in a pigsty or a barn.

"They had fleas in abundance in them days, inside the castles and out, and you can bet that the average knight-errant was pretty lousy too. You can imagine the fun a flock of fleas and cooties might have inside that iron undershirt, with no way for Sir Lancelot to scratch less'n he had a blowtorch with him."

Castles, the Old Man continued, were powerful short on central heating, inside toilets, and general comfort. They were drafty and kind of noisy, what with generally being overrun with the ghosts of all the people that had been locked up and died in the donjon keeps.

"At best," the Old Man said, "knights were a feisty lot, and would steal anything that wasn't red-hot or nailed down. They were either chronic liars or must have suffered from the D.T.'s, because they were always seeing bare hands clutching swords coming out of lakes or ladies rising up in the mists or evil sorcerers changing people into unicorns and such as that. They must of smelled pretty rank, too, as I believe they only washed every other year when the armor got rusty and they had to be fitted into another suit. You still want to be a knight?"

"I'm losing my interest in the proposition," I said. "But how did you get to be one in the olden days?" And then I could have bitten my tongue right off at the roots, because I saw he had me. The Old Man licked his chops, spread his mustache with his thumb and forefinger, and let me have it.

"Well, good blood or bad, a fellow with a hankering to be a knight got sort of sold down the river at the age of seven. He left his happy home and got removed to the castle of his future boss or patron, as they called it in them days. And oh my, didn't the fur fly for a spell! They called this little shirttail boy a varlet, which ain't anything but a corruption of valet or servant.

The varlet had to wait on tables and shine up the ironmongery and empty the slop jars. He only et what the master didn't throw to the dogs. He fetched wood and drew water, and if he didn't bow down to everybody he got a hiding. He also had to go to Sunday school every day. That was called teaching him politeness.

"In his spare time he had to learn to dance and play the harp and sing and carry on. He had to learn to stick pigs and ride horses and work with falcons and boarhounds. He had to wrestle and tilt at other varlets with sharp sticks instead of spears.

"When he come fourteen he graduated into being an esquire, and then the heavy work really begun. He was supposed to be able to fork a horse on the gallop, wearing a full suit of boiler plate, and jump streams and scale walls and such strenuous things as that, all under full armor. They used to lose a lot of esquires that way, because if a guy tried to jump a deep stream and didn't make it he plumb sank. And when a wall-scaler missed his foothold, all you heard was *clank!* and somebody had to fetch the royal can opener to recover the corpse. Next to the king the most important man in the castle was the blacksmith. He was kept busy pounding dents out of the armor after they had subtracted the esquire.

"These little chores occupied the squire until he was twenty-one, and when he wasn't too bruised he had to learn to bow and scrape and kiss hands and wear handkerchiefs tied to his tin hat and carry on with the girls. Finally he became a knight. And no sooner did they smack him three times over the shoulder with a sword than they handed him his bonnet and said, 'Git out there and play knight-errant. Go kill a dragon or something or don't come back, because we've wasted a power of time and money on your education.' "

The Old Man stopped talking and stirred the fire with his toe. He sat for a moment staring into the flickering flames. Finally he said, "You still want to be a knight?"

"I don't think so. It sounds like an awful lot of hard work

with not much reward at the end of it, now that you've trimmed off all the feathers. Maybe I'll forget it and take up some other line of work."

"I was hoping you'd say that," the Old Man said. "When you're as old as me you'll generally find that when you trim the feathers off anything there ain't much underneath but hard work and hard times, so you'd better kind of concentrate on what you got in the present and not go mooning around wanting to be an Injun or a cowboy or a lion tamer. Dogs and boats and guns and fishing rods and books—yes, I said books—ought to be enough to hold you for the present. Where do you think I learned so much about knights, for instance?"

"Books," I said. "I guess, books." He had me, right and proper.

"All right, varlet," he said. "On your way up to my bedroom to retrieve a book called Bulfinch's *Mythology* for your liege lord you might look in the closet and locate a bottle of mead. I think it's stuck in the left leg of a hip boot. Mind you don't drop it, and don't you dare to sample it. Mead ain't for varlets. It ain't even for esquires. Mead is only for liege lords and kings, and for knights when they come in from playing hooky and fetch back their first legal dragon."

15

You Don't Have to Shoot to Go Hunting

The Old Man had kind of eased up on heavy hunting and fishing in his declining days. He would say, "I think I'll send a boy to do a man's work," and run me off to the fields or waters, while he snugged himself with a dram in front of the fire. When the Boy would return, half-frozen or as wet as a drowned rat, the Old Man would smile benignly and say something cynical like, "Old and creaky as I am, I get my fun out of thinking about you freezing to death in the rain, missing those birds right and left, and wondering why I took so much trouble to teach you to hunt."

As I approach senility I find that now *I'm* the Old Man, and *I* get my kicks out of *not* hunting, but of making it possible for other people. Not that I sit by the fire, but I still receive more satisfaction in watching over people new to the business enjoy themselves—and incidentally make all the mistakes that I once made—than I used to when I was playing the lead myself.

"The best thing about hunting and fishing," the Old Man said, "is that you don't have to actually do it to enjoy it. You can go to bed every night thinking how much fun you had twenty years ago, and it all comes back as clear as moonlight.

"You can listen to somebody bragging about the fish he caught or the deer he shot or the day he fell in the duck pond, and it is a kind of immortality, because you're doing it yourself all over again. In the meantime—and I don't mean to sound like a Pollyanna—you actually *do* feel that it's better to give than to get. Also, a little healthy sermon on game conservation creeps in here, because if you've done it once and done it twice and done it three times then what's wrong with knocking off and leaving some of the raw material for the other feller?"

The old gent's sentiments kept coming back when Mama and I first took some tenderfeet to Africa. Apart from taking necessary camp meat and doing a little bird shooting I never fired a shot. Bob and Jane Low were the guests, and if you take a poll on Low I think he will sound off strong for the safari business. As for the blonde and beautiful Jane, a lady you'd more expect to see in a slim black dress at the 21 Club, well, you never saw a woman fall more speedily and permanently in love with African bush. Bugs, dust, rain, stuck vehicles, and all, the elegant Tia Juana never mouthed a complaint that I heard.

Her husband was a daily delight. Nobody else had ever been to Africa before. He discovered elephants and lions and leopards. He was the first living man to see a green plain dotted with a million antelope and gazelle. Nobody else had ever laid eyes on a buffalo. Such a small thing as the taste of an orange squash became more potent than champagne. He was nearly incoherent for a week after he killed his leopard under rather unusual conditions.

The leopard, it appears, went into a piece of bush in broad daylight, and Low and the gunbearers dived in after it. Then the leopard began to track Low (later I found its footprints atop Low's big pug marks). They beat the bush three times, and finally the leopard tore out into the open—with the gunbearers just ahead of him.

The boys turned right at flank speed, and the leopard turned left, also flat out. Low executed a snappy shoulder shot, and was back in camp by 11 A.M. with his Land-Rover full of lovely spotted cat. I had about five other toms feeding from trees, but this one had been reaped by *Bwana Mkubwa Sana Kabisa* Low on his own, all by his little self, and he was fit to bust. He broke out in a rash of babble, and I was looking over his shoulder to see how big the slain *chui* was.

Low grabbed me by the collar and shook me violently. "You're not listening to me!" he screeched. "You're not listening to me! And then the boys went back in for the last time and fired some shotguns and the cat came . . ." And so forth.

At the end of a conversationally leopard-drenched week the girls and I came to a solemn conclusion: that we wished the leopard had shot Low. But you must consider that while Low was having this high adventure, which has traveled verbally from Africa to Spain to America to London to Paris, I had more fun listening to it than if I'd committed it, having just shot a difficult *chui* myself the month before Bob arrived. I plain didn't *need* any more leopards for myself. It still pleased me to know that if Bob hadn't shot his cat on his own I knew enough about baits and the right trees to drape 'em in to have had four or five big ones coming earlier and earlier every day, so drunk with power over that reeking big pig were they.

I found that cutting down a stinking, maggoty, half-eaten wart hog can be fun. I knew that nobody else would poach on my tree, and that the leopard would be saved for another year.

Possibly I inherited a malicious sense of humor from the Old Man, but I never laughed so hard in my life as I did on Bob Low's hunting debut in Africa. I had sent the trucks and jeeps on ahead, and we flew in to a makeshift airstrip, whose boundaries were marked by strips of toilet paper held down by rocks, and the wind direction indicated for the pilot by a green-wood smudge fire. Bob and Jane literally flew from starkest civilization into darkest Tanganyika bush country.

The camp was made and ready in a beautiful new site I'd found a month before, and all the boys said, "*Jambo, bwana; jambo, memsaab.*" Low had on his new bush clothes from Ahamed Brothers and my floppy Texas Stetson with the leopard tail hatband, and he looked exactly like a white hunter as played by Stewart Granger with a mustache. The tables were set up in the mess tent with an array of bright bottles, and the refrigerators were humming happily, and the bantam chickens we used as alarm clocks—Rubi and Rosa—had already settled in, and Rosa had deposited another egg behind the refrigerator. The Grummetti River chuckled happily, the trees were green, and the fresh-mowed grass was a velvet carpet in front of the tents.

Low was fairly panting to try out his—or rather, my—weapons; so we exposed him to a topi and a tommie, and after the usual trial and error he was blooded. He came back to cool drinks and dinner, convinced that somebody had made a mistake, that we had blundered into the Waldorf, which had suddenly been moved to the Bronx Zoo.

The first serious hunting day was miraculous. We picked up fourteen lone buffalo bulls, all shootable. They galloped into a small piece of bush. Low went in after them like a little man, and he could not know that in that patch of bush were a couple of lions, a herd of buffalo, and a cobra. He also could not know that the bullets for my .450-400 double had gotten confused with the bullets from Don Bousfield's .450-400, and that our guns were chambered differently. Low was forced to wait until one of the boys hared back to my vehicle for fresh asparagus, so to speak, leaving Low more or less naked in the presence of many large, hoofed, horned, fanged, toothy things—now wondering to himself if Africa was always this way.

Eventually organization triumphed and Low shot his buff. But I shall never forget, as an innocent bystander, the picture of

Low, all the buffalo, all the lions, and the cobra suddenly spouting from the clump of bush.

I must say in behalf of Low, he quailed not and neither did he flee. He was a touch ashen at the end, but that sweet .450-400 spake happily, and Low managed to collect a better buff on his first day than it took me two safaris and six months and about a thousand miles of unpleasant walking and crawling to find. He was no good at all for anything the rest of the day, when the enormity of his achievement dawned.

I do not know many of the details, except secondhand, of the good *bwana's* achievements in the veld, as I was chief baby sitter for two girls, and it seems all I did was pour gin and tonics, explain whistling thorns and why they whistle, and whomp up birthday parties. Mrs. Low passed another milestone —I believe twenty-one is the accepted age for all ladies—and I laid on a flock of ex-cannibals to do her honor.

It was quite a birthday party. First I had to explain the basic ingredients of "happy birthday to you" in Swahili to Matisia, the Low's personal boy, who is a Wakamba. Matisia then retired to the bush to retranslate the ditty into Kamba, and emerged, beaming, with a series of grunts which ended: "Dear Janey to you."

Meantime, while the birthday toasts—Martinis, very dry— were being hoisted I managed to smuggle seventy-five Wa-Ikoma warriors into a patch of bush nearby without the knowledge of *Memsaab* Low. This is a very difficult feat, for the gentlemen had been painting themselves for three days past, wore lion-mane headdresses, had iron rattles bound to their legs, carried knives and spears, and were all slightly drunk and in a most festive mood.

They erupted as a Masai war party descending on the Kikuyu, and for the first and only time in my life I saw the cool Madame Low shaken out of her calm. Seventy-five war-painted Ikoma lads in full fighting regalia is not a sight to sneer at, especially when it erupts into your lap. I suppose a birthday party in

Tanganyika is as much a part of hunting as a fish fry or a picnic, as the lion Low did *not* shoot is a part of hunting.

We had special permission on some lions for Bob, but after he made friends with a few of my leonine friends he flatly refused to shoot one. This suddenly raised him in the community concept from tenderfoot to a member of the old gentlemen's club.

We had been more or less shaking hands daily with a couple dozen of the gracious, lazy, blasé beasts, including two youngsters that were the most beautiful things I have ever seen on four feet—one so dark he was almost blue, and the other blond as Marilyn Monroe.

"My God," Low said, "how can anybody shoot one of these lovely things? Be like shooting your best friend. No, thank you very much, no lions for me."

To see a man go from gun-happy to conservationist in a week is quite a thrill. The average first-timer says something like: "How *many* of *what* can I shoot today?" and the professionals look at the gunbearer and shrug slightly. I couldn't have been prouder as the father of twins than when Low turned down the easy lions. The entire atmosphere of the camp changed so that you could almost taste it.

It changed some more when John Sutton took Low on what John calls a "reccy-run," to see what had happened to the elephant concentration that had been disrupted and widely scattered by unseasonable rains. Fifty miles over no track is a long journey in a Land-Rover. Sutton, a serious professional hunter, conducted Low on a jaunt of over *six hundred* miles with no camp and no sleep. If Sutton was a basket case when he veered the jeep into camp, Low was an uncomplaining corpse. I felt fine. I had been bird shooting with the ladies, and Rosa had laid another egg.

But Low returned from the dead and got onto his shaky feet and took off next day with the other hunter, Don Bousfield. Living under a poncho on short ration, he didn't come back until he had a beautiful pair of tusks. This was the diploma. We

packed up and went to Mombasa and then to Malindi and simply went fishing.

Low's safari gave me more satisfaction than any of my own.
He shot out the license in both Kenya and Tanganyika inside
four weeks, and did not acquire an inferior trophy. He never
shot once to hear the gun go off. As with ships, safaris can be
difficult tests of friendship, and in the month we six white
adults—me, Mama, Jane, Bob, Don, and John—were together
there wasn't a cross word. And I have known fast friends of
years to cease speaking after three days in the bush.

My most serious hunting throughout all this was a private
vendetta with Rubi, the bantam cock. Rubi and I hated each
other on sight. He would leap onto my camp chair, crow, and
deposit droppings. Then he would crow sneeringly and swag-
ger off to peck Rosa on the head. I armed myself with a siphon
bottle and stalked him relentlessly. I may not have collected
anything for the wall, but there is one bantam rooster that
knows when he's met a better man. I got him one day in full
flight, using a duck-length lead with the soda bottle, and shot
him down in extremely moist flames. Thereafter there was no
doubt in Rubi's mind about who was running the show.

The Low safari worked so well that I decided to test my luck
a little more. I had a Spanish chum, and I thought I knew him
pretty well. I'd take a chance on Ricardo and . . . Well, we'd
see.

The Old Man had some pretty firm ideas about friends in
fresh circumstances. "A man," the Old Man once said, "ain't
no built-in hero in the woods or on the water. I don't care if he's
got ten million dollars and six yachts. He ain't a hero to his dog
if he shoots bad. And he ain't a hero to his friends if he hogs
shots. You give me just one weekend in the woods or on a boat
with a man, and I can tell you if he beats his wife or is likely
to run off with the company's money."

This was not the first time it had been said, but the truth
persists. It takes anywhere from two days to two weeks to
prove it, but in the end it always comes out. The city veneer

wears thin, and the man who is a big wheel in his main line begins to whine over a visitation of gnats. The man who might appear to be a surly heel on his native heath suddenly exhibits traits of alarming humility and tremendous consideration of others in the party.

Thinking back to when I was a boy, and the Old Man was not only younger but remarkably spry for his then considerable age, I can recall that we broke off diplomatic relations with one of his best friends. It was a simple matter of politeness involving quail. The friend was a shot-hogger, and he was always so close on the dogs' heels that if a bird got up you had a simple choice: Don't shoot or else shoot the friend in the back of the neck. When you walked into a covey past the pointing dog the friend would fire across your bows if the bulk of the birds went your way.

"I spent half my life teaching dogs to honor a point and behave like decent human beings," the Old Man said. "Now I got a friend who don't even know how to behave like a decent dog. I think maybe we don't hunt with Joe no more."

And we didn't. We spoke politely to Joe on the streets, because we did not actively dislike Joe on the streets, but we didn't hunt with Joe no more. Apart from his other unattractive habits he claimed every bird of dubious ownership, and never once, at the end of the day, had he made even a feeble effort to whack the bag fifty-fifty.

Perhaps the greatest strain on personal relations I know of is a boat trip or a hunting trip of more than one day. Perhaps the boat trip is worse, because you are a captive guest in an alien sea. However, a safari, which can stretch into weeks and months, almost invariably winds up in strife. The communion is too close, the community too big, and, generally, the people too small.

I have usually come out pretty even with the people I have taken on safari, because they have been more or less pretested under other circumstances. That's to say I've hunted and fished or visited with them before, and that way you get a pretty fair idea of what you're liable to buck.

But you still can't plan on the outcome. I've known people, who went out only to photograph, suddenly to develop a blood thirst, and people who started out wanting to shoot the entire list to wind up as bird watchers. Africa, as any reader of Ernest Hemingway will know, has a tremendous effect on personalities. The brave become cowards, the cowards become brave, the bore becomes interesting, and the practiced charmers become bores.

And it doesn't really need Africa to dredge out the true insides of a man or woman. You can do it as easily in North Carolina as on the Northern Frontier of Kenya. Somehow even the birds and animals seem to sense it too, and certainly the natives know. I was on a grouse shoot in Scotland a couple of times, and after the first day or so the local gillies could give you a pretty fair run-down on the general character of the clients involved. It would not surprise you to know that it was only a matter of time before Margaret would divorce Peter, or that Ian would abscond with his bank's funds.

And you can't depend on precedent or type or previous condition of servitude. We'd been lucky with Bob and Jane Low. Now I was taking out this Spanish friend, Ricardo, with Harry Selby and John Sutton. Again I wasn't shooting anything but birds and camp meat, and so this Spaniard had the rare opportunity of having the two best professional hunters in Africa (in my opinion) at his personal beck.

If you can meet the right people Spanish shooting is fabulous, and these people like to keep a brace of guns hot and a loader busy. I just kind of wondered if Ricardo would want to shoot the first elephant he saw or a maneless lion or a lousy buffalo, just to hear the gun go off and collect a batch of flesh.

I should not have had the reservation. Selby and Sutton said later that this was the best safari—and Ricardo Sicrè of Madrid the best client—of their combined experience.

Let me explain Ricardo. He is a millionaire and he made all the money honestly, while he was in his mid-thirties, from a standing start of two hundred dollars cash. He had a fabulous war record with the British and the Americans, when he ran the underground in southern France. He is a good writer, a fair bullfighter, a good horseman, a good shooter, an art connoisseur. He has an enormous yacht and he knows everybody of much importance from New York to London to Monte Carlo to Paris to Madrid. If ever a man had built-in possibilities to be a bum in the bush it was Ricardo.

Not a bit of it developed. From the day he hit Nairobi—with his face beat up from an auto accident on the way to the airport in Madrid—Ricardo was a smashing success. My old friend Selby has a pair of perpetual pistons for legs and the burly body of a bull buffalo. Ricardo had been sick, apart from his accident, and wasn't in the best of shape. Selby damn near worked him to death.

They were up at 3:30 A.M. every morning to drive a couple of hours to make a morning approach to a lion kill. When each of these approaches proved abortive they spent the rest of the day tracking elephants. They generally arrived back in camp, where I was living in opulent ease, about 9 P.M.

We were far north, in Kenya, and the sun smote mightily down. And the bugs bit and elephants invaded the camp and the vehicles got sick. But nary a word of complaint from Ricardo, who never had a decent lunch in camp the whole trip. He and Selby would shoot something, a bird or a small animal, and broil it on a green stick.

We—they, mostly—looked at a hundred and fifty mature bull elephants before they finally decided to shoot one. If there had been more time they'd have looked at a hundred and fifty more, on the off-chance of finding a really superb bull. As it was they collected an eighty-pounder.

They tended that lion kill and the leopard kills as reverently as though making obeisance at a shrine. They averaged two hundred rattling miles a day in the hunting car and about twenty on foot. Ricardo almost fainted from the heat one day, but he didn't beef. He got up, mopped his pale brow, and went back for more.

I confess shamelessly that most of us, when we are shooting guinea fowl or spur fowl for the pot, brass off into a clump of sitting birds with the idea of collecting meat, and we do the sporting thing with the other barrel when the birds take off. This is intelligent, because anybody who has ever hunted a running bird knows that you can't run fast enough to flush them yourself. Not within gun range.

But Ricardo would have none of this firing into a flock. He'd loose off one barrel into the air, and then take his chances with the fliers. (He was pretty lucky one day. Some birds crossed his pattern and he knocked off eight with one salvo. *Flying.*)

It is possible to murder thousands of sand grouse if you let them come close enough, tornado-twisting like teal, to the lone water hole they are forced to patronize for their daily sip in a desert land. One shot and you've got ten, twenty, thirty grouse. Ricardo shot only at the high-flying doubles, triples, and quartets. And a sand grouse, flying high and jinking, is the fastest bird I know outside the peregrine family.

Ricardo finally shot his leopard just at dark, and shot it through the left eye. He took his buffalo on the high slopes of Mount Kenya in the last half-hour of his last day. He shot the buffalo running and dropped it in its tracks.

During the entire month there was no hint of impatience, no complaint about the tremendously hard work, no whining when killing effort turned into failure. He could have shot a half-dozen lions, but none were good enough. So he didn't shoot a lion. He could have shot up the countryside, and didn't. He became so firmly fixed in the affections of the white and black hunters that Swahili is now being spoken with a Spanish accent. And we all laughed constantly, which is terribly important. I was very proud of Ricardo, and my old friends seemed a little proud of me for having produced him. I gained local status.

It seems to me that the basic theme of hunting is that word exactly—*hunting*. Not killing. Whether it's a good pair of tusks or a cloud-touching mallard or the quest of something special in any bird or beast there is a certain imponderable that separates the man from the boy. Call it a grail complex, if you will, but it sure shows up on the face of the hunter and the people around him.

As the Old Man's boy grows older he finds less and less fun in killing, and more and more fun in taking people hunting. We collected two magnificent lions in Uganda a while back on another safari, in a year when lion hunting was almost impossible in terms of mountable results. By safari rights both lions belonged to me, since they were shot on my kills—baits prepared by me and Harry. It was nice to give those lions away. It was nice to see that everybody finally had his leopard and buffalo and waterbuck and all the rest.

It was also nice to know that I, too, collected a magnificent trophy. It was a rather large rabbit, and I had to give him both barrels, but it had been a long time since I had shot a rabbit, and at least it was something to have my picture taken with. The satisfaction I got out of this rabbit fetched back acutely a remark the Old Man once made: "It's twice as much fun to see others do it if you've done it yourself, and done it well enough to where you don't have to do it again."

It occurred to me that I had had enough tigers and lions, and that I would rather watch the elephants than shoot them. Unfortunately, this does not apply to quail. Concerning quail I am still as bloodthirsty as the day my first bobwhite scared me so bad I threw up and had to be put to bed for two days.

Well, now I had two down, and another upcoming. Bob and Jane Low had departed with our friendship still firm, and Ricardo had passed all the exams. Now we had another kettle of conditions coming hard after Ricardo. Now it would be Mike and Jill from the Middle West, and a fairly difficult one to run a test on, because Mike knew a lot about his own bush country. The simon-pure amateurs put themselves wholly in your hands, and if anything goes wrong it's your fault. Sometimes the people who know a lot about their own back yard try to convert that knowledge to Africa, and in the process they do foolish things. Everybody makes mistakes, but they seem to hurt more in somebody else's country.

On this one we were in the high hills of the Masai country of Kenya, where the tame, wild lions keep you alert at night, the hippos splash in the Mara River, the tsetse flies engrave their initials on your hide, and the hyenas remind you of Saturday night in a madhouse. It was a happy camp until that day when one of the jeeps rolled in bearing a tale of tragedy of the highest order.

The Old Man had quite a few trenchant things to say about hunters, and one thing that sticks in my mind was, "No man can call himself a pure hunter until he has committed the damnedest mistake a man can make at a time when he least wants to make it.

"They laugh and carry on a lot about the big fish that got away," he'd elaborate, "and they kid you about having buck fever or forgetting to load the gun or forgetting to slip off the safety catch. But if you will prowl into the life of any man who has spent considerable time hunting and fishing you will find that everybody, at one time or another, has made a mistake that caused him to kick himself in the behind for the rest of his natural life. And it's never a big mistake. It's some damn silly little blunder that the average backward child wouldn't make, and it always happens to people that ordinarily know the hunting and shooting business backwards."

I believe I mentioned at the time, with the arrogance of youth, that so far this boy hadn't made any such stupid mistakes, and didn't think it was likely that he ever would.

The Old Man grinned his shark's grin and blew on the inside of his mustache. "You ain't home yet, son," he said. "You got another sixty years or so for the law of averages to catch up with you."

It turned out he was right, but this is not my story. It is the story of this friend whom we are calling Mike.

Mike is a man of middle years, and most of those years, since he comes from the West, have been spent hunting and fishing when time allowed. He says he does not shoot until he knows he can kill, preferring not to shoot at all rather than wound. He also wears Apache moccasins to ensure quiet stalking.

As a matter of fact, Mike is more a maniacal fisherman than a possessed hunter, and one of our more adept dry-fly flingers. But he likes bird shooting, and he has killed his elk and his mule deer and antelope, and he has caught very large angry fish on very fine thread. Mike, largely because of me, became deeply bitten by the Africa bug, and this bite festered when his charming wife Jill expressed a desire for a leopard to spread in front of her fireplace.

This Jill is a very determined woman, being of Nordic extraction, and when she sets her mouth for something to happen it had better happen. This is how Mike and Jill came to go on safari with a fiercely determined aim: Mike would shoot a leopard and Jill would unfurl it in front of the fireplace for the puppies and the children to roll on, and occasionally a Martini might be mixed to recall the good old days in the African bush. Then Jill would tell all and sundry how her man Mike dragged this lovely spotted pussycat out of the bush by his tail, just because Jill wanted a rug for her tepee.

Well sir, the safari traipsed all around, up from Kenya to darkest Uganda and then back to Kenya—long, dusty, tail-wearying miles—just to see if somehow we could not collect a leopard for Mike. Animals were dispatched and slung into trees and left to ripen enticingly. Blinds were built. Drags of defunct animals were made, the better to diffuse the scent. Water holes were inspected for leopard tracks. We constructed morning approaches and evening approaches, and crawled miles through safari ants in the blackest, bone-freezing predawn, and sat up untiringly, bug-devoured, for three hours in the afternoon, each afternoon, to jounce home, kidney-shaken, murderously weary, and fantastically filthy, ready only to stagger off into bed dirty and arise with the waning moon to do it all over again.

Weeks passed. Foot-loose lady lions climbed trees and ate Mike's leopard baits. Once a surly rhino—the only one in the neighborhood—chased a leopard off a kill and evidently scared it so badly that the *chui* never returned. But Mike was a dauntless leopard hunter, and a dauntless leopard hunter is at least one part idiot. He crawled out of bed in the freezing Masai dawn to go and inspect a couple of feeble, tawdry kills to see if any mentally retarded leopard might be feeding, and he cruised the country endlessly on the off-chance—a one-in-a-million shot —that a nocturnal slinker might stay up too late some night with the boys and go wandering home to his lair in the bright morning sunlight, when all good dues-paying leopards should be snugly abed in a thorny thicket.

Mike had been shooting a .318 Westley Richards of mine very well. It's a very flat rifle that throws about two hundred and fifty grains of lead. He had come to trust this gun, for it had killed him a fine lion. He was not really interested in the lion until he saw it sitting underneath a leopard bait, and I do believe he shot the lion so it would not hamper the leopard's chances of coming to the tree-strung kill.

The story might meander on, but I will shorten it. Clean living and high purpose paid off, and the day came when Mike had been riding along the flat top of the Trans-Mara escarpment, checking to see if any leopards (faint hope) had been feeding on a couple of topi kills. And then the million-to-one-shot hit.

A big, very big, dog leopard—an eight-footer, perhaps— meandered across the track and sauntered into a small patch of bush in broad Masai daylight. Now the search for the spotted grail was at an end, because the patch of bush was very small indeed, and the leopard could easily be driven out of it. Mike's professional hunter stopped the car, and they strolled along to the piece of bush.

Inside the bush they could hear the leopard growl. The hunters stood with guns ready, and the gunbearers began to fling chunks of wood into the clump. Out came the leopard, broad on, not hurrying but more of less meandering, presenting a target (for a man who shoots as well as Mike) as big as a spotted house. Up came the trusty .318. Jill, who was watching the show, already saw herself serving Martinis in front of the fire while sitting on this splendid, very dark, golden leopard skin.

Mike held the leopard firmly in his sights at about twenty-five yards and squeezed. The logical sequence was the sharp bark of the .318, a final growl, and a mighty leap of the leopard; then conjugal kisses, hearty congratulations, and the triumphant end of the hunt. Jill would have her rug and Mike would stand proud and tall among his clan brothers.

There was a dry half-click. The leopard melted into thick bush and was no more seen, because a leopard melting into thick bush is untrackable unless he is wounded and spraying a blood spoor. *Kuisha chui*. Leopard finish.

Mike stood there looking, as at a stranger, at the gun in his hand; this trusty gun; this marvel of rifled craftsmanship by one of the best gunsmiths in London; this burled walnut-stocked gun whose prototype has been known to speed a solid bullet all the way through an elephant, penetrating completely from stern to bow.

What had happened was simple—one of those little mistakes the Old Man had mentioned. Some years back I had affixed a very low-mounted scope to this rifle. The scope interfered with the Mauser-type safety catch, so I had the catch taken off, intending to install another type of safety. But time passed, and it scarcely seemed worth the trouble, because complete safety could be maintained when a bullet was in the chamber by leaving the bolt handle only half-thrown. All you had to do to shoot was to slap the bolt handle firmly into its bed, and she would be in vicious business.

In the truly magnificent spectacle of the leopard erupting from the bush Mike, really unaccustomed to the rifle, had forgotten to snap the bolt handle all the way home. And with leopard you are not allowed mistakes. Not even one. Not the littlest one.

There is really not much you can say to comfort at a time like that. I claim I helped some. I mentioned to Mike that he was only an amateur in the frustration league, because anybody who knows me might remember the painful story of the tiger that got away.

This particular tiger was the biggest of three in the Madhya Pradesh of India, and I killed it just as dead as I had slain the two others. He was a huge old tiger, a cattle-lifter, and I shot him, smirking the while, through the neck. He collapsed and my shikari and I congratulated each other. The shikari suggested a second, make-sure shot, but I waved him off. What need? We smoked a couple of cigarettes and had a pull at the flask. It was then that the tiger got up and slowly walked away. We never saw him again.

The tiger story helped Mike some, but not enough. The Old Man said once that you never forget a mistake that cost you dearly; so when somebody said that Mike's leopard would be a mere memory on the dewy morrow I said, No. No sir. That leopard would continue to grow, and Mike would still be hating himself twenty years hence.

"That's the real beauty part of hunting," the Old Man had said. "A hunter still finds it possible to kick himself in the tail after everybody else has forgotten the tragic incident. That separates the men from the boys in the hunting business, because a casual gent will pretend that it never happened, and even if it did, it was somebody else's fault. The mark of the true man is will he continue to hunt, instead of busting his gun over the nearest tree."

But Mike has the mark of the true man, and I was perfectly certain that before we removed ourselves from the Loita Plains he would have his leopard, and Jill might one day be able to sit on the skin in front of the fire and whip up a batch of Martinis, extra dry.

Like the Old Man said, it ain't so much talent as energy, and the bad breaks can't go on forever. The Old Man just claimed that the stature of the man was measured by how much he could smile when fate was beating him over the head with a stick.

Mike shot a big leopard later. But it'll never be as big as the one that walked across the road.

16

Lions and Liars

There is a saying among the Masai of Africa—or maybe it's the Somali—that a brave man is frightened three times by a lion: when he first sees its track, when he first hears its roar, and when he first sees the lion in the flesh. It's a pity the Old Man didn't live to see me get to Africa, because I wish to add to this generalization and I'm sure he would approve.

The first time a man comes in contact with a lion he automatically turns liar. If there is a tiny, faint shred of mendacity in a man his first lion will bring it out. This applies in a similar, if lesser, degree to male deer, giving rise first to an ague-making malady called buck fever and later to delusions of grandeur accompanied by faint falsehoods. These expand into outright fantasies that might even be medically described as an early journey into schizophrenia. Every day becomes April first.

In the bird world I believe that the bobwhite quail has done more to corrupt man's truce with fact that any other feathered friend, although a duck liar and a wild turkey liar enjoy certain phases of the moon when they take an adverse view of temperance and truth. In the exotic fields I suppose a tiger liar is almost as good as a lion liar, and the African elephant as a liar-breeder stands all by itself.

This, of course, refers only to low-level lying. People who climb mountains in search of such rich fare as ibex, tahr, mountain sheep and goats, chamois, and greater kudu are not to be included among the sea-level liars, because the altitude obviously affects fantasy. Rarefied air has a tendency to loosen the centers of imagination and also the tongue, because there are often very few witnesses to call the liar a liar. This is what generally gives rise to legends about Abominable Snowmen and such.

The Old Man had some definite ideas about sporting liars. He claimed that in his better days, weight for age, no holds barred, he could outlast anybody he knew in the solid construction of an airproof lie, although he was not so much for the gaudy fringes. The Old Man believed that when you got your mouth fixed to lie you ought to start at the ground and work up, and that a soundly planted liar didn't need a lot of fancy trimmings.

"A sporting liar," the Old Man once said, "is a truthful man turned dishonest by circumstances beyond his control. There is no real malice in him, and he is unique among all brands of liars, because with practice and careful handling his lies eventually become unshakable truth. This applies to all sporting liars except dog liars. I wouldn't believe anything a man said about his hound, his Labrador, his pointer, or his setter, sworn before a notary on a stack of Ken-L Ration."

The bare anatomy of nonmalicious lying is a complex thing. First, a silent self-deluder doesn't count, because such deception is lying on your own time and creates no harm save personal confusion, such as fanning yourself with a fly swatter. Fishermen are also excluded, because a fisherman starts lying to himself before he takes down the rod and chases the kittens out of the creel. It does no real self-eroding damage for the self-liar to add a pound to the fish or an inch to the horn or a brace to the bag.

If controlled, this self-deception is difficult to detect. You look at a pair of elephant tusks framing a fireplace and the owner says calmly, "A hundred and sixteen and a hundred and twenty." He knows better than the elephant's ghost that one weighs a hundred and ten and the other weighs a hundred and twelve, but something impels him to add a few pounds to the trophy, even though it makes no difference in their appearance or to the facts of acquisition, and his latest target for untruth has no way of weighing them anyhow.

They say that tusks have a habit of losing weight after they are thoroughly dry. My best pair is unique. Standing for the last half-dozen years by a roaring fire that operates six months a year those tusks have gone from a hundred and ten and a hundred and twelve, wet, to a hundred and twenty and a hundred and twenty-five, dry. I suppose as I grow older they'll eventually weigh a hundred and ninety-five and two hundred respectively.

An elephant is the biggest land-bound animal in the world. Conversely, the bobwhite quail is the smallest ferocious bird I know. But the quail outweighs the elephant as a corrosive influence on ordinary truth. I have long believed that one day I killed fifteen quail with thirteen shots. This is an outright falsehood, although I tell it frequently. It actually happened, but it happened to Mr. Bernie Baruch. I stole it callously, and I don't know why, any more than Henry McLemore knows why he stole H. Allen Smith's dream about the bouncing pussy-pup.

I have shot exactly two elephants, two tigers, and two lions in my life. I have shot exactly five leopards. But wind me up, boy, let me ramble, and I make Karamoja Bell and Jim Corbett look like pikers. It is a strange thing, but the tendency to outdoor falsehood generally touches on quantity rather than trophy weight or actual size. What I mean is I have hunted massive concentrations of elephants on a control operation that was supposed to thin the herds by three or four hundred beasts. Actually I never fired a shot, but unless you listen closely you might believe that I fetched back three hundred jumbo tails, was hailed as Protector of the Poor, and was duly decorated.

One of the more unusual, unvarying, and untrue aspects of big-game tale-telling is that nearly all bull elephants are rogues, and that all lions, tigers, and leopards brought to bag are man-eaters. I know there are rogue elephants. There must be, because so much is written about them. But I never saw one. Certainly there are man-eating cats, but the outsize pussies I have fetched home never sampled so much as a rasher of bacon off Homo sapiens. The leopards all seemed to relish pork, preferably maggoty, and the lions and tigers generally chose an animal like a jackass, a zebra, a young buffalo, or a cow—something with much more eatin' meat on it than a skinny human.

Possibly the main thing about lions' effect on liars is that very few people you will meet in your daily life ever saw a loose lion. This more or less prevents challenge on your veracity or lack of same. The mere fact that you are within a few feet of the unfettered king disarranges the chromosomes of your soul and everything thereafter seems bigger, more profuse. Once you've seen a wild lion at close hand, once you've shot a lion at a range of thirty yards or so your perspective changes, even when you speak of such innocuous fluffy beasts as bunnies.

I have noticed recently that I retroactively tend to shoot all lions and elephants at a range that is never greater than ten yards. Up to now I've not shot either animal from the hip, but I'm gaining, men, I'm gaining. A fellow named Harry Selby did have to shoot a wounded buff from the hip not so long ago, and I see no real reason not to steal the experience from him.

The lion that sent me darting off the narrow path of truth

was almost, but not quite, the first thing I ever shot with a rifle larger than a .22 I have to admit to a couple of zebras and a wart hog on my first day of safari, and some shocking misses on Thomson's gazelle. But I actually did shoot the lion the morning of the second day out, and a second-day lion is heady fare for a tenderfoot who is not quite sure how to load a magazine rifle. I clobbered this slightly moth-bitten old fellow medium-clean and semitruly through the ear, and he spread out into a rug midly studded with camel flies. On advice of Master Selby, who even at the age of twenty-four was a cautious professional, I walloped him again behind the shoulder before I walked close enough to pose with a prideful foot on his neck.

We slung Simba into the back of the Land-Rover, suitably padded by hastily hewn grass, and jounced merrily off to camp to show Mama how brave her little man was his second day in Africa. Mama got out of the sack to admire the beast, and I was accorded to be quite a fellow by the black boys, who had a keen nose for baksheesh on a triumphant day and broke out the formal celebration.

We propped *Bwana* Simba's chin on a rock, and Mama unlimbered her cameras. Then *Bwana* Simba's eyes opened wide, his ears perked up, and he let out a soul-shattering roar. Never before have so many people so swiftly and successfully climbed so few trees, thorns and all.

Now the truth is that the lion was stone-cold dead from the first .375 in the ear, and even deader from a second slug through the heart, and had been dead for two hours by the time we got him to camp. The opened eyes, the pricked ears came from some sort of muscular contraction as he prepared for rigor mortis. The roar was nothing but a sudden release of stomach gases.

But you check back a couple of paragraphs and you will see that I have a dandy story—if I skip the explanation. The thing is to tell it modestly and mention quietly that you ran to the jeep and got a gun and shot the lion again. (Which I did, because I hadn't figured out what made him come alive and roaring after having been dead for two hours.)

About a week later we had another bright day of derring-do, which combined the slaying of a kind of champion waterbuck in the morning, a very fine lion in the early afternoon, and a very big leopard (the first) toward evening. The lion was accompanied by several lionesses and cubs. It seems there were six or nine or twelve lionesses. I think six would be the more accurate figure, but these days I just settle for two dozen and let it go.

I wouldn't know today what happened on the rest of the trip if I hadn't written some modest pieces for *Field & Stream*, and later a less modest book about it. I find a streak of basic honesty in a writing-sporting liar. If he records the facts at the time he will be scrupulous in his adherence to basic truth—at the time. I never told any major fibs in print. My conscience dwelt among the scribbled notes. It is only age and distance that lend an added luster to the unvarnished fact.

The Old Man said he blamed whisky and open fireplaces as much as anything else for the decay of probity. Also he said no outdoor man ever touched his peak performance for tall stories before he was forty-plus.

"Lies," the Old Man said, "are like whisky. They go down better after having been aged in the wood."

I came up in a little town where the expansive yarn would have made a Paul Bunyan blush. I couldn't have been more than six when I heard the one about the bird dog who was so stanch that he froze to death on point, and when the thaw came the next year his master found a skeletal dog still standing a covey of skeletal quail. And, of course, there was one character in our town who was such a smooth and adept thief that he slid into a house one night and stole a lamp so fast that its owner kept right on reading after it was gone.

As to dogs, I certainly do not care to say whether I am an accurate witness on the prowess of some of the beasts I owned. I think it highly unlikely that any dog of mine ever pointed a live bird with a dead bird in his mouth and one foot pinning down a cripple, but wouldn't it be lovely if it were as true as it sounds when I tell it?

Sometime, when you've got a minute, remind me to tell you of the whitetailed deer I once shot in Carolina. The hounds coursed it through a friend's back yard. I shot it, and its dying leap carried it through the door of the smokehouse, and when we got inside it was hanging there, its horns caught on a hook.

17

Fishing Is a State of Mind

"The only thing crazier than a duck hunter or a mountain climber," the Old Man repeatedly said, "is a really dedicated fisherman—a man who will fish where he knows there are no fish, just as long as he's fishing. In fact, the dedicated fisherman is Simple Simon with a license."

I didn't believe a word of this, of course, because I was kind of partial to fishing myself in those days, but only when I could catch fish.

"In fact," the Old Man went on, "I think the dedicated fisherman really hates fish. Take Cap'n Ahab. You perhaps know the story of *Moby Dick*. I don't suppose you could actually call a whale a true fish, but let's say that at least a whale can't walk, and concede that he's got fins and flippers and lives in the water. Well, this here Cap'n Ahab was a clear case of a man who hated fish, and one fish in particular. This hatred for fish ruined his life and lost him a leg."

The Old Man was drawing the longbow, as usual, but there was a seed in what he said. This came to mind the other day in Spain, when a neighbor dropped in of a Sunday and announced proudly, "I caught another fish." You'd have thought he'd just won the Nobel prize.

A fish hooked this character two years ago when he moved to my occasional neck of the woods. Using a borrowed rod he landed a three-pound *dorada*—a very fine sort of sea bass. From that point on he was lost. He had a seagoing monkey on his back.

Every Sunday since that awful day he has fished, when he was in the little town of Palamós, up and down the beach in front of my house. He bought rods and reels and lines and tackle and one large milk can to keep his bait alive. He had more bait than the professionals, and more equipment than Ernest Hemingway.

Two years he fished, and the other Sunday he caught his second fish—another *dorada*, weighing a pound and a half. That, you must admit, was a long time between bites. It took him two years and three hours of lonely fishing to snag this critter, and he was late to lunch and got chewed out at home. Then he gave the fish away to a neighbor (not me).

There are a passel of fish in Spain, and in my neighborhood fishing is the major industry. But it is big-boat, deep-sea stuff with seines. Angling off the beach you might just catch a tourist or find yourself tied onto a bikini. But this does not discourage my friend Ted. He once had a hell of a day with a submerged auto tire. He is as trustingly tireless as the poor souls who fish the Seine in France. One day, the Parisian thinks, I'll catch a tuna that has strayed from the Strait of Gibraltar, or at least a large sardine.

A slightly more successful slave to the foul fishing habit is another neighbor, Artie Shaw, the reformed clarinetist. He lives on a lofty mountaintop a league or so away, and he has more equipment than Abercrombie & Fitch. He ties his own flies, hand-wraps his own rods, and makes regular pilgrimages to Austria and France and America to see what's newest and most expensive in the angling equipment dodge.

Shaw threshes the streams of the Pyrenees and the small rivers in our neighborhood. He can flick your eye out with a fly, wet or dry, at fifty yards. He hunts fish nearly every day, and from time to time he catches something, be it nothing larger than a whiskered minnow. But since he has one whole room in his castle devoted to fishing gear I keep asking him where he is going to use those platinum-mounted mammoth reels that are suitable for the tuna tournament in the Bahamas. He just mutters and ties another fly.

About the only notable trophy I ever took with a fly rod was my own ear, but occasionally the poison that invaded my veins when I was a kid in Carolina seeps back, and I can still handle a spinning reel or the old-time surf rod without seriously wounding anybody. And I came down with a craving for fishing recently that probably qualifies me to become president of the Idiots' Club.

As seems usual these years, I was in Africa, and I was sick of safari. "Let's go fishing. I need a rest," says I to Harry Selby, my professional hunter friend, and to Brian Burrows, who runs some hotels out Kenya way.

"Sure," Selby said, "I know just the place. Lake Rudolf. You'll find it fascinating. We got a permanent camp up there I built a couple years back, and a motor launch that I transported nearly six hundred miles over land. She'll do nicely if she hasn't sunk, which is entirely likely."

The difficulties involved in transporting about thirty-eight feet of specially built lake boat, on the order of the "African Queen," across the Northern Frontier District of Kenya atop a lurching lorry add up to a logistical feat comparable to carrying a ton of coal to Newcastle on your head, and I will not bore you with the harrowing details.

They even had to build a slipway to launch her and a dock to shelter her. Every nail, every plank, every piece of equipment, except thatch, came up from Nairobi by truck, for Selby to rear his village for a scientific expedition that was intent on charting the lake, its fish, and its birds.

"How long does it take to fly there?" I asked.

"Oh, 'bout an hour and a half," Selby said. "Maybe two. But we can't fly. We haven't any vehicles up there. Everybody's left, and we'll need some food and some transport for the boys. Anyhow, it's terribly interesting country, and the fish are something really extraordinary."

He cited me some statistics. One day very recently they had boated fifteen Nile perch—only one under twenty-five pounds and the rest ranging from twenty to sixty—in three-quarters of an hour. Some other people had caught sixteen perch over one hundred pounds at the south end of the lake. The record was two hundred and forty pounds.

"Sounds like action," I said.

"You'll like it. The air's so dry that you really don't mind if it gets to be a hundred and twenty degrees around midday."

Brian Burrows, an Irishman who sunburns easily, paled a mite at this information, but he had already signed on for the trip. Our noble caravan, consisting of a Dodge Power Wagon, one Mercedes diesel truck, and a dozen unhappy natives, set off to catch a fish. To catch a fish you drive about ninety miles from Nairobi until you turn right at a place called Gilgil. This road eventually brings you to Thomson's Falls, about a hundred and sixty miles from Nairobi.

If you're a lucky little chap you can go from Thomson's Falls to Maralal, another seventy-five miles, before you pitch your camp after dark. You have sent the lorry on ahead and you camp at the foot of the mountain, because it's about fourteen thousand feet high at the top, and though it is cold at the bottom it is considerably colder at the top—even in the daytime.

You will have inhaled plentiful dust and suffered a great many bumps on the base of the spine, and seen a power of dull, drab country. Juma and the other boys have made a fire, and you thank heaven for it when you dismount from the Power Wagon. You have just left a luxury safari, with iceboxes and pretty girls and mess tents and forty-odd assorted attendants. You have shot nothing, and you pitch no tents. You dine sumptuously off hot whisky, cold beans, and clammy bread, and hit the feathers without benefit of any tentage whatsoever.

Nothing is as unhappy looking as a bunch of freezing Africans loading one lonesome lorry in the cold gray crack of dawn, feeding you makeshift ham and eggs, and literally whisking the chair out from under you in order to cram it onto the truck. Nothing is as miserable as three white fishermen, who have slept in their clothes and have decided that teeth cleaning can wait for a hotter clime. Nothing is as miserable—until you check with me later.

So now we tackle the escarpment, which is really a very lovely thing, if you like driving a clanking vehicle straight up to the sky around impossible curves. We hit the summit and paused to see the view, but the wind blew us right away from the view and suicidally down a hill that twisted around the badly sutured scar of the Rift, product of a great volcanic upheaval.

We clambered down the escarpment and stopped for a drink. Burrows was pale and so was I, because no parachutes had been issued with the Power Wagon. A young Samburu warrior, who looked like Lena Horne's twin brother, stopped to pass the time of day. He asked, in Swahili, where we were going.

"Fishing," Selby said.

The Samburu *moran* shook both his head and his spear. He had now heard it all. He looked around him at the lava-strewn desert, at the escarpment behind us, and toward Baragoi, which he had left a couple of days earlier, about sixty miles t'other way.

"I have never seen a fish," he said. "I don't think you'll find any around here. Perhaps if you go far enough, my father says, to the other side of Baragoi, you will come to a great lake. Perhaps there will be fish there."

We gave the Samburu warrior a candy bar and bade him fond adieu.

"Let us press on, men," I said. "The fish are waiting." And I knew I would hate myself in the morning. I did.

We stopped off at Baragoi village to buy some gin, which the *dukah* owner naturally forgot to put into the truck. We had a small libation of cold beer and then took off, ginless in Gaza, so to speak, figuring that we would lunch when we got down the hill.

Immeasurably cheered by a couple of beers I asked the Scoutmaster how far were we from our destination, where we would fish.

"Only sixty-five miles or so," Mr. Selby said, taking a hairpin curve that headed us back to Baragoi. "It's really nothing until we come to the Valley of Death. That's something. The nice thing, though, is that we'll do it after dark. You won't be able to see where I'm driving." He chuckled darkly. "But then, of course, neither will I," he said.

I could hear Burrows gulp.

We progressed until we passed a place called South Horr. There is another place at the other end of the lake called North Horr. We played tag with a herd of elephants, and we had what could be called a miserable lunch. This was about the time we discovered that our friend in the *dukah* had forgotten to pack the gin. Even the Horr Valley, which was pretty green, was still miserable country.

"There's a police post up there," Selby said, pointing to a mountainside. "Once in a while there is a pretty good chance of getting through to it on the radio. If you have a two-way radio, of course."

"Do we have a two-way radio?"

"No," Selby said.

"That's nice," Burrows said. "It's one thing we won't have to worry about if the Gelubba come over from Abyssinia to kill us."

"Oh," Selby said, "they'd have to pass the police post at North Horr first. Unless they decided to by-pass it. They do that, you know. They can move about forty-five miles a day on foot, and generally strike and move out before the police find out about it."

"We could have fished the streams in Nanyuki," I said.

"The fishing's pretty good down Mombasa way," Burrows said.

"Oh," Selby said, "but it doesn't have the stark drama of the north. In 1957 and '58 the Gelubba concentrated on the western shore of the lake. About a hundred and sixty deaths among the Turkana were reported. There must have been more. Tomorrow, when it's light, I'll show you a hill called Porr where they wiped out a whole tribe of Turks in 1954.

"It's rather a rough bit of country," Selby went on, narrowly avoiding a plunge to our mutual deaths. "Anything bearing arms on this side of the Kenya-Abyssinia boundary, up to a line between Porr and South Horr, is shot on sight. Any government official making his rounds on the other side of North Horr must carry an escort of ten men. This makes it a bit sticky when you consider that there are only forty-eight Kenya police for all of the Marsabit District, which includes Lasames—you know how far away that is, Bob—and the whole eastern shore of Rudolf. But, of course, there's the *recoup*."

"And what exactly is the recoup?"

"A sort of flying squad, a camel corps, made up of Somalis, Wakambas, everybody—fighting people. It's an elite troop. You can't do much with vehicles around here"—for emphasis he rattled our teeth on a block of stone—"because of the lava rocks. The recoup takes off in the black dawn to the trouble spots, siestas in the heat of the day, and generally arrives at its destination from nine to ten at night. More or less like the spahis in the old *Beau Geste* books. Tell the truth," Harry said, "we are not terribly civilized around here."

"The catfishing is pretty good on the Mara River," I said.

"Malindi's nice," Burrows said. "The fishing's fine in Malindi, and you can always hop over to Zanzibar or up to Lamu to watch the dhows smuggling the elephant tusks. I hear the fishing is fine around Malindi."

"Ah, but they haven't got the real sense of the country any more," Selby said, feeling the bitter hatred that swirled around him and loving every moment of it. "Too many tourists. Not enough mythology. Now you just take the goats."

"What goats?" That must have been me speaking.

"The goats on South Island. South Island is kind of haunted. Nothing on it but goats—great big goats—and nobody really knows how they got there. Goats and ghosts. But they're there, all right. Seen 'em myself, the ghosts, and shot some and trapped some. The goats, I mean."

We clanked along in the mobile iron maiden, while Selby elaborated. "The locals," Harry said, "they believe that South Island was once connected to the mainland by a peninsula. At the base of the island was a spring where the Samburu cattle watered. The spring was sacred, and everybody was forbidden to tamper with it when it dried. But one day a pregnant Rendille woman came along with a flock of goats and started digging for water, and the spring burst forth and swallowed the whole countryside.

"She climbed the hill with her goats and eventually gave birth to a son, who, the natives said, later married his own mother and had children. As a matter of fact somebody *did* live on the island, because Sir Vivian Fuchs, in 1921, found remnants of huts and quite a lot of artifacts. And goats. Some other scientists—two men—tried to go over there and were never seen again. But George Adamson and his wife—you know him, Bob, he's the New Frontier District game warden who has the tame lioness—were over there about three years ago and they found a cairn of rocks and a whisky bottle, so the two scientists must have been lost on their way back to the eastern shore.

"Also," Harry said, "you can see firelight over there, although there's nobody living on the island."

"I don't want to see any firelight on a place nobody lives on," said I. "How about the goats?"

"You wouldn't believe them," Harry said. "They got horns twice as tall and beards twice as long as any goats I ever saw. Sort of trophy goats."

"I believe the fishing is wonderful on the Athi River," Burrows said. "And it has the advantage of being very close to Nairobi. Very few goats, though, I'm told."

"We'd better stop," Harry said. "It's about nighttime and that damned lorry seems to be too far behind us. A pity, really, that we have to get there in the black of night. As a true experiment into fear that descent into the Valley of Death really wants seeing by day."

We had come through some more horrid country and were now perched atop a high hill. Hill? Hell's delight, it was a mountain. We looked hopefully for the flickering yellow tongues of the lorry's lights. Nothing showed. The wind howled.

"I wish I was back there with the camels," Burrows said. "They at least look like contented camels." We had passed through a vast herd, numbering into the thousands, of Samburu wealth, which in that area is camels. For pure wealth you can't beat a camel. You can milk it, eat it, wear its hair, ride it, make it carry your belongings, and it has the definite advantage of getting fat on thorns and only drinking every other semester.

"Here comes the lorry," Selby said finally. "Brace yourselves, chaps. Into the Valley of Death."

It was midnight when we hit the camp on the little sweetwater stream. It had taken us fourteen hours of driving to cover sixty-five miles. The last three hours was absolutely straight

down a lava-strewn mountain, with the vehicles hanging onto
the rocks by their heels—like klipspringers. The last few miles
were along the lake's beach, which was composed of slippery
shale on which the autos skidded as though on ice.

"Home," Harry said, as we came up to what appeared to be
a thatched palace. "I'll just go cut in the generator and we'll
have some lights."

In a moment he was back, smiling cheerfully—the bearer of
ill tidings. "The generator won't cut in," he said. "I guess we'll
make it on the hurricane lamps."

Juma, the headman, came in and said something rapidly in
Swahili. I could sort out the word "Ramadan," used several
times over.

"Boys ain't pleased," Harry said. "It gets hot here, and on the
Moslem national holiday month, Ramadan, you can't drink or
eat from dawn to dusk. Also, most of the blokes spent six
months here with the expedition, and they've been out with you
for three months. Juma's face looks like an old boot."

"So does mine," I said.

"I hear the fishing is very good outside of Denver, Colorado,"
Burrows said. "In the time we've spent we could have gone
there."

"Ah, you'll love it by daylight," Harry said, "when the
freezer gets going—that's if the generator works—and we go
out on the lake in the boat. Her name's *Lady of the Lake*—
that is, if she's not sunk."

"Let's eat something before we turn in," I said. "What've we
got that is quick and easy?"

"Well, I know there's some tinned salmon and some sardines,"
Harry said.

That's when Burrows and I both bore him savagely to the
floor, intent on murder. *Fish*.

"Well," I said when Juma came early next morning with the
tea, "so this is where we are. Finally."

"*Mbaya*," Juma said. (In Swahili *mbaya* means "bad.")
"Rudolf *mbaya*."

"*Hapana mbaya,*" I said. "*Hi m'zuri sana.*" That means, "Very good, any amount."

"*Fish!*" Juma said, making a cuss word out of the noun. "All this way to go fishing. When I could be with my wives. I have been here before. I have been here for maybe six months before. The face of the place doesn't change, the water doesn't change, and the people don't change. *Mbaya kapisa sana.*"

This was the third phase of one of the longest nonfishing trips in history. We were now into the third day of torture and we had not yet wet a line. We had not seen the lake, which is a lake that very few people have seen. It is by survey 365 feet deep in spots, and 135 miles long by 35 miles wide at its broadest. It is crammed with leaping tiger fish, Nile perch, and *tilapia*, a very fine-tasting fish. Supposedly.

"*Mbaya,*" Juma said, all the laughter gone from his snub-nosed, half-Congolese Arab, half-Kikuyu face. "Bad people the other way. Gelubba that kill. Rendille that kill. Turkana that kill. Borron, bad. Samburu, bad. Locals, stupid. All bad. Also too hot. Hot as a fire all day and the *Muslimi* can't drink." Juma's face now looked like a melted rubber boot. "Not until sundown the *Muslimi* can't drink."

The staff was not only beat but frustrated rich from a year's steady safari employment, and no chance to spend any money; beat and wanting to go home to their wives and cattle and goats. Beat and not wanting to be again in the haunted hot country with its strewn lava rocks that looked like the mountains of the moon, its mysterious tricky lake full of crocodiles and hippo, and the murderous tribe called Gelubba just around the corner in Ethiopia.

"You won't like the people here," Juma said. "All *shenzis*. *Burri*. Fisheaters. Savages."

"But the fishing's good," I said. "And it's very comfortable here."

"I would rather live in a tent with the hyenas and the baboons outside," Juma muttered, and shuffled away in his working clothes.

The camp was the former site of a scientific expedition mounted by the University of Miami, and as far as I was concerned, when we got around to inspecting the area, an absolutely charming camp, by far the most lavish I have seen in Africa. Harry Selby and John Sutton, in the interest of the expedition, had created a palm-and-grass-thatched paradise in the middle of nowhere, with a chuckling stream running coolly through the middle. Great palms shaded the enormous main hut; its ridgepole must have been twenty-five feet high. There was a lab where the scientists had worked, a great dormitory for the men, a lockable kitchen, and several scattered cottages for married couples and the occasional female guests.

The generator was cut in now; the freezer and the refrigerator were humming, and all the lights working in the various buildings. The showers functioned, and the radio brought the BBC news from London. Selby and his assistants had built themselves about the deluxiest fishing camp in show business. There was even a barber's chair with a prospect of the lake and a magic island in clear view.

"We ain't so crazy," said Brian Burrows, the hotelkeeper, "now that we're here. I ain't going home no more." He gestured at the vast, cool main building with its low-sweeping eaves, designed like lifted skirts so that a constant breeze was swept in and over the thwarts to circulate air in the room. "Even if there ain't any fish," said the Liverpool Irishman, "I ain't going home no more."

"There will be fish," said Selby, appearing well-shined, shaved, and showered. "Don't fret your heads about the fish. How do you like my layout?"

"Great," said I, "if I can fly in the next time. And if there are any fish. I have to wait until I see the fish."

"You'll see the fish," Selby said. "We'll go down to the lake in a minute and see if the *Lady of the Lake* is still with us. If she's sunk we can still surf cast. The big ones come into the weeds anyhow. All you have to do is mind the crocodiles. They come into the weeds too."

"I think I shall stay clear of the weeds," Brian Burrows said. "I ain't lost nothing in them there weeds."

"Somebody's going to have to teach this chap to speak English again," Selby said. "Ever since he's known you he's a vast discredit to his rearing."

"Look who's talking," Burrows said. "I mind well that an 'ain't' or so creeps into your occasional context, me beamish boy."

"I ain't knockin' the word 'ain't,'" Selby said. "Ruark makes money off it. Let's go fishin'."

The *Lady of the Lake*, after having her bilges pumped, was an agreeable girl. We endowed Selby with the title of the Cautious Captain, because he was unwilling to go outside El Molo Bay. And smartly so, because Rudolf runs up a wind you wouldn't believe until you picked up your teeth.

"Inside is good enough for me," I said. "I ain't lost nothing outside that big hill."

Evidently we were a caravan of cowards. Nobody dissented, including Metheke, my old and trusted gunbearer, who wouldn't get on the boat at all. This gap-toothed Wakamba, who may be the bravest man I ever met, said that he was an elephant hunter and a cannibal, but he hadn't lost nothing on that big *magi* either. Metheke would sit at the shore and pluck the whistling teal and the occasional knob-nosed goose I had shot. He was content to watch the boat from a distance. He had been along when they freighted her overland. Metheke is very rich, and has a lot of wives, sheep, goats, and cattle. He wanted to live to enjoy them.

You might possibly have seen pictures of Selby and me, but I must describe Burrows, the vagrant fisherman. He looks like a cross between Brendan Behan and an Assyrian emperor, and when you deck him in shorts and the kind of floppy straw hat that Jamaican peasants wear the ensemble is, in a word, horrid. He is one of the truly brave people I know, and has the disposition of a baby lamb, or he wouldn't be off in the wilderness with me and Selby in the first place.

During the Mau Mau emergency a busload of nice old ladies arrived at Brian's hotel just as a Kenya settler shot a running native across the street in front of the opera house. One of the horrified old ducks turned to Brian. "Tell me, young man," she quavered, "is this a safe hotel?"

"Great God, no," the manager said, stripping off his jacket to display bandages. "Look what the blighters did to me last night!"

And they had, too. Old Beebee got mashed up three times in the peaceful administration of his business.

We proceeded to fish. Burrows got stuck into something we all decided was a rock, because nothing moved, even when the Cautious Captain gave the "Lady" full speed ahead. Aly, the only competent sailor among us—he's a Swahili from Mombasa, and so knows boats—went over the side and into the dinghy to see if he could unsnag the line, and then the rock came alive. Burrows had been pumping steadily for fifteen minutes on what turned out to be a sixty-pound Nile perch that had merely decided to lie doggo.

We caught fish, all right. I caught two: a tiger and a perch. I lost a mess, because these tiger fish have a way of digesting tackle. We caught more fish in the shallows. That was because we sent the local laddybucks, the Molos, fishing with nets. We wanted to freeze some fish to take home to various Mamas, and the freezer was working wonderfully.

It was working wonderfully, because we suspended fishing the following day so that Selby and Metheke could dismantle the generator, which had become temperamental again. It does not take much to please Selby. Get him greasy to the ears and surround him with displaced bits and pieces of an engine and he carols like a lark.

Once he got the generator sorted out we didn't go fishing again, because of one thing and another in the pursuit of culture, such as literary talk and the adjustment of the windsock at the airstrip on the off-chance any pretty girls might fly in to visit us. This consumed the best part of a day, and nothing ever came of it. The only pretty girl I saw was on the way home, and she was twins. I started to buy both of them as a house present for Mama Selby, but decided against it. They were more or less naked Samburu maidens and entirely too pretty to be an acceptable house present.

The generator on the boat—the "Lady" had a refrigerator too—was a bit dicky also, so that took some work, and one of the reels jammed and that took some work, and then I decided to go duck hunting and that took some work, and then we went croc hunting and that took a lot of work.

I will tell you a thing about Selby. Passing a camel through a needle's eye is child's play alongside hunting anything with Selby. If he hasn't got a mountain to walk you over he will take the year off and build one.

You would think that croc stalking could best be done in a boat. That is not so. We landed the boat around the corner of a mountain and stalked carefully over the king-size cobbles until we were in a position to miss the crocodiles and still have a decent excuse to fetch back to Burrows, who was now flag admiral of the *Lady of the Lake*, as she tugged at her anchor and threatened to break up on a lee shore.

I will say one thing for Selby, the Cautious Captain. He can shoot. He is currently in love with a tiny little toy, a Winchester .243, which has the flattest trajectory of any rifle I ever saw. Shooting well downhill off this mountain at a target area no bigger than a tangerine he nailed one croc under the bumps at a good five hundred yards. It made the water, but only barely, and surfaced at six hundred yards. Harry now had a target area the size of a small lemon, and when he squeezed off the croc turned over and showed a lot of white belly and a death thrash.

Turned out not to be the same croc. The first one was sick enough to make the same lee shore the "Lady" was headed for I took the dinghy and went away to dispatch him, and learned a cardinal truth in croc shooting. The real place to aim for is not under the bumps, but just behind the smile, where the wicked mouth turns up at the end of the long, lascivious grin.

I got a solid rest on my knees and popped the gentleman behind his smile, and you could see complete paralysis set in as his four legs spread and one long ripple went through his body. Even so he was far from being a pocketbook. I finally beached the boat and walked up and blew the top of his head off at a range of one foot, and now he was a pocketbook. We towed him home and gave him to the Molo to eat, and that was the end of another day's fishing.

The next day there were pictures to be taken and the rains were moving closer and the lodge had to be neated up and the provisions battened down and the generator secured and the local troops paid. All this time Juma and company were sulking because Ramadan isn't any fun even when it's cool, and Lake Rudolf is certainly not cool if you're not drinking ice water. We had a freezer full of frozen fish the Molo had caught for us, and a few whistling teal, which make the most delightful eating of any fowl I ever tasted. I had caught two fish, Selby had caught none, Burrows had caught three, and the Molo boat boy, using a hand line, had caught several.

The time had come to leave. We struggled painfully straight up the Valley of Death, made a camp outside of Baragoi, and it was in Maralal that we saw the twin Samburu chicks, and everybody said, "*Wacha!*" at the same time. "*Wacha*" means "No!" We had been away from home too long, especially the multiple-wived Moslems.

We developed a blockage in the oil feed that caused several pleasant stops, and some years later we arrived at Harry's farm in Limuru, magnificently filthy, bone-weary, and green-whiskery.

Mrs. Mickey Selby met the heroes at the door. "Catch any fish?" she asked.

"Some," we said. "Enough."

Next day in Nairobi everybody said, "Where have you chaps been?"

"Fishing," I said stoutly, ready to swing on anybody who would say me nay. "And I never had a better time in my life."

It was true, because as the Old Man was often heard to say, "Fishing doesn't actually happen. It just goes on in your head."

18

Voodoo in the Skillet

Along about September, when the first tart whisper of coming autumn crisps the breeze and the dogs begin to stir restlessly, I always seem to get hungrier than usual. As Havilah Babcock says, "My health is better in November," and my stomach starts to grumble a bit more vociferously when October beckons.

It is not that summer's butter beans and sweet corn are inferior to a pumpkin, even with frost on it, or that the stanch line of rich, red-fleshed tomatoes and an infinite variety of sea food are not nourishing fare, but they lack the tang of autumn, the crackling authority of anything that is flavored with wood smoke. There is still an excitement to camp cookery that cannot be counterfeited by all the back-yard barbecues in the world.

"If I had it to do all over again," the Old Man once said, "I would like to be born black and be a professional hunting cook. Seems to me that apart from being a dead pig in the sunshine there ain't a healthier way to work your way through life. And it's a heap more practical than being a pioneer."

They may possibly have disappeared from the scene, but there used to be a considerable fraternity of outdoor professional chefs. They worked only when fishing and hunting were at their height, which is to say about six months a year. They "laid up" the other six months and lived off their fat.

The specialist was by no means a servant. His cook fire gave him as much professional recognition as attaches to a good guide in Canada or a professional hunter in Africa. He was an autocrat of his outdoor kitchen, brooked no interference, took no advice, and was likely to be severely critical of the hunting or fishing techniques of his clients.

The closest modern parallel is the seasoned African safari cook, like my Aly or Mwende of recent experience. Aly is a coastal Swahili, a good part Arab, and a man I would choose to be my father if I needed a spare. He's as wrinkled as a prune, a sort of medium brown in complexion, and I should say is possibly the best cook for my tastes in the world. Mwende, who is a Wakamba, has been around so long that he was second boy when Philip Percival first took Ernest Hemingway safariing about thirty years ago.

These are Africans of great dignity, professionally grave and almost winsomely charming, as opposed to that rogue Juma, who looks like a carbon of Mickey Rooney and is a kind of priest. He is currently wearing a new set of gold front teeth, shamelessly wheedled out of me on the last expedition. This was his due, he said, because when he went methodically through my box I had brought along nothing worth stealing this trip. At last count Juma owned more of my clothes than I did.

But whether they come from Mombasa or Machakos or

Southport, North Carolina, these outdoor African chefs have a special thing in common. They can take a tin cracker box, a shovel, and a heap of glowing coals, and turn out a meal to make a French chef commit suicide out of sheer envy. I don't know how they do it, but they do.

My old Aly, for instance, uses heaps of coal of varying intensity of heat, depending on what he's cooking. He bakes a crusty, light-golden loaf in one cracker tin by heaping the coals on its top. He sears a piece of meat on a hot flame, then moves it to a back burner of damped coals, while he broils a fowl on another fire, cooks a game leg-enriched soup on a third, boils spaghetti on a fourth, or uses still another to render a chunk of fresh-killed eland suitably tender for tomorrow's broiling.

My wife is a good cook, with a lot of experience and a great deal of imagination, but she had only one try at reforming Aly's kitchen techniques. When his version of her mother's mo-lasses-*cum*-bacon-*cum*-onion special beans turned out better than the old lady's she tossed in her chef's cap and left Aly to his own devices. In the screaming middle of Tanganyika Aly gives you breast of guinea under glass and has been known to produce a soufflé so light that you have to put weights on it to hold it to the table top.

When I was a kid in Carolina we had a succession of Alys. One, I remember, was a paroled murderer, but what he did with fresh-killed venison chops over hickory coals was worthy of official pardon. He could also stick an unplucked duck into a clay mold and cook it until the clay cracked; you peeled off the clay, which took the feathers with it. He did the same thing with a fish, and its scales came off with the clay. I don't know the details of this gentleman's fit of ill temper that sent him to the jug for a spell, but given enough corn whisky and a free hand he could turn an aged shitepoke into a symphony.

Several things distinguished cooks who worked only for sporting gentlemen. I never knew one, not one, who didn't operate in a vapor of alcohol—except of course the Swahilis, who are Moslems and are not supposed to use booze. But mainly, the drunker they got off hand-hewn corn or home-stomped wine the better they cooked.

Another thing: They couldn't stand anybody in their alfresco kitchens. You went back to the cook fire and made some mild recommendation about the quail stew or the rabbit ragout, and you got a less-than-mild admonition to confine your energies to missing fewer quail or to bringing home a better brand of bunny. And there was generally some pouting crack such as: "Mah mouth waterin' for some deer liver, but ah notice ain't no-body fetched in no tender spike buck yet. How y'all gentlemen 'spects me to cook what ah ain't got ah is hard put to say. . . ."

Properly chastened, you went out and clobbered anything with horns, even a stray goat, just to keep the cook from sticking out his underlip.

If you were hunting anywhere at all close to salt water oysters always figured heavily in the menu—oysters and any fish, like a blue or a mackerel, that was fat enough to sputter his own grease into the low-blue-tongued broiling fire. The oysters got roasted in a kelp blanket, and sometimes when I think about those oysters, drowned in a peppered sea of heat-bubbling butter, I just want to sit right down and cry. There'd be a fat mackerel, his hide cracked from the heat, much of his surplus oil dissipated in his own cremation, falling apart from the sheer thoroughness of his preparation, with only a sprinkle of pepper and a slight douse of vinegar. . . . Brother, pass the plate.

Somehow the coffee made from leaf-dyed branch water had an extra-special tang, and enough smoke got mixed up in the eggs and bacon—not these silly, slim strips of bacon, but a decent hunk of hog meat—to make an adventure of it. And the sowbelly that flavored the beans had enough character to transmute a string bean into an art form.

Possibly the idea of a possum may revolt you, because he's certainly a filthy beast and horrid to look at, but a Mose or an

Ike had a certain talent for bastioning the rendered-down marsupial with enough sweet taters and onions to make an innocent believe that he was eating his way across France. In the same vein, I shunned wart hog for a long time until the white hunter Don Bousfield conned me into trying a young one. It makes American pork repulsive by comparison. Since the African wart hog is an active animal it doesn't run to fat, so the meat is as lean as fowl.

I would like to insert here that I have eaten elephant's heart, and found it nothing much but rubbery and tough. The foot tastes like pickled pig's feet, and has the same gristly cellular structure. And when once I presented my idea of how to grill a kudu fillet to Aly, even the hyenas spurned the refuse. But roast grasshoppers ain't bad; taste kind of like shrimps in batter.

I think that the bread the old-timy hunting cooks used to produce was possibly the best flour or corn-meal combination I ever encountered. There was a large, plum-black gentleman named Joe, who worked for the late Paul Dooley in a snake-infested camp in the Everglades, and he could make a golden corn bread on an open fire—a corn bread that had the consistency of cake. Joe was kind of handy with hush puppies, too, and when you scraped off the ash they went away in a bite. A hush puppy (which ain't nothing but a hoecake) dipped into the mud-and-oyster-flavored butter in which the oyster has bathed is a kind of gastronomic experience that is too good for most people and should be licensed.

Joe, like most hunting cooks, was a lover of extreme scope, but instead of orchids he took rabbits to his ladies fair. We always went hunting at Grapefruit Gulch with a stern admonition from Joe to assassinate a mess of rabbits, because he had his eye on that fat gal over the hill.

One day Paul and I, with Lee Hills and Walker Stone (the latter two sort of disreputable newspaper executives), went out in the swamp buggy and put the hounds onto an Everglades wild boar. They fetched him squealing by the ears, and we shoved him—he was only a shoat, really—into one of the boxes in the back of the buggy.

Then we went back to camp and told Joe that we'd bad luck with the rabbits, but the dogs had caught one alive and he was in the beverage box in the back of the truck. Joe went out to retrieve his long-eared calling card, and came back stricken sore and almost gray.

"Ah open dat box and de rabbit *roar* at me," Joe said. "Ah don't want no truck wid no roarin' rabbits!"

Joe had a hard time out of us ruffians. Dooley took him to the Bahamas on his boat one time, and the weather was awful. Joe got so sick that his normal purple coloration doubled.

Later he said to me, "Ah swears 'fo' Gawd and three other 'sponsible witnesses, ah ain't nevah goin' to sea wid Mistah Dooley agin!"

Joe's off-duty hours were devoted to romance, although in the Bahamas he had no rabbits to serve as entree. But shortly after he recovered from his mal de mer, a certain covey of comely maids were in evidence. I asked Joe how he arranged this collation of beauty so swiftly.

"Ah tells you, Mistah Bob," he said. "It *so* simple. Ah jes goes asho' and makes a play fo' de old, ugly gals, and in no time de word jes' spreads."

The world is so full of nobility and stupidity and other "itys" these days that I have almost forgotten the wonderful simplicity of a hickory-chip-fire smell, the tiny beacon of light presaging a massive breakfast sandwich of hot egg and bacon on fat-fried bread, with a rich African voice singing something like "Go Down Moses," and the dogs whimpering with eagerness to be off, the coffee bubbling, brownly inviting, the smell of greased gun, and the last star dropping in the sky. The whole promise of a great day was before you, the dew was wet and so were the noses of the dogs, and any one of fifty Joes was going to do something miraculous with the skillet by the time you'd come home, dead tired but almost blissfully, impossibly happy.

You know, I think the Old Man had a good idea. I can't wait to be reborn black, but I think I'll get myself a job with some rich folks as a hunting-fishing cook and lay down this weary writin' load.

19

Dogs, Boys, and the Unspared Rod

Every time I see in the papers where some young thug is up for
casual murder or senseless assault and every time I see a picture
of a man who has just made chairman of the board from a
standing start of nothing I get the same sensation: a distinct
tingling in the caboose or rear end. It dates back to being a
boy and having a respect for law, order, and eventual achievement imprinted onto my behind with a stick, switch, or limber
lath. I sometimes think we don't beat our children, wives, and
dogs frequently enough these days, or there'd be fewer creatures
who mug strangers, get divorces, and jump onto gentlemen
wearing blue suits.

That notion came into my head the other day when little
Satchmo, just turned three (which is twenty-one the way hu-

mans count time), got all excited because it was the heat season around here, and Satch hasn't met any girl dogs, formally or informally. Satchmo is a boxer who looks just like his namesake, one Louis Armstrong, who plays a trumpet and sings in graveled tones.

This juvenile delinquent Satch got all excited about a bitch across the street being in season, and he took it out on his toothless father in a completely senseless but very fierce attack. I suddenly found myself in the midst of the fray, beating a three-year-old boxer on the back of the neck with my bare fist. The beating didn't have much effect on the boxer, although I came out of the incident with jammed knuckles, a swollen hand, and two very decent accidental bites.

But what did have an effect on the sap-risen little man was a session in the back room with a very heavy Texas-type belt. It has been a long time since I really walloped a dog. I had forgotten that dogs and children can use a tanning once in a while, when they get too big for their britches, and my own rear end tingled as it remembered a few unpleasant afternoons I had experienced on the receiving end of the strap in the woodhouse. "Spare the rod and spoil the child" was a phrase I heard quite often around my house when I was a young'un, and I can assure you I was not spoiled.

Satch isn't spoiled as of today, either, and I can practically promise you that he isn't going to be chewing on his toothless papa any more. But the strange thing is that one sound licking has made a new man out of what had been a shamefully pampered puppy. Satch has fresh dignity. He also responds to commands. He also doesn't get on the wrong sofas or jump up on the guests. And he seems to look at the boss with a new, if rather puzzled, respect. I wonder if I wasn't a couple of years late with the belt business.

The two people who knew most about dog training—working dogs, I mean—that I ever met were the Old Man and a fine black gentleman named Ely Wilson. Wilson was better than the Old Man, if that's possible, and I seem to remember

now that he used to cut himself a whippy switch when a particularly headstrong puppy persisted in running up birds or
failed to respect another dog's point. Ely, a very kind man
whose animals adored him, would take this limber switch, and
in the words of the Carolinas simply "wear out" the youngster
while saying, "Whoa!" with every lick.

This was momentarily unpleasant to the puppy, but very
shortly, when Ely hollered, "Whoa!" the dog associated the
word with a limber stick and whoaed. His dogs still retained
the high spirits that made them superb in their business,
which was quail finding, but they now worked as executives
instead of free-lance hot-rodders with strange haircuts.

The Old Man had a trick about retrieving that was also a
little hard on the animal at the time, but generally turned out
feather-perfect retrievers. It was more or less a gradual process,
such as teaching the Boy to be careful with a gun first, before
he taught the Boy the business of ballistics and lead-off angles,
by merely making the Boy try to hit a running cousin with a
stream of water from a hose. (The Boy, I might say, grew up
to be a gunnery officer in the Navy, and had remarkable success in teaching lead-off angles to green gun crews with the old
hose technique of pointing ahead of what you want to hit, so
that the target and the water merge at a logical time and
place.)

"This puppy"—Sam or Pete or Tom or Joe—"is a mortal
cinch to chew up the first quail he ever lays mouth to," the
Old Man said. "So first you catch him in the act. You have
already taught him to fetch a stick or a ball, even if you have
to wind him in on a length of rope. Now you got to convince
him that this bird you shot is not a stick or a ball, but somethin' you want delivered intact when you holler, 'Fetch!' "

"Yes sir," I seem to remember saying. I had been taught to
say, yes sir and please and thank you, and I knew that little
boys should be seen and not heard at the table. I had been
taught this painfully, as I had been taught to fight a plaguing
little monster named Wendell, who wouldn't let me out of the

yard. I would run and cry when Wendell fell upon me. The Old Man took a stick to me. "It's just a matter of who hurts you the worst," he said, "me with this stick or that little boy you run from. Because every time you run from Wendell I'm goin' to lay this lath on your backside, until you go back and fight him."

Wendell and I have been friends now for about thirty-eight years, give or take a month. The battle could have been called a draw. The Old Man broke the stick over his knee and gave both us battered kids a nickel to buy ice-cream cones.

"Now," the Old Man said, "in this business of training a puppy to bring you back the bird with its feathers nice and dry and the meat unchawed there ain't no sense beating the dog for mouthing a bird. The dog is a young'un and the bird is still warm, maybe even still alive a little bit. If you beat the dog he'll figger that you're beating him for getting the bird for you. What do you do?"

"I dunno, sir," I said. One of the things you learned around the Old Man was that a confession of innocent ignorance was very often to be preferred to smart-aleck error or even to smart-aleck nonerror. The Old Man was like a boy in a way: He didn't want to be deprived of a chance to show off once in a while.

"Well I'll show you. Now, suppose you see if you can hit the next bird the dog points, and after you've shot hang onto old Frank with one hand and the puppy with the other, and let me be your bird dog."

Frank stood a covey, and I hit with the first and missed with the second. The first bird fell in a shower of feathers in an easy patch of ground peas. Frank was trained to hold a point until the fetch command came. I hollered, "Hold!" and made a dive for the puppy, managing to collar both dogs.

The Old Man went over to where the drifting feathers had settled on the peanut stalks and bent over the dead bird. In a minute he said, "Now hang onto the old dog. Holler 'Fetch!' and let the little feller go!"

Off bounded the puppy, looking for the bird, while the Old Man said steadily, "Dead, dead, dead." And the puppy located the bird and pounced on it with a hard mouth, full of sharp puppy teeth. The puppy bit down on the dead bird and let out a horrified yelp. He dropped the bird, spat out some feathers, and stood looking at the bird with his ears cocked.

"Now fetch dead," the Old Man said. "Bring it here. Give it to me. That's a good boy." These were commands the puppy had learned in the back yard training sessions, over the tin pie plate of food. The puppy picked up the dead bird very gently now and brought it to the Old Man, as if he might be very happy to get rid of it.

The Old Man handed me the bird and grinned. He had used one of the oldest dog-training tricks in the world, I guess. He had merely taken a broad rubber band, studded it with needle-pointed tacks, and slipped it around the dead quail's body. When the puppy chomped down on the dead bird the bird more or less bit back. Puppy's teeth are sharp, but half-inch tacks are sharper.

"He might forget and mouth a bird again," the Old Man said. "I doubt he will, but you keep this rubber band handy in your huntin' coat, and if he does mouth a bird again give him another dose of the same treatment. About two doses is generally enough. Dogs ain't generally as big fools as people."

The Old Man entertained some sort of premise that it was nice to try to reason with a dog or a boy, but if the dog or boy didn't listen to reason then you had to find some way to impress him that wrong was wrong, good was good, and black was not white. He was all for the initial ounce of prevention, but he generally had a long ton of cure in reserve.

I don't know if he invented the choke collar or not. But we had a magnificent lemon-and-white English setter named Sandy that had a nasty habit of stealing other dogs' points, breaking to shot, and occasionally running up coveys out of sheer jealous arrogance. The Old Man went to the local blacksmith shop and had a short consultation with the boss, and eventually, in a shower of sparks, emerged with a slip-noose collar that seemed to be constructed of sharp-nailed fingers.

"Next time Frank points and Sandy starts to steal it I'm going to drape this thing around Mr. Sandy's neck. When he bolts you'll hear me holler, 'Whoa!' Don't pay no attention. Just go ahead and shoot. I'll be in command of the rest of the situation."

It was sort of difficult to work this mousetrap operation with coveys, because Sandy was a winder and a far-ranging, high-headed genius with a radar nose. Frank was the single-bird expert, and a lot of his careful, close work was wasted by the arrogant Sandy's rushing around fool-headed in close cover. Sandy could generally manage to run up more birds out of shooting range than Frank could nail with his Swiss-watch accuracy in finding singles, after the flushed covey scattered in the broom or on the edge of the branch.

It came about one day that Frank pinned a single in a patch of scrub pine, and Sandy came up behind and—as easily, as gently, as craftily as a cat burglar—began to encroach on the point. He was so intent on theft that he paid no attention when the Old Man more or less lassoed him with this strange, cruel-looking collar. All of a sudden he made his pounce, flashed by Frank, and flushed Frank's private bird. I shot and killed the bird just after I heard the Old Man yell, "Whoa!"

Then I turned and saw the Old Man hanging onto a lead, with a half-choked lemon-and-white English setter, his eyes bugged out, on its other end.

"I believe that if there's crime there ought to be punishment," the Old Man said. "Sandy is a criminal. I have just taught him a lesson they used to teach highwaymen in England. If you steal you hang. Hanging is not pleasant, is it Sandy?" He slacked the line and took the choke collar off the dog's neck. He patted Sandy on the head. "The next time I holler 'Whoa!' you'll whoa, all right. And," he said to me, "the next batch of singles we hit we'll slap this collar back on Mr.

Sandy again, and see if we can't restrain his high spirits by exerting just a *gentle* pressure on his neck with my tailor-made gallows rope. Just sort of play him out a little bit, like you'd play a fish."

I came up through several dynasties of dogs: pointers, setters, spaniels, just plain fice dogs with back-curled tails, and even one hybrid that seemed to be at least one part muskrat, judging from his appearance. They all worked well. They answered the whistle and brought the dead birds—even doves, which they hated because of the free-falling feathers—and they back-stood each other and slowed down on singles and watched where the ducks fell and responded to a waved hand when they were hunting very far out.

Only one I remember as a natural. The rest learned it through the tough back-yard discipline: first the commands with food and the tossed ball; next the switch; and finally through such refinements as choke collars and tack-studded rubber bands. Mainly they were dogs to be proud of, and they seemed to be proud of themselves once they worked the orneriness out of their systems.

"You can't give a dog a nose," the Old Man said. "Only God can teach him to smell. But by the Lord Harry, you can teach him decent manners, and you can teach him to use what nose he's got to the best advantage of all of us.

"You might remember," the Old Man continued, "when you grow up and have some young'uns of your own, that the word *whoa* is a valuable word for a child as well as a puppy, since children ain't nothin' but puppies anyhow. And that a lecture accompanied by a sharp rap on the rear has more weight than a lecture without the sharp rap on the rear. I will ask you a question to prove it. What should little boys be at the table?"

"Seen and not heard," I replied. Man, I'd been through *that* one before, and I didn't need a choke collar.

A few years ago the first view halloo over the pooch the Russians sent winging into outer space in the sputnik aroused a strange reaction around the world. Possibly the Arabs were not concerned, since to the average Arab a dog is a miserable *miskeen* of a creature fit only for kicks and slow starvation.

But the rest of the world, even the Russians themselves, suddenly got all upset over this poor Fido whirling around the globe in an ersatz satellite, eating when his Pavlov-developed reflexes answered a bell, and finally dying in his unearthly kennel. Now indeed, in human indignation, was science fiction married to fact. Somebody was mistreating a dog. The outcry was loudest in Britain, but most of the world's journals abandoned scientific speculation for front-page evaluation of the pup's chances of homing back to this globe.

It was touching and shocking, in that it took a small bitch to bring the world face to face with reality, and all of a sudden the Old Man's figure towered tremendously in my mind over Khrushchev, Einstein, and all the scientists and technicians everywhere, who dealt in armament larger than a twelve-bore shotgun.

The Old Man would have been real mad about this mutt being perverted into a dog in the moon. He had very strong ideas about dogs, and none of them included putting a pooch in a pressureproof kennel and shooting him out of a rocket into the stratosphere to die in loneliness with no fleas to scratch and no human hand upon his head.

"Dogs," the Old Man used to say, "are a cut better than people, and should be treated according to their station and their worth. Even a trash dog has got a certain nobility about him, and should be allowed to pursue happiness in his fashion."

A trash dog, by the Old Man's definition, was any dog who had no real function by which he earned his food. A Dane, a Peke, a poodle, a pug, each was trash in the Old Man's reckoning. A yaller cur that would run rabbits, a back-curl-tailed fice that would tree squirrels, any bastard brindle of bulldog-*cum*-hound that would run a deer, even a hearty cocker spaniel that would work in the woods were borderline between trash and quality.

The quality started with purebred Walker hounds, big

springers, Chesapeakes, and beagles, hovered momentarily over setters of all breeds except Irish ("You got to relearn the dodlimbed dogs every year, and they're as flighty as a red-headed woman"), and wound up with pointers. The Old Man mightily fancied pointers, and was willing to argue that while the Carolina briers would leave a pointer's tail bloody he was better fitted for hot bush work than a heavy-haired setter. He made only one exception: our big rangy Llewellin setter named Frank, a blue-ticked genius that knew integral calculus where quail were concerned, and was haired almost as thinly as a pointer.

I reckon the old gentleman owned as austere a set of ideas about dogs as anybody I ever met. I do not say he was harsh, but he was powerful stern.

For instance, he refused to pamper a working dog—a hound or a bird dog—by turning it into a house pet. He would compromise with a retriever, though—a spaniel or a Labrador—because the retriever's work was actually fun and couldn't be spoiled by steam heat or female coddling.

"A hound dog or a bird dog belongs to live outside the house," he said. "Bring him into the house except for an occasional visit, like Christmas, and you lose a good workman and get yourself a dodlimbed lap dog that won't hunt unless he feels like it, because he thinks he's as good as you. A good hunting dog is kind of religious. You ought to mortify his flesh a little bit to keep him in line. You keep him penned so he won't waste his energy ambling around aimless, and when you turn him loose he knows he's in business. Also, you keep him a little bit thin when he ain't working, so he won't be wheezing when the season opens. Then you feed him strong, because he'll run off what extra vittles you shove into him."

I don't know what the fashionable fare for hunting dogs is today, but we never had any cases of malnutrition on a more or less steady diet of table scraps, cold hominy, green vegetables, and corn bread. Old Galena and later Big Lil used to make enormous pans of corn bread for the animals, and to the best of my memory it tasted just as good as what we had on the table.

They were fed once a day, at 5 P.M., and they were fed together but in separate plates. Mostly our dogs were males, but there was no fighting. The Old Man discouraged fighting from puppyhood, by rebuking the combatants personally with a stick and then removing their meal.

"A greedy gut," he used to say, "has got more sense than a brain."

We gave them the cheapest butcher's meat once or twice a week, and once a week a can of salmon, which at the time cost about fourteen cents. For a treat there was an occasional tin of prepared dog food, and oddly enough (for this was well over thirty years ago) the Old Man dosed most meals heavily with fish oil. This was easy to come by and cheap, too, because we lived in a community that produced a great deal of fish-scrap fertilizer from the enormous shoals of pogies, or menhaden, that provided the village with a major industry.

It seems heretical now, but we also fed them whole fish and chicken bones. The Old Man's justification was simple.

"What is a dog?" he would ask himself rhetorically. "A dog is a descendant of a wolf. A fox is his cousin. What does a wolf eat? What does a fox eat? What he can catch: rabbits, birds, small game. In Alaska the huskies eat a steady diet of nothing but fish. All of this stuff has got bones. A dog's got enough quicklime in his digestive apparatus to melt an iron bar. If he gets something stuck in his throat he just throws up. You let any one of these modern pampered critters loose, and he'll eat or try to eat anything he comes across in the woods. He'll eat it, dead and rotten—fur, feathers, bones, and all. I never knew of a dog dying of indigestion, and up to now I never heard of one choking to death on a chicken bone."

It is very possible that I learned my first lessons in general sanitation, apart from discipline, from the Old Man and the dogs. After I graduated from being Mammy Laura's "do' boy," which meant that I was vice-president in charge of holding the kitchen door open for my ancient mammy, a former slave, I achieved the adult position at the age of about six of being the dog boy.

The dog boy's job was to see that the animals got fed promptly and to train the puppies not to attack their food until the command, "Hie on!" was given. Undue exercise of appetite was prevented by holding the puppies firmly by the tails and saying, "Whoa!" when they bolted for the food. In a week's time they ate on command.

Another chore of the dog boy was to see that every kennel was aired daily and that the pine straw that made the bed was replaced weekly. We built simple kennels—a big packing box, stilted dry off the ground on bricks, with a flap top that could be turned back on its hinges to let the sun in. Pine straw, I do believe, is still the cleanest and warmest material for a dog nest, as it seems to have some sort of aromatic resistance to insects. Also, it was great fun going out once a week in the towering (to a small boy) forests to sweep bagfuls of the clean brown needles in the hushed cathedral of the pine groves. If I was feeling especially virtuous I would also lug home a crocus sack full of the fallen cones, which made magnificent kindling and issued a lovely, almost incenselike smell—to grownups, that is. Me, I preferred the smell of baking bread.

The dog boy was simultaneously in charge of defleaing, and in the rare instances when mange crept unbidden into the run it was the dog boy who cured himself as well as the afflicted animal with a tremendously potent mixture of burnt crankcase oil and sulphur. Neither the dog boy nor the dog smelled so good as formerly, but the mange generally departed.

Today I know that most things seem better in retrospect, but I cannot begin to tell you the thrill there is in taking a hand-trained puppy, a puppy you've sweated through babyhood, adolescence, manners, mange, and his natural exuberance of spirit, into the woods and have him make *you* look good in front of your elders.

"Dogs are kind of like people," the Old Man said once.

"You generally get out of 'em what you put in 'em. There's good dogs and bad dogs, dumb dogs and smart dogs that are actually too big for their britches, but, mainly speaking, you can correct up or down and get yourself a decent four-legged citizen if you go about it right. A taste of the switch and a little explanation as to why, and you got yourself a dog that won't run rabbits and a boy that won't stick up banks."

Every time I read a new headline about that poor dog in the sputnik the Old Man kept coming back stronger than the beep. It had nothing to do with the sacrifice of dogs for science or any undue sentimentality about animals, as we know that a great many animals have died that people may live. It was just a sense of outrage at the unfitness of things, at the futility of using a dog—good, bad, or indifferent—where a dog didn't belong.

"A working dog," the Old Man said, "don't belong to live in the house. A pet dog don't belong to live outside the house. A pet dog is different from a work dog, but all dogs have a dignity that ought to be respected. And any lost hound worthy of his grits will eventually find his way home."

I guess what made me real mad was that this critter wasn't ever going to find her way home, and the fault was not hers. Somehow a dog has too much dignity to get her tail caught in any kind of machine away up yonder where she can't hear a whistle.

20

Second Childhood Is More Fun than the First—I

A fellow I know turned forty the other day, and it had him mightiful down. Forty is a kind of rough year for a man. It is an October sort of year. You still wear the scars of old summer mosquito bites, but there is a prickling of frost on the pumpkin and there is more than a clammy hint of the winter crouching just behind the hill.

"I dunno what there is about forty," the Old Man said once, referring acidly to the antics of some male relative, who seemed to be trying to convince himself that his capacity for the local corn-squeezing was limitless. "Seems to afflict most fellers about the middle of their thirty-ninth year. Sort of a final fling before they give up what they think is youth and force themselves to settle down with the idea of livin' with a potbelly and a shiny head. You hear a lot of talk about women actin' flighty when they start to crowd thirty. I tell you the honest-to-John truth, a woman on the edge of what she calls middle age ain't half as fidgety and worrisome as a man."

The Old Man grinned, and fired his pipe. "Ever occur to you that you'll be forty someday?"

I guess I was about fifteen at the time, and sweating out every day that stood between me and a driving license, which became legally possible at sixteen. The idea of anybody being forty was outlandish, except for *old* people like my pa, who was nudging that ancient estate himself. It never occurred to me that the Old Man was any age at all. He had worn the same battered hat and the same shaggy mustache ever since I could remember. Even the yellow nicotine stains on the mustache hadn't changed since we started knocking around like men together, when I was summ'at sixish.

"No sir," I said. "It's too far off."

"It ain't as far off as you think," the Old Man replied. "You'll find out that it's just around the corner once you pass twenty-one and the years start to sneak up on you. The whole point, though, is not to miss nothing as they pass you by, and when you hit that real middle age don't let it fret you none. I reckon the years between forty and sixty are the best a man's apt to put in. He can do dang near anything as good as he could when he was a youngster, and what he can't jump over he's smart enough to walk around. Which would you say's the best dog we got, Frank or Sandy?"

"Frank," I said. I didn't even have to stop to think. "Sure, Frank." Our blue belton Llewellin had more bird sense in his backside than most dogs wear in their nose.

"Well," the Old Man said, "Frank's pretty near as old as me, if you average dog years into man years, and I sure ain't no spring chicken. What is the main thing you notice about Frank when he hunts?"

I thought for a minute. "Well," I said, "he don't make many mistakes. And he takes his time. And he don't run all over the place like a blame-fool puppy, pointing larks and chasing rabbits. He sure don't waste many steps, come to think of it."

The Old Man smiled approvingly. "There you got it in a nutshell. Now that Sandy's a good dog, and he'll steady down someday, but right now he's got to run a mile and a half and lift his leg on every bush in the neighborhood before you can impress on him with a stick that he's in the bird-huntin' business. When he runs up a covey it ain't because he don't know any better or hasn't been taught that it's wrong. He's just full of vinegar, and he hasn't learned to put the brakes on his spirit. When he cocks his ears and half-points a rabbit he's still playing. He knows damned well it's a rabbit and he's not supposed to notice it, but the puppy in him is just crying out loud for foolish expression and the rabbit is it."

It was beginning to look like a long day. Also it was in between seasons: too late for doves and too early for quail and ducks. It wasn't that I didn't like to listen to the Old Man, but when he started to philosophize somehow it always seemed to wind up with work, with me doing most of it. I looked hopeful and kept my trap shut.

"Sandy reminds me of you," the Old Man said. "Fit to bust with useless energy. He ain't happy with today. He's always over the next hill, looking for tomorrow. Right now you're fretting yourself sick about getting to be sixteen, so you can drive the Liz *legal*." He stressed the word "legal," knowing very well that I had been driving that old tin tragedy on the sly since I was twelve. "Sixteen'll get here fast enough, and so will twenty-one and so will forty and so will eighty, and then all of a sudden you're dead before you realize what happened to all the time you wasted worryin' about next Christmas when you ought to be happy with the Fourth of July."

The Old Man rubbed his pipe on his nose, and looked at me like he was expecting me to say something. I didn't oblige him. There didn't seem to be much point to me worrying about being forty or eighty. It was still about thirty-seven days, six hours, and forty-two minutes until the bird season opened, and about forty-nine days, seven hours, and nine minutes until school let out for the holidays, and my birthday would come during the holidays. . . .

"I know what you're thinking," the Old Man said. "You just can't wait for the time to pass until something that you can't do now gets to be possible, and then you'll worry about how long it is before you can do it again. You start to fret on Christmas Eve, because it'll be three hundred and sixty-six days until next Christmas. You ain't like me and Frank. We don't false-point and we don't run all over the place chasing stinkbirds, but we come home with the bacon more often than not, and we ain't all wore out when we get home to the fire either. You bleed for an hour if you miss a bird, and you're so busy worrying about the last one you missed, you miss the next one as well. There ain't no such animal as hindsight positive action. All you can do is wipe up the spilt milk and try to do better with the present, and let the future come up sort of gradual. You got to learn to live with what you got."

I begun to fidget. You can stand just so much high thinking on any given day when you are near-about sixteen. I wanted to *do* something.

The Old Man heaved a mock sigh. "I can see my fine-haired conversation is wasted on you," he said. "Suppose you just run upstairs to my room and get me another tin of Prince Albert, and then we'll go get arrested or something."

I came back down with the tobacco. "Let's go," I said.

"Where?" the Old Man asked. "You call it."

"Africa," I said. "I want to shoot a lion. Or India. I want to shoot a tiger. I want to do it today. I don't want to wait until I'm forty. Now, like you said. I don't want life to pass me by."

The Old Man grinned. "Purty sassy, ain't you? I reckon we don't run much to lions and tigers around here, but mebbe I can provide something in the way of one of them what-do-you-call-its for you. About time you blooded yourself on dangerous game." He grinned again and this time it was wicked.

"You ever read anything about them Bengal Lancers—the

British soldier fellers in India that go wild pigstickin'? Well, wrap a rag around your hat and call it a *puggree*, I think that's the name, and we'll go boarstickin'. Except in the case of this pig I expect we better use buckshot. We'll need some dogs. Just run over and ask Sam Watts if we can borrow a couple of his hounds. Bell and Blue'll do."

We tied up the bird dogs and slung the hounds in the back of the Liz. They lay flat on the back seat and drooled, their tongues lolloping sideways. Old Blue perked one coon-chewed ear. Cars meant guns, and guns meant hunting.

The Old Man looked at me kind of curiously. "Where's the tents? And the salt and pepper and fat back and coffee and sugar? What kind of pigstickin' expedition is this, anyhow? You don't expect to stick a pig and come home the same night, do you? It might take five, six days. You might even have to miss a little school. I reckon that'll worry you nigh to death, but sometimes you have to take the bitter with the sweet. And how about all the beaters and gunbearers and such as that? This ain't just any old kind of pigstickin' expedition."

"I don't know any beaters and gunbearers," I said. The Old Man had me on the run. "This is all new to me."

"I don't see nothing wrong with some of Big Abner's young'uns for beaters," the Old Man said, more or less to himself. "He can easy spare half a dozen. And I reckon Pete and Tom'll have to do for gunbearers. You better run down the road and tell them to be ready in half an hour. And tell Tom to bring his rifle. You can't tell what we'll run into in the jungle. Maybe a bobcat or a panther. Pity we haven't got any tigers, but I reckon you'll have to blame it all on geography. Somebody got careless and didn't apportion none of them critters to these parts."

Somebody must have got careless with Tom and Pete, too. I guess I've told you about them more'n once before. They were both lean, lantern-jawed, black-whiskered woodsmen, that some people said had a smidgen of Injun in them. They wore hip boots like other people wore shoes, in town and out, and they chawed tobacco constant. They made corn liquor in the winter, and drank it up in the spring. They fished in the summer and hunted in the fall. They worked a little bit when the menhaden—the pogies—were running and Mr. Charlie Gause's fertilizer factory was standing in the need of fish scrap. I reckon they forgot more about woods and water than most fellers ever learned, and they weren't above sharing it with me. They kidded me along, but it was gentle kidding. Pete was my special buddy. Tom, he was kind of surly sometimes. People said the Injun showed more strong in Tom, who could be a ringtailed bear cat in a rough-and-tumble, when a little homemade whisky took a firm hold of him. I never saw him cut up nasty any, though. Mostly what I remember about Tom and Pete was that they were in on the death of the first deer I ever shot, and they stuck my face into the deer's green, fodder-filled paunch.

"What's Ned Hall up to now?" Pete said, when I panted up to the house, after running all the way. The house was a weathered-gray, ramshackledy house, what paint it had flaking off in scabby stretches. The porch had a hole rotted in one end of its planking, and the steps sagged sort of slanchwise. Tom and Pete were squatted on the steps, whittling and spitting tobacco juice in the sandy yard. Seems like I never saw either one of them when they weren't doing something with a knife or a gun.

"He's decided to go pigstickin'," I said, out of breath. "You know him when he takes a notion to do something in a hurry. He said to tell you to bring the rifle, we might need it."

Tom looked at Pete, and Pete looked at Tom.

Tom grunted. "Pigs, huh?"

"That's what he said. He said you and Pete could be the gunbearers, and we could use some of Big Abner's young'uns for beaters. Something about the Bengal Lancers, I dunno, but he said get a move on."

Pete looked at Tom. He winked. "We was layin' off to fix up

the porch some," he said. "The old woman's been after us to hit a lick and fix it. You reckon . . ." He let the words drift.

"I reckon," Tom said. "It's been needin' fixin' for nigh onto three year now, and if she wasn't hollerin' about that it'd be somethin' else. Come on, Pete. If the old gentleman wants to stick a pig I reckon we best go help him out. Tell Ned we'll be ready when you come by."

I dashed off over the sand hill again, and I thought I could hear the men snickering as I ran. I didn't care if it was a snipe hunt. It was action, if it had Tom and Pete and two hound dogs mixed up in it, let alone pigs and Bengal Lancers.

The Old Man was pretty near ready when I got back. There was a stack of tentage and blankets and cooking equipment piled in a heap around the Lizzie.

"I already made some peace with your grandma," he said. "Go get your huntin' duds, and then help me load up this car. The boys coming? They ain't drunk or in jail or anything like that?"

"They're coming," I said. "They said they'd be ready when we drove by. But they seem to think there was something awful funny about this trip. Is there?"

"Not that I know of," the Old Man said. "Pigstickin' is a very serious business. A feller can get hurt with the right pig unless he handles him careful. Come on now, let's run off before Miss Lottie changes her mind."

We picked up Tom and Pete and crammed them, somehow, into the back seat of the Liz with the dogs and guns and pots and pans. We jounced along on the corduroy road on the way out of town, and suddenly the Old Man started to laugh. He laughed so hard he had to stop the car until he got his breath back. Tom and Pete, they begun to laugh with him. I sat there kind of hurt, because I didn't see anything to laugh at. I guess the Old Man must have noticed that I looked put out.

"Don't take it to heart," he said, "but does anything strike you as unusual about this trip—more than usual, I mean?"

"No sir," I said.

"Well then," the Old Man said, "look at us. Four grown men, past prime, two old flea-bit hounds, and a shirttail boy, all heading off to the jungles to play Bengal Lancer and stick pigs—at our age. I ain't apt to see seventy again any time soon, and if they'd of kept records when they whelped Tom and Pete they'd be easy fifty, fifty-two. And Bell and Blue are mighty near as old as you are, which makes them about a hundred years old apiece as dogs go. But away we rush off to the woods, like a bunch of young'uns playin' Injun. Remember what I told you earlier today about being forty years old ain't quite the end of the world?"

"Yes sir," I said. "I sure do." I looked around me at the Old Man and Tom and Pete and the dogs, and for a minute I felt older than any of them.

I told all this to my aging friend, the one who turned forty the other day, and was down in the dumps about it. He seemed to brighten considerably.

"Did you get any pigs?" he asked.

I said sure, we got some pigs, but I would tell him more later, after I soothed my old bones with a little painkiller.

You see, the Boy, which is me, had just turned forty-five, and was feeling his decrepitude in the joints.

21

Second Childhood Is More Fun than the First—II

The Old Man had squirreled away a supply of hand-hewn philosophy to fit most moods and conditions, and he was very fond of saying that a man was nothing but a boy grown old. He liked to say that if a feller was raised right it was powerful difficult to beat the boy out of him no matter how many hard knocks he absorbed in the painful process of achieving maturity.

"The measure of a grown man," the Old Man said, "is just how much tomfoolery he can get away with when he's got gray in his whiskers, without appearin' to be a damned fool. I ain't referrin' to coon chasin' and suchlike, because anybody that runs around tearing up his clothes in the woods at night behind a pack of hounds on the off-chance they'll tree a coon is just lookin' for an excuse to get drunk and fall in a briar patch."

The Old Man did not utter these sage words, however, when he and Tom and Pete, the half-Injun woodsmen, decided to quench my thirst for youthful adventure and whip me off on what he referred to as a pigstickin' expedition. We were, as I was saying, supposed to be what he called Bengal Lancers, and we were going to hunt pigs the hard way. Not sticking them with a lance, on horseback, as the Lancers did in India, but using hounds to course them, and after that it was every man— and pig—for himself.

In our neck of the woods we have what is called a razorback, a tame pig run wild and breeding to more wild hogs until he produces a wild animal every bit as mean as anything that started off in the swamps. He ain't so big as one of those Russian-y boars they have in the mountains, but he's just as ornery. He's spread out through the east Carolinas all the way down through the Everglades in Florida.

The first thing we did on this notable expedition was to stop at Big Abner's farm. Big Abner looked to be about seven feet tall. He was sort of purple black, weighed around two hundred and fifty pounds, and had about twenty children, or so it seemed. He also had several coveys of quail that used around his pea fields. He had some deer and turkey and foxes and wildcats that hung out in the big branch—swamp, that is—which ran through his property. And he had pigs. His eyes lit up when the Old Man asked him if he'd seen any lately.

"Yassuh, Cap'm," he said. "Sho is. Dey's a passel on 'em usin' down in de branch. One big old boar, too. I run him up t'other day, when I 'uz mindin' some traps, and he roar at me lak a lion. Got tushes on him turn right back to he eyes. Dat a mean hog. Got some mean sows wid him, too, and a whole mess o' shoats. I lak mighty well git ahold a couple of dem shoats befo' dey tough up lak de old feller."

"We thought we'd give the boy here a pig hunt," the Old Man said. "We got the hounds. But we need some mules and some young'uns. Come on over to the well and we'll work this thing out."

(The well, I knew, was where a half-gallon jug of scuppernong wine dwelt in the cool depths. By-and-by the grown men came back smiling.)

"We'll make us a camp," the Old Man said, "and we'll start out bright and early in the morning. We need a good night's rest for this business, You have the young'uns ready before light, hey Abner?"

"Yassuh, Cap'm," Big Abner said. "We be's ready."

We got back in the Liz and drove off the main road a few miles to a place we'd camped before, when we were after turkey or deer. It was on Abner's land, and it was a place nobody else ever used, because Abner was very strict about keeping his land posted. He leased a lot of land, mostly for the turpentine rights, and he didn't hold with strangers who were apt to set the broom grass alight with careless cigarettes and burn up a whole lot of valuable pitch pine.

It was lovely hunting country. There were big stands of tall longleaf pine, their boles chopped to make the pockets in which the big, waxy, grapelike clusters of sap gathered. If you knocked off one of these knobs of congealed sap it had the same consistency as chewing gum and was cleanly aromatic on the tongue. These big piny wood stands had very little undergrowth beneath them, because their tall umbrella tops shut out the sun. The ground underneath these great trees was strewn with long brown needles, as clean as a carpet and as slippery as glass. The sun made little golden pools and flecks of light on this carpet, but mostly the shade was as somberly solemn as a church. It got very spooky along about dusk, when the doves began to complain and the night air started to turn gently cool.

The tall pine thickets held to the high ground, but their outskirts were cutover patches of scrubby oak and seedling pine, with a lot of old dead stuff on the ground, making little hummocks and high ridges of fallen trees, lichened stumps, and shiny green gallberry bushes. These islands, for they were literally islands, were where you found most of the quail, after you'd started them out of the broom grass or the corn fields or pea patches.

Vast sweeps of broom sedge, dotted with the occasional islands, made up a rolling yellow sea. The quail roosted in the broom, away from the varmints that inhabited the swamps. Sometimes they flushed from the fields and scattered in the broom, and anybody with a good single-bird dog could shoot his limit if he was a mind to and didn't care about leaving anything for next year. But mostly the flushed birds pitched on sides of the swamps in the little islands, or sometimes flew straight through and dropped on the scrubby hills on the other side. They seldom lit in the big pine thickets—no cover—and even less seldom in the swamps—varmints.

But the deer and the wild pigs and the occasional wildcat haunted the swamps, as did the rare black bear. The deer and the pig fed out at night, wrecking the corn fields and rooting up the goobers. The pigs were particularly death on the pea fields, both peanut and black-eyed field peas, while the deer gourmandized young corn and the tender green rye.

"The plan of campaign," the Old Man was saying now, "is to pick up some pig sign and start the dogs. Then we'll send the pickaninnies in behind the dogs, some of them, and stake out some more on the flanks, and we'll beat them pigs right out into the open. We'll run 'em into the grass and ride 'em down on the mules. You, Boy," he said to me, "you're the head lancer. You're the boss pigsticker."

"What'll I stick him with?" I asked. "I plumb forgot to bring my lance."

"A pitchfork is plenty good enough to start with," the Old Man said. "If a pig gets close enough to bite you a pitchfork is all you'll need. Come in handy, especially if you fall off the mule."

"What'll *you* use?" I asked, kind of nervous. "Another pitchfork?"

"Nope," the Old Man replied. "I'm the head *shikari* of this shebang. I'm the native gunbearer. I'm too old for pitchforks. I'll stick to this old pump gun of mine. Tom's got his rifle and Pete'll back you up with his double barrel. But a real classy pigsticker shouldn't need any help from guns. It ain't supposed to be sportin', not the way I've read about it. Kipling wouldn't approve of it for certain."

Then everybody but me laughed again. It seemed to me that there was an awful lot of unnecessary laughing going on for a bunch of grown men. Mostly they were serious hunters, when it had to do with deer or ducks or quail or turkey, but every time anybody said "pig" somebody else snickered.

I won't trouble you with the camp making, because one good camp is just like another. That is to say, I did most of the work, such as chopping wood, splitting kindling, going for water, and cutting pine tops for beds, while the men lazed around investigating something ripe-smelling in a fruit jar. We had a fine meal of corn bread, fried ham and eggs, and I went to sleep wondering what devilment these grown-up children had in store for me.

I only had a short dream to wait before somebody shook me awake in the chill dawn and I scrubbed the sleep out of my eyes with my knuckles. By the time I'd been to the branch for water Big Abner and his tribe had arrived. He had evidently drummed up some nieces and nephews, for what appeared to be an army of young black faces swarmed around him. At least a dozen dogs of indeterminate breed accompanied Big Abner's relatives, and they were snapping and snarling amongst themselves. Old Bell and Blue, our borrowed hounds, looked sleepy-eyed and bored as the curs scuffled and yipped. Four mules, their ears drooping in the dawn's shifting light, were wearing battle array of wooden working hames and saddle blanket, with the reins looped over the hames. I noticed then that each of Abner's troop had a tin pot or pan of some description, and each carried a short club.

"Now," the Old Man grinned, "the idea is that you and me and Pete will ride out to the far end of the swamp, and take up stations in the broom grass. Tom will take Bell and Blue and go to the pea patch and pick up some hog sign. The hogs will naturally go into the branch, and then we'll turn the beaters and the other dogs a-loose. The beaters will pound on the pans and the other dogs will take up the trail, and if all goes well we'll beat the pigs back out into the clear. I think." The Old Man said in a loud aside to Pete and Tom, "I think this is the way you are supposed to do her. Personally, all I ever did was read about it in a book. If things go wrong I ain't responsible."

"What do I do in all this?" I asked. I wished I'd kept my mouth shut about wanting to go off to India to shoot tigers and Africa to shoot lions before I was too old to enjoy it.

"Why," the Old Man said, "it's the easiest thing in the world. You just kick the mule in the ribs and charge the pig. The pig will be charging you, of course, if he's worth the salt to cure him into a ham, and when you and the pig meet you kind of lean over the mule and stick him with the pitchfork. With all them hayfork tines I don't see how you can miss him. If you should fall off the mule I'd try not to lose a-holt of that pitchfork. These pigs can turn mighty nasty if they think they got you cornered."

I was mumbling when I climbed aboard the mule. Under that blanket the mule had a backbone any razorback hog would have been proud of. The mule turned his head and looked at me. He shook his head in what seemed to be disgust.

Tom took his mule by the reins and the dogs by their leads, and went off toward the pea field with his rifle tucked under one arm. Between the two hounds and the mule and the rifle he seemed to have considerable on his hands.

I had considerable on my hands, too, with this consarned mule. I never did put too much trust in horses, and none at all in mules, and this wall-eyed son of a roving jackass seemed to sense my lack of appreciation of his nobler qualities. He reminded me in some ways of a billy goat I had once, only he was bigger. And constructed a heap higher off the ground. They say mules have sure feet. This big gray critter stumbled and almost fell every time he took a step. It looked like half a mile from his back to the ground. Clutching the pitchfork with one hand, it was all I could do to hang onto him with the other.

We shambled along to the bottleneck end of the swamp, where the thick stuff cleared and emptied out onto the broom grass, and Pete and the Old Man didn't seem to be doing much better than I was. Mules, I reckon, ain't built to be ridden as a steady thing. Not even by Sancho Panza.

We got to the end of the swamp, and heard the dogs tune up and then settle into a steady belling as they hit a hot trail. The tune was loud and clear, and then suddenly was punctuated with angry growls and barks. Two rifle shots snapped in the keen morning air, and then there was a whole lot of yipping and yapping. Then came an unholy sound of pans and buckets being beaten with sticks, the clattering and banging relieved by squeals and growls and barking and yelling. I never heard such a mess of assorted noise in all my born days. There was a crashing of brush in the swamp on top of all the other noise, and I heard the Old Man let out a whoop and holler: "Get set! Here they come!"

And here they came, indeed. A couple of lengths ahead of the mob was a big old sow, with Blue hanging onto one ear and old Bell dug into another. The sow was making pretty good way in the grass, though, and she was squealing her head off, swinging her head from side to side while she tried to dislodge the dogs.

Behind the old sow came a litter of half-grown pigs, all squealing, and behind the pigs came all the fice dogs the Abner children had imported, and behind the dogs the Abner children were running, beating on the pots and pans and hollering fit to kill. Puffing behind the young'uns was Big Abner, and behind Big Abner was Tom, cussing steady and hauling away on his mule, which had its front feet braced and was giving Tom quite an argument.

One of the bigger pigs spied my mule and more or less charged it. I made a frantic stab at it with the pitchfork and missed, of course. The squealing pig ran between the mule's legs and the mule bucked and I flew through the air to land with a thump on the ground. Just before I was engulfed by a flood of pigs, dogs, and Negro children I heard the Old Man yelling: "Whoa, you dumb fool!" and some more sulphury cuss words before he hit the ground with a thump, too. I didn't see this happen, of course, being submerged in pigs and dogs, but Pete's mule got its head and run off under a low-hanging tree branch and scraped Pete off, knocking him cold for a minute.

It was quite a party, I reckon. Some of the smaller dogs took ear-holds on some of the smaller pigs, and the squealing increased. The problem of separating the dogs from the pigs seemed insurmountable until Big Abner produced some crocus sacks, and the pigs were sort of decanted from the dogs into the tow sacks, where they continued to kick and squeal. The big dogs, Bell and Blue, finally slowed the old sow down to a walk. She was too big to handle, so Big Abner hit her over the head with a club and tied her feet while she was dreaming. All told it was a pretty good haul: a half-dozen prime pigs and one sow for Big Abner to pen up against hog-killing time.

"Where's the boar?" I asked Tom, who finally came up without his mule. "Where's your mule?"

"Tied the damn thing to a tree," Tom said. "Shot the boar. He was too big to play with. Somebody might of got hurt. Wait'll you see them tushes. Big as a elephant. Lay a dog—or you—open like you'd rip into a sack of meal. He took two, Ned," Tom said to the Old Man. "I reckon him to be tougher'n a bear to kill dead."

"Jest as well you shot him," the Old Man said. "Our Bengal Lancer here, he fell off the mule right off, lost his lance, and got run over by the whole passel of hogs, dogs, and young'uns. I reckon that big old boar would of et him alive."

"I reckon I ain't the only one fell off a mule," I said. "I saw you fall off, and Pete got scraped off. I reckon that big boar would have et you-all, too, if Tom hadn't shot him in self-defense."

"It was either that or climb a tree," Tom muttered. "And not the first time, neither. I'd as live take on a panther as a big pig."

It turned out that the Old Man had told Tom to shoot the boar, because fun's fun and he didn't want any dogs or boys hurt in this horseplay, or pigplay, I reckon you'd call it. I understood why when we skinned out the pig. He had a hide on him nearly an inch thick. It was white like coconut meat under the thin black hair, but so tough Big Abner had to keep whetting his ripping knife when they were shucking off the hide. His tusks *did* curl up nearly to his nasty little eyes, but the tusks, Pete said, weren't what did the damage. He dug with his tusks, but fought with a jaw tooth that whetted itself sharp against the underside of the tusk, and would slash you like a knife. With his bristly reddish mane that stuck up from behind his big head and ran all the way to his haunches down his sloping spine he was as nasty a looking wild animal as ever I saw.

I guess I was a pretty sight, when we got the mules, pigs, hounds, fice dogs, pickaninnies, and other hog hunters back to camp. I was full of mud where I'd been run over by the pack, and owned a fresh set of bruises where I'd been tromped on. Tom and Pete and the Old Man seemed to think I was a very funny sight, and they kept kidding me about losing my pitchfork until the joke wore itself out.

"I reckon this boy will never make a real pig hunter in the classic tradition," the Old Man said that night, while fire warmed his feet and something else warmed his innards. "Some people are just born pig hunters; others ain't. Our young feller here just ain't a real dedicated pigsticker. We better give him back to the easy stuff, like birds. Certain sure thing I wouldn't trust him with tigers and lions."

I didn't say much then, but I was thinking just how little it took to amuse grown people. I was thinking the same thing not so long ago in Africa, several lions and tigers later not to mention years. I was having a high old time trying to get a wart hog to come out of a hole, and I wondered bitterly how the

Old Man would have managed it. This occurred to me when I was halfway up a thorn tree, after the pig *did* decide to come out of the hole. I reckoned I had finally become a pig hunter in the classic tradition, even if it was a little thorny coming down out of that tree.

22

Hold Perfection in Your Hand

There is a state of mind called October that always makes me remember a thing the Old Man once said about Christmas. "Christmas," he said, "is best remembered as the day after to-morrow."

A wealth of worldly sadness went into that one, but more than a treasury of truth. For some years now I have had my Aprils and Augusts, my Septembers and Februarys, but the only truly perfect month is October, because it is close enough to summer and close enough to Christmas and still not near enough to March to be rendered miserable. October is truly the month of the day after tomorrow.

I have been sitting here trying to recapture the elation of October and have been stumped. Do you base it on carven pumpkins or the slavering eagerness of hunting dogs who can't work until latish November or the fact that your pants hold their crease now that the unseasonable September weather has settled into cool crispness; persimmons wrinkling, perhaps, and the leaves glowing scarlet and gold against the pine green and the last of the grapes on the vines?

The Old Man said that October was the only perfect month of the year, because it was a month that really didn't have to *do* anything to justify itself. All it held was present perfection, beautiful memory, and magnificent promise. The Old Man was a great hand for cataloguing the seasons, and I'm afraid some of it wore off on me. What he really hated was March, and he was kind of bored with August until it turned into September and all the summer people went back to where they belonged.

October in my neck of the woods was a time when you had got used to the calculated torment of school once more; I mean, to where education didn't physically hurt you any longer. The football season had started, but you could still play a little side-bar baseball if you wanted to, because the World Series was still topical. And it was cold enough for a ceremonial fire at night.

We shook the bloom off the doves in September, but the trees were dropping sufficient leaves now so that you could see a squirrel, instead of just knowing he was there. We had had the big rails—the marsh hens—in the first nor'easters with the full-moon flooding tide. A few transient ducks—teal—were beginning to drop in, and you knew that the first really cold snap would fetch a mess of mallards.

Out in the back yard the dogs were going noisily, frustratedly mad. The high grass was dying, they knew, and the quail were calling, and the dogs were being restrained from hearing the pleasant sound of gunfire and savoring the wondrous odor of burnt powder on the late-afternoon air.

October was the month for torturing the young dogs. You took them out and worked them on quail, using a choke collar if necessary, and firing a pistol to get them to hold to gun. But we never worked the old pros, because they had enough problems when the season started just before Thanksgiving, and we didn't want to confuse the reflexes. Sometimes I wondered who'd go crazy first, me or the old dogs. You would nail a covey in a patch of peas and the birds would hold to a point perfectly and then fan out into an ideal singles situation in a pasture of broom grass. And there you were, stranded with a .22 pistol, a choke collar, and a puppy.

The old dogs would know it when you came back and they'd snap at the young'uns, and then you would go and take down the shotgun and inspect it for the merest fleck of rust. You'd groan and think, would it never get to be November so you and the old dogs could go out and deal with these speckled bombshells properly? It would get to be November, all right, but it would take six centuries, so in the meantime you sort of had to do something after prison hours, when Miss Clifford or Miss Struthers turned you loose on the free world.

So you took a man's knife with a sawing edge for scaling fish on its blade top, a fishing rod, and a tackle box full of such things as four-ounce pyramid sinkers and long wire leaders, and you went to the beach to start a rumble with the bluefish, which were, by now, invading your turf.

A Carolina beach in October is a thing that would have captured Van Gogh's tormented paintbrush. The wind-tortured little scrub oaks all bend in the same direction. There are long dunes of really high hills with crape myrtles helping the tiny oaks. There are vast rolling waves of sea oats, like wheat rippling in the wind, and over-all an air of wonderful loneliness that is invaded only by the silvered gulls, slanting in the breeze, and the saucily tipped-up sandpipers. And then there would be the fish.

The nor'easters start in September, and by the time October rolls around in its golden glory the wind-built tides will have cut tremendous sloughs between the protecting barrier reef and the beach proper. All manner of small fish and a great many sand fleas inhabit these sloughs. The water was icy around our knees when we stepped in to cast, because we scorned waders in those days—I doubt if they were even made, though hip boots were made—but we slung that four-ounce lead pyramid out into that slough and we didn't have to wait long for action.

We always used diagonally sliced strips of salt mullet for bait, because it would hang onto a hook, whereas the crashing waves would disengage a shrimp, a feeble creature at best. A good slab of mullet, with the hook worked through it three or four times, would withstand a typhoon. We used a double leader with two baited hooks, and when the dark evening came and the moon began to peep the local suckers came to call.

Any man who has ever tied into *two* channel bass ranging up to twenty pounds each will carry the memory of it to his grave. The big white fellows with the black spots were there, and so were the speckled sea trout, and so were the big, mean-mouthed bluefish that later sputtered so happily in the pan. A couple of three-pound blues, striking at the same time and heading in opposite directions, could create considerable diversion for the gentleman with his hand stuck into the reeling apparatus of an old-time surf-casting rig. Not so much diversion as would the puppy drum—the channel bass—but enough to stifle a yawn.

There was usually a well-weathered shack nearby, with a tin stove that was dangerously heated by its kerosene fuel. And around ten at night, with your hands freezing red and wrinkled from the sea and your body just one big goose pimple, the snug harbor of that salt-rimed shack was like a preview of heaven. But if there wasn't a shack at close hand you dragged together a pile of driftwood and built a fire on the beach, and thawed yourself out before the leaping blue flames of the salt-impregnated fuel. Hunger clutched at your belly and the cookin' was easy. You gutted a bluefish, stuck him on a stick, and let him baste himself with his own fat. His hide cracked as he cooked, but inside he was sweet as peaches.

Apart from the cold it was marvelously spooky on an October beach, with the warped, stunted oaks casting strange shadows in the fitful moonlight and the wind soughing sadly through the myrtle. All the ocean was out there, broad-striped by a moon path, and it stretched across all the world, the world you were mad to see but never really reckoned you would. Over there, somewhere, were Europe and Africa and China, and underneath the surface of that wind-tossed silvered sheet were all the secrets you would never know: sunken galleons, treasure troves, great fish, sea serpents. . . . You shivered deliciously, and not from cold.

This was a part of October. A better part was the opening of the deer season, when you took a stand in the autumn-changing woods and listened to the hounds, the bugling ever closer, now fading as the running buck changed course, the belling now rising, now falling. You always knew that the deer would be a half-mile or so ahead of the coursing pack, but you never really expected to see him when he burst out of the bushes, his rack laid back as he split the breeze.

What I mean is, it was asking too much to really *see* a deer. Other people did, maybe, but it could never happen to you. Until it did. And then the buck fever, as you stood there gawking like an idiot and just watched the deer run, with the dogs panting up a couple of minutes later looking pretty sour, because they'd done their job of work and had expected to hear rewarding gunfire at the end of it.

There was the business of retrieving the hounds that never quit running a deer until he hit the lake and left his pursuers frustrated at the edge. Sometimes one of your best hounds wouldn't show up for a week or you would get a phone call from a farmer in the next county saying that Old Bell or Old Blue had arrived in a ramshackledy condition and would you please come fetch your dog?

Come to think, there was so much to *do* in October, while you waited for the serious business of the quail and the ducks to start in November, if it was only playing Tarzan in the shrimp house. And thereby hangs the major tragedy of a life that has known considerable pain.

It was the end of October, and the dogs were fighting fit and the puppies behaving well, and soon the bird season would open. (In North Carolina when you said "bird" you meant one thing—quail.) Soon the bird season would open, and I had spotted the using grounds of every covey in Brunswick County or almost. We had a limit of fifteen in those days, and I figured that if I hunted six days a week I would average out at ninety birds a week until March 1. You cannot call me bloodthirsty; I was just optimistic.

October birds have a way of knowing when the season starts, and coveys that come when you call in October decide to spend the winter in Cuba or Jamaica or some other exotic place. No matter where or how closely you had them taped, come that fateful day of legality they leave a Miss-Otis-regrets note, and all you rouse is a fieldful of larks. No matter. Eventually you catch up with the little brown scoundrels and miss them to your heart's content.

My tragedy was this. In a spate of boredom we were playing Tarzan in the shrimp house and swinging from rafter to rafter in the best approved manner. I missed a swing, and when I got up off the floor my left wrist had a most curious-looking sag in it. It didn't hurt, but it sure was busted.

I began to cry, because here it was the end of October and November was just over the hill, and I wasn't going to be able to make opening day of the bird season. Not with this busted wing, I wasn't. I recall I cried some more when it *did* begin to hurt, but the tears were not half so hearty as when I realized that I had used October, the golden month, to cheat me of the serious business of the day after tomorrow.

23

To Seek a Bear and Find a Boy

The expectation of excitement, the Old Man used to say, is better than the fulfillment thereof, or in his precise words candy in the window is better than candy in the belly, because you can't catch a bellyache from just looking.

"But," he said, "there are certain differences between eager anticipation and ducking responsibilities. The happy medium is to approach the candy with caution, enjoy it, and avoid the bellyache. This is a perfection that very few colored folks and no white people at all ever achieve."

This had come to be known to me as November talk, when my mind was not really on algebra but was sweating profusely over the imminence of the hunting season. My nose was hot and I had a tendency to quiver, like a pointer dog that can't wait to get out of the kennel on an autumn Saturday afternoon.

"There ain't but two things really worth-while," the Old Man continued. "Anticipation and remembrance. But in order to remember, you have to include execution of the anticipation. This means, roughly, that you got to take the dare. You got to bet your hand. You got to put your courage on the block and invite everybody to take a whack at it. And a brave coward is like a force-broken retriever. He may not like his work, but he'll force himself to do it, even if he's gun shy too."

This came back to me as I was headed for Alaska to shoot a bear, and was wondering slightly if I hadn't stretched my luck a little. After achieving the untender age of the mid-forty's I have never been disappointed in anything that ever happened in the field or on the stream, and I didn't want this bear, to whom I had not yet been introduced, to let me down. He was to be the last big bugabear that I intended to shoot, except in self-defense, and I must confess I was quivering as eagerly as on the eve of opening day of the bobwhite season.

The Old Man could get real windy on occasion, but mostly there was a solid kernel of sense in his vocal finger exercises. "What you remember," he said, "is the end result of practiced anticipation. Nor do I mean just triumph. That kind of remembering is bragging. Any bum can brag, because all you have to do is remember the girl you kissed and forget the one that slapped you flat. Experience comes from an acute recall of your mistakes as well as your successes."

I caught a fair point there. That last year I had started off with a flashy streak of quail shooting. Man, I had that quail thing down to a point where all I had to do was close my eyes and loose off both barrels and at least three birds would fall into my coat pocket. Then I hit a slump. One day I missed thirteen straight birds, one of which was sitting in a tree. Old Frank, the setter, took a final disgusted look at me and went home.

Then the panic set in. Just walking up behind Frank or

Sandy or Tom was such a venture into terror that I began to invent excuses *not* to go hunting. I even mentioned that I was behind in my schoolwork, which fooled nobody at all, since schoolwork ranked next to embroidery in my disesteem file. The Old Man scourged me into what the Spaniards call the "moment of truth," and literally forced me at gun point to walk up behind those damn dogs—which I now regarded as enemies every time they pointed—and blast away. Fortunately, finally, my timing came back, and I executed what could only be called a snappy double, and then went on to fill my limit with a minimum of misses. The jinx was broken, and I was okay again.

But I noticed that I refused to remember the series of raging misses. All I wanted to recall was the first part of the season, when I could have shot a teal with a slingshot. That, as the Old Man said, was the bragging section. I had closed off the failure, in my own mind, as securely as if I had slammed and dogged down the door.

I believe that one of the first signs of mellowing is when you start remembering your failures—remembering not only with honesty but with pleasure, because they were as much a portion to the day as the mad triumphs or the competent performance. For instance, I have two enormous tiger trophies, and the bigger of the two gives me a tremendous lift every time I see him or even think of him stretched skyward on my wall. But my favorite tiger is the one that is stretched skyward only on the wall of my memory. Because he is the one that got away.

This is the one that has now grown in my reveries to be at least twenty-two feet long, with teeth like railroad spikes, and a ruff twice the size of a zoo lion's mane. It must be true, because I killed that tiger and he was dead for at least twenty minutes. Vanity prevented my giving him the other barrel as he lay slumped over the carcass of a buffalo, but I didn't want to spoil the hide. And he was dead, wasn't he, shot precisely through the neck just like the other two?

So I thought. So thought Khan Sahib Jamshed Butt, who was perched with me in the tree in the black night of the Madhya Pradesh. This tiger—at least forty-four feet long from nose to tail tip—was stone-dead, with his face pillowed snugly on the buff's behind. Khan Sahib informed me that I was a Sahib Bahadur, the greatest tiger slayer since the late Jim Corbett, and I agreed with him freely.

And then this tiger, which was eighty-eight feet long if he was an inch, got up, snarled, and disappeared. It was a very long walk home, because the cobra-filled jungle now contained a wounded tiger, and anyhow, I am afraid of the dark. I was even more afraid of facing the two Texans sitting on the veranda of the dak bungalow, who would be certain I had missed the tiger when they heard only the one shot.

It has taken some time, but I find I can now face the memory of this beast, which was a hundred and sixty-six feet long and weighed over ten tons, without cringing and even with pleasure. Because the tiger has grown and I have gotten older and can realize that a damn fool is a damn fool, and also that foolishness does not necessarily spoil the entire picture of the trip.

I could cite you some more of the same sort of stuff. I was shooting *perdices*—the big, fast Spanish partridge—a while back, and missing everything that passed. On my right my friend Ricardo Sicré was keeping two guns hot and nailing everything that approached. Señor Sicré and I had shot grouse earlier in Scotland, and here, too, I was the bum, Ricardo the star.

But late that afternoon I shot a passing bird over my shoulder, going fast and far away, and the tumblers clicked and I was on the beam again. On the last drive of these transplanted Hungarians I was zeroed in and pulled twenty-two birds out of the flight.

Now, this is nice to remember. But what makes it so nice is that I remember the morning when I couldn't have hit a trapped elephant, and the Scottish trip, which cost a fortune and from which I accumulated little but embarrassment and a magnificent hangover from dancing on the green with the locals. When I finally started hitting again I was so relieved I really enjoyed recalling the shocking state of my shooting hand before.

This also applied to greater kudu. I have spent the last seven or eight years doing everything possible wrong with that magnificent, double-curl-horned African antelope, and now that there's a decent one on the wall I remember all the mistakes and tragedies and grim post mortems, but also the beauty of the days in Tanganyika and all the wonder of the birds and animals.

I think it really takes a Pollyanna to be the kind of hunter or fisherman who gets the most out of the expedition, rather than the result. I don't think the result, though necessary, is one-half so important in retrospect as all the side-bar fun and the little incidents that go to fill in the holes. I was certain that Alaska, which I had never seen, would be fabulous.

The bears might possibly eat me, and the fish might get away, and I would fall off a mountain or into a stream, and the geese might nibble me to death, but out of the whole ordeal was sure to come a series of possible triumphs that would plant the forty-ninth state more firmly in my memory than an oil strike or a gold mine.

Whatever the outcome the Old Man remains firmly in my head. "You can't enjoy it or be sorry about it unless you try it," he said. "Whether it's bobwhites or possums, whether it's a war or a job, you got to be in it to know about it. And unless you know about it, it didn't happen, and there you are as lonesome as an old maid who never got off the front porch for fear she might meet a man."

The Australians put it more succinctly. Around the race courses in Sydney there is a saying, "You've got to be in it to win it," and a common phrase is "I'm in it," no matter what it applies to.

I was in it in Alaska, and a most unusual thing happened. I ran into a kid, who but for a change in time might have been me.

I became very young this time in Alaska, when I met a youngster named Jerry Chisum, age about fifteen. He was a quiet youngster, good-looking, blondish, blue-jeaned, and competent to be a man with a gun or an airplane or a hunting camp.

Jerry's father is Jack Chisum of Anchorage, Alaska, who runs a flying service and an earth-moving operation with his brother Mark. Both are veteran bush pilots and sourdoughs in the better sense of the word, hunters and fishermen, hardworking, gnarled-fisted men who can grease an airplane into a tricky landing as easily as they might once have handled a sled and a team of huskies.

We were goose hunting together, after a chance meeting in, of all places, a bar. I had met Jerry's father earlier in Kodiak, where I was shooting a brown bear. When we bumped into each other in Anchorage it seemed natural enough to climb into a plane and ramble off to an island to belabor a goose or so. The other members of the party were Mark Chisum, young Jerry, and Paul Choquette of Homer on the Kenai Peninsula.

We took off from Anchorage in a float plane with added wheels, a Cessna 180, and because the water was rough we switched to a true amphib, a Widgeon. And we hit a hunting camp that carried me back about thirty years. It was a rough shack, comfortable enough, with crude bunks and a heat-quivering stove, and there were the usual hurried preparations for food and drink in the local store at Homer. Nobody had shaved that day, but I noticed the pilots had taken not so much as a short beer for a minimum twelve hours before flying. Bush flying in Alaska is a sketchy business at best, and a hangover doesn't help you much when you are flying mountainous passes in a float plane or landing downwind from necessity in rough water.

At first I was a little surprised to see the kid, carrying his full share of the duffel, scramble into the plane, and figured him for a passenger. Then something struck me as vaguely familiar. The kid, young Jerry, was a full-fledged hunting partner, a man among men. Apart from being taller and better looking and of course apart from using aircraft instead of T model Fords, he might very well have been me, thirty years ago. That is, if Alaska in any way resembles Southport, North Carolina.

His father and his uncle made no patronizing effort to explain him. Conversation was earthy, and none of it was curried because of Jerry's presence. We drank and told men's stories in camp, and there was none of this "not in front of the boy" business. Young Jerry performed a certain number of chores, in perhaps a little heavier ratio than the grizzled men; but apart from the utilization of his young legs for a little firewood fetching, apart from the fact that he was not invited to share the communal jug, he was one of the bunch, equal before the law and hunting society.

The birds were not flying overmuch that weekend, and much of the hunt was conducted in the warmth of the shack. But young Jerry was off prowling on his lonesome with his gun on the odd chance that there might be some action, while parents, so to speak, slept. That struck a reminiscent chord too. One of my brightest young dreams was to slope off, while the grownups tackled the fruit jar and told stories, to come triumphantly back with the biggest gobbler, the hatrackiest deer in the entire history of hunting. This dream never matured into reality, but it was not for lack of sturdy legs and sturdier effort.

I became interested in Jerry, who is an only boy in a family that includes three sisters. It seems he has been naturally accepted as a mature man since he was about six, and has known how to fly a variety of planes since he was eight or nine. There has never been any effort by his pa and his uncle to make an outdoorsman of him, apart from certain instructions in gun handling and hunting etiquette, and a full expectation that he'd carry his weight in the camp chores. Association with the hairy adults doesn't seem to have damaged his character any, and though he is not profane I imagine his retentive store of colorful language is considerable.

Mostly I was impressed by the way the adults kidded him, and by the way he returned the kidding without being either

overbrash or what might be called smart-alecky. They joshed
him as a man, and he joshed them right back on their own
grounds, also as a man. He was polite to me as a guest, but not
oversolicitous because of the difference in our ages. He was, in
short, completely integrated to adult society and responsibility,
and some credit must go to his father and his uncle for making
a man of a boy in easy, exciting stages.

Jerry Chisum's world is a world of modern outdoor glamour,
since his vehicle is the aircraft, as everybody's vehicle in Alaska
is the aircraft. Where I once saw quail and squirrels he sees
ptarmigan and geese. My biggest game was whitetailed deer
and an occasional wild hog. Jerry has been teethed on brown
and grizzly bear, moose and wolves. He has seen perhaps the
finest fishing in the world, where I perforce settled for smaller
fry. But there is not much basic difference in the way we were
raised.

Perhaps it was luck that kept a lot of us country boys out of
jail, but I like to think that a considerable part was played by
the horny-handed adults who raised us as equals and imbued
us with a love for the bush. Pool halls and corner gangs never
interested us. A knife was not a weapon but a handy utensil
that must be kept sharp and could cut you if you whittled toward you or otherwise used it carelessly. A gun was for killing,
and at all times had to be considered a deadly weapon. It also
had to be kept clean. Camps were to be left neat, and in a
permanent camp a certain amount of basic supplies was to be
left for the next occupants.

All these rules still apply to young Jerry Chisum, but in ad-
dition, today, he knows that nobody but a fool will fly a plane
with a screeching hangover or a snootful of booze. He checks
the instrument panel as automatically as his pilot-father does.
He knows that lack of meticulous maintenance of that aircraft
will surely kill him, for he pilots in the strange and wonderful
weather that makes Alaskan flying a science unplumbed by
ordinary aviators.

In my day we watched wind and weather too, but mainly for its effect on game. In Alaska wind and weather are active enemies, positive friends. There used to be a saying among the old bush pilots that you carried an anchor in the plane. When you were flying in heavy fog you dropped the anchor, and if you heard it splash you knew you were over water. Modern navigational aids—a full instrument panel—have changed that somewhat, but even today the standard plane for travel is a single-motored job which is little fancier than the old Tin Liz of my time.

When I see a kid like young Jerry I have little use for the beat generation and not too much time for the massed delinquents of the cities. If such kids were subject to heady fare—a land where you wash gold out of the creek, wolves howl, bears rob the meat safe, tough people abound, and the close recall of the dog-sled, gold-rush days is something more than just a legend —I'm sure they'd get carried far away in the opposite direction from beat.

There is as much temptation in a frontier nation as there is on a city street corner, and an incipient bum makes his own community. I am no psychologist, but I do think that a certain rule of thumb on child-raising can be made. Give a boy a sense of fitness, of belonging, and impress him with the responsibilities that go along with that belonging, and the transition from boy to man comes without a wrench.

My early mentors—God bless them all, black, white, drunk or sober, educated or unread—never once diminished my enthusiasm because it had all been done by them before. My first deer was, in their eyes, bigger than a mastodon, and my first fox squirrel achieved the proportions of a black leopard. A coon was a tiger, a rabbit a lion. I remember being violently sick to my stomach when I shot my first quail over a pointing dog, but nobody laughed—and nobody ventured that I probably fired at the whole covey (which I undoubtedly did) and dropped a bird by accident.

There was considerably more to my inclusion in adult hunting and fishing parties than an education in caution. A lot of practical conservation was hammered into my knotty skull because, as the Old Man used to say, if you shot it all there wouldn't be any for next year, and if you were careless with fire and burned down the woods there wouldn't be any forest to hunt in.

Mainly, though—and here we depart from the modern "progressive" child and certainly from the delinquent—I think that good manners were as vital as any aspect of our training. You didn't hog a quail shot. You didn't loose off a gun across your partner's bow. You didn't deafen him in a duck blind by exploding a shell in his eardrum. The left-hand man took the first duck, and in case of a possible tie on a single bird or animal you honored your partner's presence.

"If a dog can be taught to honor another dog's point," the Old Man used to say, "there's no reason for a man to be a game hog."

I like to think that the time and trouble my elders took with me on etiquette and caution, on conservation and just plain good manners may have kept this particular youth out of the Jimmy Dean set. It is not terribly difficult to translate the first basics of the woods and waters into drawing room or business behavior.

As I mentioned earlier, the association needn't be on a Fauntleroy basis. I could have cussed as good as any stevedore when I was ten, because I knew all the words. Whisky, I knew, was for drinking, but somehow it seemed a little impolite for me to be in a mad rush to cuss and drink in front of people until I had earned the right in terms of years. My hunting partners were often crude men, fisherfolk and sailors, but a certain gentleness pervaded and always a certain discipline obtained.

I had a plain wonderful time with young Jerry Chisum and his folks in Alaska, although no trophies resulted from the weekend hunt. In this age of jets and rockets to the moon, of juvenile gang wars and what seems almost total confusion it was wonderful to see a modern rerun of what I remember so clearly as the Old Man and the Boy, even with the bird-dog homing device on the instrument panel replacing the bird dog on the ground.

24

Nobody's Too Old for a Physic

A few years back, in the Central Provinces of India, yr. ob't sv't had just climbed up a tree in the black of night. He had walked through a few miles of cobras to achieve this tree, quaking in his boots all the way, because a jungle is scary at night, even without snakes. But there was a natural kill near the tree—a big domesticated buffalo that the biggest tiger in the world had knocked off that afternoon. He had been driven off his kill before he had a chance to get stuck into it, and it was a cinch he'd return.

They still do a lot of night shooting in India, sitting up for tigers and leopards over baits, shooting indiscriminately from cars, with lights, and I didn't like it; even when hunting villainous varmints—and this particular tiger was a veteran cattle-lifter that was decimating the Gond villagers' herds and would certainly turn into a natural man eater when he got too decrepit to kill animals or eventually panic-kill a herdsman and develop a swift taste for man meat.

I was crouched uncomfortably on a rough tree-branch machan, forbidden to smoke, scratch, cough, or think, but as the mosquitoes chawed me I broke one rule and began to think about the Old Man and why I didn't care for night hunting and never would.

"If you want to hunt, hunt," the Old Man once said. "If you want to be a murderer, be a murderer. Buy yourself a cheap flashlight or a headlight for the car and drive easy through the rye fields or the corn. Pick up some green eyes with your light, fire between the eyes, and when the eyes go out pick up your deer—you won't know whether it's a buck, doe, or fawn—and sneak it home. Venison's venison. Tastes the same to a hunter or to a murderer. Only don't let me catch you at it. You might as well take up highway robbery. You ain't too old yet for a touch of hickory physic." Hickory physic was a whippy switch across the bottom.

The Old Man was a fanatic on conservation of game and obedience to the game laws, which he said were the first three rungs on the ladder of conservation. Oh, maybe we might have committed a little indirect poaching, such as the calling of somebody else's turkeys from across the road into legal no man's land which I've already mentioned, and I used to be pretty handy poaching squirrels off some government property, but the squirrels weren't doing the government any good just sitting there eating up the pecans. But by and large we were kind of model hunters, even to keeping a season tally of birds shot, and this at a time when the meat hunters thought nothing of exceeding the limit a dozen times over or murdering the best part of a covey of quail on the ground.

But like all young'uns with enough pimples to rate a driver's license I hit the nocturnal daredevil stage, and one night a bunch of us hellions decided we would go jacklight a deer, just to see what is was like.

We rigged a big searchlight, which we "borrowed" from the pilot launch, onto the new Model A Liz, loaded the shotguns, and went on the prod. Not too far out of town there were some rye fields, fresh and green, where whole herds of deer came to graze the winter crop, and we told each other that we were really doing the farmers a favor; you know, St. Patrick chasing out the snakes, St. George knocking off the dragon.

We cruised along, flashing the light across the level fields, and after an hour or so we hit onto a constellation of eyes that showed green and sometimes red under the lamp's beam. A sizable herd of deer had come out from their lying-up beds in the swamps to take on the night's provisions. They stopped grazing and stood transfixed, pinioned in the yellow trap of light. We drew alongside and I picked out the closest pair of eyes and fired between them. They went out like a suddenly extinguished bulb. At the sound of the shot the other lights disappeared and you could hear the crash of antlers as they hit the nearest brush.

The flashlight showed us a nice young spike buck, stone-dead on the ground. The Model A coupé had a kind of luggage compartment in the back. We opened it up and slung the murdered animal into it. Then we drove back to town feeling like a bunch of thugs, who had stuck up a bank and killed the teller as well.

As we hit the town we saw that the car needed some gas. Just as we pulled up to the pump the damnedest *baaaa—blattttt!* you ever heard came out of the hind end, and there was enough thumping and bumping and thrashing around to wake the dead. *Baaaa—blattttt!* Bump! Crash! Wallop! *Baaa—blatttt!* Obviously our corpse had been merely stunned and had just come alive.

The filling-station attendant looked as startled as we did, and as for me the neck hairs stood up like tenpenny nails. Old refrains of "Birmingham Jail" and "Prisoner's Song" and "In the Jailhouse Now" began to creep into my subconscious as we gunned that Model A out of there for the deep timber. Naturally we ran out of gas.

Now here was the predicament: black night with no gas on a country road and a live buck deer threatening to tear the Liz to tin shreds, and suddenly the brave freebooters were three scared kids facing a life in jail plus an extra life of shame. But in the meantime, how do you get a live deer out of the tail end of a Model A Ford coop?

When you are a criminal you seek a partner in crime. A case-hardened crook turns always to his own sort for comfort. I inspected the terrain and remembered that about a mile down the road there dwelt some gentlemen who lived by the manufacture and sale of an illegal specific against nervous tremors, namely, white mule. If one or both of the brothers were not off "working for the state," as they called a jolt in jail, we might expect some criminal assistance, since their smokehouse generally contained venison that had not been acquired under the law's strictest letter.

Junius, a lean, lantern-jawed, bristle-chinned buccaneer, was cradling a jug on the front porch of his ramshackle cabin. Eph, he informed us, was off on a romantic errand involving the nearest neighbor's daughter, Miss Sary Jane, aged sixteen, and "he'd be back when he got done." We dispatched a courier to the tumble-down manse of Miss Sary Jane, aged sixteen, and tore Eph from the arms of his beloved, for this was a tricky, technical job. Junius loaded a spare demijohn of gas into his creaky old T model, and the task force proceeded toward the liberation.

It was quite simple, actually. Eph crawled up on the top of our car with a noose in his hand. Junius opened the back end cautiously, and when the young buck stuck its head out Eph snagged it with the lasso, drew taut, and Junius dropped the compartment top back on the buck's neck. For a split second—

until Junius cut its throat with one slash of a clasp knife that had
been so frequently honed that its blade showed an inner curve
—the buck looked like a picture of a mounted deer head, only
the wall was the tail end of a car.

"You fellers want this critter?" Eph asked.

Three of us hollered together, "No!"

"We'll take him, then," Junius said.

We drove silently, guiltily back to town, and dispersed without saying good night. I avoided the Old Man the next morning, after a sleepless night, but just after the noon meal—
which I picked at—he collared me.

"Any truth in this stuff about the deer you fellers jacklit that
come alive in the car? There's different versions all over town."

I saw there wasn't any use trying to lie out of it, because the
Old Man had a beagle nose for news. "I'm afraid it's true," I
said. "It ain't gonna happen again."

The Old Man gave me a look that would have put out a
forest fire. "I'll say it won't," he snapped. "Not unless you can
manage to break jail to do it. Come on, murderer," he said.
"We're going to see the warden."

We got in the car and drove off. The warden was in the pool-
room. The Old Man waited until he finished his game, and
then he said, "Jack, if you'd step outside a minute."

When the warden was outside the Old Man said, "I just caught
a criminal for you. Do your duty. You got any handcuffs?"

The warden said no he didn't have any, but he could borrow
some mighty quick if the criminal was dangerous.

"I think he's dangerous," the Old Man said. "He's an acces-
sory to murder, car theft, night hunting, and the use of a
stolen searchlight on the murder car."

"Maybe he's repented," the warden said. "This is a first of-
fense, ain't it?"

"Yes, I suppose so," the Old Man said, "unless you count
them watermelons he stole a couple of months back—also at
night."

"Well hell," the warden said. "I got a bet on this next game. I parole him into your custody, Ned, and you can deal with him as you see fit. All right?"

"If you say so," the Old Man answered. "It'll save the state some money."

He never spoke all the way home. He said, when we got there, "You go back to the garage and wait for me." Then he went into the house and came back with a whippy Malacca cane somebody'd given him. "Take down your pants," he said, "and bend over."

Sitting in this tree, waiting for this tiger, my behind began to hurt double, and it wasn't this makeshift machan that made it hurt. The Old Man really laid into me with that cane, but even that didn't hurt as much as his icy contempt, which lasted three or four days until he figured I'd served my sentence and was due to be admitted to society again.

That cured me of night hunting until now, when Khan Sahib punched me. The tiger had come silently to the bait. We let him feed for ten minutes, and then Khan Sahib snapped the flash on him. He had a head as big as a bushel basket, and his enormous ruff was bloody. He looked balefully into the light. I drew a bead on his neck, as he lay on the buffalo eating from aft to fore, and the .470 boomed. He collapsed without moving —a rug, with his head pillowed on the buffalo's hindquarters. I started to shoot him again.

"No," Khan Sahib said. "Don't spoil the skin. He's dead, like the others." He yoo-hoo'd for the distant boys to come let us down out of the tree.

This was Tiger Three in ten days—all big, but this the biggest, and the only one shot at night. I forgot the Old Man. This was the biggest tiger I'd ever heard of, from his pug marks and the sight I had of his head. I had a flask in the tree. We celebrated.

"Let's look at him again," I said, about twenty minutes later.

Khan Sahib snapped on the light. There was a growl and I saw a tail disappear into the high grass. The tiger that had been dead twenty minutes had come to life. He'd been creased and only stunned.

We hunted that tiger for two days with buffalo, and never came close. He'd quit bleeding inside a hundred yards. The late Jack Roach of Houston, Texas, saw him a couple of weeks later, and Jack said that as far as he could make out, through the glasses, the cat had a fully healed scar a mere hair off the top of the spine.

It did me no good to reflect that Karamoja Bell, the famous elephant hunter, once cut the tail off a brain-shot bull and returned a few hours later to find the bull had got up and gone, tailless, and that everybody who ever hunted has made at least one damfool mistake. All I could think of was that buck deer carrying on and blatting in the back of the Liz, and the Old Man's rattan walking stick swishing on my backside.

From that point on you could offer me a hairy mammoth and a saber-toothed tiger staked out and tied to a tree at night and get a very sharp, profane "No!" for an answer. Daytime hunting is for hunters, and nighttime hunting is for animals. But wherever the Hunting Grounds the Old Man inhabits, I'll bet he was laughing fit to kill the night when that big tiger got up and calmly walked away.

25

Only One Head to a Customer

This happened in the Suphkar Range of the Madhya Pradesh, also in the Central Provinces of India. The dak bungalow stood on the summit of a slight hill in rolling country, beautiful country, whose crisp greens and yellows and reds were reminiscent of Connecticut in the fall or of a bright autumn day in the Carolinas. You expected to hear quail calling as they mustered scattered ranks at sunset. Instead there was the raucous *me-ow* of peacocks, the croak of ravens, the belling of a sambar stag startled by a tiger, or the sharp, biting yap of the barking deer. In the dak bungalow, which the government kindly leases to tiger hunters who rent shooting blocks, there was a kerosene-operated refrigerator and a whole sideboard of tinned delicacies and condiments.

In the main room guns were stacked aimlessly in a corner—a .470, a .308 with scope, shotguns, a scoped .220. Every time some Indian visitor would come to call—and, the good Lord knows, enough curious locals dropped in—somebody would pick up a gun and snap it at the floor or at somebody else's foot. The camp was equipped with camp managers and secretaries and clerks and a variety of nondescripts who just came to rubberneck. They all were fascinated powerfully by the guns.

The guns were not mine, but rented, and fitted tolerably well. I had already had some experience with them, especially with the .308, a really dandy little middle weapon. Dandy, that is, except I couldn't hit anything with it. This is not unusual in my case, except that once in a while the law of averages says that you're supposed to hit something if you blow off enough powder, and I was ringing up exactly nothing with the scoped weapons, including the .220. I asked the head shikari, "Anybody sight these scopes in? Graticules all checked?" And got a blank look.

"You know," I said, "scopes have to be checked—atmospheric pressure, joggling around in jeeps, too many rounds of ammunition fired, that sort of thing. They get out of alignment."

Blank look. Never heard of it. A scope is a scope is a scope. Tie it onto the weapon with a bit o' string, and the scope will kill, just as in Kenya, where the natives still believe largely that the noise kills.

"We'll stick up a target," I said, "and sight them in."

Wistful shake of head at European whim, but up went the target, a hundred paces off on a tree as big as a baobab. From a steady rest on the cushioned hood of a jeep I hauled down on the target and took a piece off the side of the tree. Repeated the shot and duplicated the hit. The gun grouped beautifully, if you liked it a foot high and two feet wide. I tried the .220 and missed the tree a couple of times.

I unscrewed the sighting apparatus and looked at the downs and the ups on the graticules, and discovered that if you wanted to shoot around corners these were the most murderous weapons I ever saw. But unfortunately if you aimed at something close-hand you were likely to kill the shikari's cousin in downtown Gondia. Evidently nobody had reshaped the sights since the scopes had been sewn on, possibly on the other side of an ocean voyage. I made the few adjustments on the screws, fired a few more sighting shots, and when the guns were on I set the sights solidly by rapping the pan with the butt end of a .470 bullet. This appeared to be magic, especially after I downed a peacock at a couple of hundred yards.

This had nothing to do with mechanics, of course. Magic. The aboriginal black Gonds and Baigas didn't believe in guns anyhow. They were very heavy on rocks and trees and iron adzes and phallic symbols, but guns, no.

"Oh my God, Old Man," said I, "you told me one day I would go to shoot tigers, but you never said it would be like this." (*This* was the shikari's venerable .577, which was wired together with baling wire.)

That business of the sighting finished, we shot some chital and sambar and pigs and one tiger. The guns were always carefully stacked in the corner of the room. One day I had a look at them and could barely fetch a mite of daylight through the muzzle.

"For the love of the Gautama Buddha and any pagan gods we have handy," I hollered, "don't nobody ever clean no bloody rifles around here?"

"Oh yas, sahib, we are cleaning immediately," and off went the artillery. To the laundry, I suppose, because the caste system would certainly demand that a dhobi (professional washerman) have charge of the cleaning detail.

Back came the guns, cleaned, to be stacked in the corner. I took them out of the corner and laid them on a table. I went to have a nap and read some enchanting fifty-year-old prose from *Blackwood's Magazine*, and when I got up there were the guns, stacked in a corner again. About the time I was smiting my brow I spied a hawk circling over the trees in front of the bungalow, and suddenly it lit. Without taking my eyes off the hawk I snatched the .220 from the nest in the corner and stalked as best I could, using trees for cover, toward the hawk.

Something of my African chum Harry Selby may have rubbed off, because I made it to easy shooting range without alerting the hawk. As is customary I started to snick the safety and discovered the safety done been snicked. I drew back the bolt to charge the magazine, and, bless pappy, I heard a tiny *chink* as a live round was ejected from the chamber. I didn't even bother to shoot at the hawk, I was that rattled. I turned and dashed for the dak bungalow.

Every gun in the cluster in the corner was loaded. Every rifle had a live round in the chamber. Every safety was off. The double .470 had two large cordite-charged softpoints in its barrels. I let out a scream that the Old Man must certainly have heard, Upstairs or Downstairs, wherever he be.

I do not believe in raising hell except when it's necessary, but the idea that anybody in the hunting business could be such a bloody fool as to stack charged weapons in a corner for any idiot to point at his foot and snap—*boom-boom*—made me so mad I went white and shaky. It was an affront to decency, as if a maiden of impeccable virtue had suddenly been accosted as an easy lady.

"Grandpa, Grandpa!" was all I could think of to say, between curses in all the six languages I swear in. And who was cursing louder than me was my wife, who had been so painstakingly trained in safety with firearms that she was almost afraid to shoot when the critical moment finally came. I never quite forgave the Indians after that one.

I went all the way back to Carolina, that first day of the gun, and remembered. The Old Man and I were out to shoot us a quail—my first. I was eight years old.

"In a minute," the Old Man said, as the dogs fanned out, "I aim to let you use this thing the best way you can. Your mother thinks I'm a damned old idiot to give a shirttail boy a gun that's just about as tall as the boy is. I told her I'd be personally responsible for you and the gun and the way you use it. I told her that anytime a boy is ready to learn about guns is the time he's ready, no matter how young he is, and you can't start too young to learn how to be careful. What you got in your hands is a dangerous weapon. It can kill you or kill me or kill a dog. You always got to remember that when a gun is loaded it makes a potential killer out of the man that's handling it. Don't you ever forget it."

I never did forget it.

During the course of my apprenticeship the Old Man ate me out. He put me through a course of fence climbing that would make the old Marine boot training look easy, and he was as mean as a drill sergeant.

"Whoa!" he'd say, like he was calling a scatterbrained dog that had just run through a covey of quail. "Now ain't you a silly sight, stuck on a bob-wire fence with a gun waving around in the breeze, with one foot in the air and the other on a piece of limber wire?"

Or: "Now, what kind of a hunter have I got here, his gun propped against a tree for any fool dog to run against and explode in his face?"

Or: "What kind of a damfool hunter stacks his gun in a corner when he comes in from hunting, so some young'un can take it to play with and blast a hole in his mama?"

And I would say to the Old Man, "But Grandpa, it ain't loaded."

"Who says it ain't loaded?" The Old Man was scornful. He walked over to the gun, took it out on the back porch, and pulled. *Bam! Bam!*

"Not loaded, huh? What was that, *mice?*"

Of course the old monster had framed me again, and stuck a couple of shells in when I wasn't looking, which was his way of making a moral lesson. He had done it before, the first day of my new gun, when he palmed a shell into the spout and told me to dry-fire to improve my aim, after I'd missed my first quail with both barrels. I cut down on a pine cone and *"Blim!"*

the gun went off and near scared me to pieces. Then he took my gun—*my* gun—away from me, and killed a quail with it, just to teach me a lesson. I was so mad at him I would have liked to palm a shell in and shoot *him*, except for the fact that I loved him and knew instinctively that he had a point. In later days my wife confessed to a desire to shoot *me* in the pants for the same reason.

But in my early pre-teens the Old Man made me uncouple the gun every time we moved from one hunting sector to another in the car. And the first thing I did when we came in, dead-beat in the evening, was to take down the piece, clean it, and stow it in its case.

The Old Man, smiling smugly over his first snort of the day, would say: "Take a mighty clever young'un or a mighty pert dog to undo that case, snap the gun together, load it, and then shoot you accidentally with it."

It may sound old-maidy, all this caution, but I confess to a breach of it. I fix my safety catches on my big guns—the double rifles, that is—so they won't slide back on to safe when the gun is broken, because I don't want to worry about forgetting to slip the automatic safety catch back on if I am reloading again in a hurry to keep something large and ugly from stepping on me. For the same reason I don't use automatic ejectors on a double express rifle. It's just one more thing that might jam when a jam is not precisely what you crave at the moment.

But one day I had to change crews and I forgot to tell the new gunbearer about this peculiarity. We were hot after an elephant and I told the boy to load the *bundouki* and he did, and when we came up to the jumbo he handed me the weapon. I automatically tried to push the safety forward and it seemed stuck, so I jerked it back and couldn't fire, because now it was on safe. In a moment of panic that lasted a thousand light-years and took a sixth of a second I fought mechanics. What happened, he had broken the gun to load it, and the safety went forward and *stayed* forward on fire, as per arrangement. I had hustled five miles through bush with that loaded cannon pointing at my head over his shoulder, and all he had to do was step in a pig hole and *"Karaam!"*—richest widow in Palamós, Spain. So the next day I took the whole safety apparatus completely off. Now when that lovely little Jeffery is loaded it shoots, and it is in my hands, and I am in front of the bearer.

It's a far cry from the Old Man and BB shots in the eye and people blowing off their heads crossing fences, but shooting some grouse just the other day in Scotland there was such a fanfaronade of pellets falling in the butts that I got down in the bottom of mine and gave up sport for the moment. The week before, one of the more tempestuous French clients had loosed a load at a grouse crossing the nearest butt, and one pellet nicked a gillie less than a quarter inch below his eye. A quarter inch higher—being one-eyed is less fun than being two-eyed.

That's why I got so tarnal mad in India, I guess. If we'd have had the Old Man for a shikari I bet you there would have been a lot of sore tails in the Suphkar camp, because the Indians have a chastising instrument called a *lathi*, and if the Old Man could lay on a *lathi* as well as he could flourish a common American stave I'd feel a touch less afraid of the guns than I was skeered of the tigers. Come to think of it, I didn't waste much time being afraid of the tigers. I was too busy keeping an eye on my friends and employees.

26

Greedy Gut

We have a shambling little orchard out in the back yard. It has an aversion to bearing anything much except spotty plums and the occasional fig, which the birds generally beat me to. But I noticed when the plums formed this year I was out there beating off the birds for a whack at the early crop. The same applied to the seldom strawberries that poke their heads up from the unwilling green around the drive. The house was a crying admonition of bellyache, but I was munching happily away. There is nothing really wrong with adolescent plums and pale pink strawberries. Even today I prefer them to their full-blown brethren. I guess it's a childhood habit I'll never kick.

"I am always surprised," the Old Man said to me once long ago, "that there is such a thing as an adult. I am surprised any young'un ever grows up to votin' age. Boy young'uns and billy goats, maybe, got less regard for their innards than anything I know of, including hogs, and a hog will eat anything, including its own pigs."

This homily was designed to justify a large dose of castor oil as antidote for the consumption of a large number of green peaches. Green peaches do not give you the bellyache as alleged; castor oil does. To my mind someone bigger than me was compounding the felony, with me as the victim.

"Green peaches, green plums, green backberries, green figs, green grapes, green apples, green pears," the Old Man said in a sing-song voice. "Why do all boys *have* to eat things when they're green? They can't taste good and they tear up your stomach and you get punished besides. Why?"

"I reckon I just can't wait," I said. "They always look so *good* when they're green. I even like the way they taste."

The Old Man grunted in disgust. "It's *your* stomach," he said. "Go ahead and wreck it."

He stalked off, muttering. I knew what ailed the Old Man. The doctor had nailed him with some sort of light diet for a stomach disorder, and had put him plumb off fried foods, desserts, and almost anything else he liked. The Old Man wasn't mad at me for eating the green peaches; he was mad at himself for not being *able* to do what he wanted to any more. He reckoned somehow that reducing him to an infant's diet was a reflection on his age.

Looking back, I expect I must have had a zinc-lined stomach, at that. I still have one today, and can only credit the early practice I had with inedibles, or a mixed bag of what was supposed to be inedible, in combination.

As a man I have withstood the kind of food you get at cocktail parties—the kind of canapés that would gag a goat. In a restless itch to stride the world I have rambled Mexico without succumbing to what is commonly called "Montezuma's revenge." The tourist in Europe generally falls afoul of what the Spaniards called the *turistas*, and blames it on a change of water, a change of diet, the local cooking oil, strange sea food, green vegetables, bad ice, peculiar wine—anything at all.

I really can't say why nothing upsets my stomach, unless it was the early training of that poor repository of juvenile whim to expect and accept anything at all. I could and did chase sour pickles with ice cream. They said you shouldn't mix sea food with sweets. If they had made a shrimp-flavored ice cream I would have been the first to ask for it. You supposedly couldn't combine watermelon with certain things, and garlic with other things. I combined watermelon with everything and I can still munch garlic by the clove. I have eaten sheep's eyes with Arabs, raw sea food with Japs, fried grub worms with Africans, and all manner of strange exotic fruits everywhere. I do not recommend this as a diet for everyone. All I can say is that nothing I eat makes me sick.

As a kid I had a sort of inventive mind. Nobody frowned on eating raw clams and oysters, fresh and salty dripping from their beds. If clams and oysters were sea food, I reckoned, then so were fish and crabs and shrimp. I never went to sea (going to sea was shoving the dinghy off the shingle and ramming home the oarlocks) without a plentiful supply of salt and a bag of fruit. The fruit nearly always included lemons and limes against the scurvy, because a solitary seafarer never knew when an exclusive diet of salt horse and hardtack would breed scurvy and inspire the crew to mutiny.

I had not read at the time that lime juice would cook fish if left alone, in the Polynesian fashion, but it did not take me very long to discover that raw fish and raw shrimp and raw crab meat were delicious if well-salted, sprinkled with lemon or lime juice, and left a short while in the sun. I got particularly fond of mullet, which we used for bait when we were surf casting. The Old Man complained bitterly that I ate more cut bait than the fish did, but the half-dried, heavily salted mullet was delicious, particularly if accompanied by a chocolate bar.

A quarter-decade later I encountered biltong in Africa. Biltong is made by slicing thin sheets of meat and spreading it on bushes to dry in the sun. It turns black and is almost un-swallowable, but is a power of comfort to chew and is most nutritious. The old Boer voortrekkers used it as a staple, much as our coon-capped trail blazers dived into the wilds with a bag of pemmican or jerky, which is practically the same thing. A really well-cured biltong will break off in short sticks, like crumbly candy, and is delicious as well as sustaining.

Biltong came as no surprise to me, nor did dried fish in the Pacific and Japan. They only tasted vaguely familiar, as if I had been there before.

As a kid I cooked the fruits of my gun about as sketchily as any savage. We made long safaris on Saturdays, which were as full of adventure as any major safari I made in later years. Even in the air-rifle stage we had attained considerable skill with the Daisies, and later the fifty-shot BB pump guns. Robins, song sparrows, jorees, thrushes, woodpeckers, and the big flickers—the yellowhammers—were regarded as major game, and the occasional dove, rain crow, or once in a long while a quail or marsh hen were placed in the elephant, lion, buffalo category. What we shamelessly slew we cooked over a hasty fire—sketchily skinned, hastily gutted, and unwashed—impaled on a green stick and merely scorched. But it tasted good at the time, and oddly it tasted just as good later . . .

. . . such as a couple of years ago in Africa. One day on a long walk after elephant we got hungry at midday, and nobody carries a chop box when he is fighting high grass after moving elephant. We called a halt, and somebody shot a small antelope, a gerenuk, I think it was. We whipped off the hide and emptied the stomach. We ate its heart and liver raw, and it was delicious. We roasted a few chops over a hasty fire. It may sound horrible, but the animal was still hot from life and tasted great after being liberally salted.

We performed a small series of experiments thereafter, and found that all birds and most small gazelle tasted wonderful, if you got them onto the fire while they were still warm with recent life. It was only after they cooled out and rigor mortis set in that they had to be aged and otherwise kitchen-treated to provide tenderness.

The birds were particularly good. We would shoot a batch of sand grouse, young guinea, doves, pigeons, or francolin, clean them while they were still quivering, impale them on a green stick, and pop them over the coals, and they were great. And these were no savage palates, either. We would go home to camp that night and sit down to a dinner which might include caviar, breast of guinea fowl, asparagus, and fresh fruit, washed down with a French wine such as Mouton-Rothschild or Chambolle-Musigny. One of the heartiest eaters of the half-cooked, only-just-dead birds was a Spaniard, who made annual pilgrimages to France merely to eat his way across the countryside and who was an expert on wines and sauces.

It did not really seem to matter what you ate, as a youngster, if you were actually hungry. One of the palatial meals I shall always remember (and still eat, when I am lucky enough to find an old-fashioned country store when I am quail hunting in the Carolinas) was what we had around noontime, when the birds had fed back into the cool of the swamp and the dogs needed water and a breather before hunting resumed around three-thirty.

A gourmet would shudder at this, perhaps, but what we ate was canned salmon (the same as we fed the dogs), canned sardines, oyster crackers or plain soda crackers, gingersnaps, and rat cheese. This was washed down with one of the enormous bottles of soft drinks they used to sell for a nickel, grape- or orange-flavored, and twice the size of a Coke. The Old Man called it "bellywash," and so it was, but it made a delicious accompaniment to the sardines, gingersnaps, and rat cheese. If belching is a sign of politeness in some countries we were more than exceedingly polite.

All through the woods in the afternoon I gnawed on dirty— and sometimes bloodstained from the pockets of my hunting coat—peppermint candies and hard cooking apples from the barrel, with perhaps an enormous, bumpy, brine-rimed sour or dill pickle from the keg that stood in the cool of the store, amongst the kegs that held the various sizes of nails, under the shelves which contained the overalls and hickory shirts. If I was in funds I might also buy a bag of assorted cakes from the slanting stand that held them—crumbly vanilla johnnycakes, as big as coffee saucers, round sticky black chocolate cakes with vanilla goo between the cake halves, and great pink things with sparse slivers of white coconut glued to the top pastry.

To go home to an oyster roast, with that sort of backlog of fodder, did not seem strange, although roasted oysters are held by some to be indigestible enough without the aid of the earlier accompaniment, without the cool-of-the-evening swill of scuppernong wine at the nearest colored man's farmhouse when your whole body is still hot from hunting.

And speaking of wine, for a man who in later life learned a little of vintage years and brand names, I was in on the birth of some of the more bizarre home-stomped beverages that ever assaulted a palate. *Or* a stomach.

With no regard whatsoever for the Volstead Act we young hellions pounded juice-oozy wild cherries into goo, fattened the mixture with sugar, and strained the fermented leavings into what we fondly believed was wine. Some wild and savage voodoo experiments were concocted in the cool of the caves we built—hideaways against the onslaughts of hostile Indians, parents, and if we had thought about it, revenooers. Dried apricots and raisins made an acceptable mash, as did grapes and fresh peaches. Mostly the stuff was nauseating to the taste, and usually contained collections of dead beetles and woozy flies, but the mere idea that we were doing something unsanctioned was sufficiently intoxicating.

I really do not know how we all lived through it. We chewed sour grass and smoked rabbit tobacco in our totem pipes. We combined sparkleberries with green persimmons and richened the mixture with all manner of nuts, from the rich tame pecans to wild hickories and chinquapins. Uncle Jimmy's all-purpose store contained penny candies that must have been confected of equal portions of ratsbane and sugar. Irey Ivans, in colored town, specialized in Brown Dogs, which seemed simply to be made of peanuts and burnt sugar. The colored folk did interesting things with blackstrap molasses in candy form, which I loved. And I never turned a hair when confronted by roast coon or a mess of chitterlings or squirrel-head stew.

We ate these oddly assorted vittles avidly. I can remember clearly drinking stickily sweet condensed milk so thick you could cut it; and the yams we roasted in the woods were notable more for their content of ingrained dirt and wood ash than for their half-raw innards.

We had only one rule on food: If it grew wild, was bought in a store, or was condemned as unfit for consumption by parents it had to be delicious. Some of the less hardy scientists occasionally went green in the face and became ill. They were greeted with jeers, the same unfeeling juvenile taunts that were hurled at the timid souls who got seasick.

When I grew older I graduated to the vile corn liquor and the viler home-brew of the prohibition era, and never batted an eye. I survived Tunisian *eau-de-vie* (ugh!), Australian whisky, South Sea jungle juice, and some illegal seagoing mixtures of compass-cleaning alcohol and grapefruit juice. I have sampled Kaffir beer and Tanganyika *pombe*, which ferments *after* it hits the stomach. And I have survived, although the Lord in His wisdom only knows why.

When he discussed the range of my gustatory habits with something more than admiring disgust the Old Man dusted off the old chestnut about curiosity killing the cat. "But in your case," he said, "it's a very large cat, and anyhow you ain't home yet."

The Old Man was generally right about most things, and these days, on some mornings, I have a queasy feeling that his record for accuracy is still unbroken, even if it's taken a long time to jell.

27

Snakes Ain't Hostile in November

Like I say, the Old Man infected me early with a feeling for the seasons of the year, and he divided the year sharply according to what the seasons had to offer. This, the Old Man said, was the way the Greeks did it. There was a season for planting, a season for harvesting, a season for suspicion and worry, and always a time to love and a time to die. March, the miserable month, had its ides, against which even the great Caesar was warned. June was soft and sweet—a woman's month—and October was full of promise and present perfection.

But the big month, at least for this boy—and I think for the Old Man—was November, a harsh, rough, tough man's month, with the threat of winter ahead but a marvelous sense of weathered magic in the woods. The quail now called only when they were scattered from flushed coveys, and you could hear the rutting snort of the buck deer as his neck swelled and see where the velvet had rubbed off—in tatters—his fighting horns.

Everything happened in November. The quail season opened, around Thanksgiving time, and the deer and turkey seasons opened. The days were crisp but still red and golden in North Carolina, and the nights were sparklingly cold and made welcome a roaring blaze. The ducks were flying legally, and sometimes it seemed that there was just too much action for one boy to stand.

Even the fishing had improved. The summer fishing was gone, but the big stuff had come in from the skimpy schools of September and early October, and November was the time for the really big jut-chinned blues and the heavy channel bass. The gray seas were chill and sad to see, but the fish flocked in close in the deep-cut sloughs, which were now almost bayous banked by a barrier reef, and the fish took up housekeeping in the sloughs.

One of the keenest memories I have is of a big shark, run almost aground and stranded on a reef when he sought to cross the barrier reef that lay between him and the feeding blues and trout and Virginia mullet. His dorsal fin wavered out of water as he literally pulled himself over the shallows on his belly.

After my first few bucks I was never much of a deer shooter, but to me November meant the beautiful belling of the hounds in the dim distance, growing and swelling to the full strength of bass and cello, almost in your lap, just before the buck burst out of the gallberries.

The dogs knew November: Jackie, the upcurl-tailed fice that was an expert on squirrels; the deerhounds, Bell and Blue; and the quail dogs, which had hunted themselves lean in early practice and now were deadly in diagnosis and steady as rocks to shot. Six days a week saw me in the woods or on the water, and if it had not been for a certain stuffy attitude about Sunday shooting I would have compromised the Biblical injunction about working on six days and resting on the seventh.

Maybe I'm too much the old man now and too little the boy when I say that modern kids—those I know, anyway—don't feel as deeply about the wondrous works of God in the forests and fields and waters; that they are completely unconscious of the present unless it involves a TV show or a red-hot car. Am I becoming an old fuddy-duddy—one of those when-I-was-a-boy types?

Perhaps, but I still think that modern kids are cheated of sensation that is not contrived. I occasionally try to talk with some of the spawn of my friends, and get the feeling they are very far away from kinship with adults. It seems to me that as a boy I didn't have many friends of my own age. My friends were mostly adults, black and white, and they raised me without recourse to hot-rods or rumbles. I can swear that the month of November was rendered delightful by my association with a bunch of hairy characters, who would be ruled off the course as improper associates in this era of the switchblade knife.

My guys fought among themselves when they got drunk on a Saturday night, and some of them manufactured illegal whisky, besides drinking it. But mostly they seemed to possess a tremendous gentleness and understanding for small boys who tagged along with them in the woods or on the boats. I can even recall one compulsive thief who threatened to beat the bejabbers out of me if he ever caught me stealing anything.

These people were as much a part of November as the sleepy possum in the persimmon tree; the cold, clotted lumps of earth in the sere cotton fields; or the delicious, frightening loneliness of the swamp on a deerstand; or the burning cold of a turkey blind on a cold morning as you waited for the big toms to come.

Perhaps I spent more time with the Negroes than with the whites, largely because in my neck of the woods there were more Negroes than whites. I was at home in the abodes of Big Abner and Aunt Florence, and they allowed no stranger to trespass on my quail reserves. I ate with them, and on occasion when caught out too late to get back to the Old Man's house slept in their tiny clapboard or rough-log houses. I suspect we were pretty well integrated before they made a law of it. At least nobody ever brought up the subject of who was white and who was colored, when we shared the squirrel-head stew or the possum and sweet taters.

The crowning aspect of my November was the big camping trip, when the Old Man and a couple of cronies permitted me— if I had been a good boy about splitting kindling and cleaning fish and gutting ducks and plucking birds—to go along some-times on a week-long campout, where I would split kindling, clean fish, gut ducks, and pluck birds, with a few additional duties, such as skinning deer and squirrels and fetching water and washing dishes. This was now the perfection of a boy in-cluded in an adult world, where men cursed openly, told man-type stories, drank whisky, and appeared to accept the boy as a man, while tactfully forbidding him to cuss, drink whisky, or tell off-color yarns.

The fruition in weather and sport was something unbelieva-ble. October had beckoned, but November delivered. Only a true idiot can appreciate the predawn misery of a duck blind. Even in the South—as far south as Louisiana—it is black and miserable in the morning, with the cold graved into your bones, and the torture of whistling wings of unseen ducks is something more than exquisite. Then comes the faint dove's breast pink of dawn, and then the rosy red, and then you can see the ducks. You can shoot. And miss. And occasionally hit.

Perhaps jubilance is the word that describes it all. There was the nocturnal stupidity of coon hunting, when the hounds were as apt to raise a skunk as a coon. The tumbles we took seemed fun, and certainly the streams we fell into were part of the ob-stacle course.

I was one time in a friend's house in Texas, where the doves were swarming like locusts and the wild turkeys consuming a ton of purloined food a week, just waiting for Thanksgiving. I was prowling around, bird-dogging some dead doves, when a remark the Old Man once made struck sharply home. I had turned up a rattler the size of a log, and just before the lady with me blew its head off with her new gun I remembered the ancient remark.

"In November," the Old Man said, "even the rattlesnakes don't like to bite people."

28

Stoicism Is Bad for Boys

"The accumulation of laughter," the Old Man said, pacing up and down in front of the fire with his hands behind his back, "comprises an aggregate of wisdom." It was raining to beat the band.

"Huh?" I said. "What was that again?" I was looking hopefully out the window, and not paying much attention to the inside of the house.

"The accumulation of . . . you heard me the first time," he said. "How did it sound?"

"Fine," I said. "What does it mean? And who made it up?"

"*I* just made it up," the Old Man said. "Maybe I might of read it somewhere, I disremember. Seneca or one of them other old Romans. Somebody or other."

"Seneca?" I said. "I always thought Senecas were a tribe of Indians, kind of like the Iroquois." If this was going to be one of those days when everybody was flinging knowledge around I was going to crowd right in there with my share.

"There's a lot you don't know," the Old Man said. "Seneca tended store somers about thirty or forty years A.D. He got famous for being a Stoic."

"A what?"

The Old Man held up his hand. "A Stoic. A Stoic is a man who practices and preaches Stoicism, which is another word for grinning and bearing it, no matter how rough times get. You could pull the toenails out of a real Stoic before he'd let out a whimper. He was calm in the face of adversity. He could stand there and take it, even though his whole life was crumbling in ashes all around him. You got to be a Stoic these days to get along in this world."

I noticed the Old Man wasn't dropping his "g's," a sure sign of something about to happen that I wasn't going to like He had a habit of leading up to these things kind of sneaky more or less for his own amusement. The Old Man was about the kindest man in the world, but there was a streak of bad boy in him still. He liked to tease me, and that's what he was doing now.

"What does it mean?" I asked again.

"It means," the Old Man said, "that it ain't going to quit raining today and if I were you I'd start practicing being a Stoic right now. I'd try to think about all the funny things that've happened, and this way you wind up wise. How's your stiff upper lip?"

When I looked out the window my lip didn't feel very stiff, and I didn't feel either funny or wise. It was raining pure pitchforks, and each driving tine stabbed my hunter's soul. I had waited nine months—and one five-day century—for this Day. Very seldom does Opening Day come on Saturday, but this year it did, combining permanent Christmas with a blue moon and a month of Sundays, with hell about to freeze over for good measure.

Now then, me and the weather had come to grips before. I had been rained out of more than one Saturday, but generally I found something to do with it that did not involve robbing a bank. Being rained out of *any* Saturday would stab you to the heart, and all the Old Man's favorite quotes about life being just a rainy Saturday didn't help much.

But I had never been rained out of a Saturday which was also Opening Day before, and I had been planning this one since I put my gun away when the season closed last February.

I had been to the hardware store and bought the shells. I was spending Saturday night out in the country, at Sheriff Knox's house. Apart from the Sheriff's birds, there were Mrs. Goodman's birds, and Aunt Florence Hendricks' birds, and Big Abner's birds, and Aunt Mary Millette's birds, and Lyndon Knox's birds, and some vagrant perimeter birds, all waiting to be shot at on this Saturday by me. The dogs had dry-hunted every Sunday since the weather turned cool, and were panting for the smell of powder. There was one six-month-old puppy who promised to be the best quail dog that ever hit the piny woods.

Monday had been bright and golden, the sky blue and unspecked by cloud. Frosts had come and killed the undergreenery. The corn shucks were sere and liver-spotted, and the persimmons were sweet enough to eat without turning you into a Chinaman. A fire felt cozy-comforting at night. The last Sunday, the dogs had worked well on the tame coveys we kept around the house for training purposes. The dogs were sharp and ready, and so, I thought, was the hunter.

Tuesday was bright and golden. So was Wednesday. So was Thursday. So was Friday. And tomorrow would be Saturday, with no school. *And* Opening Day!

But now the rain pounded down in drops as big, it seemed, as baseballs. Then the wind rose and drove the drops savagely in thin arrows against the walls and windows. The panes were steadily bleared by water, as it cascaded down in clear sheets against the sills. The rain had come about breakfast time, teasingly at first, each big drop making a little dimple in the clean-swept sand of Sheriff Knox's yard. Then the dimples turned to holes, and then the holes to little gulleys, and finally the gulleys spread to small lakes. Noah never saw a meaner rain than I had to celebrate that Saturday, the Opening Day.

Breakfast was warm inside me—a big breakfast of oatmeal and ham and eggs and hominy and coffee. The fires burnt bright in the fireplaces, but a steady gust of rain drove through the breezeway that cut the old-fashioned country house in half, and little creeks of water ran in the uneven flooring.

I opened the front door against the solid wall of sheeting water, and went out on the wide veranda. The rain was not so heavy you couldn't see across the road to the soybean field where all the doves hung out. The dogs started to follow me out of the warm sitting room, but the wet wind smote them and they huddled back against the door. The guinea fowl that always ran loose committing suicide in the road had crowded under the house, and were standing, ruffled and angry clatter-ing, with their feet hating the wet sand.

I fought the door open again and the dogs and I went back inside. The Old Man and the Sheriff were sitting companion-ably in front of the fire, which hissed from the trickles that drove down the chimney. I was dressed for the wars, but neither of the old gentlemen had bothered to put on boots. They both wore the soft-sided Congress gaiters, and you could see the white legs of their long-handled drawers pulled down over their sock tops. They hadn't even bothered to put on the long red-topped wool hunting socks they wore with their boots. The Old Man shook his head.

"You might as well take off some of that regalia," he said. "I don't think you'll hunt any birds today. How about it, John?" he turned his head to the Sheriff. "That rain looks like she's here to stay, eh?"

"Yep," the Sheriff said, spitting an amber arc into the fire. "You won't see sun today. I thought for a while she might fair off, but I don't think so now. And even if she did, the

woods are too wet. Birds are all in the branches, huddled under some brush. They wouldn't of fed out, and it's too wet for
the dogs to smell. No scent on a day like this."

I was all for dragging the dogs out by main force and fighting my way into the wet, but the Old Man shook his head.

"Waste of time," he said. "All you'll do is rust your gun
and catch a death of cold. You might as well resign yourself
to the fact that this ain't your lucky day. Even the dogs got
better sense than to go out on a day like this. This day ain't
good for nothin' but ducks, and the duck season ain't open yet.
Be a Stoic and count your past blessings."

The Old Man was right, of course. Some of the best bird
shooting in the world happens in the right kind of rain—a slow
drizzle that moistens the dry ground and helps a dog's nose
function, like a wet night makes combustion better in an auto-
mobile motor. The trailers can trail and the winders can wind,
and the coveys hang closer together. Also the singles have a way
of sticking to where they hit, so you can make them better,
and they don't flush wild all over the place when you shoot
over a point.

Some of the best shooting I ever had was on a half-wet day,
when the boys got separated from the men and the lazy hunters
stayed home by the fire, but this was not going to be one of
those days. I would have needed a boat to make it to the nearest
pea patch.

The Sheriff and the Old Man kept talking interestingly
enough, I suppose, all about war and politics and crops and the
last deer drive, but I couldn't work up an appetite for what
they were saying. I was someplace else, with the sun shining and
the dogs fanning the fields.

The Old Man watched me fidget for a while, and then he
said, "Why don't you go do something with the girls and leave
us in peace? You're about to wear out the rug. This ain't any
way to be a Stoic, and anyhow you're making me and the Sheriff
nervous."

Now as a rule I ain't got anything against girls, especially today, when I'm a sight older. But right then the only time I had for women was when they were in the kitchen cooking something that smelled good and that I would eat later. About all girls were good for was to tattle and giggle and cry if you looked cross-eyed at them. I never knew a girl who could throw a baseball without snapping her elbow, and there seemed to be a general suspicion that all girls were good and all boys were bad.

The Sheriff had a flock of gal children, and Ethel and Sally and Annie Mae and Gertrude were all twittering around about something or other, and all I could think of was that they sounded like a gaggle of geese and didn't seem to accomplish much outside of confusion. The dogs were no help, either. They just lay by the fire and looked as mournful as I felt. Altogether it was the finest study in frustrated indoor activity I ever run onto.

Lunchtime came and the rain still walloped down, hitting as hard as hammers. We sat down to eat a big country lunch—dinner, it was called in those days—but I didn't have much feeling for the fried chicken and the venison and the apple pie, the big sugared tomatoes and all the other stuff I usually loved.

After lunch the Old Man looked at me sharply, and for one of the few times in his life his voice matched the look. "All right, all *right*," he said. "Get your gun and the dogs, if you can find one that's damned fool enough to go with you, and go hunting! Anything to get you out of the house before you drive us all crazy."

I put on an old oilskin over my canvas hunting coat, got the gun, and stirred up the dogs with my foot. They were not enthusiastic about leaving the fire, and I had to drag the old boys out the door. Only the puppy thought it was fun enough to come along under his own steam.

The rain still sloshed down by the bucketful. I trudged through the soybean field, hoping to rouse a dove or so, but nothing was feeding. The gray-topped cotton soil was pure muck, now, and it stuck to my boots like cement, leaving black patches of soil underneath. Just walking in the gumbo was an effort, for your feet weighed a ton each.

Two things, I learned that day, are not improved by bad weather. One is open ocean. One is woodland. Of the two the weeping woods are sadder than the sea.

I still don't know what happens to most outdoor life when it rains. I suppose the rabbits dive into their burrows and the birds perch in the trees or huddle under brush heaps. No sign of life appeared in the dripping woods, in the sodden fields, in the soaked prairies of high grass. The dogs were draggled, cockleburred, and shivering. My old oilskin provided small protection. Rain got into my eyes and blinded me. My nose ran in time to the dripping of the trees, and the wind howled and the rain slashed down.

I forced the dogs down into the swamps, figuring it would be dryer under the heavy trees, and perhaps we would stumble on a covey of quail. We stumbled on nothing shootable, although I did manage to slip in the mud while jumping the small creek and made myself a little wetter, but not much.

After two hours or so I gave up. The dogs and I trudged back to the farm, as cold and miserable as dogs and boys are likely to get. We must have been a sight as we trudged into the breezeway.

The Old Man must have seen us coming, because he met us in the breezeway. "Get out of them wet clothes," he snapped, "and then come in to the fire. But mind you dry them dogs off before you turn them into the house. They'll stink bad enough half-dry, anyhow." Then he turned and stumped back into the sitting room where the fire was.

I nearly froze changing from wet clothes to some dry ones, and I was afraid to go in to the fire until I had rubbed the dogs with a couple of dry tow sacks from the smokehouse.

"Get any birds?" the Old Man asked sarcastically, as I stood with my back to the fire, waiting for the heat to burn my backside before I gave it a chance at the front.

"Nosir," I said.

"See anything?"

"Nosir. Nothing."

"I thought not," the Old Man said. "You feel any better for flounderin' around in the wet for the past few hours?"

"Nosir," I said.

"Prove anything?"

"Nosir."

"Have a cup of coffee," the Old Man said, "and listen to the Sheriff tell about that bad field hand that killed his wife with an ax just back there close the road near to the graveyard."

After the Sheriff had finished his tale, which was sufficiently gory to hold any boy's interest, the Old Man got up and walked to the window.

"Looks like the rain's slackenin' off," he said. "I wouldn't be at all surprised if the sun didn't set fair. Tomorrow'll likely be a nice day. Pity it's Sunday."

I muttered something, I dunno what, but it wasn't very stoical. Then I sneezed.

"You're as butt-headed as your mother," the Old Man said. "And she's as butt-headed as *her* mother. I reckon if being butt-headed means anything you got the makings of a pretty good Stoic. I don't see you handing out any accumulation of laughter, but if an aggregate of wisdom comes from being butt-headed I guess that sneeze tells me you've learned something about beating your head against a stone wall. Time and again you've heard me say that bad weather's all right if you know how to make it work for you, but on a day like today the best way to make it work for you is to stay home in front of the fire with a book."

I sneezed again.

The Old Man cocked his head. "Go get one of the women folks to give you some cough syrup and tie a rag around your neck," he said. "A sneezing Stoic is an abomination before the Lord. And anyhow, if you get sick from being foolish you won't be able to go hunting tomorrow. Tomorrow's dead certain to be better, because I can see the clouds lifting and the sun coming out."

"But tomorrow's Sunday," I said. "And I ain't allowed to hunt on Sunday." This time I managed to snuffle back the sneeze.

The Old Man grinned. "You can carry Stoicism too far," he said. "We're out here in the backwoods and you're visitin' the Sheriff. You've got the Law on your side, and I shouldn't wonder if the good Lord wouldn't make an exception in your case this time, if you don't go telling everybody about how you broke the Law. I reckon with it raining on Saturday *and* Opening Day you been punished enough, and you got a little something coming from On High."

I let out a whoop, which might have been the first symptoms of pneumonia, but I didn't care. That was the Old Man for you. He was tricky as a pet coon. One thing I had added to my "aggregate of wisdom" this day was that if I lived to be a hundred I'd never figure him out, but right then I wasn't inclined to argue. I felt so good with my accumulated laughter that I even helped the gals wash dishes that night after supper and didn't bust but one.

29

The House Comes Home

When the Old Man decided to lay down the load, a whole lot of years ago, it was depression time, and he like nearly everybody we knew had stuck a whacking big mortgage on the House. It wasn't much of a mortgage for these times, but it was computed in thousands and was as hopeless of repayment as if it had been counted in millions. Anybody in those days who had a cent squirreled off in the much-darned sock was a very rich man. Anybody who could command a certain amount of skinny credit at the store for the basic beans and fat back was richer than most folks. The earliest thirties were not a time for mortgage lifting, even if the bank that held the mortgage wasn't bust.

So when the Old Man decided that the thing he had would kill him—and it did—and with Miss Lottie already gone ahead of him and everybody broke and discouraged, the rich old fellow who held the mortgage just naturally foreclosed it, as was his right. The man who foreclosed it, some said, was a skinflint, and maybe he was.

Well, the family busted up and scattered every whichaway, and nobody looked like ever making any money at all, so the old fellow who now owned the House decided to rent it, after a decent period of mourning, but he swore he'd never sell the old place to anybody but a member of the family, so long as he lived. He loved the House, too, most as much as and maybe more than some of the people who had eaten and drunk in it and hunted and fished out of it.

It was a fine old House, and most of my life with the Old Man was spent in and around it. It was located in Southport, the sleepy little North Carolina town I've written about so much; the town with the cedar bench where the old men loafed to whittle and chew tobacco and argue; the Pilots' Association, where the men sat with spyglasses and gazed out past Battery Island and Caswell to the sea; Mr. Rob Thompson's pool parlor, where the racier element hung out on the rainy days; Mr. Price Furpless's picture show, the Amuzu; Watson's and Leggett's drug stores, and Gus McNeill's filling station; all social centers of a town which had an oak grove called The Grove and a street called The Street.

The House was square and in those days, so long ago, was painted yellow. It sat on a corner next to a smaller oak grove where we played one o' cat. It was right next door to Uncle Tommy and catty-cornered on the street from Uncle Walker, and right across the street from old Sam Watts, who had the best deerhounds in town. Some people said Sam set more store by his hounds than he did his young'uns.

The House was set up on brick stilts, and I spent many a rainy day under it, rummaging through the trove of generally nonfunctional treasure a small boy is apt to find under a house in the days before they had basements to store truck in. There were exciting things like the Old Man's hunting tents, boats hauled up from the water for a recaulk, busted oars and ragged cast nets, and crates of old yellowing magazines, and even Miss Lottie's moldy old sidesaddle.

There were some pomegranate bushes by the front door, and in the back yard behind the kitchen was an arbor with the first big Malaga grapes I ever tasted, although I had plenty of experience with black-and-white scuppernongs—experience which included the bellyache, and later a dipperful of cool, tart, homemade grape wine from the springhouses on the little farmsteads I shot over. Also in the back yard was a fig tree with huge black figs that broke open in sticky white cracks and attracted hordes of birds and June bugs and bumblebees. And a towering pecan, which hailed storms of rich nuts in the fall.

I never spent much more time inside the House than I could help, but it was very comfortable for that time. It had a big Kalamazoo stove in the parlor, where nobody but the preacher ever sat, and an awful picture of a big St. Bernard dog looking after a little girl. It had a big kitchen where Old Galena, the cook, was queen, and off the kitchen there was a pumpshelf with a graniteware basin and a dirty roller towel. On the ceiling near the pumpshelf was a rafter with two holes bored in it, where my Aunt May had a swing when she was a little girl. The holes are still there.

As a matter of fact, the whole House is still there. It was made out of fat pine so hard you had to bore holes to drive the nails in. Not being very firmly anchored to the earth it could sway its hips in a storm without sagging out of plumb or blowing away. That House is about a hundred years old, and it has weathered all the hurricanes—Alice, Ethel, Helen, and lately, Donna—that have come along since hurricanes became latterly fashionable along that part of the rugged Carolina coast. Maybe we would lose a gross of shingles, perhaps, while the modern houses with basements were skittering off in the breeze, but the Old Man's House kept stubbornly standing, as did the handful of other old houses lovingly shaped before man discovered the shoddy speed-up.

During the depression years, during the war, and after, I had a fixation about that House. It had been rented to a variety of families through the lean and the better years to follow; families careless of the love that went into its construction and the solid fun that was parcel to its planking. I saw it a few years after the war, when I went South on some business or other and took my dog Schnorkel with me. It was a sad House.

It was a sad House as so many houses become pathetic, when they are no longer filled with tumbling children and sprawling dogs. The Old Man's house had been filthed and abused. For seventeen years the strangers who lived in it beat it up. The rose-bushes died and the chandelier, with the tinkling glass prisms, fell down—that chandelier which had seen Christmas dinners with loaded boards of wild turkey and venison, standing just a whiff away from Galena's kitchen, whence came the odors of spicy fruit cake and frizzling ham and baking cookies.

The ancient slatted shutters were sagging crazily from the broken windows, banging in the wind, and the porch had rotted and fallen in. The roses were gone from the side yard, replaced by sandspurs and dandelions, and the neat borders of perennials were long-withered or shrunken brown stalks. But the mag-nolia was there, bigger and taller than ever, with one of a suc-cession of mockingbirds still shouting his silver serenade on the moonlit nights. The grape arbor was gone, its framework col-lapsed, but there was the stump of the fig tree and the tall bole remaining of a sick pecan.

At the time, the Boy was having his troubles in a man's world, but the sight of that House made me fair sick. I didn't have any loose money and I was living in New York and travel-ing all over the globe. I think having the dog with me did it. I got to thinking about all the things that had happened to me with that House as a base; all the things I had done, all the things I had learned in that House and from that House. Most of the things that I value today had started in that House, started when I was a small, fat, cowlicked boy with lop-ears, spending as much time as I could in it. That House combined Christmas and Thanksgiving and Easter and summertime, in an ordered world of guns and dogs and boats and fish and ducks and quail. It was a cathedral of ancient times, when children were accorded dignity according to how they earned it, and adults were merely small boys grown older. That was not just a House; that House was Me.

I had fallen out of the magnolia, and had shot one of the mockingbirds—for which I suffered both physically and emotionally. I had gathered the pecans and fought the birds for the figs. The oak grove was still there by the side of the House, the gnarled old branches still hung with Spanish moss, and I had played baseball under its shade. Over the hill was The Cottage and Beaver Dam and Dutchman's Creek, where I had safari-ed before I knew there was such a word as safari. From the front yard there was the water front with its Cedar Bench and the row of salt-silvered old houses, and I bet myself that I could still find the old wreck close to where the fish always bit well.

The dog ran into the weed-grown yard and laid his black square muzzle flat on the ground and stuck his bobtailed behind into the air, waiting to play. There was still a mockingbird; it attempted a scherzo. In the oak grove there was a flash of blue, a scuff of wings, and the harsh calling of a jay. The wind came up freshly from the water with its burden of salt and tar and, faintly, fish.

It was October, 1949, and the squirrel season was on. The hounds would be belling in the crisp October woods as they coursed the big buck deer, whose necks were swelling as the frost brought the rutting season and its disregard of consequence. On the beaches at Baldhead and Corncake the blues would be running in the sloughs, and occasionally the big silver slabs of channel bass would be striking. There were still quail in these parts, and the season would be opening next month, and the dogs would be whining in the back yard. Possums would be curled in gray balls in the naked persimmon trees, and the woods would be full of blue-drifting wood smoke and the evening cries of the colored children driving the cows home. Hog-killin' time was just around the corner. . . .

I was wearing a Countess Maria necktie and driving a blue Buick convertible. I was writing a syndicated newspaper column and selling stuff to magazines and going to the Stork Club and Twenty One for lunch. Toots Shor called me by my first name, and I was living in a penthouse and owed money to the bank.

And I felt like a complete fraud. I felt like I was wearing somebody else's clothes and driving somebody else's car and going around under somebody else's name, so long as the Old Man's House stood there empty and sad, lonely and despoiled of firelight and laughter.

So of course you know what I did. I had the mockingbird, and I had the magnolia, and all I needed was the mortgage.

I went to see the man people called a skinflint, and told him that I was the Old Man's boy grown considerably older. He said he remembered me; I don't know if he actually did. But this old man—he was sere and crisp-frail as a leaf before it falls —that people called a skinflint said he would be glad to sell me the House back, and for exactly as much as the amount of the mortgage for which he had foreclosed it!

Perhaps he *was* a skinflint, but he could have gotten three times as much as the mortgage warranted, for the country was fat with postwar prosperity and housing was acutely short. Skinflint or not, he had awaited death on the strength of his promise to keep the House in the family. I bought back the House, not because I could use it but because I needed it.

The House sits proud and freshly painted today on its corner. Its flowers are cherished, its interior restored. A woman who was born in the House, my mother, is its chatelaine. My father watches television in the back living room, where the Old Man used to listen to the lugubrious whine of "The Wreck of the Old Ninety-Seven" on one of those long-horned gramophones. The little girl who swung on the back porch, a grandmother for many years now, lives "down the street." There are lights and voices in the House again, and from time to time, dogs and children. Rich black laughter is heard in the kitchen, and the old-time smells still come tantalizingly into the dining room, where the old glass chandelier used to swing. Corn and butter beans and hot biscuits are still cooked in that kitchen, and the brandy is soaked into the Christmas fruitcake as in times past.

It is amazing how the time passes. There was a letter the other day from the bank that holds the mortgage, saying that we don't owe any money on the Old Man's House any more. The Old Man's House is free of strangers, and makes a happy harbor for cheerful ghosts. The magnolia and the mockingbird are safe again, and the flowers bloom, and I somehow thought that the Old Man might like to know it.

30

Even His Runts Were Giants

The death of an old dog is comparable in heartache to the death of any person, young or old, and in some respects produces more pain. The dog has been dependent, totally, and has become an extension of the man, closer in companionship than humans and certainly more blind to the master's faults. The loss of a dog is felt more keenly because a portion of the human dies with the beast, or so it seems to me.

You maybe remember that the Old Man said, "Old dogs and old men both smell bad and are better out of the house." He also said, "Watching something die is not a very pleasant process, especially if it's you."

He was referring at the time to a beast that was somewhat overdue. All we could do was make him comfortable. Then one day he died, and he died in the knowledge that he had not been abused in sharing the life of people whose lives he had richened in the sharing. When the Old Man died, he did it the same way.

Ever since I can remember I have been enslaved by dogs, and not particularly in the sentimental lap-dog fashion. Dogs and people vary in intelligence and personality. My Mickey, a cocker bitch, was meaner than a Doberman. My Frank, the blue belton Llewellin, was such a wencher that he hanged himself on a fence trying to chase a new girl, and he was well past the age of such shenanigans. My Tom, a liver-and-white pointer was the best bird dog I've ever owned, and he was queer. His voice never changed from the treble, he shrieked at the idea of being bred, and the real he-dogs never even bothered to bite him. And then, of course, there was Sandy, a lemon-and-white English setter with as foul a disposition and as accurate a nose as ever I encountered. And there was Jet, a Gordon setter who spent most of his life asleep on the sports desk of the Washington *Daily News*; and the setter twins, Abercrombie and Bitch; plus a big, rangy Rhett Butler kind of pointer named Dude, who ran away from his happy home. And finally the current crop.

The current crop is worthy of consideration. There is a spayed standard French poodle bitch named Miss Mam'selle Señorita Fräulein Memsahib, who is possibly the only stupid French poodle in the world. This one really hasn't got sense enough to come in out of the rain. There was, until recently, Schnorkel, the Old Man of the bunch, who was possibly the only brilliant boxer I have ever met. I cannot say this for his son, Satchmo, or Satch's sister, Mrs. Gwendolyn Wentworth-Brewster, otherwise known as Wendy, or some of his half-brothers and sisters, named variously Rufus and Ella and Lena.

Schnorkel, who was pressing thirteen years of dignified age, was a Warlord of Mazelaine offshoot, and like that grand old man he always bred true. There are more half-bred boxers with white shoes and white chest blazes running around Spain than you can shake a muleta at. This is known as outside work. Actually my old gentleman has been married only four times, producing forty-two pups out of the brief honeymoons. The last time—we had the bride flown in from Madrid to Barcelona —he managed to sire eleven, which is pretty good going for an old boy with a hoary face and the Reaper just around the corner. And as somebody once said of Schnork, even his runts are bigger than most people's giants.

Except Satchmo, of course. Satchmo takes after his Spanish mother. But he makes up for his smallness by being perhaps the silliest beast I've ever met. He is a comic dog on the order of a young Mickey Rooney. He sleeps on a split level and sulks if I forget his morning kick. He helps the gardener at work by biting his ankles, and suffers horribly from sinus. I can tell when the weather's changing, just by hearing Satch wheeze. I would give him away, as I gave his sister Wendy away, but nobody intelligent enough to feed him will have him. So I'm stuck with an idiot child.

It is not so bad when they are run over or succumb to distemper when they're too young to be part of the family, or even when they garrote themselves like old Frank did. But we were just in the process of watching Schnorkel die, slowly, and it was a terrible thing.

I bought this ten-week-old puppy as a gift for my wife. Paul Gallico, the writer; Bill Williams, the editor; a nonclassifiable friend named Bernie Relin; and I went puppy hunting one day after an exuberant lunch involving Martinis. We wound up in Long Island and were introduced to the baby's family. His old man, of whom the baby was the spittin' image, was unleashed and he cuffed every puppy soundly. Only one pup bared his milk teeth and charged back at Papa.

"I'll have that one," I said. "The scrapper. What's his name?"

"Chip," the owner said. "He's the dead image of his father and his grandpa. Chip off the Old Block is his square handle."

I had just made a week's run as the first civilian to test a schnorkel submarine. "His name is Schnorkel," I said. "He looks like a dog who would be named Schnorkel."

While he was kindly disposed to most people and all children this puppy was the worst dog-fighter I have ever seen. I had to pull him off a full-grown Doberman when he was just over six months old. His feet were hanging clear of the ground, but he had a tooth hold on the throat, and there was very little the Dobe could do about him until I got a stick and pried the puppy's teeth out of his neck.

This was on the same weekend that Schnork gained a lasting aversion to water. I was out fishing in a boat on a lake in New Jersey, and the puppy was on the dock. I called him, and he thought what was in front of him was pale-blue sidewalk. He strolled off the dock and damn near drowned.

From that point on all water was his enemy. You can't tell me that this is a boxer trait, because his offspring, Satch, can barely be restrained from swimming daily to Africa with old Miss Mam'selle. The Spaniards where we live had a name for Schnork. They called him *el Salvavida*—the Lifesaver. That's because he used to roam up and down the beach wringing his paws, frothing at the mouth, and beseeching people to come out of that wet old mess before they drowned.

Schnorkel was a puppy when we lived in Greenwich Village, and he had a strange set of social values. There was a nice hoodlum around the Minetta Street area, a nondescript little man who liked dogs. He approached me one day in his quiet hoodlum manner and said tightly, out of the corner of his mouth, that he had heard we had been refused insurance on personal belongings because the neighborhood was so tough.

"Don't worry," he said. "Nobody lays a glove on your joint. Leave the door open. I run this end of the town. No bum lays a glove on your joint." I waited for the kicker. "You wouldn't mind sometime if I walked your dog? I'm a sucker for pooches and I love this dog."

I said, "Fine." From time to time there would be a ring or a knock or even a lightly cast pebble against a window, and there would be Mr. Hoodlum in his form-fitting overcoat. I would shove the puppy down the stairs and the two mobsters would go for a walk.

At the time I was working late at night, and occasionally Ginny Ruark would have to walk the dog. I didn't worry about her safety in murky back alleys at 2 A.M. I had looked out the window one night. As she went into the street with the dog a shadow detached itself from a deeper, darker shadow. It flitted shadowwise down the tiny street, always melting into tiny corners.

"You shouldn't worry if your missus walks the dog late nights," my tight-mouthed little man said one day. "My boys are always around." He paused. "They got nothing better to do," he said. "Can I walk the dog now?"

Schnorkel became perceptive early. He was part of the mob, but he didn't like outsiders. It is necessary to explain here that he once owned a tame duck, and baby-sat a cat named Shortchange. This did not mean that he liked either ducks or cats. He just liked one duck, and one cat named Shortchange. The same with our tame mobsters.

Some penny-ante boys tried a heist in the neighborhood one night when Schnork was off leash, and he treed the interlopers on a fire escape. They say boxers can't smell very good, but they can sure feel. When we became a little more affluent and moved uptown to Fifth Avenue he chased one set of thieves right up on top of an outbuilding. And he really distinguished himself one night as a house detective.

This was a penthouse apartment, and the elevator opened directly into the foyer. We were having an intimate little gathering of a hundred and fifty-two people, a business-cocktail do, and Schnork leaped happily into everybody's lap. Let's just say he enjoyed meeting a hundred fifty-two people, including the cat lovers who wore blue suits and hated dogs.

All of a sudden my wife came to me in a far corner. "Schnorkel won't let two people off the elevator," she said. "He's got them bayed, like he treed the burglars. I suppose they're some loaded friends of yours that you picked up somewhere, but you better come explain it to the dog."

They were smooth enough in appearance, certainly slick enough to fit in with the other guests. But Schnorkel, legs braced and teeth showing, was having none of them. I had never seen the bums before in my life.

"What do you want?" I asked.

"Well," one said, "we thought it was some kind of club. We saw the lights on late every night, and tonight all these people came, and we thought you were maybe running an after-hours club."

"You want to go back down in the elevator or will you have some dog?" I said. "I couldn't care less."

They chose the elevator, and then Schnork went back to mingle with the party and rub his hairs off on the gentry's blue suits.

Schnorkel and Mam'selle had been Europeans for eight years when the old boy cashed. Schnorkel spoke French, Spanish, Catalan, Swahili, and English English; and Mam'selle still doesn't know her name. The help called Schnorkel *el Cocinero,* the cook, because he was always in the kitchen. Mam'selle does not associate with the help. She also refused to drink water out of anything but a bidet, which is a Latin bathroom fixture.

Both dogs were quite well traveled. They alternated between Palamós and Barcelona, and we spent one summer in Tangier in North Africa at an appalling cost in time, trouble, and money, because there was no housing readily available in Barcelona except the Hotel Ritz, and the dogs didn't care much for the noise the tramcars made outside the Ritz. So we went to Tangier and shacked up in the Hotel el Minzah and I overdrew my account again, while being involved in cat fights and the beginning of the Moroccan rebellion.

They have been well pleased with life in Spain, since they have slaves to do their bidding and a large yard in front of two houses. The yards are filled with flowers on which they make water. In front of one house there is a beach that is filled with tourists. Schnorkel, being a Kraut, was allowed to snarl at the French; while Mam'selle, being a Frog, barks at the Germans. Satchmo usually just bites me, being too lazy to *heraus* the Krauts.

You will have noticed a forced light touch to this piece. I'll tell you why. Schnorkel was gray, and he walked spraddled-legged, weak in the hindquarters, and his teeth were worn down so he couldn't even fight his son any more, and noise bothered him, and his hide was abraded, and his eyesight was going, and he had forgotten his last girl friend. My old puppy, my dog Schnorkel, was dying, in the midst of all the love he had mustered since he was ten weeks old.

It seemed to do nobody any good to see the old boy as what he was, gray and feeble, finished and useless to himself and to the others, the dogs and the people. All the ham actor was gone out of him, all of the sense of humor, all of the bounce, and all of his considerable dignity. He had a stroke and he walked around with his head down, bumping into things, and toward the end he kept fumbling for corners to die in. The facilities for modern dog destruction are few, in the backwater section of Spain I live in. We dug him a grave under some pine trees and I borrowed a pistol from one of the Guardia Civil *carabineros* and took my old dog out under the trees and shot him. The cook and the Guardia Civil and I tossed some earth into the grave, and we buried a good portion of me, that sunny morning, with the big, cockaded yellow hoopoe birds looping from pine to pine and the Mediterranean lapping softly blue almost in the front yard. We were all glad to see the old dog go, because this way we got the puppy back.

What we didn't get back was the years since the puppy came into the little flat in Greenwich Village in New York and decided to stay. We didn't get back the years which took me uptown and then Europe, to South America and Africa and India and Japan and Australia and China and New Guinea and all the other places I had hankered to see.

In his lifetime Schnorkel lived a hundred years of man's span. My grown-up friends were his grown-up friends, and so very many of Schnorkel's friends got old and sick and tired and died of it too.

I measure most of the importance of my adult life from the time I got Schnorkel until the day I buried him. I wasn't much more than a boy when I got him, just a few years out of the war and still puppyish with all the cocky confidence of youth that had been momentarily interrupted by the war. Schnork and I started growing up together and the developing project continued until time, which expands the years of a dog, stopped the dog as a wise old man and left the graying humans to profit by his past presence.

I was glad that Schnorkel had been with me the day I drove down to North Carolina and bought the Old Man's House back, not because I could use it but because I needed it. Schnorkel was still alive when I finished paying off the mortgage, and so the Old Man had his House back, as I had a good deal of my boyhood back. In between there had been a lot of living and a great deal of work, a lot of departures and homecomings. Once I was gone for nine months on a swing around the world; the welcome was the same as if I'd just strolled down to the post office.

After I wrapped my old friend in a bathrobe and put him in the earth the Guardia Civil man and I came back to the house and had a drink to the dog. The Guardia Civil looked around at the working room with the big fireplace, with some African game heads on the wall.

"He was a good dog," the *carabinero* said. "A good person. He lived a good life in a good house."

I reckon the Old Man wouldn't have minded that as an epitaph for himself.

Robert Chester Ruark was born in Wilmington, North Carolina, in 1915. He began his writing career as a sportswriter and columnist for the *Washington Daily News*, and produced a total of 4,000 columns for the United Feature Syndicate. He wrote several best-selling novels, including *Something of Value, Uhuru,* and *The Honey Badger. The Old Man and the Boy* is his most widely known and perhaps best-liked book. Robert Ruark died in 1965.